The Model Man

by

Nicole McCaffrey

The Model Man

Contact Information: info@thewildrosepress.com

Cover Art by *Tamra Westberry*

The Wild Rose Press
PO Box 708
Adams Basin, NY 14410-0706
Visit us at www.thewildrosepress.com

Publishing History
First Last Rose of Summer Edition, 2008
Print ISBN 1-60154-237-2

Published in the United States of America

"You think I set that up?"

"Yes." She placed a hand to her forehead. Between the kissing, the champagne, and the run through the lobby, she was almost dizzy. "*No*. I don't know."

The car dinged as it reached her floor, and she moved forward. Derek smacked a hand over the "close door" button.

"You're the one who didn't trust yourself alone with me."

"Trust myself?" She squeezed her purse when she would have rather tightened her hands around his arrogant neck.

"We met there to make you more comfortable, remember?"

"*Trust myself?*"

"Sweetheart, the sparks were flying from both sides. If we'd been in a room instead of the patio, we'd be in bed right now."

"What did—you self-centered, pompous—I can't even think of a name bad enough to call you!" She slapped his hand away from the elevator button. The doors opened, and she stormed past him, right into a startled Sharon.

"Hey, there you are, Kel."

Ignoring her friend, she turned and faced Derek. "I was wrong to think you could embody the heroes I create. You aren't fit to wear Captain Connery's leather pants!" Turning to Sharon, she said, "You and every other woman on the planet can have him."

Derek shoved his hands in his pockets, bracing the elevator door open with his shoulder. He watched Kelly until she reached her room, wincing as the door closed behind her with a bang that echoed down the empty hallway.

The redhead turned and gave him a wide-eyed look. "What did you do to her?"

"I kissed her." He heaved a sigh. "Things sort of went downhill from there."

She stepped on the elevator and took his arm, giving it a sympathetic pat. "Come on, big guy, lemme buy you a beer."

Reviews

Score: 4 / 5 Rising star newscaster Holland McCall returns home for the Thanksgiving holidays with mixed feelings. When she left she was overweight and unattractive, but times have changed and so has she. Tucker Callahan was a popular athlete who did not give his neighbor a second glance. Now, Holland is on her way to further fame and fortune and Tucker is a divorced father of two daughters who has returned to live in the small town of his youth. Although they both left for different reasons, an unexpected encounter wreaks emotional havoc on the lives they have created for themselves. *Small Town Christmas* by Nicole McCaffrey is a wonderful holiday story of love, forgiveness and the importance of family. The engaging small town atmosphere prompts both Holland and Tucker to rethink their priorities and their future. ~ Reviewer: Gail of Night Owl Romance

Small Town Christmas is a heart warming story of unrequited love that turns into love forever. Once you start reading you won't be able to put it down. ~ *Paty Jager,* author of *Marshall in Petticoats and Gambling on an Angel*

Nicole McCaffrey packs a powerful punch of emotion on every page. Between Holly's memories of an unrequited crush and Tucker's uncertainty of the opposite sex after a failed marriage, *Small Town Christmas* tugs at the heartstrings.~*Darah Lace,* author of *Yesterday's Desire and Wrong Number, Right Man*

Small Town Christmas is the very essence of a feel good holiday romance. Nicole has captured the imagery of a small town and brought her readers right there. The heroine's visit home has the reader nodding her head at how families can be. Tucker is a hero any woman would love to find under her Christmas tree. ~ *Roni Adams,* author of *Tales from Christmas Town*

Dedication

For Peter, who taught me that real love stories don't have endings.

Acknowledgments

Kay Sterba and Lise Horton, for help with New York, New Yorkers and life in New York during and post 9/11.

Peter, for tireless hours spent researching and discussing cars.

Wyatt and Colton, for all the times they heard me say "just a sec" or "in a minute" or "as soon as mommy finishes one more paragraph."

The best critique partners any writer ever had: Kath, Meliss, Paty and Diana for always going above and beyond...and then some.

Last Rose of Summer editor Kathryn Cottrell, who believed in this story from day one.

RJ and Rhonda, for building a garden where writers like me can take root and stories like The Model Man can blossom and grow.

One

Derek Calavicci opened the door to his penthouse apartment and stepped inside. Home, although it never really felt that way. At one time the navy and pewter color scheme, so carefully chosen by the designer, the expensive but tasteful furniture and state-of-the-art gadgets had soothed him. But not lately. He set his keys on the kitchen counter and picked up a stack of personal mail waiting there.

Gabrielle, his younger sister and personal assistant, strolled into the room. Dressed in her robe and fuzzy pink slippers, she had a toothbrush sticking out of one side of her mouth and a towel wrapped around her head. She often stayed at his place when he was gone, and judging from the clothes, shoes and magazines strewn about, she had done so this past week.

"So, how was Tokyo?" she asked around the toothbrush.

"Fine." He put his hands to his hips and glanced around the apartment. "It's a good thing I pay the cleaning lady so well."

She moved to the kitchen sink to spit out a mouthful of toothpaste. "How did the bourbon commercial go?"

"It was fine."

"Did you get lucky?"

He didn't answer her, merely shook his head in wonder.

"Okay, for other guys it's getting lucky. For you it's par for the course. So... did you?"

"Would I tell you if I did?"

"You're always so grumpy when you get home from these things."

He headed for the sofa and flopped down, finally allowing the exhaustion of the long flight and the time change to overtake him. "There's a fourteen-hour time

1

difference between here and Tokyo. I'm beat." He leaned his head back and closed his eyes, grateful that he was no longer in motion. Not in a plane, not in a limo, just sitting still.

"Hope you aren't too jet lagged, you've got an early flight in the morning."

He raised his head just enough to look at her. "Where the hell to now?"

She laughed and headed toward his desk. "You really are out of it. The Romantic Moments conference starts this weekend."

"Christ." He dropped his head back down. "Little wonder I'm more comfortable in hotels than in my own home."

"You're never here," she agreed, holding out a note pad for his inspection.

"What am I supposed to do with that?"

"It's your messages. Your voice mail filled up twice so I had to write everything down."

"I'm too tired to read them. Anything important?"

"Mmm, depends on what you call important. Or who."

"I'm afraid to ask."

"Let's see... Megan called. She'll be at the conference in Florida; she's really looking forward to 'hooking up'. She'll be in room eight-twelve. Amber, also going to the conference, is in five-seventeen. Oh, and Shannon is going to be in New York next weekend and she'd like to ... well, I'm not about to repeat it. Is she double jointed or something?"

"Damned if I can remember."

"Anyway, there's another page and a half of these."

"I'll look at them later."

"Good idea. Oh, and Frankie called. About nine times."

"What the hell did she want?"

"You. Under her tiny, little thumb. When are you going to fire her and get a new manager? One who doesn't want to run your life."

"Why bother when I can just avoid this one as much as possible?"

"She wants to make sure you two are on the same

flight tomorrow so she can go over a few things with you on the way down," Gabby spoke over her shoulder as she headed to the kitchen. "Something about the 'Flawless' campaign. You know, that new line of men's cologne and skin care products you're promoting."

He raised his head again. "And?"

She returned, holding out a bottle of water and gave him a triumphant smile. "And I made sure to book you on a different flight."

"Good girl." He unscrewed the cap and took a long drag. "What do I have going on today?"

"I canceled everything when I realized you were getting back so late. Thought you might want a little break."

"Thanks."

"Don't forget Anthony's engagement party is tonight."

"I can't believe my kid brother is getting married. Did I buy them something nice?"

"Besides paying for the wedding? Crystal. Expensive and impractical, just your style."

"I'm such a nice guy."

"Well, you'd better be prepared to answer the inevitable from the relatives tonight."

"You mean the 'and when are you going to settle down' stuff?" Now that he'd turned thirty, that was all anyone wanted to know. His younger brother's engagement had only made it worse.

"Exactly. At this point, I'm beginning to think you're commitment-phobic myself."

"I've got nothing against commitment." He raised his feet to set them on the coffee table. "But whenever the urge strikes, I lie down until it passes."

"Yeah, I know. Preferably with a blonde or a redhead."

"Gabby, I'm hurt you think I'm so shallow. I'd never turn down a hot brunette."

She swatted his feet to the floor. "You were raised better than that. And if you're going to paraphrase Mark Twain, you could at least get it right. He was talking about exercise."

"So was I."

"All right then, Mr. Super Stud answer a question for

me."

He groaned. "Do I have to?"

"Why haven't I seen evidence of a woman spending the night around here lately?"

Reluctant to get into the details, he shrugged her off. "I'm discreet."

"Since when? I used to chase them out for you."

"I would never ask my baby sister to get rid of my dates."

"Call her a cab and tell her I'll be in touch," she said, mimicking his deep voice. "And since when do you call them dates, you used to refer to them as 'leftovers'."

"I did not. Did I?"

"Hell-oo?" she sing-songed. "Who are you and what have you done with my *real* brother?"

Rising to his feet, he rolled his shoulders to release pent-up tension. Flying always did that to him. A good work out followed by a massage would take care of the kinks. Then again, so would sex.

Trouble was, he'd gotten downright choosy about the women who interested him. Probably just a dry spell, though he'd never experienced one before. Still, the last time he'd had sex—when the hell *was* that?—had left him feeling a bit... he wasn't even sure how to put it. Bored? Restless? There were no challenges anymore, everything came too easy.

"Did you hear me or are you sleepwalking?"

He turned to look in Gabby's direction. "You wanted to know where your real brother is."

She rolled her eyes. "I said I need to leave as soon as I get dressed. I have to cover a shift at the pizza shop. Aunt Ro' hurt her foot."

"What the hell did I put you through college for if you're still working in the family pizza shop?"

"Just because you're too good to do it, doesn't mean the rest of us don't put in our time. And I'd like to see you tell Dad no."

"He doesn't ask me."

"That's because you two can't talk without arguing. But hey, here's a thought. Since you still haven't given me my graduation gift yet—"

"I'm working on it." He leaned against the wall for

support and rubbed his eyes. Damn, he couldn't wait to hit the mattress.

"How about a nice vacation? I could use one."

"Take one anytime you want. On me. But that's not your gift."

"How about next week? In Florida? Sandy beaches, sunshine, the ocean."

"No way in hell."

One pink fuzzy-slippered foot stamped indignantly. "Why not?"

He straightened away from the wall, not fully awake but certainly more alert. "I can't concentrate on my job and keep track of my baby sister, too."

She gave a dramatic sigh. "You can stand around half naked and let women paw you whether I'm there or whether I'm not."

"True. But you won't be."

"Because I'm too much like you?"

He grunted. She was right—and that's what worried him.

"That's it, isn't it? Because you caught me coming out of that guy's hotel room last year?"

"A guy you barely knew."

"I knew enough to know what I wanted."

He rubbed a hand over his face. "This is not a conversation I want to have with you, Gabby."

"You haven't taken me to a conference since."

"Like I said, I can't baby-sit you."

"You don't have to. I'm a big girl. And it's not like the location will change anything. Here or there, if I see a guy I want, I go for it. What's wrong with that?"

Plenty. Although he couldn't tell her that. He didn't expect his little sister to remain a virgin the rest of her life, but he didn't want her to follow in his footsteps, either.

"You wouldn't have caught me if you hadn't been sleeping around that night yourself."

"I'm thirty years old, where I sleep is my own damned business."

"Yeah, well I'm twenty three, so—*ditto.*" With a frown, she headed into the bedroom.

He crossed the living room and paused to gaze at the

mid-morning sky through the knee-to-ceiling windows, waiting, hoping for a sense of security to envelop him. The view of the city had always soothed him, served as a reminder of his success. Yet, this morning, as it had so many times lately, the distorted New York skyline did little to improve his mood. Since nine-eleven, nothing about it had been the same.

New York wasn't the only thing that had changed in those years.

Gabrielle emerged, fully dressed but for the slippers. She must really be ticked at him; it usually took forever for her to change clothes. "I'll see you later tonight at Mom and Dad's."

"Right."

The telephone buzzed. She automatically moved to answer it.

"I'm not available," he reminded her.

She picked it up, her tone somber. "Hi, Frankie. No, he's not back yet. Yes, he knows about the conference. You're flying American Airlines? What time?" She scribbled something on her palm. "He'll be there. I'll tell him to call you when he gets in."

She hung up the phone, her dark green eyes, so like his own, sad. The wounded look tore at him, as it always did. "Call Frankie."

"Thanks." He drained the rest of the water and turned his back on the skyline that would never be the same without the Twin Towers. "Piglet—"

"One of these days you're gonna slip and call me that in public."

"I have. Several times." He moved across the room to her side. "Look, with most of the women I've ... there's been an understanding."

"What, that you're only in it as long as there are no strings?"

"Something like that. But how do you think it makes me feel to know some guy is doing my baby sister?"

"Maybe I *did* him."

He lifted a hand to brush a stray strand of chestnut hair from her shoulder. "In my mind you're still twelve. My first instinct is to protect you."

She gave a shaky laugh. "Is that why you practically

broke his jaw?"

"Probably." Hell, he'd wanted to kill the bastard.

Brightening, she flashed a hopeful grin. "So I can go?"

"Ab-so-lute-ly not."

Rolling her eyes, she grabbed her cell phone and purse from the counter and headed for the door. "You're going to be the only one at that conference without a personal assistant. I'll bet even Kelly Michaels will bring hers."

He should probably tell her she still had on those damned fuzzy slippers, but he really wanted to see if she'd—"What did you just say?"

She flashed her best cat-that-ate-the-canary grin. "Kelly Michaels. Did I forget to mention she's the keynote speaker?"

"*The* Kelly Michaels?"

"The very one who keeps you as naked as possible on the covers of all her books."

The image of the best-selling romance author he'd seen so many times, the photo that graced the back cover of her books, jumped to mind. He'd wanted to meet her for years, thank her for what she'd done to further his career early on. And find out if she was as gorgeous in person as she looked in that picture. "Now that's the most interesting thing I've heard all day."

"Don't even think about messing with her," Gabrielle warned. "At least not until you get me her autograph. She's my favorite author."

"I know."

"Which is another reason why you should let me go to that conference with you."

He held the door open for her. "No."

"How firm a 'no' is that?"

Crossing his arms over his chest, he impaled her with his best big-brother stare. He waited until she stepped onto the elevator and the doors were just sliding shut before he called out, "Don't forget about your slippers, squirt."

****

"Oh Thorn," she pleaded, voice breathless with longing. "It's been so long. Take me. Take me now!"

With a feral growl he yanked her to him, hands sliding into her hair. "Raven, my love—"

"*Mo-om!*" Came the plaintive teenaged wail. "The plane leaves in two hours. Where *are* you?"

Kelly Michaels' fingers froze over the keyboard. *Damn.* The first real inspiration to hit in days, and she had to leave. She pushed away the keyboard tray. By the time she got back to work, motivation would be long gone.

She stepped from her home office to find her daughter staring at her as if she'd grown a second head. "I can't believe you were in there," Maya wailed with all the melodrama of her sixteen years. "You know we have to leave and you're *working*?"

"Is your brother ready?"

"He's probably not even packed yet."

Upstairs, Kelly found her fourteen-year-old son sitting on the floor in his perpetually messy bedroom, earphones on, head bobbing to music she could hear from the doorway.

"Cody!" she shouted but got no response. She crossed the room and yanked the ear bud from his ear. "Cody Michaels!"

He started, then removed them. "Chill, Mom."

"Are you ready to go?"

"I got it all right here." He held up a duffle bag.

"Let me guess, iPod, laptop, two pair of shorts and no underwear, right?"

Silver braces gleamed as he flashed the smile that would always be her undoing.

On autopilot, she went to his dresser drawers and pulled out the necessary things for the summer-long stay with his father.

Twenty minutes later they were in the car, heading down the parkway. The heavier traffic thinned near the exit to the airport.

"And Mom, don't forget to call me when you get to Florida so I know you arrived safe."

Kelly slid a glance in her daughter's direction, rolled her eyes and let out a loud huff. "Oh, *Mother*."

Maya frowned. "I'm serious. You've never been away from home by yourself before. I worry about you."

"I'll be surrounded by other romance writers and the

odd fan or two," Kelly said, laughing. "What trouble could I possibly get into?"

She parked the car and stepped out. Cody already waited at the rear of the mini-van, earphones on, head bobbing.

In a surprise move, Maya reached up to adjust the straw hat on Kelly's head, then tugged the bodice of her sundress up so less cleavage showed. "It's just...well, you did great losing all that weight last year and I'm really proud of you, but..."

"But what?" she asked, popping open the back hatch and retrieving their luggage. She dangled Cody's duffel bag in front of him. He danced over, grabbed it and sauntered across the parking lot.

"You look too hot to be a mom."

Kelly stopped short as the words sank in. *Hot*? Hot was one of those twenty-something starlets that were always making headlines. And hey, she'd only lost twenty pounds, not forty.

"Who's going to ravish me at a *Romantic Moments* conference?" She fell into step beside Maya as they headed inside. "And my 'hot' days ended a long time ago, young lady. Not that I ever had any."

Maya's blue eyes flickered over her. "But your hair..."

Kelly absently reached up to the straight, shoulder length blonde bob. Gone were the days of wash and wear hair. She'd even learned how to use a blow dryer and those funny little Velcro rollers. "I thought you liked it."

"I do, it's just so....not you." Maya gave her a critical look, and sighed wistfully. "It's too bad Daddy can't see you, though."

"Sweetheart," Kelly said, pausing at the United Airlines terminal. "Daddy and I didn't get divorced because of what we look like."

"Yeah, I know," her daughter said with a snort. "He wanted to 'find himself.'"

"And he has, honey. He seems so..."

"Deranged."

"I was going to say peaceful. I think he's truly happy with your...well, she's not really your...actually, I guess she's his—"

"*Domestic partner.*"

9

"Yes. That's it." Kelly had to grit her teeth over that one. She refused to say anything bad about Alan in front of the kids, but when she saw her daughter struggling with what to make of her father and his carefree new lifestyle, she could just strangle him. If she ever dated again—and that was a big 'if'—the guy in question would have to have "Role Model" stamped on his forehead.

Maya huffed, tossed her ponytail over her shoulder and turned to her mother with misty eyes. "You think Barney will be all right?"

"After a week at Grandma's? He'll be too fat to walk."

A half-hearted smile. "Okay."

Kelly pulled her daughter in for a hug; her heart suddenly constricted. "I used to drop you kids off at Grandma's. Now it's the dog."

Maya held on for a moment before pulling away. "Oh, Mom."

A few steps ahead, Cody half-walked, half-danced. Kelly caught up to him and gave him a quick hug. "Behave yourself, young man."

Part way down the terminal he stopped and removed the earbud from one ear. "If Dad says it's all right, can I get a tattoo?"

****

Two days later, Kelly stepped out of a taxi cab and faced the Orlando Marriott hotel. Few words could describe the tropical heat of Florida in mid-June. "Hot" didn't seem strong enough.

As the cab pulled away, she knew a moment of panic. She hated doing new things. Hated to travel. Why had she let Sharon, her best friend and critique partner, talk her into this? She wanted to go home.

Her mind made up to do just that, she nodded and strode forward. She would simply call another cab to take her back to the airport. Home to the dear and familiar, her cozy writing room, her own comfy bed.

She paused in mid-stride. Home to the nagging, endless silence.

Alan would have the kids for six weeks.

Six very long, lonely weeks.

This year she had vowed to do something to distract herself, if only for a few days. Sharon had all but twisted

10

her arm to get her to attend this book lover's convention.

There were two options. She could go back home and wallow in good old comfortable misery. Or she could stay here and try something new. If she hated it, she could always leave.

Coming here was about more than challenging herself. Her latest release was an anniversary book for her, number twenty. Half the proceeds would benefit the literacy foundation. As a former English teacher, as well as a writer, reading was a cause near and dear to her heart. She'd be letting down more than just herself if she backed out.

Her stride a bit more confident, she stepped through the hotel doors. The cool comfort of air conditioning wrapped about her like a hug from an old friend. Crowds of excited women assembled everywhere, chatting, laughing. The buzz of conversation, mingled with the trickle of water from a nearby fountain reached her. Their excitement sparked her own.

Maybe this wouldn't be so bad.

A short time later, she strolled through the lobby. The convention was in full swing already. She'd changed into a lace-edged sweater, a long floral skirt and strappy high-heeled sandals she hoped would blend with what everyone else wore. She would hate to appear under or over dressed at her first conference.

"Hey, girlfriend."

Amid a cloud of perfume and a jangle of bracelets, Kelly found herself enfolded in a brief hug. She pulled back to smile at Sharon, a redhead today, though the color changed with her moods.

Her friend took her hand and gave it a tight squeeze. "I would have bet my life savings you'd chicken out."

"Almost," Kelly admitted. "But I'm here. What do we do now?"

"Happy hour." Sharon tugged her through a crowd of giddy women toward the hotel bar. "Up for a cocktail?"

"At two in the afternoon?"

"Oh come on, live a little."

They passed a grouping of poster-sized book covers promoting male cover models.

Sharon paused. "Hey, three of these are yours."

With a smile, Kelly scanned the enlarged artwork of her "babies." The same sinfully handsome man had posed for the last twelve covers. In fact, on the last four, he'd been featured alone. Not since Fabio was a male cover model paid so much attention.

"I wonder if you even realize what a little star you are." Sharon ran her index finger over the one-dimensional man. "Derek Calavicci doesn't pose for just any no-name writer."

"He was a no-name model til he posed for one of my books," Kelly pointed out. "Both our careers took off after that." She lingered in front of the cover from her latest release.

A swashbuckling hunk, dressed as Captain Pierce Connery, her swarthy pirate, stared back at her. His arrogant stance, the set of his jaw, even the look in his eyes, all seemed to convey the hero. Of course, the six-pack abs, enormous chest and flowing mane of chestnut hair didn't hurt. Neither did the way he was poured into those leather pants.

"They don't call him 'The Model Man' for nothing," Sharon sighed. "He's absolutely perfect."

"Airbrushed, I'm sure."

Squeals and applause from inside the nearby ballroom interrupted their quiet admiration.

Sharon moved to peek around the door, then waved Kelly over excitedly. "Let's go in."

"Why?"

"They're in there."

"Who, the models?" Curious, Kelly glanced inside. Five men stood on the stage, all tall and hugely muscled. And young. At forty-two, she was old enough to be mother to at least three of them.

Sharon suddenly grabbed her arm. "Oh my God, there he is."

Wavy dark hair caught Kelly's eye; she went up on tiptoe to see over the crowd. Derek Calavicci climbed the steps two at a time to join the other models at the edge of the stage. He leaned forward to accept a pen and book from an eager fan. Kelly had never seen him in person before. For a moment, she simply stared.

It wasn't just his masculine beauty that captivated

her, along with the rest of the drooling women. It was something else...that same presence he brought to her book covers, as if he truly was as rakish and dangerous as the characters he portrayed.

"I don't know what the hell 'it' is," Sharon said, echoing her thoughts. "But he's got it." She pulled Kelly into the ballroom, cocktails apparently forgotten in the wake of half-naked men.

Spellbound, Kelly stumbled along, her gaze magnetically drawn to the man who dominated the small stage.

He bent to kiss a fan on the cheek, then straightened. He scanned the crowd, as if searching for someone. Dark green eyes, so familiar and yet completely unknown to her, landed on her. A flash of something, almost like recognition, lit his face. One brow lifted, and a slow half-smile curled his lips before another fan claimed his attention.

"He saw you," Sharon whispered, giggling in her excitement.

Heat flushed through her. He'd caught her staring at him. At least she wasn't making an ass of herself by screaming and jumping up and down like some in the room. Like Sharon.

For the next half hour, while her friend screamed and cheered, Kelly observed the goings on. The phrase "mass hysteria" came to mind. It was like watching a bunch of teenagers at a rock concert. Only instead of pretty-boy musicians these men were...beefcake.

She leaned closer to her friend. "This is so embarrassing."

Fingers in mouth, prepared to whistle, Sharon turned to her. "How so?"

"They're like...trained bears or something. Paraded around for women to ogle. It's so undignified."

"Honey, turnabout is fair play. It's been done to women for years. You think Hugh Hefner ever lost a minute of sleep worrying about it?"

From what she'd heard, these men were extremely well paid for what they did. Throw in a few endorsement deals, calendars and DVDs, and she'd bet Derek Calavicci made more money last year than she had. Way more.

13

Throughout the hour-long event, his gaze strayed in her direction more than a few times. Certain he couldn't be looking at her, Kelly turned around to see who or what drew his attention. Nothing except a potted palm.

She frowned now as he once again searched her out then signaled to someone offstage. He stepped to the far edge of the platform and disappeared. She breathed a sigh of relief and turned her attention to the other models, two Fabio wannabes with long blond hair and another who looked like a Derek clone. None had his presence.

A few moments later, she felt someone behind her.

"Excuse me."

She glanced over her shoulder. A petite woman in her mid-fifties with short red hair and Harry Potter glasses stood behind her. This was no fan from the convention room. This woman wore a rust-colored suit, carried a clipboard in one hand and had pens tucked over each ear. An air of harried energy radiated about her. She extended a hand. "I'm Frankie."

Perplexed, she shook it. "Kelly Michaels."

"Mr. Calavicci would like to meet you."

Sharon let out a squeal that nearly deafened her. Kelly's stomach flipped. "Mister—*him*?" She pointed toward the stage. "Why?"

The woman shrugged. "I'm just passing along the message."

"And you are..."

The woman smiled, though the gesture never reached her eyes. "His manager."

From inside the room, the moderator announced the end of the session and assured the screaming fans the men would be available for photo ops later in the convention. Swarms of women poured from the doors, forcing Kelly to move aside or get trampled under the mass.

Frankie took hold of her arm. "Let's step over here," she said, steering her closer to the stage.

Kelly glanced behind her to see if Sharon would follow. Her friend gave her the thumbs up sign and a little wave.

"You have no idea why Mister—er, *he* wanted you to detain me?" Kelly asked, trying to will her knees to stop shaking as she looked around the room for some sign of him.

"I don't ask, I just do." She stopped as an attractive young African-American man strode toward them. "Blaine, this is Kelly Michaels. She's waiting for Derek."

Without another word, the older woman walked away, as if it were an every day occurrence for her to have to track down some female for her client.

Blaine smiled in greeting. "I'm Frankie's personal assistant. Can I get you anything while you're waiting? Water? A chair? You don't feel faint, do you?" He placed a hand to her arm as if he thought she might. Probably something he'd grown used to in his position. Swooning females.

As the last few women trickled out and the hotel staff moved in to straighten the room, Kelly began to feel foolish. Somewhere between the cab and the hotel entrance, she must have had too much Florida sun. She had to be out of her mind to stand here like some middle-aged groupie. She glanced to the far end of the ballroom where Sharon stood talking to several women.

"I have someplace else I need to be." She turned to leave.

"Don't go."

Her spine stiffened and little goose bumps popped up along her arms. An hour ago she wouldn't have recognized that deep voice. She did now. Earlier, she'd listened to him patiently answer one ridiculous question after the next. She knew he worked out every day for two hours; that he listened to Frank Sinatra, Santana, and jazz. His favorite color was green, and his birthday was January twelfth. And—there was no special lady in his life.

All this she knew about a perfect stranger. *Perfect.* Wasn't that what Sharon had called him?

She kept her back to him, waiting as his boots echoed in the nearly empty room. His size dwarfed her as he came up behind her, and she got a whiff of some wonderful, soapy clean scent.

"Kelly?"

She gave a little start at the sound of her name spoken in such deep, velvety tones. A warm hand settled on her shoulder, and she turned to face...the hard wall of his chest.

"Derek Calavicci," Blaine said, gesturing toward her. "Kelly Michaels."

"I know."

She blinked at the broad expanse of golden brown skin revealed by a white silk shirt open clear to his waist. Her insides balled into a tight knot; she lost the ability to breathe. She dragged her gaze up. Way up.

Flawless white teeth gleamed against a tanned face. When he wasn't in the tanning booth or the gym, he was probably at the dentist having his teeth bleached.

"Ms. Michaels, do you need that chair now?" offered the ever-attentive Blaine.

Kelly shook her head.

With a barely perceptible wave, Mr. Model Man shooed the assistant away.

"Ten minutes, Derek," Frankie called from across the room.

He ignored her, or else didn't feel the need to acknowledge the remark.

"So, we finally meet."

Kelly glanced down at his extended hand. She accepted it, but instead of the shake she expected, he clasped her hand in both of his. Heat spread through her, and again, she had to will her knees not to buckle.

"It seems we should have met by now."

She nodded, wishing her voice would make a comeback.

"I wasn't sure it was you." Maybe he was accustomed to women becoming tongue-tied in his presence. "I've seen your picture on the back of your books."

She winced at that. The photo had been taken at least ten years ago.

"You do know who I am?"

"Captain Connery, I'd guess," she said, taking in the pirate shirt, leather pants and black boots.

He chuckled. "It's what the fans expect."

She raised her head. "You knew who I meant?"

"The hero from your latest book. Captain Pierce Connery, former pirate. Black sheep of a proud, wealthy family. Vowed he would never wed until he met the lovely, spirited Kathryn, whose love for adventure rivaled his own."

"You *read* it?"

"It helps if I understand the character I'm portraying."

He read her books? Oh dear God. All those love scenes? Did he realize that since he had first posed for one of her covers, she created her heroes with him in mind?

She even kept his picture taped to her computer monitor.

His dark green eyes studied her with something that bordered on pleasant surprise. The fingers that grasped hers began a gentle stroking, and with every tender rub of his thumb, her knees crumpled an inch closer to the floor. Maybe she should have taken Blaine up on that chair.

"Well, um, it was nice to meet you, Pierce—I mean, Derek." She pulled her hand from his and turned to step away. Her purse tumbled from her shoulder and fell to the floor, its contents strewing every which way.

She knelt to scoop up the contents, and sensed him crouching down beside her. Her cheeks flamed so hot she couldn't bring herself to look at him, too aware of his large hands on her little vial of lipstick, her tissues, even her tampon case.

She finally managed to get everything picked up and hurriedly shoved it back in her purse. With a muttered "goodbye" over her shoulder, she headed for the nearest exit.

He followed her to the door, holding it open for her. "Will you be here the whole week?"

Try as she might, she couldn't get her gaze past that billowy white sleeve or the long, lean fingers on the door. *He's perfect.* Sharon's words rang in her head. Again. As if he had stepped from the pages of a book to stand before her.

"Y-yes."

"Then I'll see you again."

God, she hoped not. Not if she reacted like this. She slipped past him and took a few steps down the hallway, her heart in her throat until the door softly closed behind her. Knees quivering like palm trees in a hurricane, she paused to lean against the wall. A hand to her chest told her the erratic pounding of her heart wasn't only her imagination.

"Hey, you okay?"

She glanced at Sharon. Unable to speak, she nodded.

"What did he want?" The wicked grin on her friend's face said too much. "Sexual favors, I hope?"

Kelly shook her head. "To say hello. He recognized me."

"The cad. Of course he did. You said yourself, your careers took off together. So, what did he have to say?"

"Just...hello."

"Then what has you so rattled?"

"I don't know."

Sharon folded her arms and gave her a knowing look. "Uh-huh."

"What? You think this is because of him?" Kelly waved a dismissive hand. "If that were the case, then I'd be as pathetic as all those screaming women."

Sharon gave a satisfied chuckle. "You're normal."

At last, she felt stable enough to pull away from the wall. "How do you mean?"

"All this talk about not wanting another man in your life, how you're happier alone."

"I am." Even if she wanted a man in her life, she certainly wouldn't want one as young as Derek Calavicci. Or one with his reputation as a player. The tabloids followed his every move, and he never left them wanting for gossip. Not exactly the kind of guy she'd choose to bring around impressionable teenagers.

"You're normal, just like the rest of us."

"Was there a doubt?"

"I'm just glad Alan didn't totally ruin you on men."

"No," Kelly said with a sigh, "but I certainly made an ass of myself in there. Derek probably thinks I'm nuts."

"I wouldn't worry about it. He's used to women tripping over themselves."

Kelly held up a still-trembling hand for her friend to see. "Maybe it's all the coffee I've been drinking lately that's got me so jittery."

"Yeah, Kel." Sharon bumped her with a hip as they continued down the hall. "It's the caffeine."

Two

Derek leaned one arm against the bar and studied the crowd. He'd been nursing the same glass of scotch for an hour, waiting for the opportunity to make an exit.

This would be his last year working as a romance cover model. At thirty, he was getting a bit old for it and quite frankly, he'd had enough. He didn't regret a moment of his career; it had paid his way through college, allowed him to travel and had afforded him innumerable luxuries, not the least of which was the Florida retirement condo he'd bought his grandparents last year.

He was weary of the screaming, slobbering women, of the constant attention to his appearance, of always having to take his shirt off. Being valued for the way he looked half-naked. He sighed. Frankie's smothering didn't help, either. He would always have a fondness for the medium that had made him, but if he never saw another romance lover's convention it would be too soon.

His gaze came to briefly rest on Frankie across the room, chatting with other industry people. She looked back toward him every so often, making sure he was still there. Sometimes it seemed she could read his mind. She had already cautioned him about ditching this party, which was exactly what he intended to do.

He smiled in automatic response to those who approached the bar. A leggy brunette in a mini skirt on the bar stool next to him repeatedly tried to catch his eye. She was attractive enough, hot in fact. Going on instinct, he'd bet she'd be good between the sheets. But he simply wasn't in the mood. The nagging sense of discontent he'd felt lately spilled over into every aspect of his life.

She swayed toward him as she reached for her drink and something brushed against his chest. He glanced down. A scrap of bright pink lace protruded from his jacket pocket.

A thong, undoubtedly. *How original.* He had enough

of this stuff to open his own store, most of it acquired in much this same way. "Subtle, aren't you, sweetheart?"

She smiled and sauntered away, hips swaying an invitation.

Pulling the panties from his pocket, he caught a passing waiter and was about to drop them on his tray but stopped short as Kelly Michaels, flanked by several other women, entered the bar. *Whoa.*

She'd been pretty in a sweet sort of way this afternoon, a bit flustered, but nothing he wasn't used to. Tonight, however, was a different story altogether.

This evening the lovely Ms. Michaels wore a fire-engine red dress that hugged every curve. And God how he'd missed women with curves. New York was full of stick-thin paper dolls, all of them self-absorbed, bulimic, super-model wannabes.

His gaze traveled from the tips of red peep-toe pumps, up shapely legs, over her flared hips and trim waist to linger and fully appreciate the gentle swell of her breasts. A bare hint of cleavage peeked above the modest neckline of the dress, but he'd bet they were the real thing, no silicone enhancements. At last, a *real* woman.

He allowed his gaze to rest on her lovely face, wanting to make eye contact, let her know he was interested. Her eyes met his, but instead of the answering look he'd hoped for, her brows arched in amusement as she glanced pointedly in the direction of the panties that dangled above the waiter's tray.

"Ahem." The waiter cleared his throat. "May I take those for you, sir?"

He dropped the tiny garment as an afterthought, watching as Kelly and her friends found a table near the patio doors and sat down. She set her purse on the table and folded her hands almost primly. He had the feeling she was very uncomfortable in crowds, a direct contradiction to her dress, which howled for attention.

An image of her beneath him, tangled in satin sheets, caused a hot and unexpected awareness that had the fabric of his slacks pulling taut at the zipper.

A slow grin spread over his face. Perhaps he'd have to get to know Kelly Michaels a little better. Maybe there was something to the woman who created all those steamy love scenes.

A moment later, the redhead who had been with her this afternoon rose from the table and headed for the bar. He followed and found a spot beside her. She smiled warmly at him, without zeal or giddiness. Thank God. One less woman to hit on him this weekend.

"Excuse me, I wonder if you could do me a favor?" he asked.

"Sure," she said, then paused to order two white wines before asking, "Aren't you...?"

"I am."

She grinned. "You look different with clothes on."

"I get that a lot."

She stuck out a heavily-jeweled hand. "Sharon Lewis."

"You're with Kelly Michaels. Do you think I could get an invitation back to your table?"

"She'll probably kill me, but why not?"

He took up both wine glasses and offered her his arm. "Lead the way."

As Derek approached the table with Ms. Lewis, Kelly looked in their direction, glanced away and then suddenly back with an expression that bordered on horror.

"Hey, Kel," Sharon said, giving him a broad wink. "Look who I found?"

Kelly's cheeks turned flamingo-pink. He had the definite impression if she could slide under the table and disappear, she probably would. When was the last time he'd actually seen a woman blush?

He leaned close to place a glass of white wine on the table. Her eyes widened as his arm grazed her breast, and a jolt of electricity shot straight through him. "I believe this is yours."

She looked away from him and focused her attention on the glass. "Thank you."

He straightened, then pulled out the chair beside her to sit down. Her reaction peaked his curiosity. He could have sworn she felt the same spark he had, yet she seemed almost annoyed. He'd gotten over himself a long time ago, but this was a bit out of the ordinary. Most women practically begged for his attention. Clearly not Ms. Michaels.

From the corner of his eye, he saw Frankie stalk toward them with a determined look on her face. Ah Christ, she was in damage-control mode. She probably had made arrangements for him to join another group.

"We should thank you, really, Derek, for all you've done for the romance industry," Sharon said as she took a seat to Kelly's left. The other women at the table nodded.

"Not at all," he said, sensing Frankie's arrival behind him. "You ladies are the ones who do all the work. I'm fortunate just to be a part of it."

His manager placed a hand on his shoulder. "Derek brings so much class to every cover he poses for. Don't you think so, ladies?"

"He's well paid for it, too," Kelly said, her tone sharp.

Ouch. He hadn't seen that coming. She hated him. Probably hated all cover models. Maybe men in general.

"That bare chest and those abs have sold millions of books," Frankie said. Derek heard rather than saw the phony smile plastered on her face.

His aloof lady in red stiffened. "That's interesting, because the fan mail I receive never mentions him."

To his utter amazement, she lightly touched his arm. If he hadn't been so interested in what she had to say, he might have lost himself in her serious blue eyes.

"With all due respect for...whatever it is that you do, Derek. Your remarkable physique may help a new reader find her way to my books, but if she doesn't enjoy the story, she won't buy another." She turned a frosty glance in Frankie's direction. "No matter who is on the cover."

Derek glanced down at the hand resting on his arm, then into her lovely face. She eased her hand away and clenched her fist in her lap. She'd felt it too, that unexplainable sizzle between them.

"Kelly's readers would buy her books if they were sold in a plain brown wrapper," Sharon said. A murmur of agreement went around the table. "Do you know she sold even more books this year than—"

"Thanks, guys." Kelly rose from her chair. "I need some fresh air."

Derek watched her hurry toward the patio doors and slip outside. As unexpected and intriguing as the sexual pull he felt was, he hadn't meant to frighten her off. There was a reserve to her, something almost Grace Kelly-like that made her different from the women he usually encountered. Maybe he shouldn't have brushed against her when he set the glass down.

He frowned and glanced back to her friends. "I didn't mean to make her uncomfortable."

Sharon shook her head. "It's not you. She's a little homesick."

"Really." He looked over his shoulder once again, though she had already disappeared from sight.

"The first time away from the kids is rough," another woman added.

"How old are the kids?" Frankie asked in an I-couldn't-care-less tone.

"Teenagers..."

Derek only half listened, his gaze fixed on the patio doors. *Kids.* "So she's married."

"Divorced," Sharon answered quickly.

"Well, girls," Frankie said, "I hate to steal him away from you, but there are some people waiting—"

He rose from his chair, intentionally silencing her. "Ladies, the pleasure was all mine."

Frankie was close at his heels as he strode away from the table. "All right, I have it all lined up, at nine o'clock you'll join us at—"

"I'm busy."

"No, you aren't."

He stopped at the patio doors and stared down at her. "I intend to be."

"Don't you dare leave this party."

He reached for the doors and pulled them open.

Frankie followed. "What do you think you're doing?"

He paused to scan the patio for the red dress. "What does it look like?"

"You aren't really looking for *her.*"

"And if I am?"

Adopting a smug expression, Frankie crossed her arms over her chest. "I realize all it takes is a blonde in a red dress to have you snorting and pawing at the ground, but this one isn't your type."

He wasn't about to explain his attraction to Kelly Michaels. Not when he didn't understand it himself.

Besides, it was none of Frankie's business. Instead, he gave her a half-grin and said the words he knew would get her off his back. "She's female, isn't she?"

She threw her hands up in disgust. "Why couldn't you be gay like the rest of them?"

He removed a lighter from his pocket and calmly lit a cigarette. Partly because he wanted one, partly because it would further piss her off.

"Jesus, don't let anyone see you smoking," she whined, fanning a frantic hand at him. "It'll ruin your image."

Tired of listening to her, Derek strode away. If his lady in red was out here, he'd find her.

"She wasn't even interested in you!" his manager called after him.

He stopped long enough to turn around and raise an eyebrow. "I can resist anything but a challenge."

****

Muttering a curse she would have washed Cody's mouth out for, Kelly dodged a palm branch hanging low over the sidewalk. She'd been the only one wearing red while the others paraded around in the usual little black dresses. Why oh why had she listened to Sharon and Maya and bought this damn thing?

When she had tried it on, she had been almost giddy from the recent weight loss. She hadn't worn this size since before her marriage to Alan. And the woman staring back at her in the dressing room mirror had looked too good to be her. Somehow, the dress accentuated the good things and downplayed the bad.

She really wasn't the red dress type. She hadn't even packed it. Someone, and that person's name was undoubtedly Maya, had swapped the conservative black cocktail dress for this one. Her own fault for packing so far in advance.

Maya and Sharon were determined to get her out of her conservative clothing, the comfortable old navy blues, blacks and khaki's. Red had been a mistake.

Kelly glanced down at her feet. God, she felt like a hooker in these shoes. Slipping out of them, she padded barefoot across a grassy area.

The outside patio was quiet. It wasn't hard to figure

out why. Even now, hours after sunset, the temperature had barely cooled. Still, the warm breeze felt good on her face, and the gentle sway of the palm trees against the night sky soothed her frazzled nerves.

She came to the pool. On impulse, she sat and dangled her bare feet in the water.

Why had she been so rude to Derek? It was that Frankie woman's comments that had annoyed her, not him. And what was with the knot that formed in her stomach every time she saw the man? Okay, so he was handsome. More than that. God-like. He looked better in a tuxedo, more comfortable in one than James Bond.

So she found him attractive, big deal. She and about ten million other women. If nothing else, she was normal, as Sharon had observed earlier.

She had no problem with cover models. Some authors did, but Derek's manager was partially right. His pretty face and sculpted body had sold a lot of books. Many of them hers. Her sales had risen steadily since he first graced one of her covers. But she credited her own talent, not Derek's appearance, for that. Oh, sure, his looks may have attracted some new readers. But she liked to think the stories and characters she created put her on so many readers' "auto buy" list.

Heaving a sigh, she gazed upward. Stars twinkled back at her from a clear, cloudless sky. Somehow it only served to remind her how far from home she was. She wondered what Maya and Cody were doing, if they had everything they needed. The divorce hadn't been easy on them and being away from their friends for summers and holidays didn't help. She even worried about Barney, Cody's loyal golden retriever. Had she packed enough treats and chew toys for him?

The smell of cigarette smoke wafted to her on the warm night air, tickling her nose. She glanced behind her, and her stomach did that ridiculous flip-flop again. Derek sauntered toward her, so handsome with his long hair slightly tousled by the breeze, tie undone and hanging loose around his open collar.

Oh, God, he was carrying her shoes. She'd been so frazzled she'd left them behind. She supposed she should stand but had no idea how to do so gracefully in a tight skirt. She sat up straighter. Whatever he had to say to her, she deserved. He had the right to tell her off. She'd been unaccountably rude to him.

He paused to stamp out the cigarette in a nearby ashtray, then continued toward her. Leaning down, he dangled the abandoned shoes from a finger. "You forgot these, Cinderella."

"I...thank you." She took them, careful not to touch him. The odd sensation she felt earlier when they'd touched hadn't quite left her. She wasn't about to add to it.

He looked down at her, then slid his hands in his pockets. "I made you uncomfortable back there."

"No, not at all. I—" Oh, this was awkward. Both the conversation and her position. She really needed to stand up, if only to prevent a crick in her neck. She drew one foot out of the water and attempted to stand.

He took hold of her hands to help her up before she could object and waited until she had her balance before letting go. At least he was a gentleman. A very near gentleman who smelled every bit as wonderful as he had this afternoon.

She backed up a step and faced the night. "I want to apologize. I meant what I said, but I'm afraid it came out all wrong."

"No offense taken, I've heard worse," he said. "Were you heading to your room?"

"I don't know," she admitted. "I just needed some fresh air."

"Me, too."

"It's lovely out here, isn't it?" she said, attempting small talk.

He glanced her way. "Very."

Kelly flushed. Oh, he was smooth, just like his reputation. "I probably should get back to my room. I have a pretty full day tomorrow."

"I'll walk with you."

They strolled slowly away from the pool. A few floors up, the sounds of a raucous party spilled from open balcony doors. A female voice suddenly squealed *"Ohmigod*! You guys, come here!"

Kelly glanced up at the sound. A balcony full of

women were screaming in unison, "We love you, Derek!"

He raised a hand in a sort of half-hearted greeting, but no smile came to his face.

Kelly waited until they rounded the corner. "I suppose that gets old after a while."

"A long time ago." He released a heavy sigh. "But you don't bite the hand that feeds you."

The warm breeze picked up again, blowing the hair back from her face. "I wish someone would tell my kids that."

Derek slipped out of his jacket and settled it around her shoulders. She started to tell him she wasn't cold, but the heat from his body, the clean scent of him, mixed with the faint hint of some very masculine cologne filled her senses. She curled her fingers around the lapels, drawing them together. Maybe she'd hold onto the jacket for now.

"Your friends tell me you're divorced."

Wonderful. What else had they volunteered? "Yes."

"I'm sorry."

She shrugged. "We try to keep it amicable for the kids."

He paused outside the front entrance and indicated a bench. "Would you care to sit?"

Her stomach still flitted about nervously. Sharon and the others would be after her for the scoop on this tomorrow. She may as well have a seat and enjoy it. It wasn't every night she got to make small talk with a man like Derek Calavicci.

She sat, giving her head a slight shake when he sat beside her. She still couldn't get over his attention. The hotel overflowed with hundreds of beautiful young women with tight little bodies he could be pursuing. What was he doing sitting here with a forty two-year-old mother?

"What about you?" she asked. "I know you told your fans there was no one special in your life, but surely there's someone."

"I just came out of a long relationship," he said, his green eyes intent on her face. "With a woman."

She couldn't help but laugh. "I hadn't even thought *that*."

He chuckled. She liked the way his eyes crinkled at the corners when he laughed, the deep dimple in his left cheek.

"We weren't after the same things," he admitted.

"So it was serious?"

"We were living in sin," he said with a boyish grin. "Drove my *Nonna* crazy, she's convinced I'm going straight to hell."

"*Nonna?*"

"My very Italian grandmother." He reached a hand toward her, but paused when she jumped. "Your hair is caught in your earring," he explained. "May I?"

As he freed the strand and tucked it behind her ear, the back of his fingers grazed her cheek. She swallowed hard and realized she'd forgotten how to breathe again. He was so close. She gazed into his dark green eyes and found herself wondering what it would be like to kiss him. She glanced down at her hands. It was ridiculous to think she could kiss Derek Calavicci. She couldn't. Besides, she was forty-two and he...*wasn't.*

"What about your marriage?" he asked.

"We grew apart, I guess. One day we both realized we were married to a stranger."

"And?"

She shrugged. "And that's when we divorced."

The warmth of his hand covered hers. Her belly fluttered with excitement then bottomed out. She was insane. This poor guy—this gorgeous, sexy guy—was simply being nice, and here she was, half-swooning. She had to get out of here.

"Kelly, I didn't expect—"

She slipped into her shoes and rose to her feet. "I left my cell in my room, and my kids are probably trying to call. My daughter will think I've been kidnapped if I don't answer."

He stood and moved to open the door for her. "She sounds as much like the mother as you do."

"Depends on her mood," she admitted with a laugh. "Some days she needs a mother, other days she thinks she is one."

She tried not to think about the gentle hand at the small of her back as they walked toward the elevators. Or the way his chest brushed her arm as he reached around her to press the call button. She got another whiff of his cologne and breathed in the scent.

As they waited, a young, darkly-tanned brunette hurried toward them. He gave a low groan. "Do me a favor," he whispered and without giving her a chance to say otherwise, slipped his arm about her waist beneath the jacket and pulled her tight to his side.

The brunette reached them, along with a cloud of heavy perfume. She cast a pouty glance in Kelly's direction, then faced the elevator. The doors slid open with a whoosh, and all three of them climbed in.

Every nerve ending in Kelly's body zinged to life as his fingers slid over her hip to pull her closer. His breath stirred against her ear in a silken tone that hadn't been there moments ago. "Which floor, sweetheart?"

"N-nine."

"Mine, too.

The brunette's husky Demi Moore voice jerked Kelly from the trance Derek had managed to put her in while he didn't even spare the girl a glance. Instead, he bent to nuzzle her neck. "I don't think I can wait til we get to your room," he said, his fingers trailing down her arms and back up again.

"Have you lost your mind?"

He took her hand and brought it to his lips. His gaze met hers, beseeching her to go along. "I just want to be alone with you."

A disgusted huff from the other occupant followed, but Kelly couldn't drag her gaze from his.

The elevator moved with maddening slowness. Derek continued to nibble at her fingertips, his gaze intent on hers.

Kelly realized his sudden attention had to do with the Barbie doll on the other side of the elevator, but God help her, her body responded as though he really wanted her. A slow languid heat had begun to curl about her insides. Her breasts tingled, and her nipples tightened as they hadn't in years. She only hoped the jacket covered the evidence of her arousal.

The car stopped with a gentle lurch. Derek slipped his arm about her waist, ushered her from the elevator and turned left. The brunette turned left behind them.

Kelly stopped to dig in her purse for her room key.

Derek placed his hands on either side of the door frame and leaned in close. Her hands trembled so bad she nearly dropped her purse. "What are you—?"

A door slammed down the hall, making her jump. Derek swiveled away to lean against the wall. "I'm sorry, Kelly. She's been chasing me non-stop for two days."

She glanced up from her purse to look at him. "So you conveniently used me to cover for you."

He lifted a finger to stroke her cheek. "Actually, I have a preference for blondes." He traced a lazy trail down her neck, then along the bodice of her dress to gently brush the hollow between her breasts.

She suppressed a shiver and caught his hand to gently ease it away. "Oh, no you don't. Your friend is nowhere in sight, you can drop the touchy-feely stuff."

"I'm sorry, did I scare you?"

Again, her hands trembled so that she could barely hold onto her purse. God, where was that pesky little card?

"No," she said, finally finding it. "Did you intend to?"

Derek's hand closed over the key card, taking it from her. "You nearly jumped out of your skin when I touched you."

"I don't recall inviting your touch," she said, annoyed with his audacity and her reaction to it. While he only played a game, she would like nothing better than to ask him in and spend the night in his arms. Something she'd never in her whole life considered with any other man.

"Even though all I can think about is kissing you?"

"Hah! Nice try." She held out her hand. "My key, please."

"Aren't you going to invite me in?"

"Why would I?"

That devilish grin again. "Because I'd like to do more than kiss you. I thought the feeling was mutual."

Did he really think it was that easy? Just follow her to her room, and she would invite him to bed? For a moment, she studied his face. Not even one imperfection; it ought to be illegal for any man to look that good. And it was this one's job to make sure he did. "I'm a woman. I'm *supposed* to find you attractive. But no, I don't intend to let you in." She snatched the key card from his fingers.

He leaned closer. "A kiss good night then?"

She laughed. "I don't think so."

The jangling of the telephone in her room prompted her to unlock her door. She slipped inside and turned to face him. "Good night, Derek."

She closed the door, relieved to have him out of sight.

Too bad getting him out of her mind wouldn't be as easy.

Three

"Sorry, Lothario. You struck out."

Derek met Frankie's gaze in the mirror while a makeup artist carefully applied "war paint" stripes of red and yellow to his cheeks. He turned in the chair to face his manager.

"What do you mean, 'struck out?'"

Frankie shrugged and tipped back her ever-present water bottle. "She said no."

This morning the fans would get the chance to have their picture taken with the cover model of their choice. It wasn't something he minded, he always enjoyed meeting them. But today he wasn't in the mood. The Indian get-up he wore didn't help, either. It consisted of a loincloth, moccasins—and nothing else. He would be groped by women his mother's age.

"Did you send the flowers?"

The make-up girl moved around to continue working. He frowned in annoyance and flinched away.

"Yes, Derek," Frankie sounded irritated. "I sent Blaine with the flowers and the dinner invitation."

"And?"

She tipped up the water bottle again. "I told you; she said no."

"Really." Was his lady in red playing hard to get?

Frankie waved over a nearby stylist. "Do you think we could put some feathers in his hair, or something?"

"Where is she?" he asked, brushing the young man away.

"How the hell should I know?"

Derek rose from his chair and jerked the strings of the plastic cape from his neck.

His manager let out a huff of disgust. "Oh, for Gawd's sake, she's got a book signing this morning in the atrium. Leave her there. She's not interested."

He tossed the cape on the vanity. "The hell she isn't."

"Sit down and let him finish—oh, screw it."

He stalked out of the dressing room and down the hall, aware Frankie had to run to keep up. He crossed the lobby and followed the signs advertising the book fair.

Earlier this morning he'd decided to forget about Kelly; she'd made her lack of interest clear enough last night. Somewhere along the way he changed his mind. "I sent roses, dammit."

He reached the atrium. Looking relaxed, happy and gorgeous, Kelly chatted with her fans. He was struck once more by her fresh-faced beauty and mesmerizing blue eyes, especially with the sun's glow on her pale blonde hair and her face alight with humor.

The memory of her in that red dress and the soft, sweet smell of her perfume rushed back to him. The way her nipples stood at attention when she removed his jacket. He knew he'd affected her, every bit as much as she had affected him.

"If she isn't interested, she can damn well tell me why."

Behind him, Frankie warned. "Derek, don't do anything stupid."

He never slowed his pace. As he made his way to Kelly's table, an audible hush followed in his wake. She was so engrossed with the fans she didn't seem to notice the change in the atmosphere.

At the table, the women waiting in line stepped aside for him. Bright sunlight streamed through the glass walls and ceiling, casting his shadow as he loomed over her. She stiffened before she looked up. He heard a slight hitch in her breath when he shoved a book beneath her nose.

Without a word, she quickly scrawled her name, then handed it back to him. "Who's next?"

He stepped to the side, blocking her view. "Why?"

Her gaze flickered over the loincloth he wore since that was at eye level. A delicate flush crept over her face as her gaze slowly moved upward. When at last their eyes met, he was fighting the stirrings of an erection—and she seemed barely able to speak.

"I—I told your..." she waved a hand in circles, "zoo keeper, or whatever she is, I have plans."

He folded his arms over his chest, uncaring if he

sounded like an arrogant ass. "Change them."

"I can't." She peered around him and gestured for the next person to come forward.

He leaned closer, covering the books spread out before her with both palms. "Why not?"

The glance she spared him was as prim and proper as a schoolteacher. "Because I don't want to."

"Then meet me afterward."

"No."

Knowing he was invading her space, he moved even closer, his face inches from hers. "Don't make me beg, you won't like it."

"Then go away and stop asking."

A wicked thought came to mind. Before he even had time to second guess it, he moved around to her side of the table and scooped her up in his arms.

"What are you—?"

"You left me no choice." He lifted her high, tilting her toward him until she had to put her arms about his neck to hold on.

"Ladies," he said, turning to face the room of startled onlookers. "Don't you think if a man spends the night making love to a woman, the least she can do is have dinner with him?"

"Oh God," she moaned. "Don't do this..."

"I warned you you wouldn't like it," he said in a low voice.

He turned his trademark thousand-watt smile on the waiting women and winked. "I'll bring her right back."

As they left the room, a buzz of conversation exploded behind them.

"Will you put me down?"

"Not until you agree to have dinner with me." He strode toward the lobby.

"Not out there—please!"

He turned and headed down a different hallway.

"You need to learn how to handle rejection," she said in a frosty tone that didn't fit with the hot blush that stained her cheeks. "And I'm not about to stand up my friends for *you*."

Damn, she was good at slinging barbs. Still, he had to keep his eye on the prize, and sooner or later, she'd give in. They all did. "Afterward is fine."

"It will be late."

"It was late last night."

He spied the doors to the gym. A glance inside found no one there so he shouldered his way inside.

"Put me down."

"Is that a yes?"

A disgusted sigh.

He knew he should set her down now that they were alone, but her soft curves felt so good against his bare chest. He glanced down at her. "Well?"

"No."

"Why not?"

"Because I have no desire to be alone with you. I'm sure you're a very nice person. But I'm not interested."

"Thanks a lot," he said dryly. "Eleven o'clock. I'll wait for you outside by the pool. It's a public place so we won't be alone."

"That's too late, I have an early meeting."

"Ten-thirty. Reschedule the meeting."

"Ten o'clock and I'll do whatever I damn well please. Now put me down or I'll scream."

With no small amount of reluctance, he set her on a weight bench and straightened to take in her demure navy blue dress. Very professional, not at all like the soft, feminine clothing she'd worn yesterday. "Will you wear that red dress for me again?"

"I didn't wear it for *you* in the first place. But no, I won't wear it again. Probably ever." She tried to stand, but he didn't budge, effectively trapping her between him and the bench. She looked up at him, face flushed, vibrant blue eyes filled with something between anger and anguish. "Why are you doing this?"

"Talking to you?"

"This game, or whatever it is. I'm not one of your little Barbie dolls like that girl on the elevator last night. I'm a...a mother a-and I have—"

"Why are you stammering, Kelly?" He leaned in close, fully intent on having the kiss she'd denied him last night. He felt the heat rising between them. She could deny it all she wanted, but he'd bet if he kissed her, she'd melt like ice cream on a hot sidewalk.

She pushed against his chest. "Because of you, you big oaf!"

He stepped aside to let her rise, not sure if he was amused or insulted. She slid off the weight bench, hastily straightened her skirt and stalked toward the door. Without so much as a backward glance or an assurance that she would meet him, she flung it open and stormed off.

Derek wiped a hand down his face. He couldn't believe he had just done that. He never chased a woman who made it clear she didn't want to play the game.

He would apologize to her tonight, if she showed, and forget about her. Even now, the lingering smell of her perfume aroused him. He remembered the feel of her hair against his chest, the warmth of her in his arms, and groaned.

Well, he doubted he could forget his irrational attraction to the lovely Ms. Michaels anytime soon. But if he didn't stop making an ass of himself, he'd go from being the Model Man to the model fool.

****

As Kelly neared the glass doors to the atrium, she paused to pull in a composing breath. How was she ever going to go back in there and face all those women? Especially after what he had said.

She groaned when Frankie caught her eye from inside and stepped out to meet her. "Where the hell is he?"

"Probably beating his chest and swinging from the nearest vine."

"I need to have a word with you, Goldilocks. Alone."

Kelly stepped past her and reached for the door. "I have fans waiting."

"You have more than that. Half the women in that room are standing in your line now."

She glanced around the redhead to see that, indeed, a sizable crowd had gathered around her table.

"What the hell is going on with you and Derek?"

"What?"

"Don't be coy with me, Sunshine. I'm adult enough to realize some sort of love play is going on here, but you two need to keep it between yourselves. I won't tolerate any more publicity stunts."

Kelly folded her arms over her chest. "You're the one who let him out of his cage, why don't you rein him in?"

Frankie rolled her eyes. "Nobody tells Derek what to do. Whatever game you're playing, get it over with. Play hard to get for too long, and he'll lose interest."

"My only interest in your client is having him pose for my book covers."

Frankie glanced into the atrium at the women who now stood watching their exchange and plastered a phony smile on her face. "Then you'd better tell him that so he can stop acting like a jackass in heat. I can't afford to have his reputation compromised."

Kelly mimicked the smile and gave a friendly wave to the crowd waiting for her. "Is that some sort of threat?"

"You don't want to find out."

She shook her head to indicate she had heard enough and reached for the door handle. Coming here was supposed to relax and invigorate her, introduce her to new things. So far she'd been kidnapped by The Lord of the Jungle and threatened by a woman who, even in heels, stood two inches shorter than her. She just hoped no one had snapped any pictures of him carrying her off like that, it would be really tough to explain to her kids if they ever heard about it.

Kelly stepped into the atrium, cheeks burning. And stopped as a sudden silence descended. Not far away, Sharon climbed onto a table, tottering in impossibly high heels. She put two fingers in her mouth and gave a shrill whistle. The entire room burst into applause.

A cloud of strong perfume assaulted her nose and she turned to find a certain sultry brunette staring at her with an expression that bordered on envy. "So how was he?"

Kelly stepped away. This was rich. She half wished she'd agreed to meet him earlier. She could kill him that much sooner.

****

Kelly purposefully kept him waiting, casually strolling through the courtyard as if she had all the time in the world. She didn't want him to think she was eager to meet him. Better to let him squirm.

She had also made a point to wear the same navy dress she had on earlier. Changing into anything else would make it look like she dressed for him. She didn't intend to stay long, but before she left, he would know exactly what she thought of this morning's little stunt.

For heaven's sake, she'd had to leave the hotel for dinner just to get some peace. If one more woman pulled her aside to ask if he was "good" or "well endowed" or to "share her secrets," she would scream bloody murder.

The area surrounding the pool remained quiet except for the lilting strains of a Jazz clarinet. A bottle of champagne sat propped in an ice bucket atop a cart draped with white linen. Candles flickered along the patio edges, and dozens of gardenias floated on the surface of the pool. She pulled up short, scarcely able to believe her eyes. He certainly knew how to set a scene for seduction. She couldn't have written it better than this.

Derek rose from a chair in the shadows and sauntered toward her. A thousand butterflies took flight in her belly. Dark slacks and a white shirt emphasized the incredible width of his chest. His chestnut hair fell in soft waves to his shoulders, and even in the semi-darkness, she could see a shadow of stubble along his jaw, giving him the rakehell appearance of any one of her heroes.

He stopped directly in front of her. "I was beginning to think you weren't coming."

"I thought about it. But I don't need another scene like this morning."

"Right to the point, I see." He gestured for her to sit. "Go on. You've waited all day. Have your say."

She sat on the edge of a chaise lounge. He took up the champagne bottle and wrapped a towel around it. His hands were so dark against the pale linen, such long masculine fingers. An uninvited memory of his finger sliding down the hollow between her breasts last night came to mind. She forced her thoughts back to their proper course. "You have no idea how much I hate having attention drawn to me."

The cork popped with barely a sound. "Is that all?"

She drew a breath and continued. "Everyone is talking about it. They think we slept together."

He strolled over—damn him, how did he always manage to make her feel like stalked prey—and handed her a glass. He knelt before her. "And that's a bad thing?"

"Yes."

He took her hand in his, thumb stroking her knuckles. Flutters of excitement rushed through her, but she didn't pull away. Instead, she steeled herself not to be affected by his touch.

"What can I do to repair the damage to your reputation?"

She took a sip of the champagne. Maybe the alcohol would relax her. "Just tell me why you did it."

"I wanted to have dinner with you."

"And do you always get your own way?"

"Apparently not." The grin he gave her was almost boyish. "We didn't have dinner."

"I have a teenaged son who is almost as spoiled as you."

"Ah, the age thing. I was wondering when you would get to that."

"There is a considerable difference."

He gave her hand a gentle squeeze. "I'm more than old enough to know what I want. And to pursue her."

"Your method of pursuit is a bit ... over the top. Did you have to be so dramatic?"

"It got your attention."

"Mine and everyone else's. It was pretty embarrassing."

He released her hand and moved to sit beside her on the chaise. "Because people think you slept with me?"

"Everyone knows I'm not that type. Or at least they *thought* I wasn't. Until today."

"You sold a hell of a lot of books this morning."

She stared at him, dumbfounded. "I don't see how that makes a difference. They only bought them because of what you did."

He flashed that mega-watt smile of his. "And if they buy a second book it will be because of what's between the covers. Right?"

Her cheeks began to burn as he used her own words against her. "All right, you win on that one. But that woman—"

"Frankie?"

"Do you know she threatened me? She's afraid I'll say something to tarnish your image."

"I'll talk to her."

"That isn't necessary." She took another sip of champagne. "Doesn't she have a life of her own?"

"Sure. It just happens to revolve around me."

"Oh. I didn't realize—are the two of you...?"

He laughed and she was again caught up in that devilish smile and the crinkles at the corners of his eyes. "We have a mutual interest in one another, but it's purely monetary."

"I see. Look, I said what I needed to say. I'll be going now."

"Stay." He placed his hand over hers to stop her and warmth spread throughout her entire body. "I know I move too fast for you. But I'm not going to pretend I don't want to get you into bed."

A moan escaped before she could stop it. "And I won't allow you to believe that's going to happen."

He grinned. "I love a challenge."

"Then don't take it as one." She edged away from him, too aware of where their thighs were touching. "I'm too old for you. And I'm a mother who needs to set a good example for her children."

"You keep identifying yourself as a mother. When did you stop being a woman?"

For a moment, she could say nothing. She hadn't thought of herself that way in a long time. Since becoming a mother, it had been her defining role. *Had* she stopped being a woman? Alan certainly hadn't treated her like one, ignoring her in favor of work, only aware of her presence when he needed something ironed or picked up at the cleaners.

Well, she may have never stopped *being* a woman, but she sure as hell had stopped feeling like one. Until last night. With one glance, he reminded her all over again.

She rose to her feet and took up her purse. "I should go."

"I hit a nerve."

"No," she lied. He'd hit more than that; a main artery

perhaps. "I realize you think of sex as a way to get to know somebody, but I don't."

"Am I at least allowed to talk to the woman who helped make my career?"

"I don't think that's me."

He stood, and for once, she didn't feel overwhelmed by the size of him. "I posed for one of your book covers. You asked your agent to see to it that I was on all your covers after that. My career took off."

"So did mine," she admitted, moving across the patio. "So I guess we're good together." Too late, she realized how he would interpret that.

She had almost made it to the gate when his hand on her arm stopped her. He stood so close his breath brushed the top of her head. "Just think what else we might be good at."

"Derek—"

He backed away. "I'm sorry. You left that one wide open, and I couldn't resist. Come sit with me, Kelly. I certainly don't intend to seduce you out here."

She turned and gestured toward the glowing candles and the champagne. "It looks that way to me."

"I wouldn't be a man if I didn't try."

Taking hold of her hand, he led her back to the chaise. He straddled it, then pulled her down to sit in front of him.

The intimacy of their position wasn't lost on her. She tried to stay near the edge but felt the heat of his chest against her back nonetheless.

He placed one hand on her shoulder. "Have you ever studied the stars?"

"Astrology? Never."

His chest rumbled with a deep chuckle. "Not those stars, the ones up there," he said. "The sky is very clear tonight. Look, you can see Pegasus." He pointed out the constellation to her. "When I was a kid, my grandfather would take us camping in the Catskills every summer. My brothers and sisters would sleep in the tent, but I wanted to sleep right out in the open under the stars."

"The Catskills? Are you from New York?"

"My parents got a deli in Queens," he said with a wink, his thick accent mimicking that of a New Yorker.

"How does a kid from Queens become the most famous male model since Fabio?" she asked and despite his nearness, felt herself begin to relax. But it was difficult. Her heart pounded, her insides trembled. She'd never experienced this sort of attraction before. Not even to Alan. It didn't help that Derek's huge thighs pressed against either side of hers. She wished she could throw everything—caution, propriety, common sense—to the wind and give in to temptation.

The very things she warned her kids against doing.

His shoulder lifted and dropped, brushing her back. "I was six foot four by the time I finished high school. It was modeling or basketball."

"I thought you were discovered jogging on the beach while vacationing in Florida?"

"Something like that." He reached to pick up their champagne glasses. "What did you do before you were a writer?"

She took a sip and leaned against him. His arm came around to rest at her waist. "I was a mo—homemaker."

"And before that?"

"A teacher."

"I thought so."

She tipped her head to look at him.

"You remind me of my high school English teacher. Especially in that dress with your hair pulled back like that."

Self consciously, she glanced at her clothing. "There's nothing wrong with my dress."

"No, there isn't. I spent the entire tenth grade fantasizing about unbuttoning those high collars of hers."

"Wait a minute, you promised—"

"I said I didn't intend to seduce you out here. I never said I'd make it easy on you."

She sensed the teasing behind his words and smiled.

"Does your husband live near you in Rochester?"

She took another sip. Languid warmth slowly crept through her, causing her muscles to relax and a tranquil mood to settle over her. Maybe now that she'd given up caffeine she'd try alcohol. She had to have a vice of some sort. "He moved to Virginia Beach with his girlfriend eighteen months ago."

"And how about you?" He leaned against the back of the chaise and tugged her with him. "Do you date?"

"I had a blind date a few months ago. Nothing came of it."

"Was he too young?"

The soft laugh that escaped her resembled the slight buzz filtering through her body. "No, too strange. Aren't they all?" She turned her head to look at him. His hot gaze met hers. She didn't—couldn't—move when he leaned toward her.

The touch of his lips against hers, so soft and warm, sent a shock through her. When was the last time she had kissed a man like this? She couldn't recall ever feeling this with Alan. Maybe because she had never kissed a man like Derek before. Young. Gorgeous. Bent on getting her into bed.

Suddenly, she couldn't think of a single reason to deny herself. What would it hurt? Who would know? Turning, she slipped her arms around his neck and parted her lips beneath his.

He groaned and pulled her closer, deepening the kiss. His tongue slipped between her lips to tease and explore. The smell of his skin, the wild taste of him, and the feel of his hair tickling her wrists mixed with the effects of the champagne. Her senses reeled until the floor went out from under her and the only solid thing left to hold onto was him.

Somewhere in the back of her mind it dawned on her she had wanted this kiss, had wanted to be in his arms. And if she were honest, she'd admit the tingling in her belly and what it meant; he wasn't the only one who wanted more than kisses.

He eased away from her lips, his hand lifting to stroke her cheek. "Now that you finally let me do that, I'm not going to stop."

In her dreamy state, she could do little more than smile. "We'll see."

He wrapped his arms about her and pulled her closer until she lay half on top of him. His hands made slow circles on her back and shoulders. "I still don't understand how your husband let you get away."

"I'm not sure what happened, really. He worked so

hard, always the first one in the office and the last to leave. The kids barely saw him while they were growing up. I thought he was just trying to make partner. But even when he did, it didn't satisfy him."

"In what way?"

She shrugged. "We finally had the American dream, the house, the kids, the SUV. But he wasn't happy. When he said he needed to take some time to sort things out, I understood. He was over forty, after all. Mid life."

"And that was it?"

"No, he started taking yoga classes to help him relax. Now he and the instructor live together."

His finger trailed down her cheek. "That must have been painful."

"Not like you'd think." she said, trying to keep the bitterness she'd fought so hard to overcome from her voice. "Once we separated, I saw things more clearly. We'd grown apart. And I know this sounds harsh, but my career had already taken off so I no longer needed him."

"Not for anything?" he asked, his voice silken.

The butterfly clip in her hair loosened, and she barely suppressed a moan when his fingers slid into her hair. "You mean sex? That was never a big part of our marriage. By the time he left it had been over a year..."

One corner of his mouth tilted upward as he continued finger-combing her hair. "And there's been no one since, you already told me that."

She reared back, tried to sit up.

"Hold on, don't run away."

"Just because I haven't—in a long time—I'm not *desperate.*"

"No, but you've sure as hell suppressed some pretty important needs." He pulled her back down to kiss her again. She melted at the first touch of his warm lips, wishing she could give in further, give him everything. And take. She had the odd feeling if she did, it would be a night she'd never forget. But she was much too sensible to actually do such a thing.

He nuzzled the hollow behind her ear, began to nibble down the side of her neck. She let out a moan of pleasure before she could stop herself.

"Come up to my room, Kelly. I'll take care of those

needs."

When he tipped her back in his arms and again took her lips, she didn't resist. Was it the champagne, the unreal feel of this night or had she completely lost her mind?

For a moment, she indulged herself. She tangled her fingers into his silken mane of hair and gave herself up to the ferocity of his kiss.

Somehow they had become entangled, his thigh between hers, her skirt hiked nearly to her hips.

He stiffened suddenly in her arms and pulled back from the kiss. "Did you hear that?"

The only sound she had heard was the blood rushing in her head. "I didn't hear a thing."

"God dammit." He rolled away from her.

A second later he lunged from the chaise and took off on a run. It was only when he rounded the corner that she saw he was in pursuit of a man with a camera.

From the hotel parking lot came the screeching of tires and moments later, a very frustrated-looking Derek returned. He latched onto her hand, pulled her from the chaise and urged her toward the doors. "Let's get inside."

"What was that all about?"

He darted a glance over his shoulder. "Just get inside; there are probably more of them."

"More of who?" She stopped in the shadows cast by the awning hanging over the patio door to peek around him.

"Miz Michaels," called an unfamiliar voice. "Over here."

Derek stepped in front of her as a flash went off. "Will you just do what I asked?" Yanking on the doors, he scooted her through.

"Who was that man? How did he know my name?"

He had yet to let go of her arm, and she had to double her steps to match his as they passed party-goers and bar patrons on their way to the elevators.

When he stopped to press the call button, she wrenched her arm from his grasp. "What the hell is going on?"

"You don't know what that was?"

"Would I be asking if I did? Photographers, obviously.

But why would they—" Realization hit. "Paparazzi? You're their favorite poster boy."

"That's putting it mildly."

The elevator doors slid open, and she entered. "My God, you did it again."

"Did what?"

"Made it look like we were—is that why you wanted to meet me someplace public?"

"You think I set that up?"

"Yes." She placed a hand to her forehead. Between the kissing, the champagne, and the run through the lobby, she was almost dizzy. "*No.* I don't know."

The car dinged as it reached her floor, and she moved forward. Derek smacked a hand over the "close door" button.

"You're the one who didn't trust yourself alone with me."

"Trust myself?" She squeezed her purse when she would have rather tightened her hands around his arrogant neck.

"We met there to make you more comfortable, remember?"

"*Trust myself?*"

"Sweetheart, the sparks were flying from both sides. If we'd been in a room instead of the patio, we'd be in bed right now."

"What did—you self-centered, pompous—I can't even think of a name bad enough to call you!" She slapped his hand away from the elevator button. The doors opened, and she stormed past him, right into a startled Sharon.

"Hey, there you are, Kel."

Ignoring her friend, she turned and faced Derek. "I was wrong to think you could embody the heroes I create. You aren't fit to wear Captain Connery's leather pants!" Turning to Sharon, she said, "You and every other woman on the planet can have him."

Derek shoved his hands in his pockets, bracing the elevator door open with his shoulder. He watched Kelly until she reached her room, wincing as the door closed behind her with a bang that echoed down the empty hallway.

The redhead turned and gave him a wide-eyed look.

"What did you do to her?"

"I kissed her." He heaved a sigh. "Things sort of went downhill from there."

She stepped on the elevator and took his arm, giving it a sympathetic pat. "Come on, big guy, lemme buy you a beer."

Four

The early morning sun was already brutal as Kelly walked the short distance from the hotel to the restaurant where she and her agent planned to meet. She never slept well in hotels, and the conference schedule worked against her night-owl nature, adding to her sleeplessness. She'd been outside strolling aimlessly since shortly after sun up.

As she waited for M.J. to join her, she had the odd sensation of being stared at but shook it off. It wasn't likely anyone from the conference would be here to recognize her. At home in Rochester she didn't get recognized often. Still, several heads turned as the hostess led her to a table. Maybe it was the peachy-pink suit she wore; Sharon always said that was her color.

As a waitress filled a coffee mug with decaf, M.J. slid into her seat, a bit breathless. "I'm sorry to keep you waiting. Getting out of the hotel wasn't easy."

Over the rim of her cup, Kelly regarded the woman who had been her agent now for ten years. "We could have met at the hotel."

M.J. shook her head. "I'm not comfortable discussing the industry in that setting. Too many ears to overhear." She signaled for a waitress to bring her a menu and one hurried over to accommodate her.

A "plus" sized woman, M.J. carried herself with the confidence of a world leader and everyone responded as if she were. Kelly had always envied her that.

They placed their orders and settled down to business.

"I think it's wonderful you decided to donate a percentage of the proceeds from your new release to the literacy foundation."

"I thought it tied in nicely with the conference."

M.J. nodded and raised a perfectly manicured finger. "Absolutely, and it's an anniversary book for you."

"Number twenty, can you believe it?"

"I can. I talked to your editor yesterday. The publisher has agreed to match your donation penny for penny."

"You're a genius; I never would have thought to ask them."

"That's my job." M.J. reached into her briefcase and pulled out a newspaper. "Now I think we need to discuss this."

Kelly frowned at the sight of the local paper set on the table before her.

"And this."

Another newspaper followed, and then several computer-printed pages.

She picked up the first one, then gaped at the picture in the corner. Her. With Derek. Engaged in a passionate pool side kiss. The caption read "*Romance Novelist and Model Man Heat Up Florida Conference.*"

"I heard about him carrying you off at the book signing yesterday."

"It was nothing, believe me."

"What you do with your personal life is up to you," M.J. said. "But what you do that affects your career *is* my business." She pointed one finger at the pictures. "This is not a good move."

The waitress came and set a dish before Kelly. Suddenly the plate of fresh fruit and scrambled egg substitute didn't seem the least bit appealing. She picked up her water glass and gulped it down.

"What's going on with you and Derek Calavicci?"

"Nothing. We just met."

"It doesn't look that way from this." M.J. took a bite of her breakfast. "Did you have any trouble getting out of the hotel this morning?"

"No, why would I?"

"Because, Kelly Michaels, you are *the* hot topic of gossip this morning. I couldn't escape the women who all wanted to know if it was true or not. I heard it took Sharon half an hour to get off the elevator."

"I haven't seen her yet this morning." She hadn't even planned to mention the scene by the pool to Sharon; now she had no choice.

"Look, the guy's a player. You're vulnerable. You don't need to take up with someone like that."

Heat rushed into her cheeks. "I'm not taking up with him."

"Have a fling, that's fine. Just be discreet. And for God's sake, don't lose your head over him—or worse, your heart."

"I'm not having a fling." She winced at how defensive she sounded and cleared her throat, hoping it would soften her tone. "That kiss was the result of too much moonlight and champagne. I'm not interested in him. I told him that last night."

Brows arched, M.J. offered the newspaper picture a pointed glance. "That's how you tell a guy you're not interested? All these years, I've been going about it the wrong way."

"Maybe I was curious."

Her agent laughed. "You're not the only one. Okay, putting my agent hat back on now, I'm not sure how this is going to affect your career. We'll have to see what this does to your sales. These pictures have hit the national press, and they're all over the internet. If the tabloids take it and put their own spin on it, it could be very hard to overcome."

A cold chill slid through her. "*What?*" Besides the kids, her career was all she had.

"Well, this could turn out to be great. He's certainly made enough models and actresses look good by being seen with them, maybe he'll do the same with America's favorite romance author."

"Seems to me that's a title you created."

M.J. shrugged. "I haven't heard the public deny it." She took another bite of her omelet. "The man knows how to promote himself, just don't let him use you to further his career."

A knot began to form in Kelly's stomach, twisting and pulling her insides. Publicity. Was that what the candles, champagne and music had been about? She picked at a piece of pineapple, then pushed her plate away.

M.J. paused, a concerned look on her face. "Kelly, for God's sake, eat something."

"I'm not hungry."

"You're keynote speaker at the luncheon today; I don't need you passing out at the podium. Besides, you're going to need all your strength to get through the crowds of women wanting to know everything about you and Derek."

She sighed. "There is no 'me and Derek.' How can one innocent kiss cause so much interest?"

"Innocent?" M.J. gave a short cackle. "Honey, if you'd stuck a bloody hand in a pool of sharks, you'd have been in less danger."

"He's not like that."

Another laugh as M.J. picked up her coffee cup. "Denial. That's not a good sign." She swallowed, then waved a determined finger in the air. "Don't worry about this. If I play this right, you'll be a bigger name than Nora and Danielle in a very short time."

"I'd rather forget the whole thing."

"Too late now. These women smell a hot story and they want deets." M.J. smiled like a cheshire cat. "We're going to give them something even better."

****

It was after ten when Derek strolled through the lobby, sunglasses on to lessen the ache behind his eyes. Settling for a run instead of a full morning workout did little to help with the hangover. At least it had cleared the lingering memory of the nightmare that occasionally dogged him, especially when he was stressed. Living through nine-eleven had been one thing; dealing with what he had witnessed that day was quite another. But none of that had been on his mind last night.

Despite the pounding headache, a grin played over his face. Sharon and her Long Island iced teas. He couldn't remember the last time he'd had that much fun with a woman and not slept with her. There was no sexual chemistry between the two; she was a *paesano*, a friend. And half-Italian on her mother's side.

They had found a seedy little bar a few miles from the hotel and drank into the early morning hours. No paparazzi had found them there, and it wasn't the sort of place where anyone asked questions; they had been more than alone to talk.

She'd had plenty to say about his pursuit of Kelly. As

51

if he hadn't already figured out he'd gone about it all wrong. Without one bad word against her friend and without revealing anything too personal about her divorce, Sharon had let him know that pressuring Kelly would get him nowhere. Her kids were her life, and since the divorce, she had been adamant she didn't want or need another man in her life—ever. Apparently when the lady said no, she meant it.

Well, he didn't have time to chase after a woman who was genuinely not interested, no matter how strong the attraction.

Sharon had even managed to open his eyes to a few other things where women were concerned. He could still hear her slightly slurred advice, after about their fourth drink: "There's girls, there's women and there's ladies. That's a really bad country song, but it's also the truth. Don't treat one like the other."

She had also cut his hair. At the time, drunk as they were, it had seemed a good idea. He had confessed his desire to remove himself from the image he had grown to resent. Sharon piped up that she had been a hairdresser in her younger days.

He had asked the waitress for scissors and told Sharon to cut it, right there in the bar. And she had. She had even saved the shorn hair in a zip top bag and given it to the waitress, who asked if he'd autograph the bag for her so she could sell it on e-bay.

Derek had felt inexplicably free ever since. He reached a hand up, unaccustomed to the feel of his hair that short. Instead of falling halfway down his back it just brushed the top of his shoulders. It was still long enough for people to recognize him. And if he did say so himself, it looked damned good. But his manager would have plenty to say about it.

The elevator chimed. The doors opened, and Frankie stepped off. She flung one hand up in a sort of "there you are" gesture and started toward him with that determined stride. She stopped dead in her tracks; mouth open. No sound came out.

Ignoring her, Derek turned to the young girl at the front desk. "Any messages for me this morning, sweetheart?"

The poor girl, apparently struck mute, stared up at him. She gulped. To put her at ease, he winked and gave her a smile he really didn't feel. She wavered on her feet, and as he reached across to steady her, the manager hurried over with a chair. Someday he might get used to his effect on women. For now, it still amazed him.

When he'd gotten his messages—mostly envelopes with room keys tucked inside, and underwear with notes attached—and made sure the swooning teenager was all right, he turned back to Frankie. Oddly, she was still silent. Probably wondering what the hell he was up to.

"Take care of these for me, would you love?" He pressed a handful of paper messages—suggestive offers from conference-goers—into her palm and headed for the elevator.

Her screech flew all the way across the lobby. "*Where the hell is your hair?*"

He'd wondered when she would get around to that. "I cut it."

She hurried over to him. "Which one of them did it? I'll fire them all! I'll scorch their asses all the way back to New York!"

"It wasn't one of your stylists. Do you think I'm stupid enough to risk one of their jobs?" He'd also like to think he wasn't that inconsiderate.

"You're under contract," she reminded him. "Making changes to your appearance is forbidden."

He continued walking. "So sue me."

She fell into step beside him. "There are two-hundred women in the dining room—members of *your* fan club—waiting to have breakfast with you."

"I'll be down in ten minutes."

"There's not enough time to get you into costume now, not to mention hair and makeup."

"Then I guess they'll have to breakfast with the real me." He pressed the call button for the elevator.

"They don't want the *real you*, they want The Model Man."

"There are plenty of other cover models around this weekend, Francesca. If I'm not good enough, send someone else."

He stepped on the elevator; the doors began to close.

Frankie shouldered the doors open. "Don't do this to me. I've spent the entire morning dodging every frickin' tabloid in the country wanting to know about you and Goldilocks."

"Who?"

"You haven't seen the papers this morning?" She shook her head. "What am I saying? Of course you haven't. You've been with *her*."

He thumped his head against the back wall of the elevator. What happened last night with the paparazzi was such a regular occurrence he hadn't given it another thought, never considered how fast those pictures could show up.

But after what he had learned about Kelly last night, he had a feeling she would view it much, much differently.

****

As a cab dropped her back at the hotel, Kelly fully expected the throng of reporters M.J. had predicted. There were none. She had taken her agent's advice and had the cabbie drop her at a different entrance. Even so, as she stepped out of the muggy Florida heat into the icy cool of the bar entrance, no one paid her much attention. The morning workshops were underway and all was quiet as she made her way to the lobby.

Her stomach clenched at the thought of running into Derek. It was bad enough the memory of his kisses kept washing over her. But for M.J. to even suggest they might turn last night's events to their advantage was even more upsetting.

She glanced at the clock behind the front desk. In fifteen minutes she was due to sit on an agent and editor panel with Sharon. She would freshen up and then go find Sharon and make her apologies for her temper last night on their way to the panel.

The sound of chatter and footsteps signaled the end of a workshop. Hoping to avoid a mob of curious Derek fans, she slipped into a nearby ladies room.

A moment later, the door burst open.

Panic gripped her. She darted into a stall and closed the door, heart pounding as though she were being chased.

"Have you seen her anywhere yet?" came an excited

voice. Kelly watched as a pair of navy blue pumps walked past her stall into the one on her right.

"Are you kidding? She's probably still in his bed. Wouldn't you be?"

Kelly had the sinking feeling she knew exactly who "she" was. In the stall on the left, a pair of sensible canvas shoes appeared. "Let's see how tired she looks when she speaks at the luncheon today."

Oh boy.

"You think he wore her out?"

A chorus of giggles. "Maybe it was the other way around."

Another voice joined the fray. "I saw his manager; she looks fit to be tied. Word is she can't find either one of them."

Kelly groaned to herself.

"I think it's romantic."

She leaned closer to listen to this new, dreamy voice. Beneath the door she spied a pair of white sandals and pink-manicured toenails. "Why should only actresses get the hot guys? She's gorgeous, he's gorgeous, their careers go hand in hand. I saw him at the party the other night. He looked totally bored until she walked in wearing this beautiful, sexy dress."

"I heard it was drop-dead red." This from Navy Blue Pumps.

"It was," sighed White Sandals. "And she was breathtaking."

Kelly pressed a hand to her face. Right about now, her cheeks were probably as red as the infamous dress.

"I've been reading her books for years," continued White Sandals. "I hope they fall madly in love and she gets her happily ever after."

Laughter sounded from the stalls on either side of Kelly as the women finished their business and exited.

"Are you kidding?" said Sensible Canvas Shoes. "When he's done, he'll toss her aside like a used Kleenex."

"All playboys have to settle down sometime," said White Sandals as she made her way into the stall.

"Well, I hope he doesn't settle down too soon, I haven't had my turn with him yet," said Navy Blue Pumps. "Do you suppose he's as good *under* the covers as he looks *on* them?"

More giggles.

At that, Kelly chose to flush the toilet even though she hadn't had a chance to use it yet.

As she stepped from the stall to the sink, a hush fell over the room.

"Ladies." She recognized Sensible Canvas Shoes from a workshop she did yesterday on the golden age of piracy and gave her a tight smile.

Head high, she washed her hands and exited the room.

Five

"A goddamned circus. That's what this is."

Cramped beside Frankie in the back of a catering van, Derek took a deep drag on a cigarette, intentionally allowing the smoke to waft toward her.

"Do you mind?" she whined. "I'm car sick enough as it is."

He ignored her.

She fanned the smoke away with a hand. "I finally get to the point in my career where I can afford to take a limo wherever I want to go, and I end up in the back of a delivery truck to escape the press."

"You're not enjoying the ride?" He tapped the upturned crate she sat on.

"I've never seen so many reporters and photographers in one place before, not even when you dated that actress last year."

This morning's fan club breakfast was a disaster with the fans all clamoring for more news of Derek and Kelly. Everyone had seen them together—even in places they had never been. He hadn't even seen her this morning but heard the agent/editor panel she was on earlier had gone much the same way.

Frankie put a hand to her throat. "Would you put that thing out? Ever since I quit, I can't stand cigarette smoke."

"If you insist," he leaned over and dropped the butt in her open water bottle. "I've had enough, Frankie."

She picked up the water bottle, grimaced and set it aside. "Sorry, but I can't breathe with you smoking."

"You know what I mean." At her silence, he looked over at her. "You think I can't smell you all over this? You tipped off those photographers."

"Hey, if you're going to screw her, you may as well get something out of it."

"You might have given me a chance to actually do it

first."

She gave a short bark of laughter. "Don't tell me you struck out last night, Oh Great One."

He leaned against the wall and sighed. He refused to let her get to him. "Where the hell are we going anyway?"

"Someone's a little testy today. Guess I have my answer."

"She's got kids. She doesn't want them to see this kind of stuff in the papers." He shoved a plastic crate full of dinner rolls aside so he could stretch out his legs.

"Not my problem. I'm just doing my job."

"Ruining Kelly's career isn't your job. Neither is messing with my personal life."

Frankie wagged a finger at him. God, he hated it when she did that. "I haven't steered you wrong yet. If I let you, you'd just go wherever the next erection led."

"Thanks."

She laughed. "You really are testy. Why don't you do yourself a favor and get laid tonight? Anyone but Kelly Michaels."

"I don't know what you've got against her."

"It's nothing personal. I just don't like how she's affected you."

The truck turned into the parking lot of an upscale hotel. "And don't ask me what the hell this is about. Her agent set it up. Big fat witch. I'd have told her to go to hell, but I was afraid she'd sit on me."

Derek couldn't help a sarcastic chuckle. "Don't play the victim for my benefit. The only thing you're afraid of is a low bank balance. If you didn't stand to gain from it, we wouldn't be here."

"My gain is your gain," she sing-songed as the driver opened the back doors.

Derek climbed out and paused to help Frankie, though he was tempted to let her fend for herself.

She adjusted her skirt, then followed the driver through the delivery doors. "Let's hope your girlfriend got here without attracting any attention."

"Kelly is here?"

Frankie rolled her eyes and whipped out her cell phone. "Blaine? See if you can't find a playmate for Derek tonight. You know the type; blonde, big boobs, wears tight

T-shirts and serves up beer and chicken wings. Hey, is there a Hooters around here?"

Derek let out a huff of disgust and walked away. The last thing he needed was her ordering women like she was at a fast-food drive-thru.

The lobby was void of reporters, photographers and onlookers when he stepped inside. He breathed a silent sigh of relief.

A man he assumed was the concierge rushed over. "Mr. Calavicci," he said, his voice half-whisper. "I assure you, my staff is very discreet. No reporters are allowed in the hotel. Come, right this way."

Frankie caught up to him as they headed for a private elevator. "The top floor," she nodded toward the panel of buttons. The concierge dutifully pressed the call button, waited until the elevator arrived, then nodded and left them to their business.

The car began a slow ascent, made even more so by his annoyance with the woman beside him. Gabrielle was right; he should have fired her years ago.

"I must say, I'm surprised to hear you didn't score last night," Frankie said. "That little arrangement by the pool would have melted most women."

Derek said nothing.

"Actually, I'm kind of starting to root for her."

He turned to Frankie. "For Kelly?"

"Mmm," she nodded. "The one woman on the planet who doesn't want you."

"Oh, she wants me." He grunted at the thought. "She just won't admit it."

****

Kelly paced the length of the luxury suite, heels sinking into the plush blue carpet. The one at the other hotel had been overrun with fans and paparazzi. Sharon was stretched out on the tapestry sofa, moaning, an ice pack on her head, while M.J. studied the latest contracts from Kelly's publisher. A waiter had arrived a few minutes ago to set up an elaborate afternoon tea with scones, cakes, fresh fruit and cheeses.

She had no idea what her agent was up to, arranging this meeting with Derek and his manager. That, as it turned out, was the least of her problems.

Maya and Cody had seen the photos of her with Derek, not just in newspapers but on the internet as well. They were understandably embarrassed that their friends had seen them, too. They weren't the only ones with red faces. Yesterday she was just a mom who happened to write romance novels and make a living at it. Today, she was a sex-starved 'cougar'—whatever that was.

"Do you have any Tylenol?"

She arched a brow at Sharon's pathetic plea before opening her purse and handing over the pain reliever. "Little wonder you need it after the night you had."

Sharon groaned and tipped back her head to swallow the pills. "I didn't think I had that much to drink."

"Hmph," Kelly replied.

Her friend gazed up at her through pain-dulled eyes. "You aren't mad at me, are you?"

"For going out drinking with Derek? No. Just promise me you didn't say anything to embarrass me."

"I don't think I did. I can't remember all the details, but...I think I cut his hair."

Kelly stumbled to a halt. "You what?"

Wincing, grabbing her head, her friend nodded. And whimpered again.

A knock at the door made Kelly's heart slam against her ribs. *This was a mistake.*

"Don't be so nervous," Sharon whispered. "It's probably just them."

"What if it's more reporters?"

Across the room, M.J. moved toward the door. "Let me handle this."

Sharon nudged Kelly. "I wouldn't want to cross her; she'll deal with them if it is."

M.J. opened the door. Derek and Frankie stepped inside. The necessary introductions were made, and Sharon gave Derek a little wave. "Hiya, handsome."

His warm smile was cut short by a frown from Frankie. And then his olive-green gaze came to rest on Kelly.

She wanted to have no reaction to him. But her body tingled with awareness, and her stomach took a nosedive. Indeed, his hair was shorter than it had been. But damn him, it only made him more handsome.

His gaze moved over her in a now-familiar way that suffused her with heat. Something flickered in his eyes when they touched hers. Something that felt like regret.

"Hello, Derek."

Hours ago, Derek thought he'd probably never see her again other than at the book signing that would mark the end of the conference. He took a moment to drink in the sight of her, and as usual, his body reacted. It wasn't so much the way her legs looked in that skirt; she was definitely dressed for business, not pleasure. And it wasn't the lacy bra that peeked from beneath the silky white blouse. It was the whole package, right down to her red-polished toenails.

Before he ended up with a hard-on the size of the Washington monument, he turned his attention to Kelly's agent. He was more than a little intrigued she had invited him here. He'd met M.J. Rogers a few different times over the years and always found her pleasant but all business. "What's this about?"

"Why don't we sit down." M.J. gestured to a table off to one side of the room. "Anyone care for tea?"

Frankie, in full drama-queen mode, made a production of checking her watch. "Coffee. Black. I have an hour until my next appointment, so let's make this quick."

Kelly made her way to the table, purposely avoiding eye contact with him. He waited to see which chair she approached, then pulled it out for her. As she sat, he got a whiff of roses and vanilla. Different, but it suited her just as the baby powder and lavender scents he'd come to associate with her.

Her murmur of thanks sounded almost reluctant.

"You don't need me over there, do you?" Sharon asked.

"We're fine," M.J. answered. "Can I bring you some tea and crackers?"

The redhead moaned as if the mention of food caused her great pain.

Derek chuckled. "I told you not to buy that last round." He took the seat between Kelly and M.J., well aware that Kelly stiffened when he sat beside her.

She dropped a cube of sugar in her tea and stirred.

"You two must have had quite a little party last night." He didn't miss the disapproval in her tone.

"You were out with *her*?" Frankie asked. "Jeez, Derek, I have an aunt in a nursing home in Jersey, you want her number?"

Sharon pulled a face. Derek offered her an apologetic look, but she waved a hand as if to say it was no big deal.

Moving around the table, Frankie stopped behind Derek, her hand on his shoulder in the possessive gesture he was all too familiar with. "Let's cut to the chase. What's this about?"

"The mess at the hotel," M.J. replied in a cool, businesslike manner.

"So talk to hotel management."

"I'm talking about the way Kelly is being stalked by reporters and conference-goers. It's gotten out of hand."

"You want me to hire her a bodyguard?" Frankie offered.

"Let me finish," M.J. said. "Kelly just got off the phone with her kids. They've seen the pictures of her with Derek. They're understandably upset."

Derek glanced at Kelly. Her focus was entirely on her agent. He wanted to say something, but other than a pathetic "I'm sorry" there was little he could offer.

Beneath the smoked glass table top, he noticed her leg begin to jiggle. Despite her outwardly calm appearance, the crossed leg continued to bob almost nervously, her shoe dangling from the end of her foot. He watched as it finally dangled from one toe, wondering if she'd lose it. But at the last minute, she slipped it back on and started the whole process over again. She suddenly stopped jiggling, and he realized she'd noticed his interest. He raised his gaze from her shapely leg to her face, but she still refused to look at him.

M.J. took a deep breath. "So now we have two impressionable teenagers, as well as the rest of the country thinking America's favorite romance author is having a tawdry fling with a notorious player."

He resisted the urge to sigh. The tabloids were the ones who made it appear his social life was some merry-go-round of sexual conquests. Most of it had been well exaggerated.

Frankie snorted. "Tough break, Goldilocks. Tell the kids I said welcome to the real world."

Not wanting Kelly to think she shared Frankie's opinion, Derek leaned forward, effectively shaking off his manager's hold on him.

As if she hadn't been interrupted, M.J. continued, "We're prepared to take legal action against Derek. Sexual coercion. Or—" She looked pointedly from Frankie to Derek for several seconds. "We could work something out."

"What? I never—" Kelly shot out of her seat, her shocked gaze darting over him. From the sound of her voice, he could guess exactly who had cooked this up. "M.J. may I have a word with you, please? *Alone*?"

"It's all right," he said. "Let her talk. I can't wait to hear the punch line."

"The punch line," M.J. said, "is that you announced to a room full of fans—yours *and* Kelly's—as well as agents, editors and publicists that you had spent the night with her having sex. She insists it never happened, and knowing her as I do, I believe her. But the pictures that hit the press make it appear that something did. We have no choice but to defend ourselves."

"And you think saying she was *coerced* will make it all go away?" He had to hand it to M.J., she was creative. But he'd be damned if he'd let her see that. He could feel Frankie's glare settle on him, could hear the "I told you this was going to happen one of these days" lecture even though she hadn't said a word. Yet.

"No, I really don't." M.J continued. "It may not make a difference when some socialite is seen leaving your apartment in the wee hours, and no one may think twice when some B-movie actress is photographed on your arm. But we're talking about motherhood and apple pie. My client is practically America's sweetheart."

Kelly walked away from the table as if she fully expected her agent to follow. "M.J., *a word alone please.*"

He heard the ice in her voice, saw the fists balled at her sides. Clearly she didn't care for where her agent was headed any more than he did.

"Hold on, I'm not finished." M.J. glanced at each of them, but Derek focused only on Kelly as she began to pace. "The media wants to catch the two of you together. I suggest we give them what they want, let them think there *is* something going on. But not some cheap roll between the sheets."

Frankie sank into the chair Kelly had vacated. "Where the hell are you going with this?"

"Tonight my client will receive a lifetime achievement award from Romantic Moments magazine."

Halfway across the room, Kelly stopped pacing. "Did I hear you right?"

"I'm sorry to ruin the surprise," M.J. said. "I'm up against a wall here."

Derek grunted. "Seems it's *my* ass against the wall, not the other way around."

"It's no secret her fans love you, Derek. They also love a good romance."

Frankie shook her head emphatically. "No goddamn way."

"I'm listening." He had nothing left to lose by hearing the woman out. And he had a feeling where this was going.

"This is bullshit." Frankie sank her fingers into his forearm. "Blondie is just scheming to get her hooks into you."

"*Blondie*," Kelly said, moving closer to the table, "doesn't even know what's happening here."

"I'm proposing, " M.J. said clearly, "that instead of having our sweet Kelly look like some fallen angel, Derek should appear to be the bad boy reformed by love."

Frankie rolled her eyes. "Oh, puh-leeze."

Derek brushed her hand from his arm.

M.J. raised her hand, palm out. "Just for the duration of the conference. We'll find a way to gracefully end things later, of course."

Kelly shook her head. "Absolutely not." For the first time, her gaze came to rest on him. Her cheeks flushed a deep pink before she looked away. "I won't do it."

Irritation pricked at him. He hadn't expected her to agree, but she didn't have to sound as if the idea was so distasteful. Especially when that blush on her cheeks reminded him how hot their kisses could get. "Still can't trust yourself to keep your hands off me, can you?"

Fire ignited in those cool blue eyes. He had to work to keep from grinning. The effort did not go unrewarded.

She stepped closer and leaned in. "Despite testimony from swooning females who think I give a damn, I believe it's your *ego* that's the biggest part of you."

He rose from his chair, forcing her to back up or come nose to chest with him. "I'm flattered you've given it so much thought."

She took a step back. "Only someone as self-absorbed as you would think I'd given it any thought at all. Which proves my point, doesn't it?"

"Your pupils are dilated," he said. "A definite sign of sexual interest. Not to mention..." He slid his gaze down to her breasts. Actually, her nipples weren't showing, but as if he held the power of suggestion over her, they protruded through her bra against the white silk blouse. He bent to whisper in her ear. "You might want to cover those up."

She folded her arms. "A pretend affair would only mean more paparazzi. I won't subject myself to that."

He couldn't help but grin when she pulled her suit jacket from the sofa and slipped it on.

"Not necessarily," Sharon spoke up for the first time. "If you stop trying to hide and go public with this supposed romance, let them get a few pictures, maybe they'll go away."

"No."

"Derek won't even consider this." Frankie sniffed. "It's an insult. This sexual coercion talk is bullshit. I can find many, many women who will attest that—"

He tuned out Frankie's rhetoric, tuned out everything but the woman across the room from him, the electricity between them, and the inexplicable tug of attraction he still felt. "I'll do it."

"What?" Every woman in the room said the word in unison. But his gaze was directly on Kelly.

"I told you I'd repair any damage I've done to your reputation. I'll play your little game. On one condition."

He saw her spine stiffen before she turned, very slowly, to face him. "I think I can guess what your 'condition' is."

"Just can't keep your mind off having sex with me,

can you Kel?"

Shaking her head, she turned to Sharon. "You see what he's really like?"

"I have a charity ball to attend in two weeks," he said. "I'll keep up the act until then—if you agree to go with me."

"Have you lost your goddamned mind?" Frankie jumped from her chair. "This could torpedo your career. Your fans don't want to see you tied down; they want you single and available! For once stop thinking with your cock and use your head."

He took a plate and put a few slices of fresh fruit on it. "I've never been more coherent, Francesca, but thanks for asking." He moved across the room and offered some of the fruit to Sharon. "*Mangiare.* You'll feel better."

The redhead grimaced but reached for a slice of apple. "You sound like my Grandmother."

Sinking into a nearby chair, he turned his attention to Kelly. "Well?"

She returned the stare, looking both perplexed and trapped. "As if you couldn't find a date."

He draped an arm along the back of the chair. "Oh, I've found the one I want." And it was true. For some reason, he couldn't imagine taking anyone other than her. Despite his decision not to pursue Kelly any further, fate and M.J. had provided him with an opportunity he couldn't resist.

"Why?" She threw up both hands. "You're the last one I'd expect to go along with something this foolish."

"It won't be credible if it only lasts for a few days."

Sharon sat up and reached for another apple slice. "He's right, you know."

"You're just taking his side because—well, because you're... *you.*"

The redhead waved a dismissive hand. "Listen to me, if you don't do this, it really will look like you two had a hot fling. You want Maya and Cody thinking that? You want your *mother* thinking that?"

"Am I the only one who heard the woman say no?" Frankie asked.

Derek slid her a warning glance.

"You do realize what this involves, Derek?" M.J.

spoke up. "You need to be on your best behavior. No making Kelly look like a fool by bedding every female in sight while she's pretending to be in love with you."

There was only one woman he intended to bed over the next two weeks. "I'll give it my best shot."

Kelly looked from Sharon, then back to her agent. "I don't know..."

"Your sales are up by over fifty percent since this thing between you and Derek began," M.J. added.

"I don't care about that. I don't need the money."

"The literacy foundation does."

She sank onto the sofa with a sigh of defeat. He could see the wheels turning inside that pretty head. She was being strong armed, not just by him, by all of them. But he'd take her any way he could get her.

"Fine. I'll do it." She glared at him. "But I'm warning you, unless we're in public, you keep your hands to yourself."

He grinned. "If that's the way you want it." He didn't intend to make the next two weeks easy on her. There was a hell of a lot he could do to her in public, all in the name of looking like a man head over heels in love.

As if she had already dismissed him from her mind, she glared at Sharon. "I knew I should have stayed home and pruned my roses this weekend."

Six

Seated at a dinner table in the semi-darkness of the ballroom, Kelly began to wish she truly *had* stayed home and pruned the roses. A candle flickered on the linen-draped table; around her the gentle hum of conversation mingled with the soothing music playing overhead. She couldn't even begin to relax. She'd always hated black tie affairs.

Speaking of black tie...she stole a glance at the man seated beside her, devastatingly handsome in his tuxedo. So devastating in fact, that when they'd made their entrance a short time ago, a cheer had gone up from the crowd. A cheer she doubted had anything to do with her simple black evening gown or her body of work—and everything to do with the way he filled out that designer tux.

Not that she could blame them, with the way the crisp white shirt stretched across his chest. Visions of her book covers swam into her mind, taunting her with images of cut masculine flesh, rock-hard muscle and washboard abs. She closed her eyes as something else intruded; the feel of his lips on hers, nibbling their way down her neck, his hands sliding over her skin...

"Eat something."

She opened her eyes and managed a weak smile for M.J.'s comment and stabbed a piece of chicken with her fork. It looked wonderful. It smelled wonderful. But her stomach was a tangled knot of nerves. Just the thought of eating nauseated her, let alone actually making the attempt. *Adjoining rooms.* The words echoed in her brain like a jungle drum. M.J. had decided to have Derek move into the suite that adjoined with Kelly's, to make it look as though the lovers wanted their privacy.

Her "lover" chose that moment to slip his arm about her. With it came the familiar smell of his cologne. His thumb moved in slow circles between her shoulder blades.

Her fork clattered to her plate, drawing the stares of everyone at the table.

He slid a glance at her, a hint of amusement dancing in his eyes. She had seen much the same look this afternoon when he had agreed to—*insisted* on—going along with this ... whatever it was. What was it he had said about her pupils being dilated? God, what if they were right now? She quickly averted her gaze from his.

True to his word, he had acted the part of the attentive lover all evening, finding excuses to touch her, smile at her. Little wonder her nerves were strung so tight.

His hand moved up from her shoulder blade to the back of her neck in a slow caress. Almost absently, his fingers grazed the hollow behind her ear, toyed with the earring that dangled from her lobe. And he did it all the while chatting with the people seated around them, as if he touched her without second thought, like a long-married couple.

He seemed oblivious to the fact that every pair of eyes in the room was focused on them. And that was something she couldn't quite ignore. Reaching for her wineglass, she was dismayed to find it empty. Had she finished it already?

Catching the eye of her editor, who had flown in from New York for tonight's events, she forced a cheerful smile. Frankie glowered at her over the rim of her coffee cup. Ignoring her, Kelly turned her attention back to M.J. Her agent was seated next to Jared Sterling, winner of this year's Mr. Enchantment cover model contest, and beside Jared was—

"Pssst."

On the other side of Derek, Sharon motioned her closer.

"Isn't that Pink Thong girl?"

Kelly nodded, then gestured to the glass of white wine Sharon had left untouched. "Are you going to drink that?"

"No way. Not after last night. You want it?"

"Please." Wine was the one thing her stomach didn't seem to mind tonight. As she reached for the glass, Derek let out a soft groan. She became acutely aware of how she leaned across him, her upper body pressed against his chest. Heat from his tuxedo shirt penetrated her skin. Her nipples tingled with sudden awareness. She glanced up to find his dark green gaze intent on her.

"Comfortable?"

Conscious of the people at their table, and the charade they had to maintain, she gave him what she hoped was a sultry smile. "Very. Thank you."

He lowered his head, his breath warm against her ear. "Is something wrong with your food or are we on a liquid diet this evening?"

She straightened in her chair. "Everything is fine."

Pink Thong cleared her throat. "So Miss Levine," she began in a husky voice, her gaze on Frankie. "Everyone seems to think Jared will be the next break-out cover model. Maybe the biggest ever. What do you think?"

Frankie turned and quickly assessed Jared. "Who's representing you?"

"A friend of a friend."

From beneath her lashes, Kelly observed him. She had seen him around this weekend. A good five years younger than Derek, and probably four inches shorter, Jared looked like a Fabio clone, with long sun-bleached, blond hair. His face was handsome enough and his body muscular, but he lacked Derek's charisma. Even with the spit and polish that would come from the contest win, she doubted he would ever achieve Derek's level of success.

Looking half bored, Frankie tossed her business card in his direction. "Call me."

Derek gave a little grunt, as if amused.

As dinner wore on, Kelly made small talk with her editor and M.J., half-listening to Sharon practice what little Italian she knew with Derek. She tried to eat, but may as well have been chewing sawdust. If only she knew whether it was nervousness about the award, or having adjoining suites with Derek that had her stomach in knots.

That now-familiar deep chuckle washed over her. "You'd better not say that one in mixed company."

"What does it mean?" Sharon asked.

From the corner of her eye, Kelly saw Derek lean over and whisper something.

Sharon whooped with delight. "Oh, I'll have to try that one out on my husband."

Kelly half wished she could enjoy the same camaraderie that her friend did, but the rush of hormones that overwhelmed her every time he was near ruined any chance of that.

At last, waiters moved in and began to clear the tables.

"I feel like a trip to the little girl's room," Sharon said. "Come with me, Kel?"

Kelly nodded and excused herself.

"You feeling okay tonight?" Sharon asked the minute they were alone.

"If one more person asks me that..."

Her friend laughed. "Nervous about the award?"

"I think so. And this whole char—"

"Shhh..." Sharon cut in. "*Romance*."

"Right."

They reached the ladies room and stepped inside. "You sure you don't mind my flirting with him?"

"Not at all. I just don't know how you can actually eat. Sitting so close to him makes me nauseous."

Sharon slipped into a stall and closed the door. "Honey, the only trouble I'm having is keeping from nibbling on *him*."

"You and Donna. She keeps staring at him like he's her next meal."

"Donna? Oh, you mean Pink Thong. Poor girl. Jared's a hottie, but I suppose it's a little like getting stuck with Salisbury steak when you want prime rib."

Kelly groaned and checked her lipstick in the mirror. "Let's not mention food."

Sharon stepped up to the sink to wash her hands. "So what color panties do you think she used to hook Jared?"

Kelly rolled her eyes. "She probably didn't have any left."

As they exited the ladies room, more women began to filter in.

She stepped to one side to pull her cell phone from her purse. "I want to check in with the kids before I head back."

"I'll keep Loverboy warm for you."

While listening to the series of rings, Kelly chewed at her lower lip. They were probably out to dinner, but for some reason she really wanted to touch base with Maya and Cody before getting the award. They had their own cell phones, but Cody usually forgot his and Maya didn't always like to answer. Especially when the caller ID read "Mom calling."

Sighing, she tucked the phone back into her purse. As she did so she heard a giggle.

"Ms. Michaels?"

She looked up to see two giddy women. "We don't mean to bother you, but we sort of have a bet going and wondered if you would help us."

Dread landed like a brick in her stomach. "I uh..."

"Boxers or briefs?" the first woman asked.

The second one giggled behind her hand. "We're dying to know."

"Well, uh, sometimes he... that is, I mean... Derek..."

"Both," came a familiar deep voice.

Kelly heaved a sigh of relief as Derek appeared at her side. Who'd have thought she could ever be so glad to see him?

"Depends on what I'm doing. And with who." He slipped an arm about her waist and favored the two awe-struck women with that famous smile. "Of course, we haven't had much need for clothes this weekend."

Tittering like school girls, the women slinked away.

"How could you say that?" Kelly moaned, wanting to shrink under some rock.

"It was obvious you didn't know the answer."

"I would have come up with something."

He urged her forward. "Cassandra is looking for you."

"Faulkner?"

"The one and only."

Cassandra Faulkner, editor-in-chief of Romantic Moments magazine. The woman who had made Derek's career, and who, with each new release, held the power to make or break Kelly's. "Oh, God, this is it."

"Breathe."

"What?"

He took hold of her shoulders and turned her to face him. "Take a deep breath."

She tried. And failed. Probably because of him. He looked too damned gorgeous in that tux. She was just as bad as those twittering fools who wanted to know about his underwear. "Why are you being so nice to me?"

"Because I'm your lover. Remember?"

Taking her by the hand, he guided her back to the ballroom. They had no more than taken their seats when Cassandra Faulkner made her way to the stage at the end of the ballroom.

Kelly began to mentally rehearse the list of people she wanted to thank, barely paying attention as Cassandra recapped the events of the past few days. And then the woman took a dramatic pause.

"Ladies and gentlemen, it gives me great pleasure tonight..."

Her stomach clenched.

Sharon reached across Derek to grab Kelly's hand. "I think I'm going to cry."

"...it is my honor to present this year's Lifetime Achievement Award to Kelly Michaels."

A spotlight momentarily blinded her. For a moment Kelly sat stunned, overwhelmed by an entire room full of her contemporaries standing and applauding. For her. Her body of work. Her achievement.

Derek pulled out her chair and helped her to her feet. He kissed her, then stepped back. Though she was seated near the stage, it seemed like a mile before she reached it.

Keenly aware of all eyes in the room on her, her knees wobbled as she walked. She tripped over something—she had no idea what—and a gasp went through the crowd as she recovered. At last she climbed the three short steps to stand beside Cassandra and accept the award.

The magazine editor hugged her, gushing that she had been a fan since Kelly's first book, then placed the heavy award in her hands.

As if observing from outside of herself, Kelly began reciting her thank you's. M.J., Sharon, her editor, her kids. She glanced back at her table where Sharon stood beside Derek, both of them smiling at her. Her eyes momentarily welled with tears. She wished Maya and Cody were here. But she was so glad Sharon was. And there was one more person she needed to thank.

"The artists do such a wonderful job with each and every cover, and I am truly grateful to them. But I would also like to thank the man who brings my fantasies to—" She paused, cheeks flaming in mortification as a laugh went through the crowd. "My fantasy *heroes*, that is, to life so beautifully." The spotlight followed her gesture to Derek. "I know he's attracted many new readers to my books over the years. Thank you, Derek."

As she turned to head off the podium, she saw him striding toward her. His gaze caught and held hers. She couldn't move. He reached to guide her down the steps, bringing her knuckles to his lips. As soon as she managed the last step, he said, "Hold on."

A moment later he swept her into a back-bending Hollywood-style embrace. "I can't believe you thanked me."

"Don't let it go to your head," she whispered a second before his lips took hers.

It had barely been twenty-four hours since she had last kissed him, and yet it felt like a life time. For the first time all evening, her stomach wasn't in knots, and she didn't feel nervous. In fact, since this was all for show and she didn't have to worry about giving him the wrong idea, she held on and thoroughly enjoyed the kiss.

A shrill whistle that had to belong to Sharon sailed over the applause. Derek straightened, bringing her with him.

When she would have let go, he tucked his arm about her waist and walked with her back to the table. "Would you mind telling me what the hell that was about?" he asked as he pulled back her chair for her to sit.

Kelly smiled. "That kiss? Because I'm your lover. Remember?"

Sharon ran over and squeezed her in an exuberant hug. "You guys look terrific together. You're some actress, girlfriend."

Acting? If that were true, then why was her heart hammering like a runaway freight train?

****

At the end of the evening, the waiting limo seemed a welcome refuge. After the way Frankie had ripped into him this afternoon, Derek needed it.

All in all, he thought things had gone well. Beside him in the car, Kelly had a cell phone pressed to her ear, probably checking messages.

Against his better judgment he allowed his gaze to take a leisurely stroll over her. The simple black dress was elegant and sexy at the same time. Black satiny straps accented toned shoulders. Her champagne-blonde hair was swept back from her face and secured with some sort of rhinestone clip. For a moment, he studied her profile, the delicate nose and cheekbones, her dainty chin. As lovely and innocent as an angel.

An angel who had him by the balls.

Not that lawsuit threats scared him. Though he didn't resent the position he had been forced into, he disliked the way it had been handled. He'd have helped her if she had just come to him and asked. But he supposed M.J. saw dollar signs and wouldn't have had it any other way. Frankie would have done the same if she'd thought of it first.

She flipped the cell phone closed. For a split second something sad crossed her face. For some strange reason, he caught himself wondering about that. About her. The need to know more about her nagged at him. Why the hell was his mind racing to come up with something that might put a smile on her face?

She looked up and caught him watching her.

"Our first night out as a couple was a success, don't you think?"

"It was a disaster."

He laughed. "You really think so?"

She nodded. "From the minute we sat down at the awards ceremony right up until that girl threw a glass of wine in your face a few minutes ago."

He glanced down at the red stain across his white tuxedo shirt. "I still don't get what her problem was. It's not like I slept with her. Besides, she was Jared's date tonight."

Kelly rolled her eyes. "She stuffed her panties in your pocket at the cocktail party the first night of the conference, and you don't even remember her?"

He shrugged. The media had branded him as a male

slut years ago; he'd done little to dispel the notion. Maybe he'd acted that way early on in his career when the thrill of so much female attention was new. But a lot had changed in the past couple of years. For some reason, it bothered him that Kelly thought so little of him.

"Most of them do far worse than that."

Her blue gaze flickered over him before she turned toward the window. "I suppose they do."

He suppressed an amused grin. She'd been nervous and jumpy all night, something he seemed to bring out in her, which told him his plan was on the right track. Every time he had touched her she'd nearly come out of her skin.

"How about dinner tomorrow? I'll take you on a real date to make it up to you."

She flashed him a guarded look. "A *real* date?"

"For appearances sake, of course."

"I have plans."

Jesus, getting a date with the woman was impossible even when they were posing as lovers. "I did, too. Seems to me both our plans have been changed now."

"You're the one—"

He rested his head against the back of the seat. "I know. I carried you out of that book signing. I announced to the entire room that we made love."

"I was going to say you're the one who chose to carry this out even longer. The conference ends tomorrow."

"We'll have dinner anyway."

"Fine. Nothing too fancy, this is the only cocktail dress I had left, and it reeks of cheap wine, now, thanks to Miss Pink Thong." She crossed her arms and turned to stare out the window, angling her shoulder away from him.

He'd never known he could find such an innocent body part so attractive. More than once he'd fought the urge to press his lips to the hollow behind her ear, nibble his way down her neck and over to her shoulder. He shifted to find a more comfortable position in his seat after his slacks tightened unexpectedly. "I must have imagined the red one, then."

She frowned. "It's wrinkled."

He'd like to know how that happened. He sure as hell hadn't had anything to do with it, though he'd been willing.

"Just let me know what time to be ready."

Oh, any time now would be good. He doubted it would take long to get her ready if she'd just meet him half way. Even a quarter of the way. He groaned. If he kept this up, the next two weeks would be hell.

What had he been thinking, to suggest carrying this pretense on for another two weeks? Dumb question. More like what had he been thinking *with*. He frowned, remembering Frankie ripping into him after the meeting with every "I told you so" she could shriek at him. He *had* been acting like an ass since meeting Kelly; he didn't need Frankie to remind him. But it was damned frustrating to finally meet a woman who brought out all those long-forgotten sexual yearnings—only to have her rebuff him.

Forcing his mind onto safer topics, he reached beside her to pick up the heavy piece of crystal with her name inscribed on it. "What's disastrous about a Lifetime Achievement Award?"

She frowned. "My speech didn't go the way I had planned it in my head."

Guilt stabbed at him. When she'd nearly tripped on her way to receive the award, he realized his touching and stroking made her nervous.

"And then—"

"What?"

"When I stepped off the stage. You were right there."

"I didn't want you to fall."

She shot him a wide-eyed look. "I'm hardly frail."

He laughed. "You didn't eat much at dinner, but you finished your wine, and Sharon's. I thought you might need a steadying arm."

She flushed.

He grinned. "You have to admit the crowd loved that kiss."

She shook her head. "I don't give a damn what they loved. The cheers and applause were for you. For *us*. For a relationship I'm not even having."

"We both know how to change that."

"Does everything have to come down to sex with you?"

"I never even mentioned sex. But you can't seem to

77

get your mind off it when I'm around."

"How would you know? You ditched me the minute we got to the cocktail party after the awards."

"Ditched you?"

"Yes." She turned in the seat to face him. "On the way over here, you told me to follow your lead with the reporters and photographers. At dinner, you had answers ready for anyone who asked a question. You're much better at that sort of thing than I am. Yet, we got to that party and you disappeared."

"It's called being social." He'd been cornered by any number of people once they moved from the ceremony to the after-party. Some of the other male cover models, Jared Sterling included, had been slapping him on the back all day and making smart-ass comments. It bothered him that they thought he was just "doing" Kelly; that she was some cheap roll in the sheets. And when the hell had something like that ever bugged him?

Besides, he'd had to put some distance between them. She wasn't the only one affected by his *loving* attention all night, and she'd done a bit of teasing herself. Every time she had wanted to speak to Sharon, she'd leaned over him, her breast brushing his arm, his chest. He cleared his throat at that memory and buttoned up his jacket, hoping it would cover the telltale evidence. "You could have joined me at any time, but you had your feet glued to one spot. Right in front of the bar."

"What are you implying?"

He grinned. "Nothing."

She folded her arms. "I'm not a drunk."

"I didn't say you were."

"I did *not* over-indulge tonight."

"Believe me, if anyone is going to encourage you to drink, it'd be me."

"What is *that* supposed to mean?"

"It means I like you after a few drinks. Or maybe it was the way I kissed you the other night that loosened you up." He flashed his most devil-may-care grin and slid closer. "There's only one way to find out."

Her hands came up between them. "Don't you dare"

"Why not?"

She scooted farther away from him. "Because there's

no audience here."

He laughed. "You don't know the answer any more than I do."

"Answer to what?"

"Whether it was the champagne or me you couldn't handle."

"The champagne." Her nose went in the air, haughty as a queen. "You don't affect me half as much as you think you do."

He leaned back into his seat, a surge of satisfaction rushing through him. "But I do affect you."

She didn't answer, and when he glanced over at her, she was nervously chewing at a fingernail, staring out the window as their hotel came into view. "I don't know why M.J. decided we needed to switch hotels."

"We'd never have gotten any peace if we hadn't. And to make things believable, we would have had to share a room."

She slid a glance of disgust his way.

"Not that it would affect you, of course," he added with a grin.

"Well, just so you know, my side of the door will be locked."

"And mine won't." He slid a finger down her arm, partly because he wanted to touch her. And partly because he wanted to see her shiver like she always did when he touched her. That shiver went both ways though; it rebounded all the way up his arm.

He would have liked to say more, take it a step further so she couldn't misunderstand, and invite her to join him in his room anytime. But he held back. He couldn't push her too much in one night. Not that he intended to make their time together easy. She could verbally deny it all she wanted, could tell him over and over again she didn't intend to sleep with him.

He had two weeks to convince her otherwise.

****

After seeing Kelly to her suite, Derek stepped into his darkened hotel room. A strong flowery scent greeted him. He frowned. The last guest in this room must have loved cheap perfume.

From next door came the sound of running water. He

closed his eyes and imagined Kelly sliding out of that little black dress. He tried to force the image aside but was left wondering if she was taking a shower—naked and soapy wet just on the other side of the wall. Or a long hot bath. The kind he'd like to share with her.

As he removed his watch and cuff links he heard a feminine sigh.

"Derek, is that you?"

He paused and let his watch drop to the dresser. The voice wasn't familiar. A dim light went on beside the bed, and he turned.

A hiccup of laughter escaped her. "Hey, you're even hotter in person." She rose from the bed, a young Pamela Anderson clone. Damned if she wasn't wearing a Hooters uniform. "I'm Mindy."

She ran toward him and flung her arms around his neck in an exuberant hug. "It's *way* cool to finally meet you. I've been waiting here for, like, hours."

"How did you get in?"

"Blaine. He said you were looking for company tonight." She pouted, swaying from side to side. "You *are* glad to see me, aren't you?"

Well, part of him was. But that body part had already been enflamed by someone else. And despite the Pamela resemblance, she was a bit too close to barely legal for his comfort.

"So do you wanna fool around?"

He spied the half-empty bottle of champagne on the night stand and the lipstick-stained glass beside it. "Uh, Cindy..."

"*Mindy*," she corrected with another bubbly giggle. "Cindy is my twin sister. I could call her if you want."

Sweet Jesus.

Folding his arms, he leaned back against the dresser. "How much champagne have you had?"

"Just the one bottle. Well, and a glass or two from that one. Is that okay? Blaine told me to order anything I wanted."

"It's fine. Did you think to order food, sweetheart?"

Wide eyed, she shook her head. "Why, are you hungry?"

"Uh, no." And he wasn't. Not for food. And not for

Mindy. "For you."

"I don't eat anything after lunch, it goes right to my hips." She placed a hand to her shapely backside. "And I don't eat at all when I'm working." She wrinkled her nose. "I might get bloated or something."

"Right. Well you don't have to work any more tonight, do you?"

"Nope." Another giggle.

"Then why don't I order something for us?"

"I could go for a cheeseburger, I guess." Cheerleader-perky, she shrugged, breasts jiggling in a way that should have interested him—and might have, at one time.

She stepped closer and walked her fingers up his chest. "I'll go freshen up a little, and then we can have some fun while we wait for dinner."

He smiled indulgently and watched as she disappeared into the bathroom. When she closed the door, he exhaled a loud breath. Normally he'd have Frankie or Blaine handle this. But they had gotten him into this mess. He'd simply feed her, let her sleep it off and send her on her way.

He smacked a hand to his forehead. Jeez. No, he couldn't. It would look like they had spent the night together. Well, the reason he couldn't leave—whatever the hell her name was—here, the reason he couldn't even find her attractive, was just on the other side of this wall. She could damn well help him figure out what to do.

****

Leaning back in a soothing hot bath, Kelly frowned. She hadn't heard a rap at the adjoining door to Derek's room, had she? The knock came again, followed by the sound of the doorknob jiggling. Damn. She had forgotten to check that lock.

"Kelly?"

Dear God, was he in her room? She leaped from the tub and grabbed for her robe all at once. She had just belted it when he rounded the corner.

"What are you doing?" she demanded. "I was having a bath."

His gaze skimmed the length of her. "I can see that."

The reminder that she had pulled the satiny robe on over wet skin made her pull the edges tighter together.

"What was so important you had to come barging in here?"

He didn't even try to hide the fact that he was staring at her breasts. A moment later, he groaned and turned away. "Jesus, would you put some clothes on?"

She crossed her arms over her chest, and resisted the urge to stamp her foot in frustration. "Actually, I'd like to get back to my bath. *What do you want?*"

Again, that dark green gaze raked over her. When his gaze came to rest on hers, one corner of his mouth lifted slightly. "Damned if I can remember now."

A knock sounded at the outside door. "What is this, Grand Central?" she muttered.

Moving toward the door, she reached for the knob, but Derek's arm shot in front of her. "What the hell are you doing?"

She sighed. "Is there some maintenance medication you normally take? I think it's way past due."

"You're just going to open the door?"

A knock came again, followed by a voice. "Room service."

"Yes, I am." She reached for the knob again.

He leaned back against the door. "Did you check to make sure it isn't a reporter?"

"Very well." She leaned up on tip toe to look out the peep hole. "It appears to be a waiter. He's bringing up the tea bags I asked for, since there's none left in my room. May I open it now?"

"You do and you'll give him the thrill of his life." He stepped away from the door. "You get dressed; I'll take care of room service."

"Do you want my pepper spray, in case he attacks you?"

He gave her a wry smile. "In the future, remind me not to come between you and your room service guy."

"Derek?" A little-girl-sweet voice echoed from the next room.

He muttered an expletive.

Kelly folded her arms across her chest. "Who... is ... *that?*"

"She's the reason I'm here." He opened the door for the waiter. "I'll take that. Thanks."

And to think with all the teasing, she had almost let her guard down. "Well, well, well I see you ordered *room service*, too. Of an entirely different kind."

"I need your help," he said in a hushed voice. "She's drunk."

"Doesn't that make things easier for you?"

"Why do you always assume the worst about me? I want you to get rid of her."

"And why would I do that?"

"I'm not supposed to be bedding every female in sight. Remember?"

"Oh, no, Loverboy, this is *your* mess."

"I could always sleep in here."

"Nice try. Maybe you should have thought about that before you invited her up here."

"I didn't. She's sort of a...gift."

"How sweet."

A moment later, the "gift" appeared, or rather, bounced, in the doorway, silicone enhancements first. She was twenty if she was a day, dressed in a body-hugging Hooters get up.

"Oh, there you are, silly. I came out of the bathroom, and you were gone."

For a split second, Derek looked so trapped Kelly nearly felt sorry for him. But not quite. He gestured from the peroxide-blonde back to her. "Uh... Mandy—

"Mindy."

"Right. This is my friend, Kelly."

The sweet disposition instantly vanished. "Hey, I never said I'd do a threesome."

"No, no, she's my... we're um..."

"Lovers," Kelly interjected.

The girl's eyes, ringed with heavy black makeup, widened. "You ... and *her?*"

Derek put an arm about Kelly's waist and hoisted her against his side. "Yes."

"But she's like..." A heartbeat later, the girl burst into tears. "My *mom's* age!"

Kelly started forward. "Why you little—"

"Down girl." His fingers dug into her side. "Sweetheart, if I wasn't already taken, you'd be my first choice."

"Oh, please," Kelly muttered.

Mindy sniffled and looked up at him. "You really mean it?"

He winked. "Cross my heart."

"You're, like, the nicest guy I almost ever—"

Kelly held up a hand. "We get the picture."

The girl smiled, then groaned and put a hand to her stomach. "Hey, can I use your bathroom? I think I'm gonna puke."

Seven

"Your coffee, D."

Seated in a make up chair, a stylist bustling around, Derek mumbled his thanks as Blaine handed him his usual morning coffee. "Did you take one to Ms. Michaels?"

The young man hesitated. "Well, I tried."

He sighed. "I'm afraid to ask."

It was nearly two a.m. before they found Mindy's sister to come and get her. Both he and Kelly had been up early to get to the hotel for the last day of the convention. She'd barely said two words to him on the ride over. He'd sent her, by way of Blaine, the no fat, half-caff mocha latte as a peace offering.

"She said it was very kind of you to send the coffee, but next time get it yourself."

"Jesus." Did she really think he could walk across the street to Starbucks and buy a cup of coffee? That's what assistants were for. They had argued last night while Mindy went back and forth from the bathroom to resting on Kelly's bed. Kelly had wanted him to take the girl home in the limo he had at his disposal and see that she got safely inside. He had tried to explain why he couldn't do that. All Kelly saw was a pathetic young girl. He saw a tabloid headline waiting to happen. He'd just settled a bogus paternity suit, his fourth in as many years. He didn't need more of the same publicity.

In the mirror, he saw Frankie approach, beaming like a cat with a mouthful of feathers. "And how are we this morning?"

Blaine shook his head and sliced a finger across his throat.

Her smile fell. "You didn't sleep with her?"

"I'm not even going to answer that."

"Dammit, if she wasn't your type, who the hell is?"

A squeal from the other side of the ballroom drew his attention. He'd know that laugh anywhere. He leaned forward in his chair to peer around the privacy screen. There was Sharon, beside Kelly's table, smiling and laughing. He wondered whose idea it had been to couple his charity photo session with Kelly's book signing. By the smirk on Frankie's face, he could guess.

"Was this your doing?"

"Her agent is exploiting this thing for every ounce of publicity, why shouldn't we?"

He yanked the plastic makeup cape from around his neck and stood.

"The crowd waiting outside is a mile long," Blaine said.

"All wanting their picture taken for their own romance novel cover with the model man." Frankie made a gagging motion with her finger. "Can't say it's worth a hundred bucks, but at least it's for charity."

"The crowd for Miss Michaels is out the door into the parking lot," Blaine added.

"There's no accounting for taste." Frankie turned her attention back to Derek. "Would you stop staring at her like some lovesick mutt?"

He started to look away, but Kelly glanced up from the book she was signing. Her eyes widened as she took in the sight of him in his pirate costume, then flickered back to meet his gaze directly. She wore that damned navy blue dress again, the one with the collar that buttoned up her throat. He'd like to burn the prissy thing. He much preferred her as she had been last night, especially with that pale blue satin robe plastered against her body. Not to mention the fire in her eyes when he'd prevented her from opening the door for room service.

Well, she'd have to get used to that. He had four sisters and made no apologies for being overprotective around women. Not that his feelings were anywhere near brotherly. The strange surge of jealousy that had come over him at the thought of the waiter seeing her like that last night proved they were anything but.

"You're hopeless," his manager sighed. "Don't forget to see me later to go over your agenda for this week."

He turned to look at her. "Agenda?"

She waved a hand in front of his face. "Hel-ooo? Anybody home in there?"

"I had Gabrielle clear my calendar for the next two weeks."

Frankie stepped closer. "Derek," she said in a low voice, "you get that this is a *pretend* affair, right? You don't really need to spend every minute with her."

"Maybe I do." He glanced back toward Kelly, rewarded to find her staring at him. Almost as if she couldn't help it, her gaze traveled the length of him, slowly, deliberately. When she caught him watching her, a delicate flush crept over her cheeks. So she liked his pirate costume, did she? And the Indian one, if he recalled correctly. The fantasy Derek definitely appealed to her. Certainly more so than the real one. The realization stung, but lucky for her, if there was one thing he knew, it was fantasy.

A slow smile curled his lips. "Blaine, hand me the cup of coffee Miss Michaels sent back."

****

Kelly couldn't believe the crowd waiting to purchase her book. M.J. had gotten the word out on radio and in the newspapers, but she never anticipated a crowd this size. Nor had she expected to have both local and national news coverage.

Just this morning, M.J. had told her that her new release, out only a week, had already gone into a second print run.

All because of a few kisses in the moonlight.

She greeted the next fan and heard Sharon from a nearby table, "I've known Kelly for about ten years now; I really don't know Derek. Yet."

She tried to shoot a friendly warning glance her way, but Sharon was blocked from her view by the hordes of people waiting in line. Apparently her association with the Derek and Kelly romance was impacting Sharon's sales as well. Most of the other romance writers in the room today were busier than usual. She hoped the added publicity would draw in new readers for the entire genre. Much as she hated the idea of this sham affair, she had to admit, it was benefitting everybody, especially the literacy foundation.

As she handed a signed book back to the young woman, she noticed movement in the crowd. People stepped to one side, much like the parting of the Red Sea. Derek was making his way toward her. His shoulders seemed impossibly broad in that billowy-sleeved white pirate shirt, open nearly to his waist. And the way he was poured into those leather pants left nothing to the imagination. She clutched the edge of the table and prayed he wouldn't do anything as flamboyant as he had at the last signing.

Conversation ceased as he drew nearer, greeting people, squeezing outstretched hands, kissing cheeks. Like a king greeting his loyal subjects. Or a very skilled politician.

He came around to her side of the table and bent to kiss her as if they did this every day.

A murmur went through the crowd gathered around her. "Um, Derek—"

Kneeling beside her, he brushed her cheek with the backs of his fingers. "You look tired this morning, baby. Did I keep you up too late last night?"

Naturally he said it loud enough for those nearby to hear. "No." She kept her tone firm despite the nosedive her stomach took at his touch.

"I'll have to try harder tonight." He gave her a wink, then pressed a cup of coffee into her hand. "Maybe this will wake you up."

She moved to accept it and bumped his hand, sloshing hot liquid over her thumb. He placed it to his lips, his warm breath fanning her skin. With a teasing smile he pulled the coffee-drenched thumb into his mouth and sucked.

"I'm f-fine." She winced at how flustered she sounded, how her voice rose an octave when his warm tongue slid over her thumb. His green eyes twinkled with amusement.

She leaned down on the pretense of kissing his cheek. "What the hell are you doing?" Damn him, he knew *exactly* what he was doing.

At last he released her. Her thumb felt cold and a little lonely with his lips no longer wrapped around it.

Derek rose and faced the crowd of mostly women. "I'm sorry for the interruption, ladies. I just can't stay away from my girl."

Kelly resisted the urge to roll her eyes. There wasn't a female in the room who would hold it against him. And he knew it.

A middle-aged woman stepped up. "Will you sign my book, too, Derek?"

He leaned forward and took her pen. "I'd love to, sweetheart."

"Miss Michaels?" asked another fan. "May I... touch your hand? Right where he kissed you?"

Beside her, Derek handed the book and pen back to the woman.

Still another woman piped up. "I'll give you fifty bucks for that pen."

Kelly couldn't believe her eyes. He was actually taking over her book signing. She doubted it was intentional, she knew damn well he'd only come over to make her pay for the coffee remark. And to flaunt that pirate costume. And yet, unlike the first time she had seen him in those leather pants, she wasn't confused. This was Derek unsettling her senses, not some fantasy hero.

Over the next several minutes, T-shirts, posters, magazines and calendars were all shoved before him to be signed. From the other side of the room, women in costume waiting to have their picture taken with him gravitated to Kelly's line. Model Man Mania had descended. And it was a sight to behold.

A small box that resembled a Barbie doll box was presented to him. She peered down to have a closer look. Her hip bumped against his thigh, and she felt his hand slide to the small of her back. "That's the ugliest looking Ken doll I've ever seen—what's with the long brown hair?"

The woman holding it smiled proudly. "It's my Model Man doll."

Lips twitching in amusement, she turned to Derek. "Model Man *doll?*"

He looked almost sheepish. "They were big sellers a couple of years back."

"I have all three," the fan gushed. "I just bought the third in the collection on e-Bay a few months ago. This one is my favorite."

"Mine, too," he said with a wink. He scrawled a bold

signature across the box, kissed the woman on the cheek and turned to the next fan.

A pudgy, graying woman about her mother's age tapped Kelly on the arm. "I have all your books." Her smiled revealed a few missing teeth.

"How very kind of you to say so. Thank you."

"I have them with me," the woman hefted a grocery sack and plopped it on the table. "Will you sign them for me?"

All twenty? Kelly looked from the woman to the line that wound behind her and spilled out the door. "I'd be happy to, but I can't possibly sign them all right now, it wouldn't be fair to the people waiting."

"Tell you what," Derek said. "We'll both sign them later today and leave them at the front desk for you to pick up."

"I guess that'd be all right." The woman beamed a delighted smile and walked away.

"Thank you," Kelly muttered under her breath. "You saved my ass."

"Ulterior motive," he replied with a pointed glance at her backside. "I'm kind of fond of it."

"Uh oh, here comes your keeper." She could almost hear the theme music from Dragnet as Frankie stalked across the room with blood in her eye.

"Sorry to break up your little tea party, Blondie, but I'm going to have to take him back."

"You're taking your life into your hands," Kelly said. "If these women riot, I'll be helpless to do anything but stand back and watch them rip you to shreds."

"Cute." Frankie's eyes narrowed. "Derek?"

As he turned to answer Frankie, Kelly slipped her arms about his waist in a quick hug. "Darling, as much as I enjoy sharing you with my fans, you are quite a distraction."

Eyes sparkling with humor, he dropped a kiss on her nose. "That's the last thing I want to do." One more quick kiss for the sake of the fans and he was on his way.

A rumble of discontent made its way through the crowd. Kelly wasn't sure if she was relieved to have him gone. Or a little lost without him.

****

Later that morning, when the last of the crowd filtered away, the hotel staff moved in to begin the clean up.

"I think I may have a permanent case of writer's cramp," Sharon complained.

Kelly smiled. "I'd have kept signing till my hand fell off, but I ran out of books."

"We all did," Sharon agreed. "I've never seen anything like it."

"Excellent turn out," M.J. said as she came up to them. "Too bad he only agreed to this for two weeks. I'm really getting some great ideas for squeezing every dime we can out of this thing."

"Just think what might happen if you actually slept with the guy, Kel." Sharon leaned across the table with a wide smile. "*Ka-ching!*"

"I'm ashamed of both of you. That's not what—" The theme from Gilligan's Island, Cody's personal ring, interrupted Kelly, for which she gratefully excused herself. "That's my son."

She flipped open the cell phone and stepped off to one side for privacy. "Hi sweetie, where have you been?"

"Here," came Cody's sleepy voice. "I forgot to charge the phone yesterday and it died out."

"I figured as much."

"Oh. So how did your award banquet go?" he asked. "Was that guy there?"

That guy. She heaved a sigh. She hated to lie to her children, but how was she ever going to explain this mess? "Yes, he was. There's really nothing to it, honey. He's just a friend."

Even as she said the words, she glanced up to see Derek chatting with the last of his fans. Watching him gaze into the eyes of countless women today, a look somewhere between adoration and lust on his face, hadn't exactly been fun. She had spent half her time wondering how he could pull it off time after time, and the other half feeling jealous. He had looked at her in much that same way last night at the award banquet.

Cody's loud yawn brought her back to reality. "Mom? You still there?"

"Sorry, honey."

"So when will you be home?"

"In about a week. Why, is something wrong?"

"Naw, but I was hoping for some stuff from the grocery store."

She grinned. Ah, now he was getting to the purpose of his call. "Well, I'm sure there's one around here. What is it you need?"

"Junk food for the summer. Jenn's some kind of organic freak. There's nothing in this house but fruit and vegetables and green tea."

"Poor baby."

"Seriously. I asked for burgers and she bought some veggie things. I had to get Dad to take me to Burger King the other day so I could have meat."

"I'll see what I can do." A tiny thrill went through her at the thought that her kids didn't like Jenn, and missed the way Mom did things. Directly on its heels was pure guilt that she could take pleasure in such a thing. She paced to a quieter corner of the room. "Are you at least having fun?"

"Yeah, right. It's boring here. You'd be real mad—"

"*Really* mad."

"—really mad, 'cause I end up playing Nintendo all day. Dad's got some pretty cool games you wouldn't approve of."

"Why are you playing video games? I thought the house was right on the beach."

"I'm a little old for sand castles."

She laughed. "Did you ever hear of swimming?"

"That gets boring," he sighed. "And Maya's not around half the time. I miss Barney. I just want to come home."

Kelly's hand tightened on the phone. "What do you mean your sister isn't around?"

"She's got some boyfriend. She spends all her time with him."

Boyfriend? Maya was barely allowed to date, and only in groups. "Does Daddy know about this?"

"Yeah, he got mad at her last night for getting in late."

She tried to keep the edge out of her voice. "How late?"

"I don't know." Another yawn. "Around two, I think."

"If this is your idea of a joke, young man, I'm not amused."

"I'm totally serious. He's like some college guy."

College guy? With her sixteen-year-old daughter? "Is your father home? I think I'd like to speak with him."

"Naw, he and Jenn went out someplace. You should see her, Mom. What a witch. Dad doesn't do anything Jenn doesn't want him to. She bosses him around all the time. The whole house is white—white furniture, white rugs. And just try to eat or drink in the living room, she totally freaks."

"I'd love to hear all the juicy details, honey. Can we talk more later? Right now I'd like to talk to Maya."

"She's sleeping."

"*Wake* her."

Kelly tapped her foot impatiently while listening to the background noises at the house. Sharon, hearing the panic in her voice, had come to sit close by.

"Everything okay?" she mouthed.

In response Kelly rolled her eyes and shrugged.

At last Maya's voice came on the line, sleepy but wary.

"Mom?"

"Hi, sweetheart." She purposely kept her voice bright and cheery. "Are you feeling all right? It's not like you to be in bed this late."

"I'm okay, just tired."

"You sure?"

"Uh huh."

"So, is there anything you want to tell me?"

A loud sigh resonated from the other end. Kelly savored a smile of victory. Her kids would never make good spies. All she had to do was pretend she didn't know what was going on and they'd 'fess up out of sheer guilt.

"Okay, so I've been kind of seeing this guy, but Dad's okay with it and I think you would be, too."

She bit back all the "isn't it a little soon" lectures, knowing they would only cause further arguments. "Why don't you tell me about him?"

"He's so cute, Mom, and really nice. You would love him."

"Mmm hmm. How old did you say he was?"

"Well, that's the thing. He's nineteen, but-—"

"Nineteen!"

Sharon rolled her eyes heavenward and crossed herself.

"I knew you'd freak about this. He's almost as old as *your* boyfriend."

Kelly slapped a hand to her forehead. She should have seen that one coming. As a writer, one would think she'd never be at a loss for the best way to say something. With Maya, it seemed she rarely got it right. "My only concern is a boy that age would have certain... expectations. You don't have the experience to handle something like that, honey. You haven't dated enough." God, she could almost have this same conversation with herself considering the way she reacted every time Derek got near her.

"He's not like that."

"Honey, he doesn't have to be. Things can happen far too quickly, and the next thing you know—"

"Maybe it does for you and what's-his-name, but not me."

"This is not about me and what's-his—*Derek*." Since the divorce, the few times Kelly had gone out on dates, Maya had been upset, so this reaction wasn't unexpected. Especially since this "date" had been splashed all over the tabloids.

She pulled in a shaky breath, determined to redirect the conversation. "Maya, I just don't know that you have the maturity to deal with those kinds of feelings." The minute the words left her lips, she knew she'd said the wrong thing.

"Daddy trusts me, why can't you?"

Because Daddy was never a sixteen-year-old girl. "I understand you got in a little late last night."

"Cody, you snitch!" Maya's angry scream echoed over the line. Then came the high-pitched whining. "Why don't you trust me? It was a misunderstanding. We were out on his Dad's boat and—"

"*What?*"

"Mom, chill. His parents were with us. We went out on the lake to see some fireworks, and I don't know, the boat had engine trouble or something. His Dad fixed it, but it took a while. And hey, guess what? His step-mom reads you. She's got all your books."

Kelly pulled in a deep breath and willed herself to stay calm. She would have preferred to have this conversation face-to-face rather than long-distance. "That's nice, but it doesn't change my mind about you becoming involved with a boy that age."

Sharon nodded her agreement.

"He's not a boy." Maya's tone grew more annoyed.

"That's the point," she muttered beneath her breath. But she knew when to cut her losses. "Look, why don't you give me his parents' phone number, and I can call and talk to them myself. Maybe then I'd feel better about this...relationship."

"Why? They're Jenn's neighbors. Daddy already knows them. If he approves, why can't you?"

An image of her ex-husband as she'd last seen him came to mind. The thinning blond hair pulled back into a pony tail, the ever-present sandals and flower-print shirts. Like someone born a generation too late to be a hippie, but still determined to try. "Somehow, that doesn't make me feel any better."

"*Mom.*"

"We aren't getting anywhere like this. Listen young lady, until I've had a chance to speak to these people myself, you're grounded."

"Can't it wait until tomorrow night? There's a party I really wanted to go to, Trevor already asked me—"

"No."

"You can't ground me all the way from Florida."

"I just did."

"That is *so* unfair. The picture with that guy all over you is in every paper, and you're grounding *me* for having a little fun. I'm not doing half of what you are!"

The tear-making machine had been turned on; Kelly could hear it in Maya's voice. She steeled herself to remain unaffected by both the accusations and the tears even as she wondered about the "half" Maya *was* doing. "You have a twelve o'clock curfew. You also have a cell phone, if you knew you were going to be late, you should have called."

"I didn't have it with me."

How convenient, no calls from concerned parents.

A hiccough and a sob came. "What if I have Daddy call you?"

"Oh, please do, I'm dying to talk to him."

In a cloudburst of tears, Maya dropped the phone. Kelly was about to end the call when she heard Cody's voice. "Don't forget my junk food!"

****

"I want to talk to you before you go."

Derek heard Frankie's rough voice from the other side of the privacy screen set up as a dressing area. Could he never get a moment alone?

He stepped from behind the screen. "What about?"

"You cleared your schedule for the next two weeks. What about that commercial you're supposed to film in L.A. next week?"

"It's been rescheduled."

Her face went red. "Do you know what it took for me to set that up?"

He pivoted and strode toward the door. "I don't really care."

"Derek, don't walk away from me."

He stopped, turned to face her.

"I don't know what's gotten into you lately, but I've had about enough."

"That makes two of us."

She folded her arms. "What the hell is that supposed to mean?"

"I quit. I'm done."

"That's nonsense; you're under contract. I own you, body and soul, for the next two years."

"Contracts were made to be broken."

"Stop talking like a fool. You're just burned out. Take your damned two weeks if you need some time to yourself."

He shook his head. "I want my *life* to myself, Frankie. Not two weeks."

She rolled her eyes. "It must have been pure torture to have to stand there today while a bunch of twittering women fawned all over you."

That ego-stroking had worn off a long time ago. Now

it was just embarrassing. "Two fainted, one had to be pried off of me, and another went into hysterics the minute I spoke to her."

"It was hot today and some of them waited outside in that line for a long time." She shrugged. "It happens."

"What about the one who swears I cured her grandmother's cancer when I touched her hand at an appearance last year?"

She gave a snort of laughter. "I must have been in the ladies room for that one." When he didn't respond, she threw her hands up. "So what? Grandma's all better, right? Everyone's happy."

Leave it to Frankie to miss the entire point. She was so busy focusing on the money she couldn't see how ridiculous the entire Model Man image had become. "And why didn't someone talk to hotel management about putting up a canopy to keep those women out of the hot sun or taking some water out to them?"

She expelled a classic drama queen sigh. "Derek, you take this whole thing too serious. I remember when your only concern was if your condom supply would hold out for the weekend."

"Thanks a lot."

Frankie gestured to Jared, who stood across the room. "Look at him. He reminds me of you a few years back. If you're not careful, he's going to take it all away from you."

"You say that about the Mr. Enchantment winner every year."

"I was right about you, wasn't I?"

Yes, she had been. And he'd been her cash cow for far too long. He'd bet she didn't realize he knew she was trying to sell her agency and that she needed him for leverage. But this wasn't the time or the place to play his trump card. "When I get back to New York the week after next, we'll talk."

His gaze strayed to Kelly and Sharon, seated across the room. He could tell from Kelly's expression something had upset her and her friend was trying to calm her. He had no idea why that should concern him, and yet it did. Especially after the way she had laughed and teased with him earlier.

Frankie placed a hand on his arm. "Look, do whatever you have to do over the next two weeks—bombard her with wine and oysters, tie her down, drug her for Christ's sake. Get her into your bed and out of your system. She's like an albatross around your neck."

"Actually, that would be you."

"I'm going to ignore that since I'm the one who took you from dancing in a sequined G-string to million dollar endorsements."

He gave a bitter laugh.

"When you've gotten over Goldilocks, you'll see things much more clearly."

"Why, because you'll sue me if I walk?"

She favored him with a tight smile. "You always were a smart boy."

"Smarter than you think, Francesca." A short distance away, he spotted the fan who had gotten hysterical on him. She seemed calmer, and since she had waited for three hours in hundred-degree heat to see him, he started toward her. The minute she saw him, she burst into tears again.

He muttered an expletive. Blaine rushed over, poured a glass of water and knelt before the frantic girl. He looked up at Derek and shrugged as if to say he didn't know what else to do.

A glance across the room found Kelly still talking with Sharon, shaking her head as if frustrated. They looked up as Jared Sterling stopped in front of them. Sharon had been on the committee that had chosen this year's Mr. Enchantment winner, and Jared was most likely thanking her. But when he leaned toward Kelly to say something and she smiled, a possessive surge shot through Derek.

Without even thinking about it, he left Frankie and headed toward them. As he approached, Sharon gave him a little wave. "Hey, handsome."

Jared laughed. "I wondered how long it would take him to come and chase me off." He leaned toward Kelly. "If you ever decide to dump this guy, give me a call."

Derek knew the teasing was all in good fun, but he had to fight the urge to send Sterling flying across the room.

Kelly didn't look flattered in the least, more flustered and uncomfortable than anything. When she glanced up at him, an almost guarded look crossed her face as if she didn't quite know how to greet him. He wondered if she was thinking about the book signing this morning. He sure as hell was.

The look of pure desire that had come into her eyes when he sucked the spilled coffee from her thumb had stayed with him all morning. Seeing her relaxed and smiling as she had been this morning, feeling comfortable enough to joke with him, almost made him forget this was all for show.

He placed his hands on his hips and forced himself to sound casual. "We said we'd sign those books later, did you want to do it now?"

"Oh, that's right." She rose to her feet and fell into step beside him as they headed toward the table where she'd left them.

"Was Jared bothering you?"

"Don't start that Neanderthal stuff again, Derek. If he was bothering me, which he wasn't, I'd have taken care of it myself."

He couldn't help a chuckle. "No one knows that better than me." He reached down to squeeze her hand. It felt so damned good in his, he held onto it, ignoring her frown.

As she stepped around the table to retrieve the bag of books, he was forced to release her hand. She picked a book from the bag, then pressed her fingers to her temples. "What did she say her name was, again?"

"Hattie."

"Thanks."

"Sounds like you could use an assistant," he teased, trying to lighten her mood.

"I have one. She's in Virginia with—" Her voice broke, and she shook her head.

Tears? He could do that. With four sisters and about a gazillion cousins, he was practically a pro at handling emotional females. He glanced toward the still-sobbing fan on the other side of the ball room with Blaine. Well, usually.

He looked back at Kelly and slipped his hand over hers, thumb stroking her knuckles. "Kel?"

She pulled in a sharp breath, and her hand twitched as if her first instinct was to pull away. But she didn't.

"Is there something—"

"Don't." She looked up at the ceiling and sucked in a deep breath.

If she really didn't want to give in to what was bothering her, he wouldn't push her. "Do you always get so emotional over signing a few books?"

She released a shaky laugh. "Apparently so. It's a wonder I didn't have a breakdown myself." As if reminded, she nodded toward the hysterical fan now talking to Blaine. "She seems to have calmed down."

"She's fine as long as I don't go near her. Blaine seems to have made a friend for life."

"They'd look very sweet together."

"Yeah, if he wasn't gay."

Wide eyed, she turned to him. "I would have never guessed."

Derek dumped the bag of books on the table and sorted through until he found the few he hadn't posed for. He tossed two in front of her. "So is he."

Her gaze returned to Blaine. "He just doesn't fit the stereotype."

He laughed. "You've never seen him when he's on the prowl."

"I should have known. He's gorgeous and dresses so well. Those are always the ones."

"Really?" He made the best dressed lists every year.

Her gaze flickered over him, and she laughed. "Okay, you got me on that one."

He scrawled his name inside a book and slid it over to her. "I tried to talk Blaine into entering the Mr. Enchantment contest this year. I think he would have done well."

"Oh, absolutely." She wrote a little note for Hattie then moved on to the next book. "How did Frankie feel about that?"

"I didn't tell her. She'd lose the only assistant who's been able to put up with her for this long."

As if on cue, Frankie's voice echoed through the room. "Blaine—coffee! Now!"

Kelly laughed.

Convinced he'd successfully brightened her mood, he asked. "So are we still on for dinner tonight?"

"Oh, I don't know... "

"We could always stay in and order room service."

"Going out sounds good."

"I thought it might." He'd expected her to balk, but that didn't stop reality from disappointing him. "Is seven all right?"

"It's fine."

He signed the last book and handed it to her. "Are you feeling better now?"

"I'm sorry I snapped at you. I had a fight with my daughter."

"All right, you two lovebirds, break it up," came Sharon's voice. "She promised to take me to lunch, and I'm starving. Care to join us?"

"I wish I could, but I have some business to take care of."

Across the room Jared called out a goodbye, then left with his arm around a hot young blonde. Derek mentally chided himself for thinking he had been hitting on Kelly. He'd really have to watch his step where she was concerned. He was getting a little too used to thinking of her as his.

Eight

"So. What are you going to wear tonight?"

Kelly fingered through the rack of sale items in what had to be the twentieth store she and Sharon had browsed. "I think just a skirt and sweater. I didn't bring much else."

"And what are you wearing under it?"

"What?"

Laughing wickedly, Sharon grabbed hold of Kelly's arm and steered her toward a lingerie store. "Let's have some fun."

Sharon dragged her to a table of colorful lacy under things. Kelly reached to pick one up, shocked at the teensy size of it. "I've always thought of these more like dental floss than underwear."

"It's a thong, Kel. You should try one."

She dropped it back onto the table. "I'm not wearing anything that goes up *there*."

"Why doesn't that surprise me? Last time I pawed through your lingerie drawer it looked like Sears had a sale on white granny pants—buy one pair, get ten free."

"What were you doing in my lingerie drawer?"

"When Maya helped me pack the red..." Her voice trailed off. "Oops."

"You?" She gasped. "Shame on you, Sharon Lewis! You knew when I bought that dress I would never wear it."

"Which is why I forced you. And look at the results." Sharon pulled her toward a rack of bras and panties. "These might be more your speed."

Kelly eyed the display critically. "They're pretty, but it's not like anyone is going to see these."

Sharon shrugged. "When a woman wears sexy lingerie she projects a certain feeling."

"Yeah—uncomfortable."

Her friend rolled her eyes and shoved a black bra in

her direction. "Go try this on."

"Is this one of those Wonderbras?" Kelly frowned and fingered the cool, silky material. She'd never owned a bra that felt this nice. What would it be like to have the silk against her skin? What would it feel like to have Derek see it, touch it? Remove it?

Flushed at the thought, Kelly looked up and found Sharon smiling at her as if she knew exactly what gutter her mind had fallen into.

"And you thought bras only came in little cardboard boxes."

She slipped into a fitting room and tried on the bra, then slipped her blouse back on over it. She turned this way and that, both pleased and amazed at the results. And with how sexy it made her feel. "It's like I had a boob lift."

Outside the fitting room, Sharon giggled. "Wait til Loverboy gets an eyeful of your cleavage, sweetie."

"I don't think I can wear this."

"Open the door, let me see."

Kelly stepped from the fitting room, hands on her chest. "These aren't my boobs."

Sharon clapped her hands together with a squeal of delight. "You look so hot. He's gonna die."

"He'll think I'm trying to impress him."

"So let him think. Keep him on his toes. And stiff as a poker."

Kelly turned back to the mirror. "Why did you really pack that dress?"

Her friend shrugged. "To force you to wear it. You usually dress like a mother."

"I am one."

"I meant like *your* mother, Kel."

"Oh God. " Kelly peered closer to the mirror. The face cream some starlet had been hawking on QVC a few months ago was keeping the worst of the wrinkles away. Sunblock and lots of water probably helped. But maybe her wardrobe needed some tweaking. "Am I really turning into her?"

"It's time to shake things up a bit. When was the last time a hot guy like Derek tried to get you into bed?"

Her cheeks grew warm, giving her secret away.

"Hah! Never. I knew it."

She turned and headed back into the fitting room. "Okay, I'll buy the bra, that's as reckless as I get. But I'm not buying the thong. And I'm *not* sleeping with him."

"Let's discuss *that* over lunch."

****

"What do you mean you've never had an orgasm?"

"Keep your voice down." Kelly slunk low in her chair and looked around to see if anyone had overheard. The caesar salad before her suddenly lost its appeal.

Sharon sat forward, almost leaning across the table, and whispered, "I'm sorry, I just can't get over the irony. You write the hottest love scenes I've ever read. And you were married for twenty years."

"Seventeen," she corrected.

"And you—*never?*"

"Alan and I were both inexperienced when we got married. I didn't know how to ask for what I wanted. Later, after we drifted apart, we rarely bothered."

"You know, I always had a hard time believing Alan inspired all those great sex scenes. Or why you'd divorce him if he had."

"I came close a time or two. But, uh, no cigar, so to speak."

Sharon set her iced tea down so abruptly it sloshed over the glass. "That selfish little prick."

Kelly raised a hand to shield her flaming face. "I knew I shouldn't have told you."

Sharon reached across the table to take her hand. "Hey," she said in a low voice. "You can tell me anything. And you should have told me this before now. I could have given you some advice on how to take matters into your own hands—literally. Or at least helped you pick out a vibrator."

Kelly moaned with embarrassment.

"Well, it's a fact of life, honey, nature—and husbands—don't always provide for a woman's needs. You've got to know how to take care of yourself."

In spite of her unease, Kelly laughed. "I didn't really plan on this discussion today. I was more interested in talking about Maya's boyfriend."

"Maya will be fine, she's had a good mommy.

Whether she likes it or not, she's going to hear your voice in the back of her mind for the rest of her life." She wiped a napkin over the spilled tea. 'Kel, I know you pride yourself on setting a good moral example for the kids, but they're not here. I say go for it with Derek and have the time of your life. You may not get another chance."

"I'm not sure I have it in me."

"Why not? You're a grown woman. You don't have to be the good girl anymore. You can always look back later and say 'I shouldn't have done that.'"

Kelly tore open a packet of artificial sweetener and dumped it into her drink. "Are you saying I should sleep with him?"

"Do you want to?"

"I have no reason to, other than this overwhelming physical attraction." A shiver moved through her at the memory of his hot breath against her ear, the dramatic way he'd kissed her last night at the award ceremony. The image of him sucking coffee off her thumb this morning. Those damn skin-tight leather pants...

"The way I look at it, when you're old and gray, 'shouldn't have' is a hell of a lot better company than 'what if.'"

Kelly stared down into her glass. "I don't know..."

"Are you afraid of him?"

"Heavens, no. Well, not in the physical sense. Just in..."

"What, hon'?"

Tears stung at her eyes for the second time today. "Dammit," she muttered, dabbing the corner of her eyes with a napkin. "I've never felt anything like this before. The physical sensations, I mean. With just a few kisses— and when he sucked on my thumb today—"

"He *what?*"

She rolled her eyes. "I forgot to tell you about that. Anyway, I never felt anything even close to that with Alan. I'm a little afraid of what will happen if I give in to it."

Sharon gave a wicked laugh. "Do you want me to do my Meg Ryan imitation from *When Harry Met Sally?*"

"Uh, I've seen it, thanks."

"Well, *that's* what would happen. He's only in the

next room, right? Buy yourself something red and slutty and knock on his door tonight."

"I don't think so."

"You can always throw a robe on if you're feeling shy."

"Okay," she said, "suppose I did that. I'm a forty-two-year old woman who has had two c-sections and nursed two babies. Not exactly model material. What if I disappoint him?"

Sharon waved a dismissive hand. "Oh, come on. I don't know any guy who, faced with a naked, willing woman, thinks anything but 'thank you Jesus!' *You'd* be more likely to end up disappointed."

Kelly pushed a bit of chicken and romaine lettuce around her plate. "How so?"

"A guy that good looking usually isn't all that great in bed. He's probably never had to be." She shrugged. "He's so gorgeous women want him anyway."

"Oh." For Derek to turn out like Alan in the bedroom would be disappointing. Especially after the fireworks she felt when he kissed her.

"Don't look so downhearted," Sharon said with a laugh. "If he got you hot and bothered by sucking on your thumb, you'll probably go off like a rocket the minute he touches you."

"And if I don't?"

Sharon flashed a wicked grin. "I think he'd be willing to work on it."

Despite the ball of nerves simmering in her stomach, Kelly laughed.

Her friend reached across to pat her hand. "You've got two weeks, right? That's plenty of time to have an affair. You're a grown woman, you can handle this."

"What if I become emotionally attached? He's not exactly a relationship kind of guy." At least she hoped not. It wouldn't do for him to want more than she could give.

"That's the biggest hurdle. You have to go in with your eyes wide open and your heart shut tight. You tell him right up front that it's just for a couple of weeks and then you're done. You keep the ball in your court the entire time."

"And how many affairs like this have you had?"

"None," Sharon admitted. "But I've used that plot in about seven books."

Kelly laughed. "Yes, I remember. I don't know, Shar...

"Where has being cautious gotten you? Forty two years without an orgasm."

"Thanks for reminding me—and the rest of the listening audience."

"If I were you, and I mean this sincerely, I'd go buy that red negligee. One of these nights, when I was ready, I'd order up some champagne from room service." She popped in the last bite of her cheeseburger. "Then I'd screw his friggin' brains out."

****

Kelly absently ran her fingers over the condensation on the outside of her wineglass and stared into the flickering flame of the candle in the center of the table. Around her the clatter of china and the hum of soft conversation blended with the sounds of easy-listening music overhead. She smoothed her napkin over her lap, looked out the window once more at the glorious orange-purple sunset over the ocean.

And then at the man across from her.

"You look like you're about to go before a firing squad." His dark green eyes sparkled with humor, as if he found her fidgeting amusing. He probably thought she was nervous. And she was. Just not in the way he assumed.

"Firing squad, flashing cameras, it's all the same." She brought the wine glass to her lips, cringing inwardly as Sharon's tawdry suggestion replayed itself in her mind.

I'd screw his friggin' brains out.

She stole another glance at him and set the glass back down. The way he looked tonight was almost enough to sway her to Sharon's way of thinking. *Almost.* The moss green dress shirt he wore would have looked wrong on any other man, but on Derek it was incredible, emphasizing the width of his shoulders and chest, tapering down to his narrow waist. Not to mention what it did to his eyes. He had rolled the sleeves up, and she found herself admiring the muscular forearms.

"There was a small mob scene when we left the hotel,

107

but there's no one here now."

"Is that why we drove two hours to get to the restaurant?"

He slid the candle to one side of the table, then reached to take both her hands in his. "Maybe. But I wanted to bring you here. It's one of my favorite places."

"It's lovely." She attempted to pull her hands back, but instead of releasing them he pressed his lips to her fingertips. Each and every one of them. With painstaking slowness. The memory of him drawing her thumb into his mouth earlier this morning rushed back at her.

"We're being watched, you know."

"I know. Seven waitresses so far." Not to mention one who repeatedly found excuses to show off her cleavage, and another who had not-so-subtly slipped him her phone number. "Do you usually attract so much attention when you're out?"

"Mm hmm," he admitted, still nuzzling her fingertips. "But it's been a lot worse the past few days."

"Well," she leaned in to whisper, "maybe if you stopped nibbling my fingers, we'd attract a bit less." *And I wouldn't be on the verge of orgasm.*

"And disappoint all these people pretending not to stare at us?" But he allowed her to slide her hands from his.

"If they want to see more, they can read a tabloid." She slid her hand under the table to rub her sweaty palm down her thigh, hoping to wipe away the tingling he'd created, just as the waitress with the heaving bosom returned with their meal. Kelly's lobster bisque was set before her with a thunk. Derek's was carefully placed with a generous smile.

When the waitress left, Kelly broke a small piece of bread from the loaf in the basket and turned the conversation to a safer topic. "Tell me something about yourself."

She didn't care what he told her, hopefully something that would make him sound vain and shallow so she could get over this unexpected sexual response to him. Unexpected, hell. She was practically asking for it by spending time with him when she didn't have to.

"What would you like to know, sweetheart?"

"For starters, you can tell me why you call everyone that."

"What?"

"Sweetheart."

"It's just a word, Kel."

"No, it's an endearment, and you've used it on every female you've encountered this weekend."

He picked up his wine glass and swirled the contents. "It's a hell of a lot easier than trying to remember their names."

"Ah, I see. Glad to know I'm one of the masses."

"Don't read so much into it."

"Maybe you should consider using different names for those you're planning to seduce. A woman likes to feel she's special. Even if it is for one night." She took a swallow of wine, wondering if it was the alcohol that emboldened her. "What about 'darling?' How does that one feel on your tongue?"

"Not nearly as good as you would. *Darling*." He raised the glass to his lips, sipped, savored. And smiled. "And I don't recall ever hearing any complaints about failing to make a woman feel special. Even for one night."

Cheeks flushing, she turned to eating her soup. "Sorry I asked."

Forced to turn his attention to his own lukewarm bisque, Derek mentally kicked himself for handling things so badly. He hadn't intended to bait her, but she'd led him right into it. He had come off sounding like a jerk about that whole sweetheart thing, when in fact, he found it usually put his fans at ease when they were nervous.

Still, one bad answer didn't have to set the tone for the entire evening. "What was it you wanted to ask me?"

"Anything." She daintily dabbed at her mouth with her napkin, then set it aside. "I know so little about you. I just wanted you to tell me something real about yourself. Something that's not part of the whole model man mystique." She looked up as a bus boy came to refill their water glasses, waiting until he left before speaking again. "You mentioned an Italian grandmother—no, you said 'very Italian.' What did you mean by that?"

Conjuring an image of his grandmother, he felt the tension drain from his face and his lips curve upward.

Nonna was an old-fashioned woman, a relic actually, who enjoyed nothing more than taking care of her family. She still took pride in ironing his grandfather's shirts, keeping a neat-as-a-pin house. Derek had never known her to sit down to eat until she had served Papa first.

According to Sharon, Kelly was the opposite. She thrived on being financially independent, doing things for herself. He knew enough to realize her kids meant the world to her, but he doubted she would understand someone like Nonna. "She's sort of the family matriarch. Most of us would rather die than disappoint her."

"She must be a wonderful woman."

"She is."

"Do you come from a large family?"

He allowed his gaze to slide over the cleavage exposed by her soft, black sweater, the way it molded to her breasts. He wanted to do anything but talk right now. In fact, he preferred to do the whole 'getting to know you' thing naked and horizontal. As usual, she had other ideas. She seemed determined to draw him out, so he'd play the willing victim. "I'm number four of seven. Four girls, three boys."

"A classic middle child."

He raised a brow and shifted in his seat, intrigued by a sudden spark in her eyes and her playful tone. "What are you implying?"

"Well, they do have a certain...reputation."

"Attention seekers, or so they tell me."

"Wonderful mediators, masters of compromise, the confidence of a first born, the charm of a second born." She stopped and gave a self-conscious laugh. "I always consider birth order when creating characters. It's silly, I guess."

"No, it isn't." He finished his soup and set the bowl aside. "Do you come from a large family?"

"I have one older brother. We don't see each other much, he lives in North Carolina. I always wished for a larger family."

"You're more than welcome to mine. I always wanted a smaller one. We were jammed like sardines into my parents' place above the pizza shop."

"Do they still live there?"

Half-embarrassed by the admission, he nodded. "I've tried to move them, offered to buy them any house they wanted."

"What happened?"

"My father wouldn't go for it. He said when he wants a new house, he'll buy it himself."

"He sounds like a very proud man."

Derek shrugged. "Stubborn is more like it." Uncomfortable with revealing any more about his family, he rested his arms on the table and leaned toward her. "So what's your family like?"

"Well, my dad used to be a dentist. He's retired now. Mom is also retired, she was a school teacher."

"How long have they been married?"

She shook her head. "They divorced when I was nineteen. They've both remarried."

"I'm sorry."

"Thank you." She tucked a strand of hair behind her ear. "I didn't handle it nearly as well as my kids handled my divorce. And they're quite a bit younger than I was."

"Even now if I were to find out my parents were splitting up, it would throw me. It would probably ruin me on marriage for life."

Her laughter came out forced, as if she were trying not to dwell on what must still be a painful memory. "How long have your parents been married?"

"Forty-five years."

Her eyes went misty, and he wondered if she was thinking about her parents' failed marriage or her own. "That's wonderful. They must really be in love."

He chuckled. "Don't you think after being together that long it's just a bad habit?"

"Not at all. Even though I wasn't successful at my marriage, I still believe in romance. Growing old with your best friend, having someone to share the golden years with."

"Sounds like you plan to remarry someday." He could see the kind of guy she would choose, and the image gnawed at him. Older than her. Balding. Probably someone boring, like a lawyer or a doctor. Someone safe.

"Right now my focus is my kids. It will be five years before Cody finishes high school and leaves for college.

111

Maybe then I'll date again."

"Five years?" He couldn't help but allow his gaze to wander over her. Leaving herself to rot on the vine for that long was more than a shame. It was downright criminal. And the guy he'd conjured in his mind, the safe one she eventually settled for, wouldn't begin to know how to appreciate her.

"If I meet someone that's fine. If not, I'll just become one of those little old ladies with fifty cats." She shrugged as though the prospect didn't bother her.

He laughed at the image. "A little old lady with fifty cats who writes very hot romance novels."

From somewhere outside a violin began to play. He followed her gaze out the window. An orchestra had assembled on the deck below them at beach level. Several couples stood and exited a pair of french doors. Moments later, they dotted the dance floor.

He didn't dare ask. She would only refuse, make some excuse. He stood instead, and held out his hand.

She appeared ready to decline but must have remembered their charade. She rose and accepted his extended hand, wordlessly walking with him toward the patio doors.

Below, he pulled her into his arms, noticing how perfectly she fit and how they moved together, like they'd been dancing partners for years. He closed his eyes to savor her powder-soft scent. Her head fit just beneath his chin, and he bent to inhale the sweet smell of her hair.

He'd spent most of the day thinking about her. Missing her, actually. Her laugh, her smile. The way she rolled her eyes when his fans gushed about how much they loved him.

He slid a hand over her spine, mindlessly stroking, pulling her in closer.

"This is nice," she whispered on a small sigh, resting her head against his chest.

His heart sped up a bit, and he wondered if she could hear it. The song changed and still they swayed. The singer did his best, but in his mind Derek could hear the song the way Dean Martin had crooned it. When the singer began the second verse, he softly sang along in flawless Italian.

Her head lifted from his chest, blue eyes registering surprise. Her gaze locked with his, and a slow smile spread over her face.

He wanted to kiss her and suspected she would be receptive. But the moment was too perfect. Instead, he drew her head back to his chest and continued his serenade.

The slide of her thighs against his, her breasts pressed to his chest, even her hand on his shoulder were sweet torture. It reminded him of those eighth grade dances so many years ago, where he wanted to hold the girl a little tighter—but was afraid she'd find out just how turned on he was. He hoped he had better control than that now, but where Kelly was concerned, nothing was guaranteed.

The song ended and another began. She made no attempt to end the dance. When at last the orchestra announced a short break, Derek felt like he'd been wakened from a dream. They could have been dancing for hours, or maybe just a few minutes, he'd lost track.

Kelly looked up at him, one cheek reddened from where it had rested against his chest. She smiled almost self consciously, as if she, too, felt that strange sort of dreamy awareness.

His hand at her elbow, he guided her from the dance floor onto the beach. A romantic stroll by the water just might suit his cause. He intended to have the kiss he'd been waiting for all day. Tonight there would be no kissing for appearances sake. Instead he'd remind her exactly why she shouldn't leave herself on the shelf for five years. Not even another five minutes.

She paused to slip off her shoes, reminding him briefly of a few nights ago when he'd walked with her. She'd been barefoot then, too. And wearing that hot red dress. She looked every bit as desirable tonight with the moonlight glistening on her lips.

He slipped his arm about her waist, half fearing she would object. She eased into the touch, her hip brushing his thigh.

"I didn't know you spoke Italian."

"I don't make a habit of it."

The wind blew a strand of hair across her face as she

looked up at him. "Why not? It's a beautiful language."

"My Dad only spoke Italian to us. It embarrassed the hell out of me when he did it in public."

She laughed. "You want embarrassing? Try being the kid of a romance novelist."

"It must be rough for them to see you on the front page of a tabloid."

"It's just been the three of us since the divorce so it's hard for them to think I have a life apart from them."

He hooked his arm tighter about her waist and stopped, pulling her to face him. "But in reality you don't."

"N—not until now."

The breathless tone of her voice told him she was just as affected by their closeness as he. With painstaking slowness, he lowered his head toward her mouth. He expected her to dance away any moment, but he wanted to savor the thrill, the taste, the feel of her.

When his lips reached hers, she didn't hesitate. Her mouth opened sweetly, inviting his kiss, allowing him to drink his fill. Somehow the hem of her sweater became tangled beneath his hand, and the warmth of her satiny skin filled his palm. Despite the innocence of the touch, a jolt of electricity shot through him.

He couldn't remember when he had last been so turned on by the mere touch of a woman's skin. And not even the skin he desperately wanted to touch. Probably because the women he usually encountered were every bit as experienced and eager as he. There was no point in such simple contact. But with Kelly, it felt different. Even though she was older than him, she was far less experienced. The knowledge lent a forbidden air to the encounter.

His hand slid across her waist and up her back. He forced himself to move slow, not scare her away this time by pressuring her. Even when his hand brushed a silken bra strap he resisted the temptation to unfasten it.

A pleasure-filled sigh escaped her.

A moment later she let out a squeal. In that same moment, he got soaked right up to his ankles as a wave gently rolled in.

"I'm sorry," she said with a giggle. "I didn't realize we were standing that close to the water."

Catching her teasing mood, he scooped her up in his arms.

"What are you doing?"

"I'm being a romantic hero and—"

"Derek, Kelly, over here!"

A flash went off, followed by another. Temporarily blinded, Derek stumbled, but managed not to drop her. She gasped and stared at the cluster of photographers. Even in the moonlight he could see the humor fade from her face.

"Hey, Kelly," one of them called from a safe distance. They knew better than to get in his face. "How do Maya and Cody feel about your new boyfriend?"

Her grip on his neck tightened reflexively. "Put me down."

He obliged but moved in front of her. He was used to this kind of attack from paparazzi. She wasn't. True, her fame was international, but it didn't hold the same fanatical frenzy his did. "You got your pictures, now leave her alone."

"No," she protested, trying to maneuver around him. "I want to ask him how he knows about my kids."

The photographers didn't budge. Derek took a step toward them as the cameras flashed and whirred. "Get the hell out of here before I shove that camera up your—"

At that, they took off.

"You didn't have to jump in front of me like that."

Once he was sure the paparazzi were gone, he turned to face Kelly's wrath. "They were baiting you. They wanted a reaction. That would sell more papers than a few kisses."

"How do they know my kids' names?"

"They're investigative reporters, Kel, by now they know what brand of toothpaste you buy."

She stood there for a moment looking like a lost little girl.

"Maybe you'd feel better if you called your kids and talked to them."

She shook her head. "They were going to a movie tonight, I doubt they're back yet." She glanced down. "Oh, Derek, your shoes must be ruined."

The comment struck him as so absurd he couldn't

help but laugh. "You think I care about a pair of shoes?"

"Well, they probably cost more than my last car."

"So I'll get new ones." The thought that she hadn't completely lost her sense of humor warmed him. Maybe the evening didn't have to be a total loss. He reached down, scooped her into his arms again and moved toward the restaurant.

She tipped her head to search the beach behind him. "Are they back?"

"Who?"

"The photographers."

"I hope not."

"Then why are you holding me?"

"I didn't think you wanted sand all over your wet feet."

"Oh."

As they reached the car, a thought occurred to him. "Did you think when I picked you up back there it was because there were photographers around?"

Her delicate shoulders lifted and dropped. "I figured that's why you kissed me."

He set her down. She bent to brush the sand from her feet, and he caught a glimpse of her delicate arches and polished toenails. Did she really think he had been playing for the cameras when he kissed her?

She straightened and gave the roadster he'd rented earlier today a critical look. "So what's this going to be when it grows up?"

"A BMW."

"Looks like something Cody would have a poster of on his wall."

"Probably not this one. This is the Z4. The Z8 has a bigger engine, four hundred horses, six-speed manual tranny. Much more impressive. This thing's a baby in comparison."

"I uh...had no idea."

He stroked a hand over the fender. "I added a Z8 to my collection a few weeks ago. But this was all I could find today on short notice." He dangled the keys in front of her. "Wanna drive her back to the hotel?"

"I think I'll pass this time and let you handle, uh, 'her.'"

Grinning, he opened the car door. Her skirt rose a few inches as she sat down, giving him a good look at her calves. He'd gotten a glimpse of her legs when he'd held her. Apparently his little romance novelist liked to work out. The body part that had been on a slow simmer all day because of her roared to life as he pictured her in workout shorts and a tank top, skin glistening with sweat.

Christ, he hadn't been this horny at thirteen. As he moved around to the driver's side of the car, he tried to shake the nagging urge.

It didn't make sense. He'd seen more bare female flesh in recent years than most men ever would. All of it smooth, sculpted and tanning-bed perfect. Why should the sight of Kelly's bare feet and legs stimulate him so much? Even as he slid behind the wheel and started the car, the urge to run his hand up that smooth white calf taunted him. And to think the woman thought he needed a photographer around in order to kiss her.

He leaned over, not caring that the emergency brake jabbed him in the ribs, and placed a hand on her knee. "Just so we're clear on one thing."

"What's that?"

The throaty, husky tone of her voice was all the encouragement he needed. He slipped a finger under her chin and leaned in to kiss her. "To hell with the photographers."

Nine

It was after midnight when Kelly finally gave up trying to write. Nothing was flowing. Hell, nothing was even there. She couldn't concentrate.

She had heard from the kids about an hour ago. Well, Cody anyway. Maya refused to speak with her. Not that she could blame her; from Maya's point of view Kelly was the worst of hypocrites.

Rubbing her arms against the chill of the air conditioning, she pulled open the balcony doors. The night air was heavy and humid, but the prospect of fresh air was inviting. She stepped outside. The cement was warm beneath her bare feet as she gazed out over the balcony. She'd never been comfortable with heights, and at eighteen stories up, she had no intention of looking down. But the rail felt sturdy and the view of the twinkling lights of Orlando in the distance, along with the star-filled night sky was breathtaking.

Not ten feet away, Derek's doors were open, but no sound came from inside. She supposed he had gone out for the night, as any single, carefree man his age would. But she wasn't about to have a closer look.

Gooseflesh rose on her arms and neck as the memory of what had happened on the beach rushed back. She had spent most of their time together in a heightened state of arousal. Sharon's suggestion that she take advantage of their adjoining rooms had invaded her mind every time Derek looked at her. She hadn't really decided what she intended to do with that advice, but that didn't stop her mind from conjuring up images of making love with him.

Warmth washed into her belly. She had been so disappointed to think he had kissed her for the sake of the photographers. But then in the car he had made it very clear that wasn't the case. She could still feel his hand on her knee, thumb gently stroking, while he kissed her. Again. His fingertips had inched slightly over her bare knee, but even if he'd slid them all the way up her thigh, she wouldn't have objected. Couldn't have.

The man's lips were like a drug. She had wanted the kiss to go on forever, had wanted to invite him back to her room. But the invitation would have been misunderstood. He would have expected much more than kisses, and she still wasn't sure she could handle that. Or him.

Turning, she spotted the patio furniture that filled the space between their rooms on the balcony. A table, love seat, and chairs. The soft and inviting tropical-print cushions beckoned, and she moved toward them. Sinking into one of the chairs, she pulled up her knees, tucked her skirt over her toes and gazed out at the night sky.

A shrill ring sounded from next door, followed by Derek's deep voice. Her heart did a belly flop; it was after midnight. Who but a lover, or potential lover, would call him at this hour?

A moment later, he stepped out onto the balcony, cell phone pressed to his ear.

"I don't expect to get anywhere with them tomorrow," he said, pausing to light a cigarette.

She didn't want to eavesdrop on his conversation, but neither did she wish to draw attention to herself. He wasn't aware of her in the shadows, and she wanted to keep it that way. He moved to the rail and leaned against it as he spoke.

"If I have to, I'll hire someone to drive them. You're not doing anything next week, right?"

His deep chuckle washed over her like warm honey, even if he wasn't speaking to her. He was shirtless, his muscular, deeply tanned back exposed for her to enjoy. His buttocks were hidden by the dark slacks that blended into the shadows, but when he rested his elbows on the railing, she found herself admiring a side view of his taut abdomen and obliques. Not an ounce of extra flesh around *his* middle, not even when he leaned forward like that. His entire body was a work of art.

Which made her wonder about the parts she hadn't seen. What was it Sharon always said about the size of a man's thumb?

She shook her head to rid herself of the notion, but the heat pooling between her legs and the tingling in her body didn't lie. She *wanted* Derek. Physically. Wanted to know what it would be like to spend one hot, uninhibited night with him. Just one. But she wasn't the sort of woman who could take something like that lightly. She needed emotions, feelings. Commitment.

Didn't she?

She had always been so practical. First as the good girl, straight-A student and perfect daughter. Then the loving, devoted wife. And now the selfless mother. She had never tried to be anything else. Some people liked to experiment with their wild side; she didn't even know if she had one. Which had always been fine. Until now. Now the thought of what she might be missing taunted her.

"While you're rearranging my schedule," Derek went on, "don't forget to leave the week before Labor Day open. I promised Ben and Noah I'd take them camping."

He took a drag on the cigarette. "I never even thought about Caitlin. Don't you think she's too young?" As if feeling the weight of her stare, he turned and looked directly at her.

"Gabby, I'll talk to you later." He tapped the screen on the mobile phone, ending the call without so much as a good-bye, and extinguished the cigarette in an ash tray near his door. For a moment he stood there, watching her watch him. Electricity arced across the short distance separating them.

She lowered her gaze. Even though the shadows hid her face, she didn't want to risk him reading anything in her eyes. "I didn't mean to eavesdrop."

"No, that's not your style."

If he only knew her style. The one that had her secretly ogling his body whenever possible.

Okay, that was it. She was out of here. Uncurling her legs, she rose. "I was just going inside."

"You don't have to go because of me."

Oh, yes I do. "I should get back to work. I do my best writing this time of night."

He folded his arms over his chest. "It's past midnight."

"This is when I write. Usually until around two. And I'm near deadline." She glanced down at his bare, masculine feet. Damn the man, even his toes were sexy.

"I won't see you until tomorrow night so you should have plenty of time to write. I have an early tee time in the morning. Then I have to take care of some family business."

She couldn't help but smile. "With a last name like Calavicci, 'family business' sounds ominous."

He laughed. "We'd be more likely to make a pizza for someone than break their thumbs."

Thumbs. She refused to give into temptation and look.

"I'll leave the limo in case you want to go somewhere."

"I won't. I really should spend the day working."

He smiled. "I always had this image of you holed up in a cabin in the woods somewhere with an old typewriter."

Derek had always had an image of her? The thought warmed her just a little. "No cabin, no typewriter. Just a golden retriever at my feet." Sweet, lovable Barney. She hoped he wasn't giving her mom too much trouble. "Are you getting ready to go out somewhere?"

He slid his hands into his pockets and stepped closer. "Where would I go?"

"I don't know, out to a club or something."

"When the whole world thinks I'm here making love to you?"

Heat flooded her cheeks, but then she suspected that was his intention. "I'm sorry. You're doing this for me and here you are stuck in this hotel room."

"I thought I was doing it so I wouldn't get sued." He closed the distance between them. Instead of sitting on the love seat or one of the other chairs, he sat on the table directly in front of her. The position brought his naked chest to her eye level, and she had to force her gaze to settle elsewhere. It flitted up, over his abdomen, his lips, his eyes before finally landing on the balcony railing over his shoulder.

"I had no idea what M.J. was up to. I didn't know about any of it."

"I know that." His voice took on a gentle tone. "And I wouldn't have agreed if I hadn't wanted to do it."

She pulled her gaze back to his and found the fire

simmering there. "Because you didn't want to get sued?"

He smiled almost boyishly. "No." He reached out, capturing her wrist to pull her forward between his open legs. "Hell, no." He brushed his fingertips from her cheek to her chin, his thumb tugging at her lower lip.

His gaze darkened, focused on her mouth. He bent toward her, and she tilted her head for his kiss. But he stopped and lifted his gaze, eyes locked onto hers. The thumb on her lip slipped lower, knuckles slowly brushing down her throat to follow the deep vee of her sweater.

She caught her breath as he grazed the hollow between her breasts. The touch sent a shockwave of pleasure straight through her.

"Am I still moving too fast for you?" His voice sounded strained, tight.

Swallowing, she could do little more than shake her head.

His fingers brushed the tiny heart-shaped buttons that lined the front of her sweater. Her breath quickened to match his as he unfastened the top button. He reached for the second, hesitated. Then that button fell away beneath his deft fingers. As did the third. He released the fourth button and her sweater fell open.

He lowered his gaze once more and immediately her nipples tightened. With a groan he bent his head to nuzzle her neck, fingers stroking the exposed swells above her lacy bra. She closed her eyes and leaned into him.

A tremor went through her as his fingertips skimmed lower, stroking over the black lace, lingering to tease her nipple.

He raised his head.

"Open your eyes, Kelly."

She could barely react.

His hand came up to cup her cheek. She opened her eyes and nearly drowned in the desire staring back at her. Her eyelids felt hot, heavy, and it was all she could do to keep them open. She focused on his mouth, how close it was, how much she wanted it to touch hers. Touch her skin.

He pulled her to him. His mouth was hot but undemanding. She had the sense he was giving her room to retreat. Unsure of where to put her hands, she held them above his shoulders, hesitating. She had wanted to touch him for so long. But she didn't trust herself to stop once she started.

"Touch me," he whispered against her lips.

Awkwardly she settled her hands on his shoulders. Emboldened by the hard, hot feel of his skin, she slowly eased them down, sliding over that magnificent, sculpted chest. The very chest she'd watched countless women grope and paw at all morning, as if he was some exotic animal on display in a petting zoo. Something selfish and possessive rushed over her. For the moment he was hers to touch. She wanted only to give and receive the pleasure that came from her hands moving over that taut, golden flesh.

She continued her exploration, slipping over his rock hard abdomen, then back up and over his biceps. In the back of her mind the thought echoed that to touch and be touched like this was playing with fire. But she was helpless against the sensations swirling inside her, pulling her under like a rip tide.

His hand slid to cover her breast, molded it through her bra. As the earth shifted beneath her feet, she steadied her hands on his thighs, acutely aware of heat and solid muscle beneath her palms.

He nuzzled her breasts, his hair brushing her bare skin. She moaned in pleasure and eased closer. His hand closed gently around her wrist, and a low groan came from his throat. He pressed his forehead to hers, and for a moment she could only hear the rapid intake of breath, though she wasn't sure whose. She glanced down. Her fingers were less than an inch from the telltale bulge in his pants. How had she traveled so far up his thigh without realizing it?

"Kelly," he whispered. "If this goes much farther, we won't be able to stop."

Stop? But she didn't want it to stop—oh, God, this was what she had warned Maya about. And exactly what she had feared would happen if she was alone with Derek again.

So much for being uninhibited.

She took a step back from him and tried to pull her sweater together. Her fingers trembled so badly she couldn't grip the buttons. All she could manage was a cry of frustration.

Derek brushed her hands aside and fastened the buttons as quickly as he could—but not nearly as fast as he'd unfastened them. "I must be out of my mind. In front of me is the most desirable woman I've ever met and I'm helping put her clothes *on*."

"Desirable," she laughed. "After the women you've known, that's a joke."

She started to leave, but he grabbed hold of her arm. "You honestly don't realize what you do to me." Knowing he shouldn't, he slid his hands into her hair and looked into her passion-darkened eyes. "Do you?"

He kissed her hard, hot, then released her, afraid if he lingered he really would try to change her mind.

"I should go back inside," she murmured.

Take me with you. "Think about what you'd like to do tomorrow night."

Her eyes closed briefly, her tongue darting out to moisten her lips. "I will."

He watched her go, then turned and entered his room. The first thing to greet him was the bed. The big empty bed. Groaning, he closed the balcony doors behind him and leaned against them. He'd never done anything so goddamned noble in his life. Kelly, who had been like a drug in his system for days now, had finally given in to desire.

A perfect, star-filled night. A beautiful, willing woman in his arms. And what had he done? *What the hell had he done?*

Had it been any other woman, he wouldn't have a problem with a hot encounter on the balcony. But not Kelly. Even at eighteen stories up, there was no way he'd do that to her. With his luck, the paparazzi would fly by in a helicopter and catch them.

Besides, seduction was no longer enough. He didn't just want her warm and willing, overcome by desire. He wanted her fully aware of what she was doing. And with who. No fantasizing he was one of the heroes from her books.

An image of creamy breasts spilling from that lacy black bra, pure desire in those blue eyes and kiss-swollen lips would haunt him all night. Along with the almost shy way she had touched him. After being mauled by strange women all day, it was amazing how her gentle hands had both soothed and aroused him.

He stepped away from the doors. What the hell had she done to him in the past twenty-four hours? Last night he'd only been concerned with how long it would take to coax her into bed. Tonight he was putting it off when he easily could have had her. Something had changed. He just wasn't sure what. Or when.

Oh, who the hell was he kidding? The first time he'd seen her picture on the back cover of a book, he'd been interested. Of course, the blurb beneath it had mentioned a husband and kids. But the years had changed that picture. Gone was the sweet, fresh faced young mother; in her place was a sexy, confident woman. This time without a husband. He'd looked for her at every conference, watched for her the other day when the entire hotel was buzzing with news of her arrival.

If he was honest with himself, he had to admit it wasn't only her body he wanted when he made love to her. He wanted all of her.

Which did nothing to relieve the throbbing hard-on he was stuck with. He headed toward the bathroom, hoping a cold shower would take the edge off.

Noble should feel a hell of a lot better than this.

****

Crystal blue skies outside the window. A lone cloud, white and puffy, floated slowly with the wind. A bird swooped past, whimsical, carefree. He followed its course as it moved past him.

Not a bird. A plane. Flying too low. Too close to the buildings. He yelled for it to go higher, but his voice bounced off the glass. He tried to pound the window.

Unable to move. Helpless to do anything but watch.

An explosion. A man and woman jumped from an upper floor of the tower. Then another burst of orange flame and black smoke. Glass and paper exploded like confetti in the sky. The building collapsed, pancaking one story at a time.

So many lives lost. Hurtled from this world into the next before his very eyes.

"Derek."

Like a vision from heaven, she was there. In his bed, laughing that husky laugh, welcoming him into her arms, her soft rose and vanilla scent filling his senses. His body. Christ she felt good. Making love to her was just like he had known it would be.

She wrapped her legs around him, urging him inside. He paused to savor the moment. He'd never waited so long for a woman in his life, and he wanted to appreciate the victory. Any moment she'd be wrapped around him. Tight. Wet. Hot.

The phone at his bedside rang, jarring him from sleep. He fumbled for it and snarled an expletive into the receiver.

"Geez, freaking ask me to wake you at six a.m. and then bite my freaking head off," Gabrielle snapped.

"Sorry. I was in the middle of a dream."

"Well, I know you weren't having sex 'cause you wouldn't have answered the phone."

Having sex? Hell, close enough. He hadn't had a dream like that since his teenaged days. Another second and he'd have been on very intimate terms with the mattress. Meanwhile, he was hard as a brick again.

"Why didn't you have the hotel staff wake you? Let them have the pleasure of you at this hour, it's their job."

"It's your job, too, Piglet." He wiped a hand over his face. "Besides, if I told them I needed a six a.m. wake up call, the photographers would be sitting outside at five."

She yawned into the phone. "As long as you're awake, can I go back to bed now?"

"Did you have any trouble moving my schedule around?" He flopped onto his back to stare up at the ceiling.

"I still have a couple calls to make. I'll get to it later today. So how are things with my favorite author, is she there with you?"

"No, I told you what was going on with that."

"Yeah, but it's been a few days. I figured you'd have worn her down by now."

He rubbed his eyes, willing the memory of that hot dream to leave him. "Kelly's not like that."

She gave a knowing laugh. "You wouldn't be sticking

your neck out if you believed that. By the way, you should see the e-mails coming in on your web site. Half these women want you to marry her. The other half don't like you having a girlfriend. They're pissed as hell."

"Hey," he scolded. "Watch your language."

"Yes, *big brother.*"

He could imagine her rolling her eyes at him. "Go back to sleep."

Derek hung up the phone, then on impulse, went to the door adjoining his room to Kelly's. As he'd promised her, it wasn't locked on his side. He checked the knob. Just as she'd promised, it was most definitely locked from hers. He placed a hand on the door, imagining her sound asleep on the other side.

With a weary sigh, he let his hand drop and headed for the bathroom. And his second cold shower in less than twelve hours.

****

"This is absolute garbage."

With a huff of frustration, Kelly crumpled the paper she had just pulled from the printer and tossed it in the general direction of the wastebasket. It landed beside it, in a pile of discarded attempts she'd already accumulated.

"It's this place. I can't work here!" There was no answering thump of a tail, no wet, cold nose touching her bare foot. No kids banging through the door yelling *"Mo-om"* in search of pool-side towels, sunblock, snacks, or whatever else.

Resting her elbows on the table, she placed her head in her hands. "I can't be homesick now, I have a deadline."

A knock on the hotel door sent her heart to her throat. He'd said he would be gone most of the day, and it was barely past noon. Rising slowly, she took even longer getting to the door. She still wasn't sure how she could ever face Derek after the way she had behaved last night. Heat pooled between her legs at the very thought, and her knees nearly buckled.

Reaching the door, she dutifully checked the peep hole. She jerked back, blinking. It was him. But it wasn't. She looked again. Derek, or at least his one-dimensional likeness, life-sized and dressed in an Indian costume, stared back at her.

A knock sounded again, and this time she nearly jumped out of her skin. "Who is it?"

Sharon stepped into view. "It's me and M.J."

Shoulders slumping in relief, Kelly pulled open the door, grateful it wasn't the real-life version. And grateful for the distraction the two women brought to her non-productive afternoon.

"I'm leaving for New York in a few hours, but I wanted to see how you were doing." M.J. said as she entered the room.

Sharon followed, awkwardly lugging the cardboard Derek through the door. "I don't want to leave this baby in the hallway for someone to steal."

"What the hell is that?"

"You like?" Sharon asked. "I won it. There was a drawing at the end of the conference. I was hoping he'd sign it for me."

"Did you stuff the ballot box?"

Sharon gave cackle of delight. "I spent close to an hour filing out little slips of paper. But it was worth it. I just don't know how I'm going to get it home."

"Marv won't let you bring that thing in the house."

She gave a little pout. "I could always keep it in the garage."

"That's a good place for it." Uncomfortable with the sensations even the cardboard version of Derek evoked, Kelly turned her attention to M.J. and found her frowning at the small mountain of paper near the wastebasket.

M.J.'s gaze met hers. "I take it you're not having a good day."

Kelly shook her head. "Terrible. No matter what I do, these characters won't cooperate." She gestured to her lap top. "Thorn is acting like a sex-starved animal every time he's in a scene with Raven, and she's even worse. The more she tells him she doesn't want him, the more she's melting at his slightest touch." She flopped into the chair. "This may be the first time ever I miss a deadline."

"Well, there must be something you can do." M.J. glanced behind her to Sharon. "You're her critique partner, suggest something!"

Kelly turned to glance at her friend, who smoothed one of the crinkled sheets of paper. She read in silence for a few minutes, then frowned. "I don't think I can."

"What? Why not?"

"Nothing," Sharon said with a grin. "This is the best thing you've ever written. I always knew you had it in you, Kel. The sexual tension leaps right off the page. I can feel how much these two want each other, and the conflict is right there in front of them. There's no way they can get past this and be together."

She grabbed the page back. "Let me see that."

Slipping on her reading glasses from where they dangled on a chain around her neck, M.J. leaned over Kelly's shoulder. "Oh my. Do you have more of this?"

Kelly shrugged. "Only about twenty more pages. Why?"

"Sharon is right. This is wonderful. I want more. And since you're writing so well, I won't bother you any more today. Before we go, would you mind if I use your bathroom to freshen up? I've got a long flight ahead of me."

When she was gone, Sharon pulled a white paper bag from her oversized purse. "I brought you a little something, just in case. I should have mentioned this yesterday."

"These aren't..."

"Condoms. I got you a nice assortment. Some lube, too. You know, sometimes you get to that fifth or sixth time and nature doesn't provide. Of course, saliva works better, so he could always—"

"Uh, I get the idea, Shar. Thanks. I think."

"Well, I knew *you'd* never go out and buy them." She glanced back at the bathroom door as the toilet flushed. "I'm sure he'll have protection, but it'll look better if you're prepared. Did you give my suggestion any more thought?"

Oh, practically all night. "Sort of."

Sharon tossed the bag on the bed, and Kelly grabbed it, quickly stashing it in the bedside drawer before M.J. could see it.

"By the way, Kelly," M.J. said, stepping from the bathroom. "I think you should know several other writers were approached by tabloid reporters yesterday and offered money."

"For what?"

"Information. They're really starting to take an interest in you. This whole Derek thing has turned out even better than I expected."

"Great."

"Would you consider doing any of the morning talk shows? I have a feeling after the insanity we saw yesterday, they're going to come calling."

Hell, why didn't she and Derek have their own reality show? "No."

"Are you sure?"

"Positive."

"Well, okay then." She leaned in to kiss Kelly's cheek. "Are you ready Sharon? Who knows how long we'll have to wait for the security checks."

"Oh, they always stop me." Sharon moaned and headed for the door.

"Aren't you forgetting something?" Kelly asked.

Sharon gave an embarrassed laugh and headed back for the cardboard cutout.

"He's not here right now, but I'll give him your message about signing that atrocious thing for you, Shar."

"What's atrocious about it?"

Kelly glanced back at the picture of Derek in the Indian costume, her eyes helplessly drawn to the hard-muscled chest and sculpted abs. A tingle crept up her cheeks and spread through her as she recalled how that body had felt beneath her palms last night.

"Oh ... my...God," Sharon said. "You really *did* take my advice."

"About what?" M.J. asked.

Kelly immediately averted her gaze, afraid of what her perceptive friend might read in her expression.

"Nothing." Sharon studied her, a half smile on her face. "I think you're right, though. Let's give Kel some space."

Scooping up her life-sized model man under one arm, she headed toward the door. "E-mail me any pages you want me to read over, Kel," she said. Once M.J. was safely out of earshot, Sharon turned back and gave Kelly a knowing wink. "You want me to run back downstairs for another dozen rubbers?"

****

Sauce, heavy with oregano and basil. Coffee that had been percolating half the day. And starch on cotton after a hot iron had been applied. The smells in his grandparents' Florida condo were the same as they'd been in the small, cramped apartment over the family pizza shop in Queens.

While Derek sat eating lunch with his grandfather, Nonna stood nearby ironing pillowcases and humming along to the Mills Brothers playing on the radio. She set her iron aside and moved toward him with her pain-ridden, shuffling gait.

"More *gnocchi*, Dante?"

Like the rest of Derek's family, his grandparents refused to accept the name change he'd made for the sake of his career. If he'd changed his last name, they'd have probably disowned him.

"*Si. Grazie, Nonna.*"

Before he could specify an amount, she heaped a ladle full onto his plate, followed by three meatballs the size of tennis balls. A moment later an enormous glass of milk was plopped in front of him.

His grandmother sank carefully into a chair beside him, then patted his hand. "*Mangiare*," she said. "A man your age should have a little belly. Women like that you know."

She'd get her wish if he kept eating like this. He'd have to exist on nothing but lettuce and air for the next week or he'd never fit into Captain Connery's leather pants again. Not that he really wanted to, unless it was to give Kelly a private show. She seemed to prefer him in costume. But not last night.

Finally, *finally*, he had gotten her to respond to him sexually. And for the first time in five days he was forced to spend the day apart from her. He should have canceled everything and spent the day with her instead, to hell with golf and to hell with her writing. It was more important to keep her on edge, aroused.

Aroused. The sight of her nipples straining against black lace and satin, pale breasts glowing in the moonlight, barged into his mind. He forced himself off that track. He couldn't even go there, couldn't even wonder what tonight might bring or he'd never be able to get through the rest of his visit with his grandparents. And he was here on a family mission.

"So are you driving up to New York this week, Papa?"

Over his own full plate, his grandfather nodded.

"I was thinking you might want to fly this time." He tried to keep the words nonchalant, but his mother and sisters had all expressed their concerns to him over the past few weeks. According to Nonna, Papa had been more tired than usual and having dizzy spells.

He winced inwardly as his grandfather paused, fork halfway to his mouth, and fixed dark eyes on him. "I take the car."

"You'd get there a lot sooner if you flew. Come on, I'll get you first class tickets, you'll love it."

"I take the car."

To press the matter any further would be disrespectful, at least that was how Papa would see it. His grandparents made the trip from Florida to New York twice a year, and they'd always been fine. Still, he had to admit Papa looked worn out.

"I hear you've been tired lately." He tried to sound as casual, as if they were discussing a Yankees game or the weather. "You feeling all right?"

"Papa is an old man, of course he's tired." Nonna protested. "More coffee, Angelo?" His grandfather shook his head, and she turned to Derek. "Dante?"

"I can get my own coffee, Nonna."

"Bah," she said and began to rise. She grimaced and paused for a moment. His grandmother's osteoarthritis was another thing that concerned him, but she refused to do anything about it.

Derek rose to his feet and put a hand on her shoulder. "Sit."

The coffee pot was on the stove, as always. He'd never known his grandparents to have an electric coffee maker, just a little ceramic pot that sat on the stove all day. He poured some into a cup and savored the strong aroma. He had to admit, there was no coffee like Nonna's. Even if he would have caffeine tremors for the next five hours.

He turned to lean a hip against the counter. "Are you taking your medicine?"

"She don't take not'ing," Papa said.

Nonna rubbed a hand over her knee. "If I need them, I take them."

"You're supposed to take them every day or they won't work," Derek reminded her.

"I don't like to waste them."

"Is it the money?" He set his coffee cup aside. "I'll buy you a truck full of them." From the stubborn set to her chin, he knew this was another pointless argument.

Nonna nodded toward the box he'd set on the table when he had arrived. "What new toy did you bring your Papa this time?"

Engrossed in his newspaper, Papa barely looked up.

"I thought you might be a little stubborn about driving to New York, so I bought you a phone. Just for emergencies."

His grandfather looked up from his paper. "What's that? One of them shell phones?"

"Satellite, but—never mind.' He took the phone from the box and handed it to Nonna, since Papa hadn't expressed much interest. "I programmed in all the numbers for you, and you can always use it to call nine-one-one if you have to."

His grandmother placed a hand to his cheek. "Such a good boy."

He could tell by her vague expression that this gift, which was supposed to give him peace of mind, would end up sitting on a closet shelf along with countless others. At least the Cadillac he had bought them had a global positioning system. Not that he believed they even knew how to use it. He'd wanted to buy them something better than the caddy, had given his grandfather stacks of car brochures wrapped up as a gift one Christmas and told him to choose whatever car he wanted, the price was no object. Papa had chosen a white Cadillac. Said as a young boy he'd always wanted one. He'd done the same for his parents. His father had refused. It seemed no matter how hard he tried to spoil his family, they wouldn't let him.

"Finish your lunch," his grandmother admonished.

Feeling like an obedient kid, he slid back into his seat and tucked into the food, mostly because she'd nag him to no end if he didn't. Besides, he seldom got to eat like this anymore.

By the time she had set a plate of Italian pastries on the table and refilled the milk glass, he was stuffed to the gills.

When Nonna again sat beside him, she put her reading glasses on. He knew what was coming the minute she picked up a folded-over newspaper that sat beside her coffee cup.

"Model Man and Romance Novelist Turn up the Heat," she read aloud. Her broken English made it sound even worse than it was.

He sighed as she presented him with a tabloid picture of Kelly at the pool side that first night. In the upper corner was a photo of him dressed like an Indian with her in his arms. The memory of her on the balcony last night stole into his mind again. The sweet taste of her lips, the feel of her warm, soft skin beneath his hands, the sound of her sighs when he'd touched her...

"Who is this lady?"

He jerked himself guiltily from the memory. Christ, why did he feel like he was twelve years old again? "Just a colleague."

His grandmother studied the picture. "Uh huh. And what does she do?"

Here it comes. Much like his father, his grandmother hated the books he posed for, hated that he took his clothes off to make money. "She's a ... writer."

"Does she write them dirty books you pose for?"

He sighed. Kelly's novels were well-written and very emotional love stories. Yeah, the love scenes were sensual—okay over the top steaming hot—and he wouldn't mind acting out a few with her, but there was nothing dirty about them. "Nonna, they aren't—"

She leaned across the table and whacked him with the rolled up newspaper. "Have you no respect for women, Dante Giovanni Calavicci?"

"Let me see that, Theresa." Papa took the paper and studied the picture a second or two. "There is not'ing wrong here, at least the girl has clothes on."

Derek mentally rolled his eyes at the reference to Simone, the lingerie model.

Nonna shook her head, upper lip stiff. "In my day, if

a man kissed a woman that way, she was his wife."

Papa chuckled. "Old woman, I kissed you like that *before* we were married, not after."

"Angelo, such talk in front of the boy."

Derek rose from his chair. Much as he loved his family, he'd had enough. He'd done his best to convince them not to drive home, to no avail. Nonna still wasn't taking her medicine, nothing new there, either. In another couple of weeks Nonna and Papa would be in New York and the entire family could harp on them.

And Nonna's negative attitude about Kelly had done strange things to him. On the one hand, he couldn't help but think how much Nonna would like her. She was a devoted mother who lived for her kids, his grandmother could relate to that. And she was very old fashioned, a true lady stuck in a new age where most women were anything but.

On the other, he'd be embarrassed for Kelly Michaels to have a glimpse at his old-world family. The plastic slip covers on the sofa and lamps, religious statues half his size in the living room. Not to mention the shrine to the Blessed Virgin just inside the front door. She'd probably turn up her dainty little nose at all of it.

Still, the thought of her left something warm spiraling in his belly that had nothing to do with Nonna's *gnocchi*. He'd been away from her all day and for some inexplicable reason, was eager to get back to her.

"You're leaving?" Nonna asked, eyes misty with disappointment. "But I never see you anymore, my Dante. You just got here."

"I've been here half the day," he said with a gentle laugh. "Long enough for you to feed me three different times."

"Leave him alone, Theresa. Let the boy get back to his girlfriend."

"Girlfriend," Nonna spat the word as if it was evil. "Always a girlfriend with you. Why not a wife?"

Derek hugged his grandmother and kissed her soft, wrinkled cheek. Over the top of her head he gave Papa a wink, then favored Nonna with the same smile he'd used to charm an extra cookie out of her when he was little. "Cause Papa already stole my best girl."

Ten

After writing most of the day, Kelly was emotionally drained. She hoped she had gotten a handle on Thorn and Raven's problems. If only she could do as much with her own.

Talking to the parents of Maya's boyfriend hadn't helped. The conversation had gone well; they seemed very nice. But she still preferred her daughter not spend quite so much time with just one boy, especially one so much older. What was more uncomfortable was the boy's stepmother coming on the line to ask her if all the rumors about her and Derek were true. She was getting better at hedging and putting people off, but it was damn hard to do when the man in question's hands and lips had tormented her all day.

In fact, more than a few times today she'd caught herself describing Thorn's lustrous chestnut mane and olive-green eyes. Only to remind herself that Thorn's eyes were blue and his hair a sandy blond.

It was a little before six when her cell phone rang, the Gilligan's Island theme telling her it was Cody.

"Hi sweetie."

"It's not sweetie," came a familiar, angry voice. "I understand you've been talking to my neighbors."

"Fine thanks, Alan. How are you?" She'd been dreading this conversation, knowing her ex would make it as difficult as possible. "And yes, I spoke with Doctor and Mrs. Bradford. So nice of you to decide it was all right for our daughter to start dating."

"You've all but humiliated her now, calling and checking up on her like that."

"I'm her mother. If I don't embarrass her at least twice a day, something is wrong."

"I wouldn't think you'd have time for that sort of thing since you've been keeping so busy. Nice pictures in the paper, by the way."

She had wondered how long he would take to get around to that. "Let's not throw stones, shall we? There are several I could hurl in your direction."

"How am I supposed to keep her grounded?" Leave it to Alan to change the subject to avoid admitting he wasn't perfect.

Kelly sat down on the bed. "It's called 'parenting'. Not that you have much experience with it."

There was a long sigh, and she could picture him running his hands through what was left of his thinning hair. Could even picture the ragged, chewed up cuticles and bitten-to-the-quick fingernails. "She's really being difficult."

"Of course she is, she's sixteen."

From next door there came the thud of a door closing. A moment later, a knock on the adjoining door. Her heart slammed against her chest, and a tremor of anticipation skimmed her from head to toe. She hadn't seen Derek since last night.

She'd felt the pull of desire before, but never like this. This was an actual *need*. As though she might go insane if her body didn't get what it craved. Her gaze strayed to the bag of condoms lying innocently on her bed. Could she go through with it?

Only one way to find out.

She pulled open the door and motioned to Derek that she would just be another second. She felt, rather than saw, his gaze move over her and wondered if the yellow tank top and tropical print wrap skirt was too much. It had seemed a better choice than the black mini dress Sharon had helped her pick out yesterday. Or the very naughty red negligee.

After changing her clothes twice, Kelly still had no idea why she took extra care with her appearance tonight, but she wanted to look good—without giving the impression she had dressed for him. She had thought of little else besides what happened between them last night.

Alan's whining brought her back to the conversation. "What am I supposed to do with her?"

"Here's a novel idea, spend some time with her. She needs her father."

137

"You don't know how difficult she's being," Alan insisted. "Argumentative, sarcastic. It's really driving a wedge between Jenn and me."

"I'm *so* sorry your children are getting in the way of your love life."

"When did you get to be such a bitch? Is this some menopause thing?"

Don't take the bait. She pulled in a deep breath. When that failed to calm her, she closed her eyes and pictured herself on a beach. Any beach but the one Alan lived on. Peaceful. Serene. The sun warming her skin, the ocean lapping at her toes. It still didn't help. With a wicked smile, she added her ex into that vision, bobbing contentedly on the waves. And a great white shark. *Ah, much better.*

"I have to go now. Someone is waiting for me."

"Go ahead, pass the buck to me. But don't think I'm going to hold Maya to a grounding I don't agree with."

"That you don't agree with or don't want to deal with?" A moment later a buzz of silence told her he'd hung up. "Nice of you to use Cody's phone so you didn't have to pay for the call, you cheap bas—" She looked up and saw Derek leaning in the doorway, looking mildly amused. He also looked incredible in a golf shirt and tan shorts. The sight of his darkly tanned muscular legs brought back memories of digging her nails into those thighs last night.

Heat that rivaled the tropical Florida air bathed her insides, sending a sharp pang of longing into her lower belly. And effectively pushed away the worst of her anger.

"Ex husband?"

She nodded.

"I'm sorry I got back so late, traffic was backed up. Do you mind waiting while I grab a shower and change?"

Another one? The man took more showers than anyone she had ever met.

"That's fine."

Once he had gone, she paced the hotel room almost restlessly. She'd never felt so on edge before in her life. Irritated with Alan. Concerned about Maya. Worried about those damned pictures. Nervous about what the night ahead with Derek would bring.

I'd screw his friggin' brains out.

What seemed like only minutes later, the sound of a door opening and closing startled her. She lurched to a halt. Derek stood in the adjoining door again, this time with a towel slung low about his hips, another in his hand as he briskly dried his hair, as if it were no big deal that he was naked except for the towel. Droplets of water clung to his chest, and despite her inner voice's warning, she watched in fascination as one lucky drop made its way down his taut stomach toward that towel.

"Did you think about what you wanted to do tonight?"

"Non-stop." She forced her eyes back to his face. Was he doing this on purpose?

He grinned. "Dinner, a movie, a long drive? What did you have in mind?"

None of the above. "Oh, I don't know."

"Did your ex upset you? You seem tense."

"Maybe a little." She walked over to the balcony doors, anything to break the sudden spell he had cast over her. "Why don't I give it some more thought while you get dressed?" She pulled them open. "I'll just be right out here."

Derek gave a low groan. That couldn't have gone much worse. Most women wouldn't have walked away from what he'd offered just now. But Kelly had yet to do anything most women would. For a second, something had flickered in her eyes that almost made him think she'd come around. He'd never doubted for a second that she found him physically attractive. And she had never denied the fact. But getting her to act on those feelings was another thing entirely. Maybe last night had been just a fluke.

He dressed hurriedly, and paused to pull a bottle of chilled wine from the mini refrigerator in his room. A few seconds later, telling himself he hadn't rushed for any real reason, he found Kelly on the balcony.

Elbows resting on the waist-high rail, she stared out at the hazy sky. She looked deep in thought, probably reliving the conversation she'd had with that asshole ex of hers. Not wanting to startle her, he set two glasses and the wine bottle he carried down with a soft clink—just enough to let her know he was there. She turned as he splashed a vintage chardonnay into each one.

"Looks like it might rain," she said.

Great. The weather. Exactly what he wanted to talk about. As it had earlier, her gaze flitted over him as if looking for a place to rest. Down his chest and stomach to his pleated slacks, lingering as if she couldn't take her gaze from ... *there*. Hell. If she kept that up, she'd be keeping *him* up. That would scare her off for sure.

Her gaze finally settled on the two wineglasses he held in his hand.

"Now why didn't I think of that?" she asked, smiling and accepting one of the glasses. "A drink to calm my nerves."

He'd love to know just what she was so nervous about. Business, first, however. He pulled a folded manila envelope from his back pocket and tossed it on the patio table. She leaned back against the railing, and he stood waiting for her reaction. None. He slid his hands in his pockets, feeling fidgety, tense. Things he hadn't felt around a woman in a long, long time. "I should probably warn you, there are about fifty photographers outside the hotel."

She groaned. "Now what?"

"We made a big impression yesterday." He studied her face for a reaction before zeroing in on her mouth. Full, wet, inviting. He wondered if she was remembering the same kiss he was. *All of them.* "The tabloids always come out on Friday. I don't know what the headlines will bring, but I'm sure we'll be on the cover."

"Great. Undoubtedly one of the pictures they took last night."

He moved to join her at the railing, taking a sip from his glass before speaking. "Those won't ever be seen."

"How do you mean?"

He nodded toward the envelope. "The negatives are in there."

"How did you—"

"I have my means. Your kids are officially off-limits to the paparazzi."

The relief evident in her blue eyes was worth any inconvenience spent chasing around as he had today. "Derek, I don't know what to say. When you said you would take care of it, I didn't expect it to be so soon."

"I called in some favors." About a hundred of them, actually.

She laughed. "Via Blaine or Gabrielle?"

"Neither." He supposed she'd find it hard to believe he occasionally handled things himself. But certain things, like promises made to Kelly, just couldn't be trusted to anyone else. Not even Gabby.

"I didn't mean to imply—"

"You didn't." He lifted the glass to his lips again, and this time her eyes were intent on his. "Do you have a publicist, by any chance?"

She shook her head. "I've never needed one."

"You might want to look into it."

"I'm almost afraid to ask why."

He sighed, not really wanting to get into it but knowing they had to. She needed to know, had to be warned ahead of time. "Because this thing is bigger than we realized. I think it will only get worse when our time together is over."

Something like regret touched her eyes before she looked away. "I haven't even thought that far ahead. Could we please not discuss it tonight?"

Was there some significance to this night he didn't know about? First the reference to her nerves, now this. He had to hand it to her; she knew how to keep him guessing.

A humid breeze blew a strand of hair across her face. It caught on her lip gloss, and he reached to brush it away. "There is one little catch to getting my hands on those photos."

She stilled. Her posture went rigid. The look she cast him was guarded. "What sort of catch?"

Jesus, did she really think he'd try to bargain for sex? He tried to keep the edge from his voice when he spoke. "I had to promise we'd give them an exclusive interview. It was the only way I could get the negatives and the guarantee they won't try to photograph your kids."

"Oh."

"You thought I was going to suggest something illicit?"

"No. Yes. I mean... I don't know why I always think

the worst where you're concerned. I just do."

Maybe because he hadn't given her reason not to.

"So when is it?"

"The night of the charity ball, in New York. I thought that would give us some time to decide what we want to say."

"We? Now we're doing an interview together. This is all starting to spin out of control."

"A little. We may need to stage a very public break up when the time comes." But he didn't want to talk about that either. "Maybe tonight isn't the time to discuss it. Have you decided where you want to go?"

She took a gulp of wine, turning away from the railing to face him fully. "How would you feel about just staying in?"

Every nerve ending in his body went on high alert. For a long, silent moment he couldn't speak. Not one damn word came to mind. What the hell was she suggesting? It couldn't be what *he* was thinking. Like a slow motion replay, last night's events moved through his mind. The feel of her warm, silken skin, the image of her standing before him with her sweater open, moonlight bathing her bare skin with a pearly glow. Her soft moans and sighs.

A scorching blush crept over her, and she looked unsure of herself. "Maybe not."

He placed a hand over hers before she could turn away. Dammit, any other woman and he'd know exactly what she was up to. But not Kelly. "Staying in sounds great."

"Why don't I call the concierge and see what I can come up with for dinner?" She gave his hand a little squeeze before releasing it. "My way of saying thank you."

With that, she hurried back into her room. Was she running again or simply taking care of dinner as she said? And what the hell was with the crazy signals she was sending his way? Asking him to stay in, then darting off like she couldn't wait to get away from him.

There was only one way to be sure. A little push would send her in one direction or the other. Past experience with Kelly told him exactly which way she'd go. She'd run like hell. But he had to know. Had to try.

He had just topped off their wineglasses and taken a seat on the love seat when she returned.

"The delivery man from the Chinese restaurant should be here soon," she announced.

He patted the seat beside him. Much to his surprise she didn't hesitate or refuse. He shifted as she sat, taking up more room than was necessary, so that her body pressed against his from shoulder to thigh. He stretched his arm along the back of the seat, fingertips brushing her bare shoulder. He'd have his answer soon enough. If she wasn't interested, she'd take off once he started the touchy-feely stuff. And if she was, it might hurry things along a bit when he took the initiative.

"So, do you golf often?" Her voice was too bright, too forced. If he hadn't guessed she was nervous, he knew it now.

"Not as often as I'd like." His fingers continued to brush her shoulder, slipping beneath the strap of her tank top and along her skin. All she had to do was turn toward him, look at him, and he'd take it from there.

But he needed some sort of starting point. "M—my ex used to spend most weekends on the golf course."

Oh, Jesus, was she comparing him to the ex, now? If she needed to make conversation, he supposed he could play along. Besides, if there was one curiosity he had about Kelly, it was her former husband. "Did he spend much time with the kids?"

"No. Being an accountant, he worked most weekends in the winter, of course. And by the time tax season was over, it was golf season. As long as there wasn't snow on the ground, he could golf right through December."

The thought grated on him, her husband leaving her alone all that time while he worked. Much like his father had done to his mother, though in his father's case it had been a necessity. "So you were basically a single mom."

"It felt like that sometimes, yes."

"Do you two argue often?" He had to wonder if any lingering passion fueled those arguments. It hadn't sounded that way from their phone conversation.

"Only when he has the kids. Right now Alan is a little more interested in trying to be a buddy than a dad."

God, he hated this, hated having to talk about this

with her. He'd rather just kiss her. "I'm sure the break up must have been hard on all of you."

"Sort of. We were in therapy, trying to save our marriage, when he began his affair."

"An affair?" Anger bubbled inside him. What the hell kind of husband was this guy? "I hope your father and brother beat the hell out of him."

"No," she said with a soft laugh. "No. I never even told them."

He stopped stroking her shoulder. "Why not?"

"Well, Daddy has high blood pressure and David... I just didn't think it was any of his business."

Derek's sister Angela's husband had screwed around on her shortly before their divorce. No one had told his father because they had known how angry he would be. But he and Anthony had tracked the guy down at his favorite bar and taught him a thing or two about how to treat women.

"Was it the only affair he'd had?"

"As far as I know. But I didn't have any fight left in me at that point. Trying to save a marriage from a younger woman and a man in the throes of a mid-life crisis seemed pointless. I gave up, even though I'd sworn I wouldn't make the same mistake my parents had, wouldn't put my kids through it."

"But you wouldn't have stayed with a man who could do that." He held his breath, waiting for her answer.

"If my children were younger I might have. I mean, I stayed all those years in a dying marriage because I knew what would happen if I left. I'd have become a single mom for real; I'd have had to go back to work full time, I wouldn't have been home with my kids anymore. Their entire lives would have been turned inside out and..." She reached for her wineglass. "Why are we talking about this?"

He hated to think of her feeling trapped like that. But it sure as hell explained her reluctance to take that kind of chance again. Unless... "Are you still in love with him?" He hadn't meant to blurt it out like that, but it was too late to take the words back now.

She gave a little choking sound. "Are you inquiring about the competition, Mr. Model Man?"

"What if I am? A man's got a right to know what he's up against."

"As if any man could compete with you." She laughed. "And for the record, no, I'm not. Alan killed any feelings I had left a long time ago." She raised her glass to her lips again, then paused as though a thought had just struck her. "How about you?"

He flashed a grin. "I'm not in love with him, either.

"No, your ex girlfriend, the one you lived with. What was she like?"

He shrugged. Simone and her many issues was the last thing he needed to think about right now. "Just a girl."

"A model?"

He wasn't going to get into this. Didn't need her to get insecure over women in his past. Every woman he met compared themselves to the models he'd dated. "She was a lingerie model. I'm sure you know the catalog."

"What happened?"

"In the first place, it wasn't recent." He leaned forward to set his glass aside, noting her appreciative gaze on him. "It was a couple of years ago. And living together was more just a progression of her leaving her things around my apartment."

"So it wasn't really that serious."

Only to Simone. "We were hardly ever together. One of us was always out of town or out of the country working. Then I started to hear things about her and a certain photographer." He shrugged. "That was the end of it. I found out later the photographer was just a fling to get me jealous." Way more than that, she'd tried to pass off the other guy's baby as his, but no way was he going there. Not tonight.

She took a sip of the wine, favored him with a mysterious little smile. "One might wonder if you're afraid of commitment."

"One might. But they'd be mistaken."

"That isn't exactly an answer."

"It doesn't seem fair to ask someone to sit around and wait for me when I'm gone so much." He took the wine glass from her and set it aside, doing his best to close the whole subject of ex's—his *and* hers. "And it seems like a waste of time to talk about this."

"What would you rather talk about?"

When he pulled her into his arms she didn't resist. "I'd rather not talk at all."

"Derek, about last night..."

He'd thought of nothing else all day. He wondered if she had. "It won't happen again," he said, his lips hovering over hers. "Unless you want it to." Please God, let her want it to. And then some.

"I meant the pictures," she whispered. "I can't tell you how grateful I am."

"Maybe something will come to you." Unable to wait another second, he brushed her lips with his. To hell with tentative kissing. He poured his hunger for her, his entire day spent moping like a horny kid without her, into the next kiss. She opened for him without hesitation, her tongue meeting his in an intimate dance that left no question where this night was headed.

A knock sounded on the hotel room door, and she jumped like she'd been caught with her hand in the cookie jar.

"That would be dinner."

As if he cared about food right now. With a groan, he rose from the love seat. "You stay right there."

Kelly reached for her wineglass and drained it. If she was going to go through with this, she needed to shut out that nagging inner voice that proclaimed good girls—good mothers—didn't do this sort of thing.

A moment later he returned, holding up two large grease-stained bags. "Did you order enough food?"

"Your web site says you have a weakness for Chinese food."

"Among other things." His gaze deliberately fixed on her mouth. One corner of his lips turned upward as he began to remove the small white cardboard boxes from the bags. "So why were you looking at my web site?"

She was used to working with a picture of Derek taped to her computer monitor and had needed a picture of him to better describe Thorn's magnificent chest. Of course, after tonight she could just describe it from memory. Just when she'd thought her love scenes couldn't get any steamier, staring at his picture, remembering the way she had touched him last night, had inspired what was probably her hottest love scene yet.

He pulled out a chair, motioned for her to sit. As she did the touch of his palms warmed her shoulders. "It's all right. I visited your web site last night."

She looked up at him in surprise.

"It hasn't been updated in a while." He took a seat across from her. "Don't you think your fans are curious?"

"Probably," she admitted. "I'll have to get my web guy on it." No point in mentioning the "web guy" was her fourteen-year-old son.

She frowned when he handed her a pair of chopsticks. "I've never used these things before." Her fingers couldn't seem to grasp the concept of having extensions. She'd kill for a fork. She hated feeling uncoordinated, especially in front of him.

Derek watched her struggle with the chopsticks. He still couldn't believe she had chosen to stay in tonight. Any other time, he might have thought he'd misunderstood. But there was something different about her tonight, and not just the sexy clothes. She was ready. Or at least every signal she sent his way declared she was. "Here." He leaned across the table and took hold of her hand, molding her fingers around the little wooden sticks. "Like this."

Intentional or not, as his fingers stroked hers, he heard her breath catch. "I'm... not doing too well with this."

Whether she meant seduction or eating utensils, it was time to lay his cards on the table. "I'm a very good teacher."

Her gaze moved from his fingers to his face. In the flickering candlelight her blush warned him he had to move slow, let her set the pace.

He eased his hand away and motioned for her dip the sticks in the bowl. "Now try."

She failed and set the chopsticks aside with an embarrassed giggle. "No wonder the Chinese are so thin, they can't eat."

He dug into the bag and produced a plastic fork. "Maybe you gave up too soon."

She scooped a forkful of Lo Mein noodles into her

mouth. "It's this or starve, and I haven't eaten a thing all day."

In that case, he'd better let the lady eat. The last thing he needed was for the wine to go to her head and cloud her senses. Besides, if things went the way he hoped, she would need her strength. "Why didn't you eat?"

"I forgot."

"Forgot?"

"It happens sometimes when I'm working."

And to think his grandmother had pumped a week's worth of calories into him today. Tomorrow he'd make damn certain she ate. Starting with breakfast. In bed.

She pointed her fork at his plate. "You haven't touched your food."

"I'm enjoying watching you." He'd lost track of how many times his eyes had returned to her mouth while she ate or sipped her wine. He'd only had a taste of her before they had been interrupted, but it was enough to whet his appetite for more. His gaze dropped to her breasts, then slowly returned to her soft lips. Much more.

This time he didn't have to wonder about the blush staining her cheeks as she cleared her throat and looked up at him. "Tell me about this charity ball, whom does it benefit?"

"People who worked at Ground Zero after the nine-eleven attacks." He picked up his own chopsticks and began to eat. "A lot of them have lingering health issues and lack the insurance or financial means to pay for their medical care. Some are too sick to work."

She tore a piece off of an egg roll. "It sounds like something you feel strongly about."

"It's sort of a pet cause. They worked their asses off, they deserve to be taken care of."

"That's right, you're from New York. Did you—"

He had to clear his throat before he could speak over the tightness in his chest. "My brother-in-law was a firefighter. He was in the North tower when it collapsed."

Her soft hand covered his across the table. "I'm sorry. I didn't mean to dredge up unhappy memories."

"My sister Bianca's husband. He and I used to take the kids camping every summer. Mike couldn't wait until the baby was old enough to come. She was only eight months old when it happened." He had no idea how Kelly always managed to get him to open up about things he seldom talked about. But this was no time to dredge up pain, suffering, and loss. He gave the soft, pale hand on his a squeeze. "I think you should try those chopsticks again."

She laughed. "No way."

"It just takes practice." He stood, then came around the table to kneel beside her. This time he wrapped his fingers around hers and guided them.

She was able to get a small bite to her mouth, but ended up with a grain of rice stuck to her lower lip.

He caught it on the pad of his thumb and brought it to his mouth. "Delicious."

When her eyes met his, they'd gone soft and serious. If food held little appeal for him before, it had none now.

"You're nothing like I thought you would be."

He reached up to tuck a stray lock of hair behind her ear. "Neither are you."

She turned her head so that her cheek rested in his palm.

He couldn't look away from her mouth, from the lips that pulled him in like a magnet. "Kelly, are you sure about this?"

"About what?"

"You know damn well what."

Derek wasn't sure who moved first, but she was in his arms, her mouth hot against his. Fingers laced through his hair, pulling him closer, demanding more. His own hands roamed from her hips to her waist before easing up to cup her breasts.

She unfastened the tiny buttons up the front of his shirt, her hands smoothing over his chest. Her fingertips were soft, cool, yet the sensation they left behind scalded him. Just like last night, he couldn't get enough of her touch. But he couldn't make love to her on the cement floor of the balcony.

"Not out here," he whispered.

Blue eyes, dark with passion, stared up at him. "What?"

"I'm not taking any chances with photographers tonight." With her in his arms, he rose to his feet and carried her through the open doors into her room. He closed them, then leisurely eased her down the front of him, keeping their bodies in constant contact. The feel of her soft curves against his arousal, the knowledge that she didn't move away, honed his need to razor sharp.

Until that moment, Kelly had envisioned giving herself time, working up her courage, taking things slow. *To hell with that.* She cupped the back of his neck and yanked his mouth to hers. Lord, he tasted good. No, better than good. But it wasn't enough. She wanted more. He shrugged out of his shirt, his mouth never leaving hers. She flattened her palms against his bare, hard chest, gliding them down to his hard muscled abdomen, fingernails skimming across his ribs.

His hands roamed over her hips, molding her body against his. She was unprepared for the wave of desire that washed over her at the feel of his hard, thick arousal against her belly. A pleasant trembling began deep inside, pressing her closer still. Her hips shifted to better accommodate him.

For a moment, his lips left hers. He pulled back just enough for her to see his green eyes, heavy with lust, questioning her.

Just in case he needed confirmation, she whispered, "Yes." Beyond that no other words came to mind.

With a moan, he took her mouth again. One hand slid slowly up her side in a feathery touch that might have tickled at any other moment. But the shivering sensation in its wake was no tickle. The cool air that brushed her bare skin as he eased the tank top up was followed by an incredible heat from his hands. He bent to nuzzle her breasts.

Something bumped against the back of her thighs, throwing her slightly off balance. She hadn't even realized they had moved. She put a hand out to steady herself. A table, though for the life of her, she couldn't say exactly which one.

His hands molded both breasts, caressed the lacy white push-up bra she was now terribly glad she had bought on her shopping spree yesterday. The front clasp gave to his skilled fingers; her breasts sprang free. He kissed his way along her skin, fingers traced the sensitive sides of her breasts; thumbs teased her nipples. A thousand shivers danced over her skin at the touch of his calloused thumb. Somewhere in her brain it registered that she wouldn't have believed the man could even have callouses, had ever known physical labor. But Alan's hands had been smooth as a baby's, and she couldn't help but appreciate the difference. At last, he took her into his mouth.

She couldn't contain a cry of pleasure when he drew on her nipple. And with one hand on the table to maintain her balance, she could only tangle the fingers of her other hand in the still-damp hair at his neck and arch her back in pure contentment. The movement brought their lower bodies even closer together.

He pressed against her, cradled right at the very place between her legs that throbbed with a need she'd never felt before. If he moved just a little, or if she had the nerve to part her legs just a bit more, she'd probably climax. For so long she'd only written about it, had half-envied the heroines in her books. But this was real, not something based on her imagination.

His mouth left her breast to glide up her throat and drag across her lower jaw. Hot breath brushed her ear. "Do you want me to stop?"

"No," she breathed. *Don't stop. Please don't stop.* She pulled his mouth back to hers, twining her tongue with his. He shifted again. And she knew a moment of disappointment as the erection she had been writhing against moved away. A hand slipped beneath her skirt to begin an unhurried journey up her inner thigh. She wanted to move, to open herself to his touch, but didn't dare. A whimper escaped her as his fingertips brushed the damp lace between her legs.

"It's all right," he whispered. "I'm going to give you everything you need."

His lips hovered over hers, so tempting she lost the ability to speak. His fingers rested idle between her legs. She needed only to grant him access.

"Just let go, Kelly. Trust me."

With effort, she relaxed the rigid control she'd always maintained and let her thighs fall apart. His finger hooked around the material at her hip and began to ease her panties down.

From a distance she heard the familiar tinkle of computer-generated wind chimes. Her first instinct was to ignore it, but then it came again.

She tore her lips from his, listening. Wind chimes? Maya's personal ring. "My cell..."

"Leave it."

"It's my daughter." Looking back to Derek, she nearly changed her mind. But she was a mother first. "I'll be back, I promise."

Insides in knots, knees trembled as she headed across the room, searching for the ringing phone. Her hands shook so bad she could barely flip the damned thing open to answer it.

"Hello?"

"Mom?"

Kelly's heart jumped as she heard her daughter's tearful voice. "Honey, what's wrong?"

"Dad won't let me go to that party with Trevor. He'll probably meet some other girl and dump me. This is all your fault."

Across the room, Derek leaned against the table, arms folded over his chest. Suddenly aware that she stood there with her shirt up around her neck, Kelly tugged it down. "I—I know you're upset, sweetie, but if he really has feelings for you, it won't matter that you aren't at this party. It might even make him miss you."

"It's not fair! You get to spend time with your boyfriend, and I don't." From the change in tone, Maya must have realized tears weren't working and decided to change tactics.

From the corner of her eye, Kelly saw Derek pace to the balcony doors. As if needing something to do, he stepped outside and lit a cigarette.

"You just don't want me to be happy."

"That's right, you've figured me out. I don't want you to be happy. It's my job as your mother to keep you miserable."

"That's not funny!"

She held the phone away from her ear for a moment. "Honey, we'll have to talk more about this later. Right now I'm in the middle of something."

"Work?"

"Sort of." If nothing else, she could always call it research.

"And that's more important than me?"

Kelly's heart fell a bit. This wasn't the first time Maya had accused her of letting work come before family. And *this* wasn't even close to work, no matter what she called it. Her daughter's accusations never failed to wring guilt from every corner of her soul. But she didn't want to get into that discussion. Not now. She felt trapped between returning her attention to Derek and Maya's need to take her anger out on her.

"Oh my God," Maya gasped. "You're with that guy, aren't you?"

"Yes, but—"

"I can't believe you. I'm grounded, and you're out having fun."

"I'm not getting into this with you, right now. Get some sleep, sweetie, we'll talk more tomorrow."

"Mom!"

"Love you, Maya. Bye."

Derek came to stand in the doorway as Kelly ended her call. He didn't have to see her face to know their tryst was over. He'd known the minute he heard the hysterical screaming over the phone. The moment wasn't just ruined; it might as well have never existed.

She turned. The guilty look was immediately followed by a blush that turned her cheeks scarlet. What a contradiction she was. In a million years he'd have never believed she would come onto him like that. He'd had aggressive women; he'd had shy women. But never both in the same package.

He shoved his hands into his pockets. She had straightened her clothes, though her hair was still mussed from his hands, her lips swollen from his kisses. But the fire was gone from her eyes. The seductress had left the building.

If only his throbbing hard-on would be as merciful.

She was having trouble looking him in the eye, and truth be known, he felt just as damned awkward.

"She would have kept calling if I hadn't answered."

"I know." A long silence hung between them. She

didn't move. Neither did he. "I should probably go."

Did she have to look so damn relieved?

"Derek, I'm—"

The last thing he wanted right now was an apology. For that matter, he didn't know what the hell he *did* want, other than to throw that phone of hers off the balcony. "I'll talk to you tomorrow, Kelly." He strode across the balcony and back into his own room.

Two cold showers in the past twenty four hours had done nothing to relieve his frustration. At this point, he doubted even jerking off would help. And the thought of another woman right now didn't even appeal to him. That was a real kick in the gut. He couldn't have the woman he wanted—but he couldn't seem to want another.

He couldn't blame Kelly for the way things had played out this evening. Sure, he wished she would have turned off the damn cell phone before things heated up. But her kids came first; she'd made that clear from the start. And honestly, he wouldn't want it any other way.

Heading for the closet, he yanked out a change of clothes and running shoes.

Only one thing would alleviate the physical discomfort and sexual frustration he felt right now. Exhaustion.

Eleven

"Aw, Christ." Derek rolled over and glanced at the bedside clock. Seven a.m. He sat up, groaning when overworked muscles protested. He'd gone straight from a late night run in the tropical Florida heat to the hotel gym and hadn't gotten to bed until three a m. It had worked. Tired and sore as he was, she wouldn't be able to get a rise out of him today. He hoped.

A gentle tapping sounded on the adjoining door. Probably coming to finish him off. She'd float in, wearing something lacy and see-through, work him up only to leave him hanging again. Or maybe she'd just carve his heart out and roast it in the mid-day sun.

"It's open." Today would be the first they spent entirely together. At least he assumed so. He hadn't exactly taken the time to ask her about that last night. Maybe he'd been a little overzealous with the workout. Hell, it'd be just his luck if she wanted to crawl in beside him and keep him company.

"A—are you alone?"

Did she really think he'd gone straight from her arms to another woman last night? "Yes, dammit."

She opened the door a crack as if to make sure, then entered the room. Her gaze flew over him and the bed, then darted away. "I didn't wake you, did I?"

"No." He rolled one sore shoulder and winced. He didn't usually bench that much weight, but last night he'd been too frustrated and wound-up to care. He'd definitely overdone it. A soak in the hot tub, some Advil, a Ben Gay rubdown and he'd be fine.

"I came to apologize for last night."

Regret? That was a hopeful sign "That's not necessary. It happens."

"Not to me." Standing there in black Capri slacks and sleeveless sweater, her hair pulled back in a ponytail and a pair of very trendy little glasses perched on her nose,

155

she was adorable. Sexy. And completely in control. Not even a slight resemblance to the seductress who had all but ripped his shirt off last night.

He wondered how different this morning might have been if they weren't interrupted last night. He felt a familiar tug down below and suppressed a frustrated groan. *Not today.*

"I—I need to leave, Derek. I need some of my research books and..." she wrung her hands together. "I never intended to be away from home for so long."

"You *what?*" He hadn't expected this at all. He tossed the covers aside and stood, his overworked gluts and quads howling at the movement.

She turned away like a shy school girl. "You're naked!"

"You asked if I was alone, not if I was dressed."

"You might have mentioned it."

"I'm perfectly comfortable this way."

"Well, I'm not, so please put something on."

He moved to the bathroom and pulled the pants he'd worn last night off the back of the door. Every muscle involved in the act of sliding them on objected, but he was too pissed to care. Leaving? What the hell was she thinking, she couldn't leave now.

She cautiously turned as he emerged from the bathroom, her gaze following his movements as he zipped and fastened. "I—I'll still go to the charity ball with you, of course. But I won't hold you to this pretense any longer."

"Is this because of last night?" Dammit, was she punishing him or herself for what almost happened?

"No, no. I'm just ... homesick, I guess." She paced across the room, arms folded protectively over her chest.

"I've turned my schedule—hell, my *life*—upside down for you for the next two weeks, and now you're leaving because you're *homesick?*"

She reached the end of the room, turned and began to pace back. "Don't raise your voice to me."

He purposely blocked her path, forcing her to either go through him or stand still. "If this is where I'm supposed to beg you to stay, you're going to be disappointed."

"You think this is some attention-getting ploy?"

"I'm not sure what I think right now."

"Let me put your mind—and your ego—at ease. This isn't about *you*."

"Why don't you sit down?" He sure as hell needed to, but he wasn't about to tell her that.

She glanced from the bed to the chair across from it and walked toward the chair. But didn't sit. "You only agreed to this whole thing because you thought you could get me into bed, anyway."

"And because I actually came close, you're out of here?"

"No." She abruptly sat. "No. I wanted..." She glanced at her hands. "I wanted the same thing you did last night."

Like a fast forward replay, the entire evening sped through his mind. He closed his eyes, forcing himself to picture anything else—the nuns from the Catholic schools he'd attended; his grandmother in her underwear, anything but the memory of Kelly's soft moans and sighs, her beautiful rose-tipped breasts... aw *hell*. "How did we get from tearing at each other's clothes to this in the space of twelve hours?" He sank down on the foot of the bed.

The tinkling of wind chimes sounded from Kelly's room and like Pavlov's dog, she rose.

"Leave it."

"That's my daughter."

"I know who it is."

"Then you know I need to get it."

"Is the world going to end if she gets your voice mail?"

"She's upset right now, it's important that I be there for her."

"So that's what this is really about?"

"What?"

"Your daughter guilted you last night for what's going on between us."

The wind chimes stopped and a frown creased her forehead. She sank back into the chair and shook her head. "No. You don't know my daughter."

"Maybe not, but I have teenaged nieces. Six at the

last count. The world revolves around them and everything is a crisis."

"Maya isn't like that. Well, not usually."

"Fine. So let's get back to last night."

"Last night was... curiosity on my part. I was experimenting with my wilder side. But as it turns out, I don't have one."

The hell she didn't. "So I was an experiment?"

She glanced back down to her hands. "I just thought... for one night..."

"Jesus." He rose to his feet, grimacing as his battered body objected. "I was there and available for your use, so what the hell."

"How is that different from you trying to charm your way into my hotel room a few nights back?"

"It just is."

"Really." It wasn't a question. "So you can use me, but I'm not allowed to do the same to you."

"Kelly, we've been over this. At the time, I thought you were..." He hesitated, not sure how to put it into words that wouldn't make him look like an egocentric jackass. "Like most other women."

"I think it's safe to say I'm far less sophisticated than the women you're accustomed to. There's certainly no revolving door on my bedroom. I've never been intimate with anyone other than my ex-husband."

No one but her ex? That explained two things. Sex couldn't have been worth much or she wouldn't be so willing to go without. And taking a lover wasn't something she would do lightly. But that didn't change the fact she had turned him inside out and upside down in this past week, and he was beginning to wonder if it was intentional. "So you decided to try me out just for the hell of it, is that it?"

"You certainly made it clear you were willing and able."

"And this morning, out of the blue, you're over it."

"I'm beginning to think I am."

"I'd prove you wrong, but I'm just not up for it this morning, sweetheart."

"Don't you 'sweetheart' me." The cell phone rang again, and she crossed the room in angry strides, stopping when she reached the doorway between their rooms. "And yes, I'm well aware you had a late night. You made enough noise when you came in."

"Have a little trouble sleeping last night, Kel?" The knowledge that she couldn't sleep nearly made the sore muscles and exhaustion worthwhile.

"Only because I was worried about Maya." She hurried through the doorway to the still-ringing phone.

Derek leaned around the door frame and watched her pull in a deep breath before chirping a bright hello. She came off sounding more like she'd been lounging on the beach instead of arguing with her would-be lover.

After a few seconds of listening to the screaming and crying that even from a distance was loud enough for him to hear, she sank onto the sofa. "Oh, honey, don't cry. It's early yet, maybe he's still sleeping."

The hysteric wailing and crying continued. Derek glanced around the room, noting the slightly rumpled bed and the bags packed and waiting by the door. She was really leaving.

"Is it possible his cell phone isn't turned on right now?"

He turned his attention back to Kelly; she looked almost helpless, chewing at her lower lip, frowning. Her daughter sure knew how to push her buttons.

Not wanting to eavesdrop, he wandered back into his own room and picked up the work-out clothes he'd left on the floor last night. He paced restlessly, half listening to the sounds of Kelly trying to soothe her daughter.

"You try to get some rest sweetheart. I'll call you when I get home." She glanced up when he stepped back into her room and met his gaze. "Yes, I am. In just a little while." She set the phone aside with a heavy sigh. "I don't know this boy, but right now I'd like to castrate him."

"That bad?"

"It's just... she needs her mother now, not—" She put her face in her hands.

Derek moved to sit beside her, and she looked up at him out of teary, woeful eyes. "She used to tell me everything."

He pulled her into his arms. "You thought she did. Think about it; did you tell your mother everything when you were her age?"

She sniffled. "No, but ... you'd have to know my mother. I'm nothing like that. Maya and I have a good relationship."

He leaned across her to reach the box of tissues on the end table. She removed her glasses and pulled out a couple. "I feel like I'm losing my little girl." That set off a torrent of tears.

Lacking any words that might make her feel better, he held her while she sobbed, uncaring that her tears soaked his bare chest. Guilt nagged at him for how selfish his reaction had been earlier. She was right; it wasn't about him. Yet he had reacted without thought for Kelly and how hard this must be for her. Practically from the moment they met he had been pressuring her to sleep with him. Then M.J. and Sharon had talked her into agreeing to this pretend affair. The paparazzi descending on them like vultures hadn't helped.

Now Kelly was having trouble with her daughter while working close to her deadline. The one common thread in all of it? Him. He had only been thinking of himself and what he wanted.

Little wonder she was so upset. This was too much for her to handle. The knowledge, and the realization of his own role in her troubles, made him hold her that much tighter.

Her sobs began to quiet, and he stroked her hair, smoothing back strands that had come loose from the pony tail at the back of her head. He hated to admit it, but it was time to let her go. If she needed some space, some time to herself, he owed her that. More, actually.

He caught the moisture from her cheek on the edge of one finger. "Are you all right?"

Nodding, she raised her head to look at him, eyes watery, nose red. She took another tissue from the box and wiped at her nose and eyes. "Embarrassed more than anything."

"About what?"

"Losing it, like this. I'd hoped to at least make it home before I fell apart."

He laughed again and slid a hand down her bare arm, skin cool from the air conditioning but silk and velvet in a way that was uniquely Kelly. "After the week you've had, I think you're entitled.'

She shifted to right herself in his arms. "Maybe, but you shouldn't have to deal with it." She pulled another tissue from the box. "And look at the mess I made all over you with tears and make up."

As she dabbed at his chest, he studied her face. The red around her eyes only made the blue in them more brilliant. Had she always been this beautiful or had he been so consumed with getting her into bed he had failed to notice?

Her hand slipped lower, the tissue grazing along his stomach, down to the waistband of his slacks. His abdominal muscles flinched at her touch, and not because of his abuse of them last night. She went still and ever so slowly glanced down. Her breath caught in her throat. He followed her line of vision, knowing all too well what she saw. Yep, it was there. The tell-tale bulge just under his zipper.

Her hand hovered for a moment, as if she longed to continue the exploration. He held his breath, tempted to move her hand, wishing she'd take the initiative. One touch and they would both be goners.

A knock came at the hotel room door.

She glanced toward it but made no attempt to move. "That's probably the bell boy for my things."

He swallowed. If he had thought exhaustion a good defense against her, he'd been wrong. His physical reaction was the same as always.

"Derek, I'm really sorry for the way things worked out. After the last two nights, you must think—"

He suppressed a groan. Did she have to remind him when he was struggling to maintain control as it was? "I don't think anything." He took the hand still resting just over his waistband, brought it to his lips and kissed it. The knock came again, this time a bit louder. He disentangled himself from her and rose. "I'll get that." Anything to put some distance between Kelly and his growing condition.

"What about the charity ball?"

Hand on the door knob, he paused. He should just tell her to forget it, but he had promised an exclusive interview. And it would be another chance to see her. A chance to say goodbye. "It's a week from tonight."

She nodded. "I'll look for something to wear."

"Why don't you let me take care of that?" He'd rather not dwell on the idea of dressing her just now. It would only lead to thoughts of undressing her.

"You don't know what size I wear, and I'm certainly not about to tell you."

"You don't have to wear it if you don't like it." Didn't she realize he had already memorized her shape? And after the years he'd spent modeling in Milan before coming back to the States, he probably knew better than she did what would look good on her and what wouldn't.

A third knock came, and Derek pulled the door open.

"Good morning, sir," the bell hop greeted. "I'm here for Mrs. Michaels' bags."

Derek watched as the young man began to load Kelly's suitcases onto a cart. As he worked, his gaze swept the room more than once.

No doubt the tabloids would pay the little weasel for whatever he could scrape together. Both their rumpled beds could easily be seen through open doorways, and with Kelly's tear-streaked face and him half dressed, it didn't look good. He could offer to pay the kid twice whatever the reporters were offering, but there were never any guarantees. He'd been burned that way before.

Just last night he had warned her that the fall out would be bad when the end came; he hadn't been expecting it quite so soon. Something heavy settled in his chest, and he tried his best to ignore it.

She bent to retrieve her purse and lap top case. The sight of the computer hit him like a slap in the face. She had spent yesterday writing, hadn't she? Was that what had changed her mind about sleeping with him? A day spent writing hot love scenes?

It hadn't worked out so he supposed none of it mattered now.

"I guess this is... goodbye. For now."

"Just for now. I'll be in touch in a few days." He picked up her phone from the sofa table and handed it to her. "While you were making dinner arrangements last night, I programmed some numbers into your phone. My place in New York and my cell number. The third is Gabrielle's. If you can't reach me, she'll know where I am."

"I'm sure it won't be necessary." Her still-watery gaze locked onto his face.

"Once the paparazzi finds out we're apart, they're going to devour us. Promise you'll call me if you need me."

"I will. Derek, I'd like to kiss you good-bye, but—"

Instead, he pulled her close and pressed his lips to her forehead in an almost brotherly gesture. No, he'd never be able to stop at just a kiss.

****

With a huff of frustration, Kelly rose from her chair. She stretched and glanced at the clock. Half past ten. She never did her best writing in the morning and today was no different. She just couldn't concentrate.

She was right at the black moment, where the lovers were parted by insurmountable differences. And she couldn't write it. Glancing down at her notes, she read for the thousandth time: *believing the child Raven carries to be his brother's, Thorne accepts the marriage his father has arranged with another woman. Raven cannot tell him the truth without revealing his brother's darkest secret. A secret she has vowed to take to her grave.*

As the couple parted ways, Kelly could see only Derek in her mind. The look on his face when she had left, as if he couldn't believe she was actually doing it.

"Oh please," she said aloud. "He's probably glad to be rid of me, already moved on to some younger, less complicated woman."

Barney, her loyal love-the-one-your-with canine companion, raised his head and looked at her as she wandered restlessly around her office. The dog hadn't left her alone for a minute since she picked him up from her mother's house yesterday.

"Poor Barney," she soothed, pausing to stroke his soft head. "You're lost without the kids, aren't you? I guess that makes two of us."

He put his chin back down on his paws and regarded her with soft, sad-sack Golden Retriever eyes.

Moving across the room, she paused to study framed artwork from her book covers. Usually they filled her with a sense of pride and accomplishment. She had never before seen them as anything but the living embodiment of her characters, her work.

Now all she saw was Derek. She turned away as the memory of touching that incredible chest, those solid thighs flooded her. The feel of his hands, his mouth against her skin. Her breasts.

A moan escaped her. She wasn't even sure why she had left. Ran away, was more like it. Well, that wasn't quite true. She did know why. Guilt. Not your regular old run-of-the mill remorse, either. Pure one-hundred-percent mother guilt. Maya had been so upset and what had she, Kelly, been doing? Exactly what she had told her daughter not to. Oh sure, there was a world of difference between a sixteen-year-old girl and a forty-two-year-old woman. That didn't help the guilt any.

Of course, her own mother's comments added to the mix, since she had picked her up at the airport last night. As if the stares she had encountered on the plane hadn't been enough to rattle her. She had wondered why everyone kept staring at her. It wasn't until someone seated nearby had set their magazine down and headed for the bathroom that Kelly had seen it. A tabloid featuring her and Derek on the cover with a very suggestive headline.

Even now, she grimaced as she recalled climbing into the back of her stepfather's Lexus while he loaded the suitcases into the trunk, and seeing a copy of each of the current tabloids there waiting for her.

And her mother's terse comment. "I don't know whether to ask for autographs or an explanation."

The evening went downhill from there.

A cold, wet nose nuzzled her leg, breaking her from the unpleasant reverie. Kelly glanced down at Barney. "What do you say we try some gardening? I can't get into too much trouble out there."

The weeding, pruning, and deadheading always helped to unravel the blocks and tangles that affected her writing. There was something very therapeutic about working in the dirt. She liked to think if she hadn't discovered writing, she'd have gone into landscaping or opened a florist shop.

Minutes later, gardening tools and gloves in hand, she and Barney headed for the flower beds.

Across the street, Mrs. Horner swept her driveway. Again. The neighborhood busybody spent most of her day cleaning the driveway, and when she finished that, she worked on the street. Kelly had told herself many times the older woman was simply bored and trying to keep busy. But she certainly knew everybody's business.

She gave her neighbor a little wave and knelt in the grass. Her spade had barely broken the ground's soft surface when the woman crossed the street. Kelly groaned. Why did people always want to chit-chat when she was trying to sort out plot ideas?

"Mrs. Michaels, how was your trip?"

Kelly glanced up at her and smiled. "Lovely, thank you." Oh God, she hoped her neighbor didn't read the tabloids.

"I thought you'd like to know those men were here while you were away."

Her hand froze over the weed she had been about to pluck. "Men?"

"Yes, dear, those ones over there."

She followed her neighbor's gesture to a four-door blue sedan parked a couple of houses down. Two men sat inside, watching her.

"They wanted to know all about you, what sort of neighbor you were, what your social life was like."

"Mrs. Horner, you didn't...talk to them, did you?"

"Well, not really." Her hand fluttered to the neckline of her housecoat. "There isn't much for a shut-in like me to tell, I certainly don't mind my neighbor's business. I explained to them that with my cataracts, I can barely see my own hand in front of my face."

"Mmm hmm." Kelly continued digging, unsure of what to do. Photographers had been outside the gym this morning when she had come from her Pilates class, but she hadn't seen these before. Instinctively she knew they were reporters, probably the tabloid variety.

"Do you know your house was dark the entire time you were gone, dear?"

No, but I'm sure you do. "I guess I forgot to leave a light on."

"You should be more careful. My Herbert caught those men digging through your trash. What you need is a good alarm system."

Ah, is that your son's line of work these days? "I'll keep that in mind, thank you."

"I just don't like the idea of a woman living all alone. And with your husband gone, you can't be too careful. You know, my Herbert always keeps the lights on in the driveway at night. Says anyone with a mind for mischief would be easily spotted that way."

"I have Barney for protection."

They both glanced at the dog, who sat contentedly gnawing a dilapidated old football. He thumped his tail happily. Kelly sighed. He was about as ferocious as a gold fish.

"You know my Herbert, Jr. is in the home security business. He'd be more than happy to come by and talk to you. Did I mention he's single again?"

"I believe you did." *Nearly every time I see you.*

"You just can't be too careful these days. By the way, there were some very flattering pictures of you in this week's scandal sheets."

Kelly bit her lip to keep from cursing. Now she knew the real purpose of this neighborly visit.

"Well, of course, with the type of books you write, I'm not surprised these things go on. I suppose with the children away, a woman your age needs to kick up her heels now and again. Quite the young stud you were photographed with."

"Yes, he was. Hung like a race horse and the stamina to match." Oh God, had she said that out loud? She'd thought about it, but hadn't meant to actually say it. If nothing else, for the first time in fifteen years, Mrs. Horner was speechless.

"Wh—what did you say dear?"

Kelly sat back on her heels and watched as one of the reporters stepped from the car and started toward her.

She rose to her feet. "If you don't mind, Mrs. Horner, I'd rather not talk to these gentlemen. Will you excuse me please?"

"Kelly, wait—a few questions!" called the reporter. "Where's Derek? Did you two have a lover's spat?"

"Barney, come." The dog at her heels, she beat a quick retreat around to the back of the house. Stumbling up the steps to the deck, she slipped inside the open door, closed it and snapped the blinds shut. She had hoped by coming home things would return to normal, after all, if they weren't together, then there was no story. Was there? She leaned against the door, her heart pounding like a jackhammer.

What would happen after the charity ball when this thing was truly and finally over? Would her life go back to normal then—or would it take weeks of being hounded like this before the reporters gave up and left her alone?

A noise on the deck started her, a sound much like someone knocking over one of her flower pots. Barney began to bark. Through the slats on the blinds she could make out the silhouette of a man in her backyard. Should she call nine-one-one? How did one report being stalked by paparazzi? Did the police handle that sort of thing?

"Dammit." A sigh of frustration escaped her. There was only one person she could think of to call right now. Only one person who could tell her how to get rid of them. She hated to bother him, hated to even admit she needed him. But need him she did.

In more ways than one.

****

Derek stepped into his darkened apartment and flicked the wall switch just inside the door. Dim light bathed the room, illuminating the usual disarray that signaled Gabrielle's presence. He checked his watch. Ten p.m., but there was no sign of his sister. It wasn't like her to be in bed so early, so it was possible she had gone out.

He moved across the room, dodging the books, magazines and other things Gabby had left lying around. Her sloppiness should probably annoy him, but it was better than coming home to an empty apartment time after time.

Across the room, the lights of New York twinkled against the night sky, beckoning to him like an old friend. A slightly battle-scarred old friend, but a familiar one. He moved to stare out the window. Far below, the traffic on 42nd street moved along at its usual pace, the red tail lights and blue-white head lights little more than tiny dots.

His youngest sister hadn't been around when he dropped Nonna and Papa off at his parents' place a couple of hours ago. He groaned. Two straight days in a car with his grandparents left him exhausted and irritable, but at least he had gotten them back to New York in one piece. A little rattled, maybe, but no worse for wear.

Naturally, once word had spread that his grandparents were home and he along with them, various brothers, sisters, nephews and nieces descended on his parents' place. He'd had no choice but to stay for dinner. Not that wild horses could have dragged him away; it had been too long since he spent time with his family.

He'd indulged the usual questions about reality versus the tabloid stories but hadn't told anyone what was really going on with Kelly, deflecting their questions with relative ease since everyone always talked over everyone else when they gathered like that. Instead, he'd soaked up his family.

The loud conversation, the abundance of food, the laughter, even the arguing had relaxed him. His father seemed relieved that he had cut his hair. And his mother and sisters had carried on that he never came home anymore, all the while waiting on him hand and foot. Odd that he didn't mind their fussing when lately it irritated the hell out of him for women to fawn over him. Now if a certain romance novelist wanted to fuss over him, that would be a different story.

Just the thought of her caused warmth to spiral into his belly—plus an annoying little pull of disappointment. They had only been together a few days; it was impossible to think he might actually miss her. But somehow the lady had wrapped herself around his brain so that everywhere he went he saw those big blue eyes, heard that throaty laugh.

The sound of a door latching drew his attention, and he turned to see Gabrielle, rumpled and sleepy, belting her robe as she came out of the bedroom. She looked toward the front door, then back to the living room.

"Hey," he greeted softly, trying not to startle her.

She turned to the sound of his voice. "Hey, yourself. I wasn't expecting you for a few more days."

He shrugged. "I ended up with some time on my hands so I drove Nonna and Papa in from Florida."

"You mean you *hired* someone to drive them."

"No, I did it myself." He moved past her into the kitchen, ruffling her long, curly hair as he passed.

"You should have called and told me you were coming, I'd have cleared out of here and let you have your privacy."

"I think Nonna would have had a stroke if I'd made a call while driving. She prayed the rosary non-stop as it was." He opened the fridge and reached for a bottle of water. He stopped short at the six pack of beer with one missing and the half bottle of wine. Water bottle in hand, he straightened.

"Papa let you drive?"

"Not willingly. I talked him into letting me take the wheel for a while, then I never stopped. Another twenty-four hours of Nonna's back seat driving, Papa passing gas and daily mass was more than I could bear."

"He must have been pissed."

"A little. When he wasn't snoring." He opened the water and turned to toss the cap in the trash. An empty beer bottle sat on the counter near the sink. Domestic stuff. Couldn't she have found a guy with better taste than that? He glanced toward the bedroom door that she'd closed behind her. Come to think of it, Gabby never closed the door unless she was in there.

Leaning a hip against the counter, he studied her. She fluttered about the kitchen, straightening stacks of papers as she went, wiping down the countertop with a paper towel, reminding him of their mother. "So, where is Kelly Michaels in all of this? She wasn't in the car with Nonna and Papa, was she?"

"No. She went back home to Rochester a couple of days ago."

"A couple of days?" She rounded on him, her eyes wide. "Why didn't you tell me?"

"I've been in a car for eighteen hours straight." He moved past her into the living room.

"I had no idea you two had split up. I went on Good Morning America this morning—I told them it was the real thing for you this time. Dammit, Derek, I *lied* to

Diane Sawyer for you."

Chuckling, he sank onto the leather sofa, the comfort of it welcome after the long drive. As he raised his feet to rest them on the table, he spied two empty wineglasses, one with pink lipstick on the rim.

Gabby followed him to the living room. "So?" she prompted, one hand on her hip. "What happened?"

"Nothing. Kelly had family obligations, that's all."

She threw one hand up in a gesture that was uniquely Italian. "You finally got her in bed and then you dumped her, didn't you?"

"I told you before, she isn't like that." His gaze returned to the wineglasses. Tired as he was he'd have to leave soon, give her time to get rid of lover boy. He really needed to look into getting a bigger place.

"This from the guy who claims that with enough convincing, they're all 'like that.'"

He winced. "That was a long time ago."

"Yeah, a whole six months at least." She moved around the sofa and began to pick up her shoes and magazines. "Last I knew you'd committed two weeks of your life to this woman. With your track record, that's practically a long-term relationship."

"Things came up."

She straightened. "Oh my God. *She* dumped *you*."

"Come on, Gabby, women don't dump me." Had she? It hadn't felt that way at the time, but he was beginning to wonder. Had she played him with the tears, the anguished mom routine? And he'd fallen for it.

"I don't believe it. She got you in bed, took what she wanted and left you high and dry." She smirked. "I have *got* to meet this woman."

Got him in bed? Hell, he should be so lucky. "Like I said, Kelly isn't like that." He finished the water, then leaned forward to pick up one of the wine glasses. "You might try it yourself some time."

She went suddenly still. "Try what?"

"Being hard to get."

"What's that supposed to—" She snatched the wine glass from his hand and picked up its mate from the table. "Are you saying I'm easy?" She hurried away from him, muttering Italian curse words under her breath.

He rose and followed her, stopping to lean against the door frame. "I'll give you half an hour—hell, take a whole hour if you want, just get him the hell out of here. Unless you want me to do it for you."

"You never said I couldn't have people over."

"I know you're an adult; I probably should have called and told you I was back early, but I didn't think about it. I'm just not in the mood to make small talk with the guy my baby sister is sleeping with."

The bedroom door opened. Eyes wide as saucers, Gabrielle hurried across the kitchen.

"Hey babe," a male voice said. "I woke up and you were gone. What's up?"

Something about the voice was familiar. Recognition dawned and Derek turned to see Jared Sterling, standing there in nothing but underwear.

The same Jared he had watched play musical bedrooms with at least five other women this past weekend. Without thinking, he strode across the living room, grabbed the asshole by the arms and shoved him against the wall. "You didn't get enough women at the conference? You had to come here and fuck my sister again, too?"

"Derek," Gabrielle screamed. "Let go of him!"

Jared put up a hand. "Look, man, it's not what you're thinking."

"Really?" Derek jerked him a bit harder against the wall, ignoring the discomfort of muscles still recovering from an overzealous workout and being cramped in the car. "Cause I'm thinking about rearranging your face." He pulled back his fist, but Gabrielle wrenched at his arm.

"Not the face," she screeched. "He's having head shots done tomorrow morning."

He glanced at his sister. "You think I give a damn about pictures?"

"Jared—don't!"

Derek blocked the fist Jared threw in his direction and landed a jab to the younger man's ribs, followed by one to the nose. Spurting blood, Jared muttered an expletive and returned a blow to Derek's jaw. His lips smashed against his teeth, and he tasted the tang of blood. But somehow it felt good. The anger and frustration he'd ignored for so long bubbled to the surface, and he lunged again. Jared hit the wall with a thud but straightened and rushed at Derek like a charging bull.

"Stop it, both of you!" Gabrielle picked up a shoe and wielded it like a weapon. "*This*," she shrieked at Derek, volleying the shoe in his direction, "is why I don't bring guys around my family. Because you're just like Dad."

He sidestepped the high-heeled missile, but her words stung long enough for Jared to land another punch to his midsection.

"You're just as bad as my brother!" Gabrielle cried as she stepped between the two, shoving each to one side.

Slightly dizzy from the last punch, Derek stumbled backward. "What the hell does that mean, 'just like Dad'?"

Gabrielle turned to Jared, jabbing his chest with the toe of another shoe. "You told me it was only one or two women last week—we are *so* going to talk about this."

"Babe—"

"Don't you 'babe' me. Now go put some clothes on and stop embarrassing me."

Derek wasn't the least bit surprised when Jared retreated to the bedroom like an obedient pup. When Gabby was mad, you didn't argue. And she looked fit to be tied.

Gabrielle turned furious eyes on him. "I meant what I said—you and Dad and Anthony are the whole reason I don't bring my boyfriends around."

"*Boyfriend?*" He propped himself on the back of the sofa.

"The three of you treat me like I'm a child, questioning every decision I make," she went on as if she hadn't heard him. "And you're the worst hypocrite of all. You trust me to make decisions about your life, but you don't think I'm capable of making decisions about my own!" She raised her chin defiantly. "And, yes. Boyfriend."

Derek ran a hand over his throbbing jaw. "Jesus, Gabby. You don't think just because you slept with him—"

She gave him a shove that sent him sprawling over the back of the couch onto the cushions. "There you go again! As if I'm too stupid to know the difference between screwing someone and having a boyfriend."

Derek righted himself in time to see Jared emerge

from the bedroom fully dressed. But he couldn't quite get up because his younger sister leaned over the back of the couch wagging her finger in his face.

"I spend all my time working—for you, for that damn pizza shop, and up until graduation a couple weeks ago, at school. Where do you think I'm gonna meet guys?" She jabbed him in the chest. "Huh? Where else?"

He swatted her hand aside and straightened. "I can't say I ever thought about it."

"Well, it sure as hell isn't the pizza shop with Dad breathing down my neck, scaring off every guy who tries to make small talk. I meet them when I'm working with you. Photo shoots. Promotions. Conferences. Jared and I flirted for months before we hooked up at the Romantic Moments conference last year."

"Where the hell was I through all of this?"

She put a hand to her hip. "Do you really want me to answer that?"

"Oh, Jesus." He raked a hand through his hair. That had been right around the time his "dry spell" had hit. He'd spent way too much time bed-hopping, trying to find a woman who could hold his interest more than a few hours.

"Anyway, Jared moved to New York, and we've been seeing each other ever since."

Jared stepped behind Gabby. "Until she dumped me."

"I got scared," she said with a shrug.

"Of what?" Derek asked, eyeing the younger man. If he'd laid a finger on her, he'd kick the fool's ass to Kingdom Come.

"Would you relax?" Gabrielle sighed. "Scared. You know, of my feelings. But I changed my mind right before you left for Florida."

"That's why you wanted to go with me?"

She glanced down at the floor in a rare attempt to appear demure. "Kind of."

Derek peered over the top of her head to Jared.

"I was trying to forget her, that's what was up with all the other women."

Gabrielle whirled around. "Yes, but you said one or two."

A guilty flush crept over the blonde man's face. "I—

uh—I..."

A day. One or two a day. Derek knew the routine, had been there a few times himself. But in the interest of hurting his sister's feelings, he held his tongue.

Gabrielle came around to slump on the sofa beside him. "Can you see why I can't bring him around Dad? What would he say if I brought home a guy who does what you do for a living?"

The comment grated, but only because it was true. "I'm sorry, Gabby."

"I didn't mean to take advantage of you letting me stay here," she said. "But think about it, I'm twenty-four years old, I'm not allowed to move out until I'm married, and Dad would kill me if I stayed out all night at a guy's apartment. When I'm here, it's our only chance to be together."

"Dad probably doesn't approve of you staying here, either."

"He knows I'm safe here, but no, he doesn't like it. Mom's got him convinced it's better than taking the subway home every night."

He rubbed her shoulder affectionately. "Stay as long as you want, I told you, it's no big deal. I just wish you had better taste in men."

At that she grinned up at Jared.

Derek cleared his throat. "Before I take off and leave you two alone, I want to have a talk with your, uh, *boyfriend*."

"What, you want to know his intentions?"

"As a matter of fact, I do."

"You're kidding me."

"Dead serious. Go on. Go pretty yourself up or something. You look like hell."

She rolled her eyes. "Only if you promise you're done throwing punches."

Derek slid a glance at Jared. "I won't damage anything ... *vital*."

Gabrielle headed for the kitchen. "I'll hear if you start another fist fight."

"She'll be listening to every word we say anyway," Derek said.

"I heard that."

Jared took a seat in the recliner across from him. "Before we get started, I think you should know I'm in love with her."

"I told you to get over that," she called out.

Derek sat back on the sofa and rested his ankle on one knee. "I'm listening."

"I've never met anybody like Elle."

Elle?

"I've been head over heels since I first set eyes on her," Jared went on. "I finally got up the nerve to tell her a few weeks back. That's when she dumped me."

"And you decided to drown your sorrows in other women?"

He blanched. "I tried. But it didn't work."

"It didn't look that way to me."

Jared leaned forward in the chair, resting his elbows on his knees. "It was stupid. I know that now. Look, eighteen months ago I was driving a tractor on my folk's farm in Nebraska. Now I have women throwing themselves at me like I'm something special. It's a lot to take all at once."

Derek briefly studied the solemn brown gaze that stared up at him. He well remembered the feeling Jared spoke of, but it didn't change the fact they were talking about his baby sister. "I hope you have it out of your system if you're planning to make any sort of commitment to my sister. And get yourself checked for STD's before you so much as breathe on her again, or I'll kick your ass clear back to Nebraska."

The other man nodded. "I will. And it is—out of my system, I mean. If I learned anything last week in Florida it's that I want to marry Gabrielle."

"I told you to get over *that*, too," she called from the kitchen. "Derek, your cell's ringing, want me to get it?"

"Go ahead," He watched Jared gingerly touch his nose. "Sorry about that. Make up should cover it." He sighed, resigned to the fact that like it or not, this could well be his next brother-in-law. "You realize you'll have to formally ask my father if you can marry her."

Jared nodded.

"Convince me you're sincere, that you'll treat her right, and I'll put in a good word for you. But I have to warn you, my word doesn't carry much weight." He rubbed his jaw. "You're pretty fast with that fist."

"Comes from chasing weaner pigs around the farm."

"I'm not even going to ask what that means." He glanced up as Gabrielle strolled out of the kitchen, cell phone to her ear. The smug look on her face peaked his curiosity.

"No, it's not too late to call. He's right here. I don't know what you did to him, but I've never seen him so on edge." She stuck her tongue out at Derek. "And grumpy. He's like a different person." She laughed and walked closer, taunting him. "I hope to meet you soon, too, Kelly."

Kelly?

Derek vaulted over the back of the sofa and grabbed for the phone, but Gabrielle danced away. "He's really anxious to get this phone away from me. Any idea why?"

He grabbed her about the waist and wrestled the phone from her. "Kelly?"

There was a hesitation. "I'm sorry to bother you."

"It's no bother." His heart started to hammer a hundred miles an hour. Hell, faster than that. *Kelly had called him.*

"I don't know what to do… they're everywhere."

"Who, baby?"

Beside him, his sister pulled an exaggerated frown, then mouthed the word "baby?"

"Paparazzi. Reporters. At the gym this morning and outside my house all day."

"Where are you now?"

"Home." A deep "woof" sounded in the background. "But I'm sitting here with the lights off and the blinds drawn. They're still out there. Derek, I couldn't even get out to get my mail this afternoon. How do I make them go away?"

"They won't until they find a better story somewhere else. Have they said anything to you?"

"They keep asking where you are."

"I was afraid of that." He pulled in a deep breath before voicing his next thought. But two days away from her was enough. "I can be there in a few hours."

"I can't let you do that."

"I'll take you some place where they can't bother you

for a few days."

"Wi—with you?"

His heart sank at her hesitation. He'd decided to no longer force his will, his attention or his attraction on her. He wouldn't push her if she didn't want his company. "Only if that's what you want."

She gave a nervous-sounding laugh. "I've kind of gotten used to having you around."

He couldn't help the smile that stretched across his sore face, despite his sister watching him with way too much interest. He paced to the other side of the room for privacy. "Is that your way of saying you miss me?"

"Maybe."

"Did you get things straightened out with your daughter?" Damn it, why did it seem so good, so right to talk to her like this, as if they were old friends?

"Her boyfriend called yesterday. All is right with the world once again—at least for now."

Then maybe all would be right with them since a certain sixteen-year-old girl was happy. "I'll see you in a few hours." He ended the call and found Gabby grinning at him, eyes dancing with laughter. "What?"

"You are *so* into her."

"Why, because I'm helping her out of a mess I made?"

"I saw the look on your face when you heard her voice. And you didn't call her sweetheart." She shook her head. "Derek, you aren't just hot for her, you're—"

"Shut up, Piglet."

"When are you leaving?"

"Soon."

"Where are you going to take her?"

"Someplace private where we won't be disturbed."

"Not that God-forsaken cabin you built in the Catskills."

"That's an idea. And what's wrong with my cabin?"

"It's ... primitive." She folded her arms and gave him a knowing grin. "But I suppose if I was looking to be alone with my lover, it might be the ideal place. You better hope she's into roughing it."

Across the room, Jared laughed. "Would it matter to you as long as we were together?"

Derek was amazed at the soft way his sister looked at

her boyfriend. And a little nauseated.

"Well, you'd better get some rest if you're leaving in the morning."

"I'm leaving now." Damn right he was. He wasn't dumb enough to give Kelly time to change her mind.

"It's four hundred miles to Rochester, and you've already driven for eighteen hours."

"I had three espressos after dinner; I'll be up for a week straight."

He picked up his keys from the kitchen counter, and his bags from where he'd set them just inside the door. "The place is yours for the next few days, Piglet, but you'd better introduce Jared to the rest of the family before someone else catches you two together." He opened his wallet, pulled out his American Express black card and slapped it on the counter. "And do whatever you can to make the cabin less 'primitive.' Fill it with whatever you think a woman would like, champagne, candles, bubble bath stuff—whatever."

Gabrielle frowned as if deep in thought. "I didn't think there was a tub there."

"I guess you'll have to add it to the list."

"So if you trust me to know what a woman wants, does this mean you're admitting I *am* one?"

He resisted the urge to roll his eyes as he opened the door to leave. "That remains to be seen, Piglet."

Twelve

Kelly gave up on ever sleeping again. It wasn't just her body refusing to let go of the sensations Derek evoked. It was her mind. Fueled by sheer paranoia.

Barney barked until late into the night, so she knew the reporters were still out there. By the time they finally gave up for the night, she was exhausted. Yet when she lay there in bed, all she could do was stare at the ceiling.

So, just as she had yesterday morning, she greeted the sunrise on the deck off her kitchen, stealing a few quiet moments outside before the paparazzi descended for the day.

Derek would be here some time today. The thought alone should have her on edge with nervousness. It didn't. It had her on edge in an entirely different way. For two nights now, what little sleep she'd had was haunted with dreams of making love to him. She'd awakened in near agony, her body writhing with need. She had allowed guilt and fear to chase her away from that feeling the other day, but she wouldn't make that mistake again. This might be her last chance, the one and only hot love affair she would ever have.

Though her heart would probably come to regret it, she intended to make the most of what little time they had left together.

She rose to go inside and warm the too-cold coffee left in her cup when she heard a car pull into the driveway. It was just a little before seven; these reporters were getting bolder. Stepping down from the deck, she padded barefoot across the yard. As she rounded the house, she noted Mrs. Horner across the street sweeping the front walk already—no surprise there.

An unfamiliar grey sports car with tinted windows and a BMW emblem on the grill sat in her driveway. Setting her coffee cup on the front step, she stalked down the blacktop, intent on giving whoever it was a piece of her mind. Hell had no fury like a sexually frustrated woman who'd been denied sleep.

The driver's side door opened just as she reached it. In the same instant she recalled Derek comparing the BMW he'd rented for their dinner date to the one he owned. Before she could even register the sight of him stepping out of the vehicle, he pulled her into his arms, crushed her against him and devoured her lips with his.

Just over thirty-six hours had passed since she had seen him, yet it felt like a lifetime. His familiar taste brought back memories of tropical breezes, champagne and Chinese food.

She forgot about everything but him. Her fingers refused to stay still, roaming lightly over his chest, reveling in the feel of him. The kiss deepened, and her hand moved with a mind of its own to caress the hard wall of muscle under his shirt, sliding over the flat male nipple, skimming across his ribs. A low sound from deep in his throat, half groan, half growl reached her, and his hand at the small of her back tightened, as if he forced it to remain still rather than mold her closer.

Something cold, wet and familiar tickled the back of her knee. Barney. Realization dawned through her fuzzy senses. She was kissing Derek like a drowning woman clinging to a lifeline. In her driveway. In front of Mrs. Horner, who was probably waiting to greet the reporters. Kelly pulled back from the kiss.

He didn't release her but held her so close she had to tilt her head to look up at him. The searing heat in his green eyes focused on her mouth, telling her he would have let the kiss go on endlessly. "I'm glad you're so happy to see me."

Frowning, she placed a fingertip to the swollen corner at the left side of his mouth and followed it down to the faint bruise on his jaw. "What happened to you?"

He moved to one side to close the car door he had left open. "I had a little misunderstanding with Gabrielle's boyfriend."

"And he hit you?"

"Only in self defense." He stopped and stared up at her little house; she wondered what he was thinking. For someone as wealthy and accustomed to the finer things in life as Derek, her little blue house, which she loved to think of as a little cottage in the woods, must look pitiful. The plants that overflowed the boxes at every window were ones she had planted herself. She even painted the white shutters with their little heart-shaped cut outs. And there wasn't a flower in the yard that she hadn't put there and nurtured into bloom. It was home.

He glanced back down at her with a warm smile. "This is exactly what I would have pictured your house like."

Suddenly aware she was still in the nightshirt she'd thrown on after her shower, with no make up and air-dried hair, she pulled away, smoothing her hair in embarrassment. "I'm a mess. I wasn't expecting you so soon."

Derek had a hard time forcing his gaze from her. Actually she was very cute in a rumpled sort of way, in her knee length oversized pink T-shirt and bare feet. "It was a shorter drive than I thought." Well, that wasn't quite true, but she didn't need to know he'd wanted to see her so much he'd left New York at two a.m. At Gabrielle's insistence, he'd showered and changed out of his blood-stained shirt, but that had been it. He'd gotten in the car and driven straight through.

The golden retriever, who had been patiently sitting nearby, put its paw up on his knee in a playful gesture, and he bent to ruffle its fur.

She tugged at the dog's collar, and it sat obediently. "I guess I should thank you for coming."

He grinned. "These reporters are good, they're so well hidden I can't even see them."

A delicate flush moved over her cheeks. "Well, if Barney could talk he'd tell you they were out here until well after midnight. It was kind of creepy."

Derek knelt in front of the dog. "I take it you're Barney." His answer was a good slobbery tongue in the face.

"I wasn't sure if I should even call you."

He straightened. "I had a feeling they'd start hounding you once we went our separate ways. It'll get worse before it gets better."

"Why don't we go inside before they show up for the

day. Can I get you some coffee?"

As she called to the dog, she bent to retrieve a coffee cup. The sight of her pink polished toes, the comfortable way she moved, stopped him. He wasn't used to seeing her so at ease with herself, so relaxed in his presence. He glanced up at the house again. He lied when he said this was exactly how he'd pictured her house. This wasn't even what he'd expected. Instead of a new subdivision with small trees and matching houses, hers was a street so heavily lined with trees it almost put him in mind of being in the forest. And her house didn't look like a replica of the others. It looked like...Kelly's house.

As he watched her, she poured the contents of the coffee cup at the base of a rose bush, then paused to admire the blush-colored blooms. He'd only been away from her for a day or two, and yet he couldn't bring himself to stop looking at her.

Halfway up the steps to the front door, she stopped and glanced over her shoulder. "Coffee?"

He forced his feet forward and followed her into the house. If he kept staring at her, she'd think he'd lost his mind. And maybe he had for a minute or two. But for some reason it felt too damned good to be with her. He shook his head to keep himself from digging any deeper into that.

The entry way, at least from what he could see, seemed like it could be none other than Kelly's house, with its dried flower arrangements and dozens of artfully arranged pictures on the walls. Most were of her children, though there was one of a much younger Kelly, flanked by two pudgy toddlers and a pale, blond man.

"My ex, obviously," she said as she moved past him. "I tried not to take down all the pictures of their dad, so they feel like he's still part of the family."

In the kitchen, she moved to open a cupboard door and leaned up on tiptoe for a coffee mug. He considered reaching them for her, but instead stood back to admire the expanse of thigh revealed when her T-shirt rode up. As she eased back down, the soft material settled against the curve of her backside and if he had any lingering doubts about whether she wore anything beneath that shirt, they were erased.

"How do you like it?"

"Exactly the way it is."

She set the cup down and turned to face him. "You mean black?"

"No, I mean you."

"I'm not even dressed yet." She ran a hand self-consciously through her hair.

He moved in front of her and settled his hands on her shoulders. The lingering scent of lavender from her hair teased him, but another scent, familiar and unique to Kelly, lured him. Despite his resolve to move at her pace, give her some distance, he needed to touch her.

"Derek." Her voice had taken on a husky quality. "The coffee."

"What coffee?" For a long moment he did nothing but watch the rise and fall of her chest, the way her lips had gone soft and parted. A strand of hair fell over her cheek, and he tucked it back behind her ear, his knuckles lingering to caress her skin. "So are you still ... over me?"

"No." Her lips formed the word, but no sound came out. Her gaze remained fixed on his mouth. She took a step back.

He followed.

"Wait." Her hand came up to rest against his chest. "Derek, I want you. But we need to get some things straight first. At least I do."

The clouds parted. Heaven's gates opened. A chorus of angels sang Hallelujah. Had Kelly just admitted to wanting him? Had she really liberated him from his self-imposed restraint? He took her hand and brought it to his lips. "We can talk all you want. But first do me a favor."

"What?"

"Say you want me again."

She let out a whoosh of air upon hearing his request, as if she had feared he would ask something obscene. "Didn't you hear enough of that from the women at the conference?"

"I didn't hear it from you." Still holding her hand, he tucked it at his waist and moved in closer, pressing tighter to her. "In fact, all I heard were denials."

"I never said I didn't feel it. Just that I couldn't act on it."

"What changed?"

"I realized I may never feel this way again—the way I feel when I'm with you." Her cheeks went pink. "L—like I said, we need to set some things straight first."

"We will. But I asked you for something, and I'm still waiting." Without giving her time to answer he bent to nibble her lower lip, then gently sucked it. She let out a small moan and parted her lips beneath his. He pulled her against him, his hand sliding over her behind, molding the material to the shape, the crevice. Her hips moved against him, finding his erection and cradling it between them.

Backing her toward the counter, he braced her against it. Deliberately, since she still hadn't uttered the words he wanted to hear, he slid a hand over her breast. A rush of heat shot through him at the feel of her swollen nipple against his thumb, and he stroked it until she moaned and rested her forehead against his shoulder.

"Say it," he whispered.

She murmured something incoherent against his shirtfront. He shifted, then lifted her against his throbbing erection until she cried out and threw her head back. "I didn't hear you."

"I ... want... you." The words were slow and held a note of desperation.

It was more than just his ego that needed the gratification of hearing her say it. He had almost believed she didn't. "What was it you wanted to talk about?"

A cry of almost frustration escaped her. "One night. We can only have one night."

"Why?" He removed his hand from her breast, then lowered his head to take the peak into his mouth through the thin cotton T-shirt.

"I ...have my reasons."

Her nipple between his lips, he could only moan his disapproval. Her hands laced into his hair, and he raised his head. "It won't work."

His fingers grazed the hem of her T-shirt. He eased his hand beneath, palm gliding over her smooth thigh, up and over her hip, the shirt rising with his movement. She moaned aloud as he continued his slow journey. At her rib cage he paused and met her gaze. "It'll take more than one night to do what I intend to do to you."

He echoed her moan of pleasure as he eased his hand the rest of the way up and soft flesh filled his hand, taut nipple brushing his palm. Their mouths fused together once again as he stroked and caressed her. He drew lazy circles around her nipple with the pad of his thumb until she shuddered and pressed tighter against him, if such a thing was possible.

Her fingers twined in the hair at his nape as she arched toward him. "Don't stop," she pleaded against his lips. "Please don't stop."

He hadn't intended for it to happen this way. He hadn't even come here with this in mind. Well, not for this morning anyway. Yet he couldn't take his hands from her, couldn't bring himself to turn back now.

Deliberately, he let his hand trail over her ribs, fingers grazing the underside of her breast before sliding down to the curve of her waist and over one hip. Still no complaint. He was dangerously close to the point of no return. He'd never had a woman ask him to stop before, but he fully expected this one to. For that matter, he'd like to know where that damned cell phone of hers was.

Her lips moved over his chest, fingers skimming his stomach. Her knuckles brushed his abdomen as she reached for his belt. Between them his arousal ached almost painfully. If she touched him now, he'd either take her right here in the kitchen or embarrass himself by going off like a horny teenager.

To put some distance between her hand and his throbbing need, he shifted a hand behind her and cupped the delicate flesh of her buttocks, hoisting her to him. He lifted her against the counter and pressed even more intimately against her.

A startled cry was torn from her throat. Her eyes opened, lids heavy with passion, then closed like a china doll as he slid the T-shirt up to her shoulders. Unable to wait, he bent his head to her breasts. She moaned, her fingers moving from his nape up over his scalp. As his tongue slipped over a sweet nipple and her sighs echoed in his brain, he eased her down from where he had hoisted her. He needed her. In that moment, he wanted her more than he wanted his next breath.

His supporting hand now free, he trailed it slowly over her hip, across her soft abdomen and down. He shuddered when his fingers grazed the soft curls and felt the moisture just inside the folds. Too long. He'd wanted her for far too long.

He parted her with one finger and slipped it inside. The slick, velvety warmth was nearly his undoing. She was so ready he wanted to bury himself inside her. Hard. Fast. Now. But he steeled himself against the urge. This was one woman he needed to take his time with. And taking the edge off her need now would prolong both their pleasure later. He wanted to give her that, along with the release he could offer her now. He began to tease that ultra sensitive little bud ever so gently with his thumb. She arched against him and gasped.

His mouth returned to hers, while he stroked her. Her moans sent something powerful, almost protective, surging through him. His own need seemed secondary as she responded to his touch.

She pulled her mouth from his. "Derek, please..." she rasped. "I can't...I've never..." He slid another finger inside, thumb stroking.

"Oh God." She tensed. Her fingers dug into his shoulders. He continued his sweet torment, rewarded when she began to move in perfect rhythm with his touch. A cry tore from her throat. Her body quivered around him. Soft sounds, somewhere between a whimper and a sigh followed.

Moments later, her body relaxed, and she sagged against him.

She rested her forehead on his chest. He cradled her head with one hand, his heart pounding. The sweet smell of her hair teased his nostrils, and he nuzzled the golden strands.

He became slowly aware of a damp sensation on her cheeks, against his chest. "Kel?" He leaned back, but she refused to look at him. He heard a hiccup and lifted her chin.

"What's this?" he whispered, a chill slicing up his spine. God, had he hurt her somehow?

Tears ran down her cheeks. She merely shook her head and again sought refuge in his chest. He held her while she sobbed, uncertain whether he had caused the weeping, or if it was good or bad.

At last, she quieted. "Why did you do that?" she asked, her voice muffled against his chest.

"Seemed like a good idea at the time."

She finally looked up at him, her eyes red-rimmed and watery, her nose pink. "You must think I'm insane with all this crying."

He pressed his lips against her forehead. His enthusiasm had cooled when she started to cry. Seeking his own release seemed unimportant right now. He couldn't recall another time when that had been the case. "Just tell me I didn't hurt you."

A bubble of laughter burst forth. "I promise, you didn't." She looked up at him, two bright red splotches on her cheeks. "I always thought there was something wrong with me. I was never able to..."

Realization hit Derek like a sledgehammer. Was she saying she had never had an orgasm? "Maybe you were with the wrong man."

She laced her arms about his neck. "I think I was." She smiled up at him, and his heart constricted at the sparkle in her blue eyes.

He scooped her into his arms and carried her toward the stairs. "Which way to the bedroom?"

****

Kelly couldn't believe they were finally doing this. It didn't seem real, and yet it was easier than she would have imagined to just let go and give in to emotion, to passion. And to Derek.

At the top of the stairs, he paused.

"Left," she said.

He shouldered the bedroom door open and stepped inside, setting her on her feet just inside the room. He lifted her chin on his finger. "Are you sure this is what you want?"

She nodded and wrapped her arms about his neck. He kissed her, his hands roaming, straying to her breasts, over her hips and buttocks. The sound of Barney's deep, insistent bark came from downstairs.

He pulled back enough to look into her eyes. "Are you expecting someone?"

"Just the reporters. And you." Not wanting to let go of him, even for a moment, she took his hand and led him to a window across the room. She pulled the lacy curtain aside and peered through the closed slats of the blind. He wrapped his arms about her from behind and rested his chin on her shoulder.

"The blue car," she said. "They've been here every day."

"I recognize the type."

She pulled back as one of the men trained a pair of binoculars on the house. "Now that they see that fancy car of yours in my driveway, they'll really settle in and stick around."

"You never know." He trailed one hand up and down her arm. "The hot story was that we were apart. If we stay together and lay low, there's no real story."

She turned around to face him and settled into his arms. "And how do you suggest we *lay low*?"

He grinned. "I think I can come up with something."

She moved closer to the bed and sank onto the mattress, pulling him with her. "Tell me about this *something*."

He knelt on the mattress beside her, then abruptly straightened. "Well, for starters..." He picked up the phone from her bedside table.

Puzzled, she watched as he switched the ringer to the off position. Then he reached for the cell phone that lay beside it and turned that off, too. "What are you doing?"

"I'm not trying to come between you and your kids, Kel, but right now you're mine. I don't want any interruptions." He placed his hands at either side of her head on the mattress. "Anything else? Pagers? Walkie talkies? Web cams?"

Eyes still on the cell phone, she shook her head.

"Good. Because Mommy is unavailable for the next few hours."

Heat threaded through her stomach, drawing her attention from the phone back to him, to the promise simmering in his olive-green eyes. "The next few ... *hours*?"

A slow grin spread across his face. "You didn't think we were only going to do this once, did you?"

"But I thought we agreed—"

"*I* didn't agree to anything."

She rose on an elbow and placed a hand to his chest. "Derek, wait a minute—"

"We've done enough waiting." He kissed her. Gently at first, but the kiss deepened as the passion between them flared. She laced her fingers into his hair as he explored her mouth thoroughly. His hands caressed her breasts, her waist, her hips, following the length of her thigh and the curve of her bent knee.

He caught the hem of her T-shirt and eased it up. She sat up to allow him to remove it, and as he pulled it over her head, her face met his chest. Moaning at the soapy clean smell of his warm skin, she pressed her lips to his chest, flicked her tongue over his nipples. His groan emboldened her, and she smoothed her hands down his taut abdomen. And lower. The sizable bulge in his pants that had so intrigued her the other morning was back, and she wasn't about to shy away from it this time. He let out a small hiss of breath as she traced the length of it, then fit her hand around him. Wanting to touch him, see him, feel him fill her palm, she unfastened his belt and the button at his waistband.

She gave a little squeal when he threw her back down on the mattress. "You're going to make things happen way too fast."

Fast? Ten minutes would be a record for her ex. But she wouldn't allow thoughts of Alan to intrude on this.

Hovering over her, he held her arms above her head with one hand. "If you're entertaining any fantasies about making love to one of your heroes, or The Model Man, now is the time to get rid of them. It's just me and you."

Working her arms free, she wound them around his neck. "I want you, not some fantasy who doesn't exist."

With a primal groan he bent his head to her breasts. His warm, wet tongue slid over her skin, followed by a caress of breath. She arched in pure pleasure as he took her nipple between his lips. He tugged at it slowly, deliberately. She tangled one hand in the silken strands of his hair, smoothed the other over the back of his neck and down between his shoulders, pressing him closer, urging him to take more.

She couldn't have written it better than this, couldn't have imagined the way her body came alive at his touch, the sensations he stirred.

His mouth left her breasts to trail over her stomach, his hair falling forward to brush her skin. The sensation of his hair tickling her was almost too much to bear.

A brief moment of uncertainty came over her as he neared her cesarean scar. He had made love to lingerie models and movie stars, probably none of whom had ever given birth or gained forty pounds during a pregnancy. She couldn't hope to compare favorably. She opened her eyes and stared up at the ceiling, holding her breath.

His face hovered over hers. "Kelly," he whispered, "you're beautiful. Don't be shy with me." His gaze still on hers, he trailed his fingers back down over her breasts and stomach. Her legs automatically parted for him, and she was half embarrassed he would find her so eager for him again. Her hips rose off the mattress as he stroked her. He bent his head, spreading kisses over her belly. And down. She held her breath when he nuzzled the soft curls between her legs. Felt the kiss he placed to the inside of her thigh. No one had ever kissed her so intimately.

She tried to put her legs together, but he braced them open with a forearm. She gave a cry of surrender when his breath fanned against her. His tongue probed, entering her, flicking over her most sensitive places until her mind became a kaleidoscope of pleasure. She hid her face behind her hands and surrendered to sensation.

White-hot need coursed through her, centering on her lower body. Her hips rose from the bed of their own accord, and he slid a hand beneath to cup her bottom. When release would have come, he backed off, kissing her thighs, her knees, her abdomen, hands stroking in a way that soothed rather than aroused.

When her breathing slowed, he kissed his way along her inner thighs once more, and the sweet torture began all over again. But she'd had enough. Her body demanded release. Grabbing a fistful of his hair, she gave a gentle tug.

With a soft chuckle, he came to her, propped up on his elbows, his body half covering hers. He bent to nip her chin. "Did you want something?"

Cradled between her legs as he was, she could feel his erection pressed against her. She'd never wanted anything so much in her life.

"You," she breathed, then, knowing he'd probably make her say it anyway, she added, "Inside me. Now."

His eyes darkened. He sat up to finish unzipping his slacks, but she didn't want to be denied that right. In fact, there were many things she wasn't ready to be denied, and the sight of him completely naked was one of them.

Rising to her knees, she slipped her arms around him from behind. Now it was her turn to make him suffer, if only for a few minutes. She rained kisses along the back of his neck and across his broad shoulders, rubbing her breasts against him as she went. She paused to taste the salty tang of his skin, to inhale the uniquely male scent of him, to savor every fantasy she had ever had about him.

She ran her hands over his shoulders and purposefully down his stomach. His breathing changed, and she knew she had his complete attention. Finding the zipper half undone, she eased it down the rest of the way and the entire length of him sprang free. Her fingers stroked him tentatively, but she couldn't grip him from this angle, couldn't reach to touch him the way she wanted to.

He caught her hands, brought one to his lips to kiss it, then rose and eased out of his pants. Lying beside her on the mattress, he rolled to kiss her again. This time her hands found what they had sought before. Smooth, silken heat met her palm. She stroked him, closed her hand around him, watched his face change from playful to pure hunger. Now she was the one in control, and she flashed a triumphant smile. She couldn't recall the last time she had this much fun; she almost didn't want it to end.

He twined a hand in her hair. "Kelly, you're driving me crazy."

Her hand around him went still. "Is that a good thing?"

At the sight of her wide, innocent eyes, Derek laughed. "It's more than good. But if you keep touching me like that, we're going to be in trouble."

He didn't want to stop touching her, but at the same

time, some primitive need wouldn't be satisfied until he was inside her, until they had completed the act. Or maybe he just wouldn't believe it until it actually happened.

As much as he wanted to feel her beneath him, feel her legs wrapped around him, there was something more he wanted to give her. Control.

He leaned back against the head board and reached for her.

"Aren't we forgetting something?" she asked.

"There's one in my wallet."

She gave him a triumphant little smile and leaned forward to kiss him. Her hand trailed over his cock, proudly erect and ready to serve. "I have some, hold on."

"You what?" His laughter sobered as she reached over and opened her night stand drawer and produced a familiar little foil packet.

He cupped a hand behind her neck to pull her in for a kiss. "You have no idea how much it turns me on to think of you going out to buy these."

"Actually—"

"Don't ruin it for me," he said with a laugh. "I don't want to know if you didn't." He tore the package open with his teeth. He rolled it on and pulled her half on top of him, kissing her, tongues twining and dancing mindlessly. He lifted her, placing her astride him. His erection pressed against one soft buttock cheek

"Um... Derek, I think I'd be more comfortable if we did this the traditional way."

"Trust me, Kelly." He pressed a finger tip to her lips. "I want to do this at your pace, not mine." With her legs over him, every naked inch of her from her roses and cream breasts to her soft stomach and the blonde triangle of curls below was on display for his enjoyment. He leaned forward to flick his tongue over one pink nipple. "If we did things at my pace, we'd have done this the night we met."

Her laugh turned to a moan when he drew the peak of her breast into his mouth, molded his hands down the length of her spine and over her hips, urging her to take the initiative.

At last she rose to take him. Erotic as the sight of her easing down onto his shaft was, he threw back his head and closed his eyes. Slick, tight heat sheathed him with agonizing slowness. Tight. She was so damn tight... He fought the need to take over, to grasp her hips and thrust deep.

"I've never made love this way before."

He raised his head to look at her, saw the heat and need reflected in her eyes. "Remind me to beat the hell out of your ex-husband if I ever meet him."

"No, it's me. I'm too self-conscious. I told you, I'm not as sophisticated as the women you're used to."

"Kel, I wouldn't want you to be."

She laughed, but the sound quickly changed to a little "ooh" of delight when he placed his hands on her hips and guided her. Her body began to move with his. Uneasily at first but then she found a rhythm and allowed it to overtake her. He steeled himself against the need to let go, held back as much as he could.

Her cries and moans grew louder, more frantic. Just when he thought he couldn't last another second, she cried out his name with a note of desperation. Her muscles clenched around him, the spasms wringing a like response from his body. Release, sudden and violent rocked him.

She shuddered one last time then sagged against his chest, and he knew the satisfaction of having given her not only her first orgasm, but several.

Even if the effort had nearly killed him.

Thirteen

Kelly sagged against Derek's chest, conscious of her own rapid breathing. For long moments she simply lay there, comforted by the pounding of his heart beneath her ear. She felt the rapid rise and fall of his chest and stomach, scarcely able to believe what they had just shared. His hands slid down her spine in a soothing caress, and he pressed his lips to her temple, her hair.

Utter contentment washed over her. She couldn't recall ever feeling so relaxed or complete. And at the same time so alive.

Lifting her head, she glanced up at him. "Is this what would have happened if I'd let you into my hotel room that first night?"

A rumble of laughter came from deep in his chest. "Probably not."

She skimmed a fingernail over the solid pectoral muscles that so fascinated her. She suspected the same thing; what happened just now was from pent-up wanting. And waiting.

A finger brushed her cheek, then slid over to twine in her hair. "Are you okay?"

"Mmmm." She sighed. "More than okay." She traced a circle over one rock-hard bicep, marveling that at least for now, this masculine beauty was all hers to touch and enjoy. Resting her head back on his chest, she lay content in the silence, though a million questions played tag through her head. Had she disappointed him? It hadn't seemed that way. Had he compared her with other women he had been with?

The connection she felt was probably one-sided. He had bedded dozens of women; this was nothing new to him. But she'd never felt this way before, so much a part of someone else, at least not since her children were tiny little babies. She should have asked Sharon what came after the lovemaking, what was acceptable and what wasn't. Closing her eyes, she tried to remember how it had been with Alan in the early days. Had they cuddled after sex? No, she couldn't remember ever doing that. He usually just went to sleep while she lay there, frustrated and restless.

She opened her eyes, surprised to find him watching her. This was probably not the time to pull the "what are you thinking about?" stuff guys hated so much, but she'd love to know.

He smiled and brushed the hair back from her face. "Are you comfortable like this?"

As a matter of fact, she was. Straddling him, resting on him. It was heaven. "Mmm hmm." Maybe *he* was uncomfortable. "Are you?"

"I meant with me still inside you."

A flush of embarrassed heat stung her cheeks. No wonder she was so darned content and fulfilled. She eased off of him. "I'm sorry, should I—"

"No, you're fine." He maneuvered her back against the pillow beside him and tugged the rumpled bedspread over her, almost tucking her in, then bent to kiss the curve of her neck. "I'll be right back."

She snuggled deeper into the pillows as he slipped out of bed but resisted the pull of sleep. She wanted to turn and look, see every glorious naked inch of him. Not that there was much she hadn't seen already. Giving into temptation, she peeked just in time to see him disappear into the bathroom. *Perfect.*

Sated and drowsy, she scooted to the opposite side of the bed. She had just begun to doze off when the mattress gave beneath his weight. He hooked an arm about her waist, dragging her across the bed to him. "Where did you go?"

"I… can't sleep with someone so close," she admitted. "I'm not used to it." Not to mention it had taken her two years to adjust to sleeping alone. She didn't need him to undo in a few hours what had taken years to get used to.

"I'm not used to it, either," he admitted, tucking her against his chest and wrapping his arms securely around her. "But for you I'm willing to make an exception."

She shifted restlessly, trying to find a comfortable position. But with the heat of his body curled around her, his breath tickling the top of her head, it was no use. Over the sheet, his hand slid up to cup her breast. "I must not have done my job very well; you should be asleep by now."

"Just having trouble drifting off."

"Can I help?"

She rolled onto her back and gazed playfully up at him. "What did you have in mind? Sleeping pills?"

He pressed a kiss to her chin, then worked his way down her neck. "Something better."

He had barely touched her, hardly even kissed her and already with a will of their own, her legs were wrapping around him, her body arching to urge him inside.

"Wait," he said, his voice sounding strained. He rolled away from her to reach for his pants and fumbled in the pockets for a condom.

"You certainly came well prepared." She sat up to wrap her arms about him and watch over his shoulder as he deftly slid on the condom. Funny it didn't embarrass her so much this time, it was merely a means to an end. "One would almost think you had this in mind."

"Oh, it was on my mind all right," he said, turning to sweep her beneath him once more. "Practically since the minute I met you."

She wrapped her arms about his neck, her legs opening for him. "I do remember having that impression."

He gave a low grunt, which turned to a groan as he eased inside of her. "And you sure made me work for it."

"Mmm." Losing her train of thought to sensation, she smoothed her hands down his bare back to grab hold of his buttocks. Her gaze locked with his as he moved, setting a pace that almost matched the beat of her heart. The tension began to build once more until her train of though stalled and gave way to sensation. She cried out as she climaxed, just as intensely as she had before, heard his cry of release.

When he lowered himself on top of her, she closed her eyes to savor the smell of him, the feel of his weight on top of her, reluctant to let go.

Long after he had fallen asleep half on top, half beside her, she lay cocooned in his warmth, surrounded by the musky smell of lovemaking, his arms and one leg wrapped around her.

She *had* made him work for it.

And he had been worth the wait.

****

The growling of his stomach woke him. Derek didn't have to wonder where he was, the lacy curtains liberally sprinkled with roses belonged to no one but Kelly. Her scent surrounded him, on the sheets, on his skin. She had moved to the far edge of the bed again, but he resisted the urge to retrieve her. They had so thoroughly loved one another, worn each other out so completely, he wanted her to rest.

Even if he wanted to move her, they had been joined by Fido. *Barney.* Whatever his name was. When he sat up, the dog raised its head to look at him, half-curious, half-wary. Derek had the feeling he was sleeping on the dog's side of the bed. He wondered how long they had slept, but there was no clock in sight.

Waning sunlight filtered through the curtains, tinged with the pinkish glow of early evening. He turned on his side to watch her as she slept. He fingered a strand of blonde hair, savoring the texture of it, admiring the way the light played through it. She lay on her stomach, hair veiling her face, the sheet down about her waist. The smooth, creamy expanse of skin called to him. On impulse, he bent to kiss the small birthmark just below her right shoulder. She murmured something in her sleep. Not wanting to wake her, he tugged the sheet up around her and rose carefully from the bed.

He found his pants and slipped into them, then headed down the stairs. In the kitchen, he found his shirt still crumpled on the floor and the long-cold cup of coffee sitting on the counter. He glanced down, surprised to feel carpeting beneath his bare feet. He'd never met anyone with carpeting in their kitchen before, but somehow it suited Kelly. Her love for gardening was evidenced by the variety of plants, hanging, climbing, creeping, and otherwise, that filled the windows around the breakfast nook. Next to the small table, a set of french doors opened onto a multi-level deck.

From what he could see the backyard enjoyed the same meticulous care as the front, topiaries and flower

197

beds bordering a brick pathway that led to a garden. All of it, the loving attention to detail, the colorful burst of flowers and greenery, was pure Kelly. In a way he couldn't describe, it was her signature.

More than anything he wanted to slip outside and have a cigarette. But he didn't dare take that chance with the paparazzi still lurking, didn't need to tarnish Kelly's reputation anymore than he already had. In fact, just standing half naked by the doors was probably a bad idea.

Moving away from the window, Derek paced restlessly across the kitchen and pulled out his cell phone to check his messages. For the first time in—hell, forever—there were none. Which was probably a good thing, it meant Gabrielle had people working on the cabin and no one else wanted him. Of course, he still hadn't mentioned retreating to the Catskills to Kelly. He wasn't even sure how they were going to get out of here, unless the reporters planned to take a dinner break soon.

He stepped into the dining room, just off the kitchen. The blinds were pulled, proof that the paparazzi had been stalking Kelly as she'd said. He headed toward the largest front-facing window and peered through one slat. And stopped short. There were no longer just a few photographers; half the damned city lurked outside her house. The local news, a cable entertainment channel, tabloid reporters.

And women. Hundreds of them.

A memory of the last time he'd worked in the family pizza shop sprang to mind. Once word had gotten out he was there, hordes of screaming fans stormed the place. He'd tried to reason with them but had gotten pulled into the crowd, crazed women grabbing at his hair, his clothes, his skin. A knot curled around his stomach and tightened. How the hell was he going to get Kelly out of this in one piece?

The dog bounded into the room, and Derek turned to find her leaning in the doorway. She'd freshened up, her hair pulled back in a pony tail, her lips still swollen from their lovemaking. One shapely thigh was visible where her bathrobe parted, and he found himself wondering what, if anything, she had on beneath it.

"Are they still out there?"

He let the blind fall back into place. This was probably not the best time to tell her the flower beds she so lovingly tended had been trampled by thoughtless fans. "Still there."

For a moment something hesitant crossed her face, as if she wasn't quite sure what to do. Neither was he. This was usually the part where he made his excuses *Sorry, sweetheart, can't stay for breakfast. Gotta hit the gym.* Or, his favorite, *I'm leaving tomorrow for an out of town shoot. I'll call you when I get back.* But he felt none of that now. Just … relaxed. As glad to see her standing there in that blue robe as he had been when he'd seen her in it the first time. And nowhere near ready to accept her one-night-only ultimatum.

She stepped into the room. "Is this the awkward part?"

"Do you feel awkward?" He closed the distance between them and took her into his arms.

She rested her forehead against his chest. "No."

Taking her face between his hands, he bent to kiss her. Gently. Tenderly. Careful not to stir up any more passion until they had both had a chance to rest. And eat. And figure out what the hell to do about the crowd outside on her lawn.

"Do you?" she asked. "Feel awkward, I mean."

"No." A moment's panic hit him at the truth of his statement, but the strange new calm she'd brought to him over the last few days stifled any need he might have felt to run. Even now after having had her a few times, he wasn't tired of looking at that face, was still intrigued by the way her robe gaped in the front, offering a tantalizing view of her breasts. Breasts he was very well acquainted with. His stomach roared loudly, reminding him he needed food first.

She laughed. "I'm starving, too. But with those photographers outside, it would be impossible to order anything in."

He'd let her eat before telling her those few photographers had turned into a full-blown circus. He followed her into the kitchen, the dog leading the way, and leaned against the counter. "I guess you'll just have to cook for me."

She gave a short laugh. "Trust me, you don't want that to happen." She moved to a cupboard and tugged it open. "I can't cook."

"Can't or don't?"

"I ruin microwave popcorn." She bent at the waist to poke around inside the cupboard, offering him a view of her backside that nearly made him forget his complaining stomach.

She emerged, holding up a blue cardboard box. "How do you feel about mac and cheese? I might be able to scrounge up some hot dogs to go with it."

"Do you have any idea how much fat and sodium you're talking about?"

"Models." She heaved a dramatic sigh. "Does it even matter what you eat? Aren't you going to throw it up anyway?"

He laughed. "I'm choosy about what I put in my body."

"Nicotine, alcohol and caffeine not withstanding, I suppose." She tugged open the fridge.

"We all have our vices," he teased, following her. Unable to keep from touching her, he slipped his arms about her waist and bent with her to peer into the refrigerator.

She moaned, as if she found the contact as pleasant as he did. He gave her ear a playful nip. "That's one very empty fridge, Kel."

"I only buy the bare necessities when the kids are gone."

"If I wasn't starving, I'd show you how much I like your *bare necessities*."

Laughing, she moved to the freezer door. "Just a few frozen dinners, more sodium, I'm sure."

"Mmm hmm," he agreed.

She reached for a lone package of frozen stir fry vegetables. "I'm not sure how old these are."

He chuckled at the way she eyed the bag, as if she'd never seen vegetables before. "How do you manage to feed your kids?"

"They're both wonderful cooks. Maya takes right after my mother, she's phenomenal, she made Christmas dinner last year by herself, crown roast with all the trimmings. And Cody can make a meal out of just about anything." An almost guilty look crossed her face. "More often than not, they cook for me."

"You're kidding."

"No, writers are terribly selfish people, Derek. When I'm on a roll, I completely lose track of time. Necessity being what it is, my kids have been able to cook since they were young. Otherwise, I'd forget all about dinner until eight or nine o'clock at night. Or until Alan came home and started nagging me."

He took the bag from her and tossed it on the counter. Then he reached in the fridge and pulled out the eggs. He was just about to close the door when he noticed a bottle of wine and set that on the counter as well.

"What are you doing?" she asked.

"I'm going to cook for you."

"*You* cook?"

"I do. I happen to be pretty damn good at it."

She searched through a drawer until she came up with a corkscrew. "There's just no end to your talents, is there?"

He gave a slight grunt. "Do you want to find out or are you sticking to your 'one night only' ultimatum?"

With suddenly trembling hands, Kelly set a frying pan and olive oil on the counter before Derek. She watched as he poured two half glasses of wine, fascinated by the sight of his tanned, lean fingers on the frail stem of the wine glass. Her stomach knotted and a familiar ache began in her lower abdomen. It wasn't possible he could still arouse her without even touching her, not after everything they had done to each other this afternoon.

One night only? Had she really believed it would work? One night didn't seem nearly enough now. Which was exactly why she should send him packing.

She busied herself feeding Barney and setting out place mats and utensils while Derek began to sauté the vegetables.

Every so often, Barney would look up toward the window and growl so she knew without looking the photographers were still lurking about.

"You aren't going to answer me, are you?" He asked.

"I'm still weighing the pros and cons."

"I must not have been very convincing upstairs."

She sank into one of the chairs at the table and took a long sip of wine, watching while he separated the egg yolks from the whites, whisking the mixture with the ease of one quite comfortable in the kitchen. "I didn't mean it like that." And she didn't. But what did they have to gain—hell, what did *she* stand to gain—by continuing this fling? As it was she'd never be normal again, not after today.

A few minutes later, he set two perfect vegetable omelets on the table, then took a seat opposite her.

Nerves still fluttered in her stomach, but the food on her plate smelled so inviting hunger pangs gnawed at her.

"Eat."

"I ... I will. It's just... Derek—"

"If you want to get away from the photographers and reporters, I'll take you away from them." He didn't look at her and from the tight set of his jaw she knew her indecision bothered him. "You're a prisoner in your own house if you stay here."

"You're sure they won't just give up and move on?"

"It doesn't look that way."

He was right about that. More than anything she wanted to be with him, but she wasn't sure she should take the risk of involving her emotions.

"Your food is getting cold, Kel."

Obediently she scooped up a forkful of the omelet, surprised to discover just how hungry she was. For several moments silence hung heavy and awkward between them as they ate. Finally she dabbed at her lips with a napkin and took a deep breath. "I'm not sure spending the next few days alone together is wise."

He reached across the table and placed his hand on hers. "Every time I get a little too close, you retreat. You're doing it now."

"I have to think about my work. You're a distraction. I'll never meet my deadline if we're..."

He removed his hand and picked up his wineglass, green eyes regarding her with amusement. "There won't be much to distract you. Just sex and the great outdoors."

"As long as you understand I'll need to spend a great deal of time working." She was already addicted to the pleasure she had found in bed with him, was already wondering how she would ever live without it. She'd be a fool to turn down the chance to spend more time with him. And twice the fool to actually do it

Fourteen

After emerging from the bathtub, Kelly leaned heavily against the sink to reach for her robe. She still marveled at the things they had done to each other. Her rubbery knees barely supported her weight after their watery workout. She had just belted the robe when Derek, still naked and dripping wet, came up behind her, and tugged at her ear lobe with his teeth.

She turned toward him with a giggle. "Is any of this even physically possible?"

"You were married to what's-his-name for too long."

She laughed. "Maybe I was. Anyway, it's nearly midnight; shall we go see if our paparazzi friends have given up for the night?"

"Actually, I'm kind of enjoying being trapped in here with you."

She slid her hands over his firm, naked buttocks with a satisfied moan. "If you don't get some clothes on soon, I'm going to show you how much I like it, too." She shoved a towel in his direction.

"That hardly counts as clothes," he said as he wrapped it about his waist and knotted it over one hip.

She leaned in for a quick kiss. "Mmm, but I like it."

"Come to the Catskills with me and we can be naked all day long." Mischief danced in the gaze that met hers. "Or do I still need to convince you?"

"First I think we should find that bottle of wine we left downstairs." She slid a hand over one wet, bulging bicep. "Then you can work on *convincing* me."

With a playful growl, he scooped her off her feet and headed for the stairs.

"I *do* know how to walk."

"I can't help it if I enjoy having you in my arms." As they reached the last step, the dog came to greet them.

"Hey Barn,'" he greeted, then looked at Kelly with a puzzled frown. "I thought you put him in the backyard before we went upstairs?"

"I did. I can't imagine how he got in."

"*Kelly?*"

"*Mom?*"

From the kitchen, three voices spoke in unison. Still in Derek's arms, Kelly winced as an overhead light was switched on.

There stood Maya, open-mouthed; and Cody, half-kneeling on the floor, as though he had just been playing with the dog.

And Alan.

****

Kelly could only stare as her brain skittered between delight at seeing her children—and utter mortification at the circumstances. Derek set her on her feet rather unceremoniously. She started to step forward, then remembered he was only in a towel and stayed firmly planted in front of him. Was it possible Cody had grown another six inches over the past few weeks? Or that Maya's legs were suddenly a mile long?

"What the hell is going on here?" Alan demanded. "There must be fifty people outside."

She adjusted her robe and moved her gaze from her children to her ex-husband. "It's my house—*I'll* ask the questions."

"Why is *he* here?"

Kelly winced at Maya's question. Her daughter's expression bordered somewhere between disbelief and disgust. "He's with me." She hoped her tone was as light and unaffected as she tried to keep it. But doubted it.

"I can *see* that."

Derek stepped forward, hand extended. "I'm Derek."

Alan shoved Maya behind him. "Tell him to put some clothes and get the hell away from my daughter."

Kelly wanted to scream that it was high time he started acting like a father, but knew he was grandstanding. Besides, she really did need to find a way for both of them to get some clothes on. If she could only remember where they'd last left them...

Cody moved toward Derek. "Yo dawg," he said by way of greeting, extending his hand for a quick shake. "Hey, is that your Beemer in the driveway?"

"Sure is. What do you think?"

"*Sweet*," Cody replied. "What's she got under the hood?"

"You want to check it out?"

Cody's face could have lit up the room. "Dude, are you serious?" He turned to his mother. "Do you mind?"

Kelly flashed her son a grateful smile. He may not have realized it, but he had just given Derek an excuse to slip out of an awkward situation. And truth be known, she didn't need Derek to witness this.

Derek moved past her and gave her arm a little squeeze. "Just give me a minute to change."

"Don't put clothes on for our account," Alan sneered. "You do your best work without them, don't you?"

Kelly glared hard at him. She didn't dare look at Derek, too mortified at her ex's behavior, but sensed he was holding back a response.

"You are such a hypocrite!" Maya shrieked. "You did everything you could to break up me and Trevor, but you're still seeing that guy. He must be, like, twenty years younger than you—and you're *sleeping* with him!"

"Honey, we'll discuss it when—"

"Trevor dumped her," Cody spoke up with an amused-little-brother grin. "For some other girl. Very hot."

"Shut up, Cody."

Alan gestured over his shoulder. "What the hell is going on around here?"

"Last time I looked, Alan, your name wasn't on the mortgage. What I do in my house is my business and I wasn't expecting the children home for another two weeks."

"So he, like, lives here now?" Maya demanded.

Kelly glanced at her scowling daughter. "Of course not, we were just..." There wasn't a word for it. Well there was; but she couldn't say it to her children. She put a hand to her forehead in an effort to think. "The point is, Alan, you should have called."

"We did!" Maya bit out. "Like a hundred times. I left a bunch of messages on your voicemail."

Kelly's cheeks flamed. She half wished the floor would open up and swallow her whole. "I didn't have my phone on."

"Yeah, I'll bet." Maya stormed past her to stomp up the stairs. "I'm calling Heather." Derek had just begun to descend the stairs; Maya made an exaggerated gesture to avoid any contact with him.

"Jenn threw us out," Cody piped up.

"She *what?*"

"Not just us. Dad, too."

Kelly folded her arms over her chest. "Really."

Cody nodded. "I spilled grape pop on her rug."

"It was a white rug," Alan added.

"So she puts my children on the street?"

"It was hardly like that," Alan said. "She was upset about some other things, too. This was just the last straw for her."

"You let that woman throw my children out of the house?" Kelly could barely contain her fury.

"Oh, they're *your* children now," Alan sneered. "A couple of days ago they were my problem. If *your* daughter hadn't come home drunk maybe Jenn wouldn't have gotten so fed up."

He stopped speaking when Derek cleared his throat. Kelly heard a jangle of keys. His green gaze met hers before he stepped fully into the room.

She knew a perverse moment of pleasure when he paused next to Alan, the size of him positively shriveling her ex. "Derek Calavicci, this is Alan Michaels."

Again, Derek extended a hand and Alan chose to ignore it. He shrugged and tossed his keys to Cody. "Just keep it under seventy, bud."

Cody's face lit up like a fourth of July celebration.

"Don't even think about it," Kelly called as he turned to exit the room. Cody flashed her a grin.

"Is it all right to take him for a ride?" Derek asked.

She nodded.

Before leaving the room, he stepped over to her and placed a quick but possessive kiss to her lips. "You okay here?"

She nodded.

"Do you want me to stay?"

"No, you'd disappoint Cody. Go on, I'm all right."

He gave Alan a long look before he left the room. She

sensed he wanted to say something more but supposed he didn't exactly know his place just now. Well, that made two of them. She closed her eyes, wishing more than anything it was an hour ago, that she were still in Derek's arms, that anything but this had happened.

"There are enough candles in the living room to light a city block."

"It's none of your business."

"So is it just a sex thing or are you in love with that guy?"

"A sex thing?" She threw up her hands. "What difference does it make? You never cared about my sex life when we were married."

"Oh, here we go."

"Maybe if you'd have cared just a little bit about my needs, my feelings I would have understood—wait a minute. What was that you said about my daughter coming home drunk?"

"Last night. She snuck out after we'd all gone to sleep and went to some party. She came home at four this morning, staggering drunk, throwing up everywhere."

Kelly's mind swam at the information. Oh God, any number of things could have happened with her in that state. What if someone had slipped something into Maya's drink? She had never done anything so rebellious before. "How could you let this happen?"

"Would you guys keep it down?" Maya appeared at the top of the stairs, cell phone cradled on her shoulder. "I can hear you all the way up here."

As her daughter turned to go, Kelly caught a glint of gold peeking from beneath her T-shirt. "What is that?"

Maya tugged at her shirt. "What?"

"Oh, my God, tell me you don't have a belly button ring."

A guilty flush crept across Maya's face. She put the phone to her ear. "I'll have to call you back."

"What's wrong with it?" Alan asked. "Jenn has one, I don't see what's the big deal."

Kelly held out her hand. "Give it to me."

"No way."

"Take it out and give it to me."

"*No.*"

"Maya!"

"Daddy," Maya cried and ran down the stairs to her father.

Alan put an arm about his daughter's shoulders. "Don't you think you're overreacting?"

Kelly rounded on him, her temper no longer under control. "Not only did you let her date a boy far too old for her, but you allowed her to run wild with no discipline whatsoever. Now she has a belly ring, something she knows I don't approve of, and you think I'm *overreacting*?"

"You know, your boy toy is welcome to that shrewish temper of yours."

With a shriek, Kelly picked up the nearest thing in reach and hurled it toward him.

The box of tissues hit the wall with a loud smack just as Derek appeared in the doorway.

He looked from the wall to Kelly, then back to Maya, who cowered behind her father. "What's going on?"

"Mom's freaking out," Maya said. "Not that it's any of *your* business."

"Go to your room." Kelly wasn't sure whether she was more embarrassed for Derek to see her out of control, or that she had lost her temper.

"I came to ask Al to move his car, it's behind mine."

"It's *Alan*," her ex said through clenched teeth.

"Right. Anyway, I think maybe I'll wait on that ride."

Kelly put up a hand. "I'm fine, really. Maya, please go to your room so I can speak to your father in private."

"The way you guys argue, I'll be able to hear every word anyway."

"*Now*."

"I want to live with Daddy."

"What?" Suddenly pale, Alan turned to his daughter. "Maybe you should just go to your room, Princess. We can talk more about this later."

With an annoyed sigh, Maya stormed back up the stairs.

"I'm sorry." Kelly said, moving across the room to Derek. "She's not usually like this."

He took her hand and gave it a reassuring squeeze. "It's okay. You told me you weren't allowed to date. Now I can see why."

She wanted to fall into his arms as she had the other day after fighting with Maya on the phone. It had been so nice to let someone comfort her. But she had to stay strong. The battle with her daughter had only just begun. "Alan, I think you should leave."

He checked his watch. "It's kind of late. I was hoping I could just crash on the couch or in one of the kids' rooms."

"Absolutely not," Derek said.

Kelly looked up at him in surprise.

"Well, I see who wears the pants around here. Now that he's finally put them on."

Derek pulled her close against his side. "I'm sorry, Kel, but there's no way I'm leaving here tonight if he's staying."

"I lived in this house for seventeen years," Alan sneered. "I think I'm entitled to sleep here if I want to."

"You aren't staying," Kelly finally said. "And you can't either, I'm afraid."

"I know that." Derek whispered. "Al, as soon as you leave, I can take Cody for that ride. He's outside waiting."

"It's *Alan*."

"Right."

Kelly was amazed at the way Derek stood there, his hands on his hips, waiting for her ex to leave. Amusement warred with annoyance; she wasn't used to letting anyone else fight her battles. And Alan wasn't used to being ordered around. But a moment later he pulled an annoyed face, reminiscent of Maya, and sulked off.

"I'll be back tomorrow morning to talk about this. Maybe Boy Toy can go to the park up the street and play in the sand box while we grown ups talk."

Kelly followed him to the door, Derek right beside her. As he opened it, she hung back, remembering she was still in her robe. "Wh—where are the paparazzi?"

"There were only a few diehards left. I gave them some money to go get a pizza and leave us alone for a while."

"I didn't know you could do that, or I'd have tried it myself."

He gave her elbow an encouraging squeeze. "Yeah, well, they'll be back. Most likely with friends."

Outside, she found Cody with his head beneath the hood of the BMW. "Man, this thing rocks."

Kelly hid a smile.

Alan paused to consider the small but flashy convertible. "Not very family friendly, but then I guess you'd have to consider the owner."

"It's just a toy." Derek said, leaning against the car and folding his arms. "As long the golf clubs fit, I'm happy."

"Dad golfs," Cody offered. Kelly could have kissed him for trying so hard to find common ground for the two.

Derek turned toward him. "Is that a fact, Al? We'll have to get together and hit a few balls sometime."

"All right, but be warned, I've got a fourteen handicap."

Kelly was sure she saw a smirk cross Derek's face. "I'll do my best to keep up."

A few minutes later, Alan's SUV pulled out of the driveway and roared down the street.

"Is he always so high strung?" Derek asked.

"That was mellow, actually."

He pulled her into his arms and lifted her chin. "He sure had you riled up."

"He's known me too long, knows what buttons to push."

Embarrassed at his possessive display, she glanced over her shoulder to see if Cody had seen. He appeared completely absorbed by the car. As she watched, he pulled out a long silver stick and dabbed at it with his fingers. "She's down a quart."

Derek chuckled and stepped forward. "I've been abusing her a lot lately, I probably should change the oil."

"I could help you."

Kelly held her breath. Despite Cody's off-handed tone, she knew he would love nothing more than to get his hands good and greasy, especially on a hot car like Derek's. She prayed Derek wouldn't disappoint, but then, it wasn't as if he had kids, he wouldn't understand.

"You're on. How's tomorrow morning?"

Cody grinned from ear to ear, braces glinting in the light from the garage. "Awesome."

"Let's take her for a spin."

211

Kelly turned back to Derek, unable to contain her smile. "You just made his entire year."

He glanced at Cody, now gently closing the hood and strutting toward the driver's side door, keys in hand. "I was fourteen once too."

She sighed and rested her forehead against his chest. The soapy clean smell of him surrounded her. She began to relax. "I'm sorry the night turned out this way."

"It's okay. But I'm still waiting for an answer from you on that one night only thing."

"Oh, God."

"I said I was in this for two weeks, Kel. But I could be persuaded to stick around longer."

"I can't ask you to do that."

"You might have to. You don't want your kids to get the wrong idea. And Al." He gave a low chuckle. "He's something else."

"I'm sorry about the boy toy stuff. Look, can we talk about this tomorrow? After I've had some sleep—and about nine hundred more screaming matches with my daughter?"

He bent to drop a kiss to her nose. "Tomorrow it is."

"Where will you stay tonight?"

He shrugged. "I'll find a hotel."

The car roared to life then with a lusty purr. Within seconds the radio was blaring.

"I guess you'd better take Cody for that ride before he goes without you."

He walked toward the driver's side and motioned for Cody to put the window down. "Got your learner's permit pal?"

Cody shook his head.

"Then climb over."

Moments later, the vehicle pulled out of the driveway. Somehow she wasn't worried about Derek doing anything foolish or driving too fast to impress Cody. He wasn't like that. Hopefully some time tomorrow she'd figure out what to do about this entire mess. She couldn't ask Derek to play the boyfriend role any longer than he already had. She wasn't sure she could keep her heart out of it if things went on much longer. Besides, his interest would wane now that the kids were home, and she wasn't as available as she'd been in Florida.

For now, though, she still had the wrath of a sixteen-year-old to deal with.

Fifteen

Derek hoped eleven a.m. was enough time for Kelly to talk with her daughter—and get a little rest.

He'd hardly slept a wink all night himself, which was unusual—after a marathon of extremely satisfying sex, he should have been out for hours. Kelly's kid problems weren't any of his business, and she'd never welcome his intrusion. At the same time he wanted to let her know he was there if she needed a shoulder. Not that he expected her to take him up on it. She didn't need both the ex and the daughter ganging up on her.

He'd stopped at a local auto parts store and picked up a few things. He had a gut feeling the kid would be thrilled to help him wash and wax the car. Since he'd gotten in and out of there unnoticed, he chanced a stop in a nearby bagel shop, he didn't want to show up at Kelly's empty handed. That hadn't gone nearly as well, and by the time he'd posed for pictures with fans, signed autographs and kissed some lady's Chihuahua, his coffee was cold and it was nearly noon.

Now, standing outside Kelly's front door, he hesitated. Angry voices drifted out from the kitchen. Al's dark blue SUV was parked in the driveway, so he suspected a full blown family feud was underway.

Kelly's voice, weary and hoarse, drifted to him. "Just tell me you didn't have sex with Trevor."

"Tell me you didn't have sex with *what's-his-name.*"

"I'm forty-two years old young lady. There's a difference."

He knocked on the screen door; a second later Cody appeared. "Dude, you *so* don't wanna go in there."

He stepped inside, tousling the kid's hair as he moved past. Kelly sat at the kitchen table, staring blearily at her coffee cup. He didn't have to ask to know she'd had no sleep. The urge to wrap her in his arms and protect her from the onslaught was overpowering.

The ex looked up and pulled a face over the rim of his coffee cup. "Oh goody, Opie is here."

"Mornin', Al."

"It's *Alan.*"

"Right."

Kelly rose from her seat at the table. "Would you like some coffee, Derek?"

Ignoring her formal tone and assuming she was as unsure as he about how to do this, he stepped forward and kissed her.

The daughter huffed in disgust.

He slipped a finger under Kelly's chin, assessing the dark circles and red, puffy eyes. "Everything all right?"

She nodded and gave him a half-hearted smile.

"I'll be right outside; my car has a hot date with your kid."

This time her smile was genuine, and he dropped a kiss to her forehead, cast a warning glance at Al and headed toward the front door.

Outside, Cody waited on the steps, gazing at the BMW with lust and adoration. Derek grinned. It was as if the kid was looking at a naked woman for the first time. He dangled the keys in front of his nose. "You want to pop the hood and get started?"

As he strode toward the trunk to remove the jack, he spotted two paparazzo waiting patiently across the street. An older woman in a house coat and slippers stood talking to one of them. With a sigh, he strode toward them. Right now, it was only the same guys who had been plaguing Kelly all week. By this afternoon there would be more.

He favored the older woman with a well-practiced smile. "Who is this beautiful lady?" he asked, tongue very much in cheek. "Your wife?"

The heavier-set of the two reporters blanched.

As hoped, the woman twittered like a school girl. "I'm your girlfriend's neighbor."

"Ah, yes. Kelly speaks of you often." Half true. In fact, Kelly had pointed the woman out in the crowd yesterday, mentioning she was the one feeding information to the press.

He winked, then turned his attention to the reporters waiting patiently for something photo-worthy to capture.

"Guys, could you give us a break today?"

The man gave an apologetic shake of his head. "No can do, Der'. Boss' orders. Your face sells papers, and he smells a story here."

"There's no story except a woman and her teenaged daughter having issues. You need to back off and leave them alone."

"You in love with her?" asked the second one in a thick New York accent.

Derek sighed. "It'd be nice if you guys would leave us alone long enough to find out."

"There certainly was a lot of activity going on over there last night," the woman said.

Derek arched a questioning brow in her direction. "I have insomnia," she explained, looking a bit sheepish. "Awake all night sometimes."

"Yes, I have that same problem," he replied with the same naughty-boy grin that worked on his *nonna*.

The second man reached for the pencil tucked over his ear. "So you two are up all night going at it, is that it?"

Derek closed a hand around the pencil. "Don't write that. She's got kids, for God's sake."

The heavier man looked toward the house where Cody stood by the car, waiting. "Okay, we'll give you a day or two. I'll put the word out you two have gone away. But you're going to owe me an exclusive at some point."

"Kelly and I are doing one for another paper next week."

"When you break up," the man emphasized. "I want the dirty details, the scoop on who dumped who and why." He gestured toward the house. "My money's on Mommy."

"Nah, *him*," the other guy nodded in Derek's direction. "He can't keep it in his pants long enough to be faithful to one woman."

The reporter's comment stopped him in his tracks. What was that tightening in his gut? It wasn't the first time he'd felt it. "Done."

By the time he returned to Cody, the paparazzi were climbing into the car and pulling away.

"How'd you do that?" Cody asked. "They've been driving my mom crazy."

Derek turned to watch the sedan pull away. "I sold

my soul."

The boy laughed and pointed toward the hood of the car. "Ready?"

"We need to jack it up to get underneath, I think."

The boy's blue eyes—the exact same shade and shape as his mother's—flickered over him. "You're gonna get underneath the car dressed like that?"

Derek glanced down at his pleated slacks and designer shirt. "You think I'm going to get dirty?"

The kid laughed. "Let me grab some old towels from the garage."

Minutes later he had jacked up one side of the vehicle and slid underneath. Cody squatted down beside him. "Okay so you didn't get dirty. How'd you do that?"

"Years of practice."

"So why *are* you dressed like that?"

He glanced over at the kid's earnest expression. "You mean why am I wearing Armani?"

"Yeah. If that's what that is. I mean, are you going somewhere?"

He wasn't sure whether the kid *wanted* him to go somewhere or liked having him—and his car—around. "I always dress like this. When I'm not in costume."

"No jeans and T-shirt?"

"Sometimes." Derek unscrewed the oil pan plug and sticky black goo began to ooze into the drip pan.

"So you dress like that because women like it?"

Derek chuckled. "It doesn't hurt." He could tell by the thoughtful expression on the kid's face he was making a mental note of that.

"Is that what my mom liked about you?"

He slid out from underneath the car and rose with a groan. "I'm getting too old to do that, kid. Next time you'll have to." He accepted the towel Cody handed him and wiped his hands. "And no, that's not what your mom liked." He gestured toward the oil filter. "You wanna take that off?"

"Sure." The kid picked up the oil filter wrench and leaned over the engine. "So what was it...your muscles?" He slid him a shy glance, reminding Derek of how he'd felt at fourteen. Scrawny. Trapped somewhere between little boy and not quite man. Certain if he were ripped enough all the girls would want him.

"Nope. I pestered her until she agreed to go out with me, but it wasn't easy." Well, that was sort of close to the truth. "She shot me down. About four times."

Cody grinned. "Sounds like her." He stepped back and gestured to the filter. "It's too tight."

Derek leaned in and gave it a twist.

"So...are you in love with my mom?"

He paused, hand still on the wrench. He'd been half expecting that question, something along the lines of a 'what are your intentions' interrogation. He couldn't tell the kid the truth, and he wouldn't offer a sugar-coated version of it, either. A lie was the only plausible option. "Yeah, I guess I am."

The grin that spread over the boy's face almost made the lie worthwhile, except he knew Kelly would kill him for saying so. Then again, she'd kill him if he'd told the truth—they'd acted on an overpowering mutual attraction that couldn't be denied any longer. Lust, not love, had been the deciding factor.

"I thought so. I could tell by the way you looked at her."

As Cody spoke the words, the front door banged open. Derek, finished with the wrench, straightened just as the drama-queen stormed past him, Kelly at her heels. "Where are you going?"

Red face screwed up with anger, Maya turned. "To Heather's house." She took off across the lawn at a brisk walk, sobbing, cell phone pressed to her ear.

Indecision crossed Kelly's features. Derek supposed she was weighing whether it made sense to keep her daughter home and continue the fight, or give them each a much-needed break. He waited for her to look his way; instead, she turned and went back into the house.

He met Cody's gaze over the engine. "That happen a lot?"

"Kinda, yeah."

He picked up an old rag and wiped his hands again. "Should I go in there?"

The kid considered his words, then shrugged. "It's your funeral."

Derek gave him a little pat on the shoulder as he

moved past. "I think I can handle it."

Inside, the house was too quiet. He'd expected to find Kelly and Al talking but there wasn't a sound. Then again, he'd half expected Al to have something to say to his spoiled brat of a daughter, but he hadn't. His old man would have had plenty to say to her. All of it in Italian, and none of it pleasant.

A noise from the kitchen led him in that direction. Inside, he found Kelly scrubbing the sink with a vengeance.

"Wouldn't throwing something make you feel better?"

She let out a little yelp, then turned to face him. "You startled me."

He grinned and moved toward her. "Everything okay?"

"Fine," she chirped, eyes suddenly welling. "I'm just—"

He stepped closer. "Where's Al? Wouldn't he make a better target?" He was rewarded when she let out a small laugh. "I'll hold him down if you want."

"I'm sorry, Derek. You don't deserve to be caught up in this."

"What am I caught up in?" He slipped an index finger beneath her chin.

"This mess with Maya, the jabs from Alan. You didn't ask for any of it."

He pulled her into his arms, and for a moment she held herself rigid. "Maybe. But I'm not complaining." He heard her release a fractured breath and pressed his lips to her hair. "Would it kill you to let me comfort you?"

"No," she whispered against his chest. "But I don't want to get used to it."

The words sank in with ice cold clarity. Damn, why did he keep forgetting this was all a pretense? Especially since *she* didn't forget it for a second.

"Have you ever considered just putting your foot down with her?"

She stiffened again. "What?"

"Don't get defensive, just hear me out." He leaned back far enough to look at her. "The woman I met in Florida—who didn't hesitate to tell me to go to hell—is letting a sixteen-year-old girl walk all over her. How is that possible? Where's my strong, sexy lady in red?"

"Don't," she picked up the brillo pad and resumed her attack on the sink. "I've told you before, I'm not what you thought I was that night. And I don't need advice on raising my daughter."

"Looks to me like you do."

"Thanks," her voice had gone husky. "Like I need childrearing advice from a guy who has never been married, never had kids, isn't even a grown up yet."

He leaned a hip against the counter. "I told you about my brother-in-law dying in the towers, right?"

"Yes."

"He left behind four kids. The oldest was nine."

She glanced up at him. "Your poor sister, I'm so sorry."

"She got through it; she had my mother, aunts and sisters to lean on. But those kids needed someone to play the role of father in their lives. My youngest brother was still in high school, and my oldest brother had a family of his own."

She stopped scrubbing. "You?"

"Me. I'm not home often, but I spend as much of my free time as possible with those kids."

"That's nice of you—"

"Anyway, last summer Bianca—my sister—met a great guy. You want to guess how my fourteen-year-old niece reacted when her mother started dating again? It only got worse when they got engaged a few months ago."

She frowned up at him. "Why? She's old enough to know her father isn't coming back, why wouldn't she want her mother to be happy?"

"She's already lost her father, she's afraid of losing her mother, too."

"Wait a minute—are you saying *Maya* is worried about... that's ridiculous."

"Think about it, Kel." He closed the distance between them. "She doesn't know what's really going on with us. She managed to break up Al and his girlfriend, and I'm standing in the way of you two getting back together."

"But that's never going to happen."

Damn if he didn't breathe a sigh of relief at those words. He pulled her into his arms and tipped her head back. "You're damn right it's not."

"Derek, I'm sorry for what I said about—"

He didn't wait for her to finish. It had been too damn long already. He kissed her slowly, gently, trying not to stir any embers, but he could taste the longing in her kiss, feel it in the way her hands came up to caress his shoulders, slide over his biceps. Her tongue slipped out to meet his and he couldn't hold back, couldn't keep the raw desire he felt from intruding.

"Hey, Kelly?" Al's voice from out on the deck, penetrated his consciousness. "Could I get some more coffee out here?"

She pulled away to look at him, humor lighting her eyes.

"You suppose he knew what he was interrupting?" Derek asked.

She shook her head.

"You aren't really going to bring him coffee, are you?"

"No," she said with a laugh. "Those days are long gone."

"Good." He eased away from her and headed for the coffee pot on the counter. "Because I'd be glad to bring him some."

"Derek, don't—"

Kelly watched as he took the pot from the burner and pushed open the sliding glass doors that led to the deck. She put her hands over her mouth, half dreading what she'd hear next.

"Nice out here, isn't it Al?"

"It's Alan," her ex bit out.

"Right. Boy, Kel sure does have a way with plants doesn't she?"

"Guess so. That my coffee?"

"Sure is, buddy. Hold out your cup."

Kelly winced, mentally ticking off the seconds until she heard a howled expletive.

"Damn that was clumsy of me, Al. Let me get you a towel."

A moment later, Alan stomped through the doors. "I'm going back to my hotel. To change."

Kelly pursed her lips together to keep from giggling. A moment later Derek stepped through the doors, winked, and set the coffee pot aside. "I've got a car to wash and wax."

****

By the time evening fell, Kelly was feeling more like herself. While Cody and Derek played with his car most of the afternoon, and Maya hid out at Heather's house, she did some grocery shopping so she could actually feed her family. Alan spent the day visiting his parents so she hadn't had to contend with his whininess, either.

Now, seated on the deck with Derek as darkness descended, listening to the rhythmic thump of a basketball and male laughter as Cody and some friends played a game, she was almost content.

Derek slipped an arm around her; she rested her head on his chest. It should have relaxed her, should have soothed, but the smell of his skin and the caress of his hand along her arm only made her long for time alone with him—and that wouldn't be happening anytime soon.

"You seem more relaxed," he whispered against her hair.

"I am," she sighed. "Is that bad? A day spent apart from my daughter and my ex and I'm feeling better?"

His deep chuckle rumbled just below her ear. "I can see where Al would keep you on edge."

"He wasn't always that bad. At least I don't think he was." She fingered the buttons down his crisp, white shirt. He'd gone back to his hotel to change before dinner. She didn't think she'd ever get tired of how good he smelled, the way he dressed. "Dinner was nice," she added.

"Yeah, it was." He pressed his lips to her hair again, and for a split second, she could almost forget this wasn't real. "I'm sorry we couldn't go out."

Unwilling to face more fans or paparazzi, they had opted to stay in and grill steaks. Alan and Maya were both gone; it was just her, Derek and Cody. Things were relaxed and casual, and she still couldn't get over the way the two had taken to each other. They talked sports, cars and laughed like long lost friends. Derek didn't seem to be putting on an act, it was a side of him the likes of which she hadn't seen before. And at one point, when he stepped inside to take a cell call from Gabrielle, she asked Cody if he was really all right with things, if it was okay with him that his mom was dating someone.

True to his good nature, he had simply shrugged. "Dad has Jenn. Why shouldn't *you* be happy?"

Now, with Cody playing basketball with his buddies, joyfully reunited with Barney, who had yet to leave his side, and things the way they were with Derek, life seemed simpler, almost perfect. And it would have been, if any of this were real.

"It's only another few days until the charity ball," Derek's deep voice broke into her musings.

"With all that's happened the past few days, I'd nearly forgotten about it."

"Me too. Are you still planning to go—now that the kids are home, I mean."

How could she? "Oh, Derek—" She raised her head from his shoulder to tell him she couldn't. But her gaze met his and that familiar heat zinged between them. But there was more than just desire in his dark green gaze, there was something else. Disappointment?

"The day after the ball, I leave for L.A. for a month."

"A month?"

Cold realization dawned. She wouldn't see him for a month. Wait a minute, who was she kidding? She wouldn't see him again. Probably not ever. Not that he wouldn't be glad to be rid of her and all the baggage that came with her. She couldn't let it end like this, on a whimper rather than a bang.

He traced a finger along her nose, then her lips. "Al can babysit, can't he?"

"Yes," she whispered. "That's a good idea. He can stay here and it'll save him money on a hotel for a couple of days. That'll appeal to him."

He chuckled but the humor faded. "Kel." His Adam's apple bobbed for a moment. "I'll be back just before Labor Day. I always take my sister's kids to the cabin for a week. Ben and Noah are Maya and Cody's age. Maybe you and the kids could come..."

"We wouldn't be alone."

"We'll find time." With that he leaned in for the kiss she'd been desperately craving, his lips tender against hers at first. It wasn't enough. She wanted to touch and be touched, to feel every glorious inch of his body slide along hers.

"Can we find time tonight?" she asked, pulling away just far enough to speak.

He groaned low in his throat. "I thought you'd never ask."

The sound of the front door opening and banging shut, the laughter of teenaged boys debating over who beat who had her jumping away.

Cody's gaze met hers through the sliding glass door. "We're hungry," he said, reaching into the fridge and tossing out a few cans of iced tea to his friends. He straightened from the fridge, pointed in Derek's direction. "That's my mom's boyfriend. It's his car."

"How many dents did you put in it with the basketball?" Derek called back.

Cody laughed as he and his friends converged around the kitchen table with a bag of chips and their drinks. "Just a few, but that paint we spilled on it didn't help."

"I think I'm gonna use you for bait tomorrow, kid."

"Oh," he poked his head out the door. "Mom. I forgot to ask. Can I go fishing with Derek tomorrow?"

Kelly frowned and looked at Derek. "Fishing?"

"Yeah, I stopped at the marina this afternoon and rented a boat, I didn't realize you were so close to the water here. I mentioned it to Cody, and he said he'd like to go—with your permission of course."

"Sure, I—" Alan had never been much for activities with the kids. But why had she never realized her son wanted to go fishing? And why did it please her that Derek and Cody had become fast friends at the same time it worried her that her son was getting too attached too soon?

"You should come with us," Cody spoke up. "Maya's sleeping over Heather's anyway."

"She is?" Alarm bells went off for a moment, but then Heather had always been a grounded, sensible girl. Maybe Maya needed time with her old friends. "Why didn't I know this?"

"She called and asked Dad," Cody said around a mouthful of chips. With that, his attention returned to his friends, someone mentioned Playstation, and they were off for the living room.

"Of course she did," Kelly muttered. Still, she would call Heather's parents and confirm that bit of information.

"I'm sorry, Kel. I should have asked you first."

"No, it's fine," she said. "You two have a lot in common, you both like the outdoors and cars. Those aren't things he can share with his dad. I just... Cody thinks you're here to stay and..."

Derek winced. "Yeah, he asked me about that today. I told him we were in love."

"What? Why would you do that?"

"Would you prefer the truth? The kid's looking out for his mom, that's all. He wanted to know my intentions."

"My little boy is worried about me?"

Derek laughed. "He's a good kid, Kel."

"But what am I going to tell him in a few days, when..."

"That I'm in LA for a month and we don't want to do the long-distance relationship thing."

"Well, it certainly didn't take you long to come up with that."

"It's the best I've got." He pinned her with a serious gaze. "And if it makes you feel any better, I've got a date with Al tomorrow afternoon for golf."

"Why?"

He shrugged, but she saw the smile playing at the corners of his mouth. "He asked."

"You're better at golf than he is, aren't you?"

"I guess that remains to be seen. So are you going fishing with us?"

"Oh, I don't..." Then again, there was precious little time left to spend together. "Sure. What time?"

"I told the kid I'd pick him up at three thirty."

"In the afternoon? That'll give me plenty of time to—"

"In the *morning*, Kel. You fish really early in the morning."

"Oh. Sounds like *fun*."

Sixteen

The sun was nowhere to be seen when Kelly followed Derek and Cody down the path toward the pier. He lit the way with a flashlight, but she was grateful for the warmth of his hand around hers. A hundred "girlie girl" questions rushed through her mind at the absurdity of this adventure, not to mention her body's protest at doing something completely against her natural rhythm. She should be just heading for bed now, not beginning her day. Especially since, instead of sleeping, she'd spent the night working and had yet to get to bed. And since Derek had promised Cody he'd pick him up at three thirty, she'd made a date with Derek for two.

They'd met in the gazebo that housed the hot tub. While a day spent unable to touch one another lent a frenzied pace to their lovemaking, she had no regrets. Even now the memory brought a tingle to her skin. A month ago, if someone had told her that she, Kelly Michaels, good mother, would be sneaking out to her backyard gazebo in the middle of the night for an encounter with a very hot guy, she'd have laughed in their face.

But now, as Derek led her down the wooden dock, cautioning her to step carefully over a loose plank, she pushed aside the shadow of guilt whispering in the back of her mind. He seemed relaxed, at ease, and excitement radiated from Cody. They were both eager to share this with her.

She stepped gingerly into the small rowboat. "I would have expected something closer to a yacht from you."

"I've been on enough of them. Besides, we don't need one just to go fishing." He held her hand until she had her balance and had taken a seat, made sure Cody was safely in, then stepped in himself. He put the oars to the water and began to row.

Kelly hunched over, hugging her knees to her chest,

listening to the rhythmic motion of the oars cutting through the water, the sound oddly loud in the calm of pre dawn. The strong smell of the bug spray she'd doused herself and Cody with met her nostrils, and she wrinkled her nose. "Tell me again why we're out here at this hour?"

"The fish bite better early in the day when the water is quiet," Cody explained. "Later when people are out with boats and jet skis and stuff, it disturbs them."

"Ah, I see." Though she really didn't. She glanced toward him, barely visible in the faint light from the moon.

"Do you want me to take you back?" Derek asked.

"No, not at all." While she knew next to nothing about fishing, it was apparent from the conversation between Derek and Cody all morning that this was important to them.

Besides, she still had that burning need to know more about him, to peel away yet another superficial layer and find the man beneath, maybe glimpse something his other girlfriends hadn't. Not that she was technically his girlfriend. She wasn't sure just what she was. In fact, the only thing she was sure of was that she didn't want to label it right now. "So this is something you did with your grandfather," she said, glancing around as they moved farther form shore toward the middle of the lake. "Every summer at the lake?"

"Every summer. Now I bring my nephews. "

"I'll bet they love it."

"They do. It's always been sort of a guys-only thing, but now some of my nieces are complaining they don't get to go."

"No girls allowed," Cody spoke up.

"Well, that hardly seems fair," Kelly reasoned.

In the semi darkness she saw one broad shoulder lift and fall. "Sometimes guys just want to be guys. You can't relax with women around. And I'm not driving anyone back to the city for a broken fingernail."

A loud snort of laughter from her son surprised her.

"Now, that's downright chauvinistic. Not every female is that way. Maya has always been more the type to get sweaty and dirty playing soccer than to go hang out at the mall." A pang of sadness pierced her at that thought. She hated how things between her and Maya were still unresolved and hoped the time spent with Heather would bring her back down to earth.

"She'll come around." Derek said, as if sensing the maudlin direction her thoughts had taken. "Maybe you should think more about what I said. Bring the kids up to the cabin this summer; she might make friends with some of my nieces. And I've got a couple nephews her age, maybe she'll forget all about that college boy you're so upset about."

She couldn't begin to imagine ending their affair, then spending a week with him while her kids camped, swam and fished with Derek's nieces and nephews. Being forced to listen as he took calls on his cell phone from a new lover? And what if Maya fell in love with one of his nephews, married him—she would be tied to Derek's family for life, see him at every holiday, every family event. She couldn't bear the thought of hearing about him getting married, having children, building a new life—

"Mom, did you hear what Derek just said?"

"Bring the kids to the cabin this summer?" She bit her lip, still pondering the consequences. "I'll have to think about it."

Cody laughed. "She zones out like that when she's thinking about her books."

"Then let her zone out, she's entitled." Derek's soft chuckled floated to her in the darkness, sending a hot rush of awareness through her. "All I said was let's stop here."

Kelly felt an embarrassed flush creep over her and was grateful for the cover of darkness. It had to be lack of sleep that had her brain wandering in a dozen different directions.

Derek set the oars aside and the boat stayed relatively still on the calm water. "How about some coffee? It might wake you up."

She reached for the cup he poured from a thermos. He poured one for himself and scooted closer to her. The tell-tale gasp of a soda can sounded from Cody's direction, and she squelched a motherly instinct to chide him for drinking pop at this hour of the morning. She settled tentatively against Derek's shoulder, still shy about any physical contact in front of her son. She closed her eyes, enjoying the gentle rocking of the water. "So this is fishing."

"Not even close."

"What's missing?" she tipped her head up to look at him.

"I haven't even baited a hook yet."

"Oh." She shifted, trying to get more comfortable on the hard bench seat. A gentle breeze blew across them, and she wrinkled her nose. "Derek? What is that ... smell?"

"Probably some old bait left over from who knows when, and lots of fish guts."

She squelched the shriek that rose to her throat and lifted her feet to rest them on the seat across from her.

Cody's belly laugh echoed on the water, accompanied by another deep laugh from Derek.

"You're a terrible tease."

Derek leaned in close. "Funny, I thought the same thing about you at one time." She flushed, wondering if her son had overheard.

Cody seemed intent on a box he'd pulled from beneath the seat. Kelly straightened when she realized it was a donut box. "When did you find time to get breakfast?"

"Last night after D left. You were working."

Expecting to see jelly-filled confections, she nearly gagged when he opened the box and shone the flashlight on a mass of wriggling night crawlers. "Breakfast for the fish, anyway." He grinned, braces glinting in the light.

She tried not to grimace as Derek showed Cody how to bait a hook, then cast a line into the water. He turned to her. "I suppose you want me to do yours, too?"

It was a test; she knew it was a test. He wanted her to do it, to prove something to him. No way in hell was she touching that... *thing*. "Er, yes. Please."

"Just this once." He baited and cast once more.

"Now what do we do?"

"This is the hard part. We stay quiet so we don't scare the fish."

She lowered her voice to a whisper. "Okay." After a moment or so she glanced over at him. A Yankees cap was pulled low over his eyes. Dressed in hiking boots, cargo shorts and a well-worn T-shirt advertising a bait and tackle shop, he'd be unrecognizable to even his most rabid fan. Not because he didn't look handsome, there was still that athletic, hot young guy thing about him. But because he looked so normal. "You know, I'll bet this is not what your fans think you do in your free time."

"Yours either."

She smiled. "I'm serious. You just don't come across as the simple life kind of guy."

He sighed and shifted in the boat so that he was beside her. "I didn't used to think I was. I tried all that other stuff, the ski trips to Aspen, scuba diving in the Caribbean, yacht parties in the Mediterranean, the club scene in New York. None of it relaxed me the way this does. It took me a while to learn how to just be still, listen to the water, to nature. Now five minutes after I leave my cabin, I'm in a hurry to get back."

"Where's the cabin at, D?" Cody asked after a slurp from the soda can.

A shadow of a smile tugged at Kelly's lips. Just this once she'd let her son's poor grammar choice slide.

"Catskills." He slid a worm on his own hook and cast the line into the water.

"You been going there long?"

"About eight or nine years." He leaned back and put his arm around her once again. "What about you, writer lady? What do you do when you want to relax?"

"She doesn't know how." Cody snorted.

"I enjoy gardening," she spoke up in defense of herself.

"Yeah, but it doesn't relax you," her son pointed out. "You get all freaked out over weeds, or bugs nibbling your leaves and what the deer and the rabbits got into."

"I do not." She frowned as he gave her an exaggerated wide-eyed look. "Do I?"

Derek squeezed her shoulder reassuringly. "We still have a couple of days to work on that."

She had the uncanny feeling that for once he wasn't talking about sex.

He pointed toward the eastern sky, which was beginning to steadily brighten. "Watch this."

For the next several minutes she didn't speak. She watched, spellbound, as the sky changed from pink to orange to golden until at long last the sky was utterly and gloriously a radiant pale blue.

"I've never seen a sunrise quite like that," she whispered. "It's like the sun rose right up out of the lake."

"I thought you'd like it." His voice was soft, his touch at her shoulder even more gentle. "I'm glad you came with me this morning."

"Thanks for bringing me." She inched closer to snuggle against him. "You're right about this fishing thing, there's something so calming here. I almost feel like the whole world can go on with its business and I don't mind."

"Sure you say that now," he teased, "but you thought I was crazy when I said I'd pick you up at three-thirty in the morning."

Cody laughed, apparently enjoying the teasing between them.

"Maybe just a little."

The grin Derek gave her was boyish, as if she'd said something unexpected. He bent his head closer to hers. For a moment her breath caught at the sight of that face, so beautiful in its perfection. Everything about him, in fact, was perfect as far as she was concerned; she loved everything about the man. A bizarre sensation rocked her, as if the world had just pulled the rug out from under her feet. Good Lord, of all the people she could feel this way about... *not him.* Definitely not him. This was a game to Derek, she was just another bed partner. And she didn't want to feel this way about anyone again. Not ever. It would only lead to misery.

Instead of kissing her, he pulled slightly away. "What was that?"

"Wh—what?"

"Your face just went totally serious."

"I uh... got a whiff of some fishy smell. Must be something in the air." Damn she was a lousy liar. She resisted the urge to chew her lip and looked for something—anything—else to talk about. "My coffee must be ice cold by n—oh!" She gave a cry as the world beneath her, or at the very least, the rickety row boat, really did rock and sway.

"Looks like someone has beginner's luck," Derek said, rising to grab the pole he had baited for her. "Here, it's all yours."

"Wh—wait a minute, I have no idea what to do with this thing."

"Same thing you did with me, Kel." He gave her a playful wink. "Reel him in."

"Is that supposed to be funny?" She gave another yelp as the line jerked, and nearly dropped the pole.

"Hold on." He pulled her down in the boat and sat behind her, straddling her hips with his legs, covering her arms with his. After a few moments he had managed to lift the line from the water, revealing the biggest fish Kelly had ever seen... okay, the *only* fish she had ever seen, other than at the supermarket. It twisted and struggled as it dangled in the air.

"What do we do now?" Kelly asked, watching as Derek unhooked it.

"C.P.R., usually."

"On a *fish?*"

Another round of belly laughter from her son. "Mom, it means catch, photograph, release."

"How do you know this stuff?" she asked. "I thought your knowledge of fishing was limited to which aisle in the grocery store the Gorton's box is located."

Derek shot her another one of those boyish grins. "Here hold him."

He didn't give her a chance to refuse, merely shoved the flopping thing into her hands and grabbed his camera from the bottom of the boat. "Smile, Kel."

"How can anything that spends so much time in the water smell so awful?" Naturally the camera flashed on her grimace.

"Care to try again and give me a smile this time?"

"Derek, take this God-awful thing out of my hands before I scream."

Laughing, he did as she had asked. "He's keeper-sized, Kel. Probably a good twenty inches, a real nice large mouth bass. You sure you don't want to keep him?"

"The picture will be memory enough, thanks."

Moments after Moby Dick had been returned to his

watery home, Kelly sank down onto one of the uncomfortable seats again. "So that's it? You come out here to catch fish, take their picture, and then throw them back? You don't eat them?"

He shrugged. "I prefer my fish cooked in a restaurant. I just come for the relaxation, the fresh air, the peace and quiet."

"At three thirty in the morning."

"Yep. But, if you want me to take you back in, I will."

Truth was, as unpleasant as the whole fishing experience was, she enjoyed being with him. There was something so down to earth about the Derek she had known the past few days, so normal... she couldn't get enough of it. "No, this is fine. I brought a book like you suggested, and I have my notepad and pen, I can jot down some ideas." She poked through the bag she had brought with her.

"I'm glad to hear you say that."

She raised her head to look at him. "Really?"

"I haven't brought a woman fishing with me in about ten years. You were starting to remind me of exactly why."

"Who was it?" Cody asked, echoing her thoughts. She hated that she was glad he'd asked, but in the same instant she felt sort of special for being the first woman in a decade he'd shared this with, she had to wonder who else had been so special?

"Well, she was hardly a woman. My sister, Gabby. I think she was all of thirteen. She barely lasted an hour."

Kelly felt foolish for having wondered, for the smidgen of jealousy that had crept over her about something that had happened ten years ago. She needed to give herself a serious reality check. Maybe later today she should call Sharon for a dose of common sense, it was lawn service day in her neighborhood after all, and Sharon loved nothing more than coming over to ogle the hot young landscaping guys as they worked on the lawns. Pulling a book from her bag, she settled back to read.

As the morning sun grew hotter, Kelly set her book aside and shrugged out of her sweatshirt, a movement Derek noted with much appreciation. Then she scrounged in her bag for a tube of Sunblock and squeezed the sticky white goo onto her arms and legs. Then rubbed, in that uniquely female way. Long smooth strokes up and down her slender calves, over her forearms and upper arms. Slow circles around elbows and knees. He swallowed and shifted on the hard seat, darting a glance in Cody's direction, hoping the kid didn't notice his discomfort. His eyes were closed, brim of his hat pulled low, a half smile on his face as he listened to his iPod.

He drew his attention back to Kelly and stifled a groan as she continued to smear on Sunblock. One day of non-stop sex and one without any—he wanted her as much as he ever had. He was still waiting for the sense of claustrophobia to descend, the sense of being smothered by all this togetherness. But Frankie's suggestion he get her out of his system didn't seem to be working. And that's what worried him. Somewhere along the way, Kelly had become his in a way he'd never expected when they'd planned this charade.

Finishing with the lotion, she held the tube in his direction. "Want some?"

He swallowed, wondering how she had managed to read his mind. Then he noticed the tube in her hand. He shook his head. "No thanks, I don't burn."

"Suit yourself," she said. "I was going to offer to rub it on."

He couldn't help the chuckle that rose and died in his throat. It still amazed him she could tease like that. His gaze strayed back to the line in the water. Another movement from Kelly drew it back. She pulled her hair from the pony tail at her nape. The movement lifted her breasts, thrusting them forward, but it was her hair, highlighted by the early morning sun, that held him fascinated. She placed the elastic band between her teeth and fluffed the blonde strands with her hands.

The flowery smell of her shampoo wafted toward him. She combed through it with her fingers, catching it back into a tail again with one hand before taking the band from between her teeth and securing it. Blue eyes regarded him before she slipped her sunglasses on. "Is something the matter?"

"N—no. Uh—"A tug on his pole drew his attention, and he was grateful for the distraction. What was it

Frankie had said about him staring after Kelly like a lovesick puppy? He pulled the line from the water far too easily. The small fish dangling from it flopped angrily but was too small to put up much of a fight.

A snicker from Kelly's direction had him glancing her way, but she pursed her lips and pretended to be engrossed in her book. "I've seen goldfish bigger than that. On the cracker aisle."

Without thinking about it, he unhooked the little guy and tossed him on Kelly's lap. She shrieked and leaped to her feet. The fish fell to the bottom of the boat, flopping wildly.

"Sorry about that. I must have butterfingers."

She glared at him, then bent to pick it up. She started to toss it overboard, but at the last second lunged forward and dropped it down his shirt. Settling back, she gave him an innocent look. "Oops, I guess I do, too."

He rose and untucked his shirt, freeing the fish. He scooped it up, dangling it by its tail in front of her. "I think he'd find what's down your shirt much more interesting."

She crossed her arms over her chest. "You wouldn't dare."

"Wouldn't I? " He slid off the seat to his knees in front of her.

Laughing, she scooted to the other side of seat. He advanced again.

"Derek Calavicci, stop teasing." She backed up again but had retreated as far as she could in the little boat.

"Who's teasing? He probably *would* find it interesting. I sure do." But the way she said his name had him longing to hear his real name from her lips. Whether she was laughing as she was now, or fisting her hands in his hair and pleading.

"Won't he die soon if we keep torturing him like this?"

He lifted one shoulder in a nonchalant shrug. "He'd die happy."

Her lips twitched in amusement. "I meant the fish, not you."

He closed the distance between them until he loomed over her. "Kiss me, and I'll forget about dropping him down your shirt

"I'm not kissing you when you smell like fish."

"I don't smell any worse than you do."

She raised a hand from where it dangled over the side of the boat and smeared a palm full of lake water over his face. "You do now."

With a flick of his wrist he tossed the little fish back into the water. "I've still got a donut box full of bait over there."

Her eyes widened. "You wouldn't dare."

"Probably not, but..." he paused, drawing out the word while he trailed his own hand in the water. "I'd do this."

She shrieked with laughter when he retaliated with a handful of water over her face. She wriggled to get away from him and slid partially off the seat. He caught her about the hips. "Now about that kiss..."

Still giggling, she offered, a quick, chaste brush against his lips.

"You call that a kiss?"

"It's the best I can do at this hour."

Hands still about her waist, he tickled her. She gave another screech of laughter and tried to wriggle out of his embrace.

"I didn't know you were so ticklish."

"I'm not," she said, gasping with laughter. "Only when I'm tired."

"Why are you so tired?" he teased, knowing damn well why she—they—had no sleep. But she was so beautiful with her head thrown back, smelling of fish and water and early morning sun, he wanted to keep tickling her, keep her laughing so he could hear that sound again and again. Instead, he could only stare at her.

She placed her hands over his and pulled away from him. "We're probably scaring the fish. Besides," she nodded toward Cody, arms folded across his chest and slack-jawed, his chest rising and falling rhythmically, "you'll wake him. And we're not the only ones out here anymore."

He looked out across the water. Another boat sat quite a distance away, but the two men in it were staring at them as if they were insane.

Kelly gave them a friendly little wave, and they waved back somewhat awkwardly. "Here," She handed him one of the fishing poles, then picked up her book again. "You fish. I'll read."

The sun rose higher in the sky as the morning wore on, the warmth from its rays growing more persistent. Feeling the heat against his shoulders, Derek shrugged out of his shirt. It was less a reason to show off to Kelly, though he noted her eyes raking him appreciatively every so often, but he couldn't afford tan lines. He hated having make up sprayed on to cover them and wasn't about to waste his time in a tanning booth either.

She seemed engrossed in her book for the most part, he was gratified to see he wasn't on the cover; it was one of those contemporary ones with cartoonish characters. He supposed too many books like that could put him out of business, but he was relieved not to have his own likeness staring at him all morning.

The activity on the lake had begun to pick up, and he pulled his hat lower and slipped on a pair of sunglasses.

"Going incognito?" she asked.

She was half right. Most likely no one would recognize him unless they came in close. Not his face anyway. His body was a different story.

Not that he cared. Right now Kelly was the only woman who interested him. A thought that grated and intrigued at the same time. He pondered once again the fact that he had made no progress in ridding himself of his fascination with her, or worse still, that it no longer mattered if he did.

The more he made love to her, the more he wanted her. And that had never been the case with another woman. Ever. Usually it was just the opposite, once the mystery was solved, his interest waned. Rapidly.

It had been that way even with Simone, whom he wanted from the first time he'd ever seen her on a billboard in Times Square. But then Simone had been about something else. He hadn't wanted her because she fascinated him, the way Kelly did. He'd wanted her in much the same way he'd wanted a Ferrari when he was a teenager. With legs a mile long, silver blonde hair down to her waist and a flawless face, Simone had been more about status than anything else. *Every* man wanted her. If he had her, then it was true; he could have any woman he wanted.

Like Kelly, she'd been content to let him pursue her. He'd asked her out through her agent. She'd turned him down and the chase was on. But very much *unlike* Kelly, she hadn't been worth the time and effort. He'd been enamored enough of her beauty to overlook it at first, but it hadn't taken him long to tire of his prize. Her personality ran from self-obsessed and shallow to an insecure little girl in need of constant reassurance. No in-betweens.

"You're staring at me." Kelly didn't even look up from her book.

"I was just noticing your shoulders are starting to look pink."

She rolled a shoulder forward and turned her head. "I burn more than I tan."

"Why don't we head back now?"

"Are you sure? You haven't found 'the one that got away' yet."

Hadn't he? Then again if there was one thing he could say for Kelly, she kept him guessing. Maybe he hadn't. He picked up the oars and began to row, noting with a grunt of satisfaction her gaze on his bare chest and arms once more. There was no doubt what they would spend their time in New York doing.

She retuned to her reading, and he found his thoughts wandering back to Simone. Hindsight being what it was, he could see now he hadn't exactly been supportive. He'd been riding his own career high and hadn't had time to hold her hand and coddle her through her self doubt. Once their relationship had soured, even though Simone refused to let go, he'd thought nothing of sleeping with other women. Anything in a skirt.

But Simone, nor any of the other women, had fascinated him the way Kelly did. A smile played over his face as he remembered their first night at her place, just before Al and the kids had shown up. They'd had one hell of a time in her oversized bathtub, even long after the water had cooled. And it hadn't been all about sex, either. They had lain there contentedly together, staring up at the stars through the skylight, talking. And laughing.

He knew she was still somewhat mystified by his attraction to her, and every so often something almost like shyness came over her. How would he ever explain to her that her body, more curvy and womanly than any woman he'd ever been with, was sexier to him, more of a turn on than any six foot tall, size two model?

He drew closer to shore and eased the boat near the dock, reaching over to pull it closer. He jumped out to secure the line while she roused Cody.

She helped her sleepy son out of the boat, then stepped carefully onto the dock. "I don't know about you but a hot shower to wash off this fishy smell is the first thing I want."

He glanced at his watch. "I've got a couple of hours before I have to meet Al."

"What I'd give to have a bird's eye view of *that* game."

He laughed and slipped an arm about her waist. "I'll tell you all about it afterward." He stole a kiss before retrieving the leftover bait and coffee thermos from the boat. Cody, zombie-like and quiet, walked back down the pier toward Kelly's waiting mini van.

"I think the poor kid's going to sleep the rest of the day," Derek observed. He slid his arm around Kelly's waist, and she fell into step beside him.

"I was thinking I might take Maya shopping with me. I need to pick up a few things before the charity ball, and I thought it would give us time to talk."

"I think it's a great idea," he said as they headed down the dock. "Give her some time, Kel. She'll come around."

"I hope you're right."

"So what is it that you need to buy? Anything I might find interesting?"

Her throaty laughter warmed him. "Not with my sixteen-year-old daughter present."

"Ahh, that's true."

"Besides, that stuff is already packed." She went up on tiptoe to give him a lingering kiss

"*That stuff?*"

With a mysterious little smile, she hurried back down the dock.

Nicole McCaffrey

He couldn't help the fool's grin that spread over his face. His lower body hummed with the interest she'd piqued while his brain conjured up all sorts of pleasant images. He put the pole over his shoulder, whistling, and started forward. He'd have never guessed he could be so content to wait to make love to a woman, he never had been before. And even though he'd have preferred Al and the kids stay in Virginia a bit longer so he and Kelly could have had more time alone, he was perfectly willing to wait.

From the first sparks that had flown between them in Florida, he'd guessed making love to her would be incredibly satisfying and fulfilling. But it was more than that, more than just lovers in perfect sync having hot sex. Making love to her felt like coming home.

So much of that had to do with her personality, the warmth she radiated. He smiled at the sight of her waiting there by the van with Cody. His heart tripped ridiculously at the sight. Damn it was almost as if—
"Jesus."

As understanding dawned, his foot caught on the loose plank he'd walked around earlier—the same one he'd warned her about. The dock rushed up at him with a thud. Like a graceless fool, he sprawled face down at Kelly's feet. For a moment he couldn't move, but it had nothing to do with having taken a fall. And everything to do with the realization that had hit him like a bolt of lightning.

"Derek, my God are you—"

"I'm fine." If his voice was harsh, it wasn't from the embarrassment of the fall he suffered. Kelly hurried over to him. He looked up to see a mixture of emotion on her face. Concern, bewilderment, a hint of amusement. He rolled to a sitting position, felt the blood trickling down his chin, saw a similar trail on one knee, but oddly didn't feel the pain. "I'm fine," he repeated in a gentler tone and rose to his feet.

"Dude," Cody called, now fully awake and laughing. "That was classic."

"Thanks, kid."

Kelly straightened as he rose to his feet. "Did you lose your footing?"

240

"More like my mind." He chanced a glance at her once again and saw only the worried look, the teeth sinking into her lower lip as if she wanted to say something more.

And it *was* temporary insanity that had tripped him up. It had to be. No way in hell was he falling in love with Kelly—the one woman, as Frankie had so eloquently put it, who *didn't* want him.

****

It was late afternoon by the time the golf game was over. As players went, Al wasn't bad. But Derek had birdied the last three holes while Al had hit into the rough. Watching Al's frustration grow had given him an enormous sense of satisfaction. Especially since Al had only invited him along with the intent of showing him up.

Now, seated at the bar in the country club lounge, Derek nursed a scotch on the rocks, while Al stared morosely into his Manhattan. He supposed there were worse things than getting bested at your favorite pastime by your ex-wife's new lover. He just couldn't think of any at the moment.

"Al, look—if you want to play again tomorrow..."

"No, I'm good." He raked a hand over his thinning blond hair and glanced over at Derek. "So are you serious? About this whole thing with Kelly?"

Concern from the self-absorbed ex? Say it wasn't so. "We're talking it slow, seeing where it goes."

Alan shook his head. "I don't buy it."

Derek took a swallow of his drink and set the glass aside. "Why not?"

"I don't know. Kelly hasn't looked at a man, hasn't had an interest in life outside of writing and kids in... well, pretty much her whole life. Now all of a sudden she's with some pretty boy model? It doesn't make sense."

"It took us both by surprise, believe me." He absently rubbed the now-scabbed-over spot where he'd landed on his chin this morning. He'd been surprised all right, but the more he tried to figure it out, the more he came back to the same answer.

"Did she throw something at you?"

"Naw, boating accident."

The other man swirled the ice in his drink then

signaled for the bartender. "So I guess I can see what a woman Kelly's age would see in you, but—come on. What's a guy like you doing with her?"

Derek's hand stilled on his glass. "How do you mean?"

"Well, she's pretty, but she's not beautiful." He picked up his drink and downed the last of it. "The bloom is long-gone off that rose, if you know what I mean."

"Is that a fact?"

Alan nodded his thanks as the bartender set another glass in front of him. "The thing about Kelly is... I don't know. She comes off all sweet and easy going, but believe me, she's a raging bitch."

Derek swiveled in his seat to face him, content to let him keep talking.

"And be warned, my friend, if you marry her—she'll waste no time letting herself go."

"*Letting* herself go?"

"Yeah, you know, gaining weight, not fixing herself up anymore."

"Did she do that, Al?"

"Oh yeah." He snorted. "I bought her exercise videos, but she never seemed to appreciate them. She was only looking after two kids for God's sake. You'd think when they were napping she'd have exercised or done something with herself. But no, instead of trying to look good for me, she started that writing crap."

"So this *letting herself* go... you think that was a conscious choice?" An image of his sisters, his mother and grandmother and how tirelessly they cared for their loved ones came to mind. "Maybe she was too damn busy putting everyone else first to take time for herself."

The corners of Alan's mouth turned to a bitter grimace. "She never put *me* first."

"From what I've heard you weren't around enough for her to do that."

"No siree." He took a hearty swallow of his drink. "I found it much more gratifying to be in the office, where people appreciated how hard I worked and didn't just nag me to take out the trash or spend more time with the kids."

A thought that had been nagging at Derek practically

since he'd met Kelly leapt to mind. He leaned closer. "Tell me about the girls in the office, Al. I'm sure they looked better than what you had waiting at home."

Alan groaned. "Every summer the college interns would come in. God they had such hot little bodies. Why would I want to go home when I could stay in the office and stare at them?"

"Exactly," Derek reasoned. "And I'm sure they were more than willing to do whatever it took to get ahead."

Al's smile faded. "Not with me," he admitted. "I was only a supervisor back then. But I heard stories."

"So you never cheated on Kel?" he nudged him with an elbow. "C'mon, it's just us guys, you can tell me."

"No," he insisted. "I was always afraid I'd get caught. Not by my wife, but by the upper management. Sexual harassment. I wasn't about to risk my job."

"So you were just unfaithful in your mind, working late hours, drooling over women you could never have, while Kel was home wiping up baby puke and changing diapers?"

"That's pretty much it." He took another long swig of his drink. "Til Jenn came along and opened my eyes to what I was missing in bed." He set the glass down with a thunk. "But I've got to hand it to you, Boy Toy, you found Kelly at the right time. She hasn't looked this good in years."

"Really?"

"Yep. Just don't marry her, if you get what I'm saying. She'll get comfortable and the next thing you know..."

Derek had heard enough. "Al," he said with a sigh. "Stand up."

"Stand up?" he frowned. "What for?"

"Because I can't do this while you're sitting down."

He slid off the barstool "Do wh—?"

The feel of his fist connecting to Al's jaw was more satisfying than Derek had thought it would be. As he'd expected, the blond man collapsed in a dazed heap. He half hoped he'd get to his feet and come at him just so he could deck him again.

"What the hell was *that* for?" Al slurred.

"For Kelly. She should have done it years ago." He

pulled out his wallet and slapped a stack of bills on the bar. "Call him a cab and send him home."

Seventeen

Kelly had probably held her hopes too high for the shopping trip. It had gone well for the most part, with Maya being surprisingly helpful while she browsed shoes and dresses and the all important undergarments. Derek may have insisted he was capable of picking out the right dress, but she didn't trust him not to choose drop-dead red. Besides, a man who only dated models wouldn't know a thing about the type of undergarments that tucked, lifted and basically reversed the pull of gravity. And at her age, those were the kind she needed.

She ended up choosing a midnight blue gown with a touch of sequins on the straps. Understated and simple, it hugged her curves in all the right places. Now, standing on the dais outside the fitting room, studying it in the three-way mirror, she hoped she'd be able to hold her own against all those New York women in another few days.

Maya glanced up from entering a text into her cell phone. "Those sandals we looked at in Macy's—the strappy sliver ones—would look good with that."

"Would they?" Kelly asked, going up on tiptoe to see how the dress would look with heels. "Since when am I allowed to look good?"

"Whatever." Maya glanced at the cell phone, smiled, then thumbed the buttons again.

Kelly twisted her hair up and turned her head side to side, trying to decide if she'd have to wear her hair swept back or loose. "Who are you texting?"

"Huh? Oh just Heather."

The sales woman poked her head around the corner. "Oh, that looks *divine*."

Maya rolled her eyes.

"I wouldn't have chosen that color, Miss Michaels, but you were right. It's perfect for you, it darkens your eyes."

Kelly smoothed a hand down the front of the dress

and turned back toward the mirror.

The woman moved closer to finger the hem of the dress. "And with heels it will be just the right length."

"I'm still not sure," Kelly murmured. "Do you think it clings too much?"

"Spanx," she whispered discreetly.

"Sa—say that again?"

"Spanx undergarments. We sell them in the lingerie department. They are absolutely the best for camouflaging all those ...*little areas*. Wait here, I'll go find some."

When she had gone, Kelly stepped down off the dais and waited for her daughter to make a comment, but she seemed intent on the cell phone.

"You know, honey, after this, I probably won't see Derek much. Our schedules are going in different directions."

"You mean *his* schedule."

She arched a brow in her daughter's direction.

"*You* never go anywhere. Your schedule is always the same. He's the one in the tabloids with all those women."

Kelly didn't miss the censure in her daughter's voice. "I know you don't approve—"

"It's your life." She shrugged. "Do what you want. Or *who*."

"It's not like th—" She swallowed back the words. What *was* it like? Though Maya wasn't paying attention, mother-guilt nagged at her. Was she sending the message to her teenaged daughter that it was okay to have casual flings?

"From your point of view, I may appear to be the worst hypocrite in the world." She reached behind her to unfasten the dress. Emboldened by the fact that Maya had yet to interrupt, she continued. "But I meant what I said about the differences between forty-two and sixteen. I'm a grown woman, and what I choose to do and what you're *allowed* to do are—" A glance in the mirror showed her daughter hunched over the phone, busily pressing keys. "And if I want to date a purple-people eating monster from Mars, I'll do so."

"Cool, Mom. Whatever."

Kelly suppressed a sigh and made a mental note.

Next time she grounded her daughter, the damn phone was getting locked in a drawer.

****

She barely had time to put her purchases away before she heard a car pull in the driveway. But it wasn't the familiar hum of Derek's fancy sports car, and it was too early for Cody to be home from the ball game. Most likely it was Alan. And from the way he slammed the car door, she sensed the golf game had not gone well. She glanced out the window, surprised to see a taxi pulling away.

She descended the stairs, noting Maya sitting on the sofa, texting again, a dreamy smile on her face. What was it Cody had said this morning about a text from an ex-boyfriend? Surely she wasn't talking to—

"Oh...my...God."

"What?" Kelly followed her daughter's line of vision. For a split second she could only stare horrified while Alan gestured to the left side of his face. A bluish purple bruise was evident at the corner of one eye, the surrounding tissue so swollen, his eye was half-closed.

Maya leaped up from the sofa, the phone forgotten for once. "Daddy, what happened?"

"Your mother's idiot boyfriend."

"Derek did that?" Kelly clamped a hand over her mouth as possibilities raced through her mind. But none made sense. "What did you do to him?"

"Nothing," Alan grumbled, heading for the kitchen and pulling open the freezer door. He yanked a dishtowel off the stove handle and began to pile ice cubes into it.

"Daddy probably beat him at golf."

Alan folded the towel and lifted it to his eye, wincing.

"Well?" Kelly asked.

"It wasn't about the golf game. I said something he didn't like and he punched me."

She had never known Derek to be hot-tempered, in fact he seemed more in control of his emotions than anyone she knew. "What did you say to him?"

He pulled the towel away for a moment. "Just that I don't buy the two of you together."

"Don't *buy*? What on earth is that supposed to mean?"

"I can guess what you see in him. But what's a guy like that doing with you?"

A knot of anger unballed in her stomach. She'd been holding her tongue—her temper—for two days for the sake of the kids. No more. "Give me that." She yanked the towel away from him, uncaring that ice cubes scattered across the floor. "Why are you here?"

"I don't know." He shrugged. "Where else would I go?"

"Your mother's house."

"She's not home."

"Well, since you don't seem to know why you're here, I'll fill you in. You want to make trouble. It's what you do best, and you saw this as a prime opportunity." She moved closer, jabbing his chest with one finger. "You think I'll dump Derek and come running back to you out of guilt or obligation. Even pity."

"I never said—"

"Do you really want to know what he's doing with *me*?" Aware of their daughter in the next room, she leaned in closer. "Sex, Alan. Mind-melting, soul-scorching, unbelievably *hot* sex. Multiple orgasms so intense my brain feels like it's going to explode." When his mouth dropped open, she couldn't resist adding, "All. Night. Long."

His pale blue gaze flicked over her as though he'd never seen her before.

She folded her arms and stepped back. "Satisfied?"

"No," he murmured, side-stepping away. "But apparently *you* are."

"For the first time ever." With that, she turned away from him to see Maya standing in the kitchen doorway, looking horrified. Kelly swallowed, wondering just how much her daughter had overheard, but it was too late now. Add to that the fact that she had just defended a guy she wasn't really even dating. Or was she? They had never clarified that point.

Alan moved toward the refrigerator and tugged open the door. "I'm hungry. What's good to eat?"

"Try a restaurant." She pushed the door closed, leaving her hand on it for emphasis. "My days of feeding you are over."

"What's your problem?" he asked. "You don't need to get all touchy, I was just trying to look out for you."

She couldn't hold back a short bark of laughter. "Oh, that's a good one." She pointed to the shiner. "I guess Derek thinks *he's* looking out for me or he wouldn't have slugged you."

"I can't believe you're laughing," Maya piped up. "Look at Daddy's eye. How can you just take Derek's side?"

"I've known both of them long enough to know whose side I'm on."

"Daddy, can't you have him arrested for assault or something?"

"Probably." Alan replied. "I've already left a message with my attorney."

"Oh *please*," Kelly huffed. "Were there were any witnesses to this *alleged* assault?"

"Possibly," Alan hedged. "Maybe I'll just sue. My attorney will have to figure it out. But I'm guessing Boy Toy can afford it."

"You sleazy, opportunistic, worthless son of a—" She bit her lip, unable to complete the thought with her daughter standing there. "You don't really think this will make it to court?"

"No," Alan scoffed. "I assume he'll want to settle to avoid the publicity."

"You're despicable."

The familiar throaty purr of Derek's BMW reached Kelly's ears.

"Speaking of despicable," Maya muttered.

Kelly turned to her daughter. "Enough! Not another word out of you, young lady."

"Hand me the phone," Alan barked. "If he comes near me again, I'll have him arrested."

"Go home, and you won't have to worry about it." She moved to the front door, intent on telling Derek this wasn't a good time. She couldn't let him in with Alan and Maya acting like temperamental toddlers. She slipped out the front door just as Derek stepped out of his car.

She had no idea why, except perhaps to reassure him, but she quickly closed the distance between them and all but threw herself in his arms.

He wrapped his arms around her, lifting her off her feet. When he set her down, there was a question in his amused gaze. "I don't get greeted like this very often."

"That must have been some golf game. Did my ex get hit by a fly ball?"

Derek groaned and pressed his forehead to hers. "I can explain."

"You don't have to."

He frowned. "I don't?"

"He's been at you non-stop the last couple of days. I'm sure you'd had enough of the boy toy stuff."

He chuckled. "You think I hit him because of *that*?"

"Didn't you?"

"No." He took hold of her hand and they walked toward the house. "I think I'll let Al tell you why."

"Oh, he started to; he just hasn't figured out his story yet." Kelly opened the door and ushered him inside. Despite earlier thoughts about sending him away, now that he was here, she couldn't bring herself to do it. He was the only sane thing left to hold onto at the moment.

As Derek entered the kitchen, Alan backed up a few steps. "I want you to know I've called my attorney."

"I'm glad to hear it," Derek replied noncommittally.

"Next time those tabloid reporters show up, Dad, you should talk to them." Maya sneered. "Let them find out what The Model Man is really like."

Kelly flashed her daughter a warning look. "Maya, I told—"

"How can you stand to be near him after what he did to Daddy?"

"Go to your room, I'll be up to deal with you shortly."

"That's hardly fair," Alan argued. "She's just upset about Boy Toy taking his frustrations out on me."

"He doesn't belong here!" Maya screamed. "He's just messing everything up."

"Messing everything up? What are you talking about?" Surely she didn't think that because Alan was available again, they'd reconcile.

A ring sounded from Derek's pocket. He excused himself and stepped out onto the deck.

"When Derek comes back inside, Maya, you'll apologize."

"Not until he apologizes to Daddy."

"I'm sure your father had it coming."

Angry blue eyes welled with tears. "I can't even believe you said that, Mom." With that, she ran from the room, feet pounding up the stairs.

Kelly heaved a sigh, listening until the bedroom door closed with a wood-splintering bang. A movement outside caught her gaze as Derek paced across the deck. A frown creased his brow and he had one finger in his ear as if Maya and Alan's arguing had drowned out his conversation.

She stepped out onto the deck and slid the doors closed behind her.

"Gabby, just slow down and tell me what happened."

Derek glanced up at her, and she was shocked at the stricken expression on his face. "What hospital—St. John's?" He nodded, as if the answer was what he'd expected. "I'll be there as soon as I can, just sit tight—and keep me posted." He hung up the phone and turned to face her.

"What happened?"

"My grandfather's had a stroke."

"Oh, Derek."

"Gabby tried to book a flight for me, but the next plane to New York isn't until eleven o'clock tonight. I can get there faster if I drive."

"You can't drive when you're upset."

"I don't have much choice." He stepped closer, taking hold of her shoulders. "I don't know what's going to happen with the charity ball, Kel."

"Don't worry about that right now."

"I'd better get back to the hotel and pack up my things."

Kelly glanced inside the kitchen. Maya had come back downstairs, most likely because her tantrum hadn't gotten the expected attention. Though their voices were drowned out, she could see both her daughter and Alan; Maya on the phone—probably to Heather—gesturing wildly. Alan, on his cell, nodding and looking thoughtful. Most likely his attorney. Her stomach clenched at the thought of going back in there to face them.

"I'll call you as soon as I know anything." Derek

251

dropped a quick kiss to her forehead. "I'm sorry, Kel."

The sight of him heading toward the driveway had her feeling suddenly lost and alone. She glanced back in the kitchen once more, and her stomach clenched again. Her bag for New York was already packed and sitting in her bedroom.

"Wait!" she called, running after him. "I'll go with you."

****

Traveling the New York State Thruway at eighty-five miles an hour wasn't exactly Kelly's idea of safe. The sporty roadster, built for speed, held the road remarkably well. Despite the lighter traffic of the early evening hours, as Derek switched in and out of lanes, passing tractor trailers and slower moving vehicles, Kelly had to admit it; she was terrified. One of the lessons of motherhood that had surprised her was her sudden interest in her own well-being. It wasn't enough to know her children were safe and well, added to that was fear of her own mortality, lest her children ever be left without her. This experience didn't lessen that fear in the least.

She glanced over at Derek whose gaze was fixed ahead on the road, occasionally glancing toward the mirrors. Then over at her. His cell phone was cradled in her palm. Silent. She had yet to decide if that was good or bad.

After they first left Rochester, the phone rang several times. She had refused to allow him to talk on it while driving, citing the law as an excuse. But in reality she just didn't like the idea of him being distracted while driving at such a high speed. So she had fallen into the role of relaying information from his family to him.

But it had been more than an hour since the last call.

Recalling her father's heart attack from a few years back, when she'd been Christmas shopping with Sharon and the kids, she remembered how Sharon had kept her talking the entire way to the hospital. They had been at an outlet mall about forty-five minutes from the city and Sharon had talked her ear off the entire way, never giving her a chance to wander into "what if" territory. She was still grateful to her friend for that. Perhaps she could do the same for Derek.

"So you've always been close to your grandfather?" She phrased the statement as a question, even though it wasn't one.

He was quiet for several seconds, and she wondered if perhaps she had said the wrong thing.

"More so than with my father," he finally said, his voice low. "We seemed to have more in common. My dad was always working. Papa had handed over most of the family business—the pizza shop—to my dad by the time I came along. We spent a lot of time together, camping, fishing. Yankees games."

"What's he like?"

"Old and stubborn." Derek glanced over at her with a half smile. "He's had a hell of a life. He came here from Italy alone when he was just fourteen and worked his ass off to build a life for himself and provide for his family. I always wanted to make things easier on him. The minute I started making decent money, I offered to buy him a house."

"I'll bet he was thrilled."

"No, he liked his old one." He laughed, as though remembering the event. "He lived over the pizza shop. There are three apartments over it, my parents' place, my Aunt Ro, and my grandparents. He didn't see anything wrong with that. I ended up buying him a condo in Florida so he could spend winters where it was warm." His voice trailed off, and the clicking of the blinker filled the silence as he signaled for another lane change. Kelly held her breath and prayed, but she had to admit he was a skilled driver.

After successfully switching lanes, he glanced over at her. "Look, I know what you're trying to do, and I appreciate it."

"I'm just keeping you company."

"No, you're trying to keep me from thinking about why that phone isn't ringing."

"You know how slow hospitals are, I'm sure your family doesn't know anything more or they would have called." *Unless it's bad news.*

The look he gave her told her he thought the very same thing. She decided a change of subject was in order. "I'm sorry if I didn't give you a choice about my coming along." He hadn't said a word about it so far, and she had wondered more than once if she were really welcome.

His familiar deep chuckle washed over her. "The look on Al's face when you told him he'd have to take care of the kids the next few days was priceless."

She smiled. "Well, it won't hurt him to spend more time with them."

He reached between them to cover her hand with his. "It's fine, Kel. I was just hoping to have time to spend with you, show you around, try to impress you, that sort of thing. And now..." His thumb stroked over her knuckles, sending a flurry of shivers through her.

"I know."

She covered his hand with her other one, then held her breath as he changed lanes to pass a semi. She released his hand and nudged it toward the steering wheel.

"Maybe you should have both of them on the wheel."

****

A short time later, they reached New York. It had been years since Kelly had been there, and she found herself mesmerized by the changes in a skyline she'd only recently seen in photos.

A tinge of sadness struck her as she gazed at the changed skyline and remembered that terrible September day. She knew Derek had lost friends that day, but wondered if he had seen the terror unfold. He hadn't offered any more on the subject, and she supposed this would not be the best time to ask.

A short time later, they pulled into the parking garage of St. John's Hospital and began the task of trying to find his grandfather.

At last they reached the ICU. The minute the elevator doors opened, Kelly spied them. She'd never seen so many dark-haired, olive-skinned people talking over one another in her life. If it wasn't the Calavicci family, then it was an open casting call for another Godfather movie.

They all flocked around one woman in particular, who dabbed a handkerchief at her eyes, both laughing and crying. When she spoke, they all stopped to listen.

A strikingly beautiful dark-haired girl spied them

and broke from the group. "He can barely talk, but he's swearing at the nurses in Italian."

Kelly stepped back as the girl flung herself at Derek.

Derek's shoulders visibly relaxed. "He's all right then."

The girl sniffled as he hugged her close. "I was so scared."

By now, others had begun to move toward them. Derek was briefly lost amid a storm of hugs and kisses. A flurry of Italian and English followed with everyone talking at once. When Kelly was about to be swallowed up by the crowd, he grabbed hold of her wrist and dragged her to his side.

More than once the younger girl's assessing gaze came to rest on her with a knowing smile.

"You can see him in just a few minutes," an older woman said, her words directed at Derek. "He's been asking for you."

He gave Kelly's hand a gentle squeeze, then pulled his sister toward them. "Gabby, take care of Kelly for me until I get back."

She knew a brief moment of sheer panic when he walked away with his mother and grandmother, leaving her with this crowd of strangers. But Gabrielle wasn't really a stranger; they had talked on the phone before.

Gabrielle smiled at her like a cat with a mouthful of feathers. "Guys, this is Kelly,' she said to the group. "Derek's new girlfriend."

She was sure her face was about to burst into flames. Another girl a few years older than Gabrielle, and so heavily pregnant she could only waddle, stepped forward. "I'm Gina." And so it went until she had been introduced to every last one of them. There were too many to possibly remember all their names.

Someone mentioned needing coffee, another had to make a phone call, and soon it was just the two of them.

The younger girl giggled and took hold of both Kelly's hands, pulling her toward a grouping of chairs. "Alone at last. I want to know *everything.*'

****

Derek was exhausted by the time he emerged from his grandfather's hospital room. He'd spent the past hour talking to nurses, physicians and heart specialists.

His grandmother held tight to his arm as she made her way down the corridor. He had to adjust his steps to match hers, made slow by painfully arthritic knees. His mother and father were directly behind them.

His grandfather needed surgery to clear a blockage in a neck artery. He had a long road ahead for recovery and would need to make significant changes in his lifestyle, including his diet.

"That'll never happen," his mother said, echoing his own thoughts. "Did you understand what that doctor said?"

Derek glanced at her over his shoulder. "Ministrokes," he said. "Has Papa been acting confused lately?"

She reached his side and paused. "You know, the other day he told me he wanted a cup of macaroni when he meant coffee. I asked him about it, but he said he was just teasing. It did seem a little strange, now that I think about it."

"Bah," Nonna snorted. "Papa is old. Old people get confused."

His father came to stand beside them, hands in his pockets. "He said he was having trouble seeing."

"His eyes are fine," Nonna insisted.

"The surgery will keep him from having a full blown stroke," Derek added with a look at his grandmother.

"Lady doctors don't know nothing." She scoffed. "Papa is all right. Tell them I take him home now."

Seeing the watery eyes and slumped shoulders, Derek slipped an arm about her. "He's going to be okay. Don't worry, Nonna, I'll see that he has the best of everything."

She gave his arm a gentle squeeze. "You're a good boy." She gestured toward a nearby chair. "I need to sit."

Derek helped her into the chair. She rubbed her knees, a pained expression on her face.

"Can I get you anything?" he asked, kneeling down to her level. "A pill? Some new knees?"

She laughed and placed an affectionate hand to his cheek.

He noticed his father glance at his watch. "I have to go light the ovens soon."

Derek rolled his eyes. The phrase would haunt him to his grave. His father's entire life revolved around making sure the pizza ovens were lit at least two hours before the shop opened for business. "They don't even know when they'll get to Papa's surgery and all you can think about is work?"

His father shrugged. "I gotta light the ovens."

"You can't close for one day?"

"I close Christmas and Easter," his father replied in his thick Queens accent. "That's enough."

Still crouched down, he half turned toward his father. "What, you're open on Thanksgiving now?"

His mother nodded. "You'd be surprised how many people would rather forget the hassle and order a pizza."

"The real meaning of the day is about spending time with your family," his father added with emphasis. "If you were ever around, you'd know that."

Derek resisted the urge to laugh. "When the hell did you spend time with yours?"

"I'm busy taking care of them," his father snapped, his voice raising an octave with each word. "I don't have time to spend with them. And I don't have time to go off on fancy vacations like some people."

"All you ever cared about—" Derek stopped when his grandmother delivered a sharp rap to the side of his head.

"Don't disrespect your father," she said in Italian.

She gestured for his father to come closer, and when Rocco leaned in, she rapped him as well. "This is not the place."

His mother flashed Derek an angry look, then took hold of Nonna's arm. "Let's go sit in the waiting room."

Derek helped his grandmother to her feet. When she'd gone, he found his father looking at him almost apologetically.

"I'll send Gabrielle to open up today."

"Gabby's life shouldn't have to revolve around the pizza shop."

"I can't afford to close, I'll lose too much business."

"I'll pay you the difference."

"I don't want no money my son earned taking his clothes off." He jabbed an angry finger toward himself. "I take care of my own family."

Derek had heard that conversation too many times to count. Mindful of the attention they attracted with his father's booming, heavily-accented voice, he sighed. "All right, Pop. Let's just forget it for now."

Together, they stepped into the waiting room. Most of the family had gone home by now. His younger brother Anthony snored softly in a chair at one end of the room, and Gabrielle was sprawled on a sofa, sipping a cup of coffee and reading a novel. He barely recognized the blonde curled up on a two-seater sofa, head resting on her arm, sound asleep. And then he remembered.

A wave of tenderness washed over him at the sight of her. He had been certain having her here would be awkward, or that she'd get in the way. But right now he was ridiculously happy to see her, comforted in some small way by her presence.

Gabrielle held up the book and gave a triumphant smile. "She signed it for me."

Fully aware of the watchful gaze of his family, he strode across the room and knelt down beside Kelly. "Hey, sleepyhead," he said, stroking her cheek.

She stirred, then looked around in confusion. Her blue eyes focused on him, and she gave a sleepy smile.

"Let me get you home."

"You can't drive, you haven't had any rest," she protested, her voice sleep-slurred.

He chuckled. "*My* home. I need to stay here a while longer, but Gabby will take you. She has to light the ovens at the pizza shop anyway."

"The ovens?" Gabrielle groaned. Nonetheless, she swung her feet to the floor.

His mother leaned in to whisper something to her.

"It is *too* her." He heard Gabrielle whisper. He glanced up at his mother who held a book about eight inches from the end of her nose. She could barely see without her glasses, but she had the back cover open to compare Kelly with her picture.

"Is she the one who writes dirty books?" That from Nonna. In English.

He sighed. They would have a million questions for him later. It was rare for him to bring a woman around his family, and natural for them to be curious. But right now he wanted to shield her from the full-blown onslaught of the Calavicci's.

Pulling the still-sleepy Kelly along by her hand, he approached his mother. He pulled the book from her hand and dropped a kiss to her cheek. "Yes, it's her. Gabrielle's taking her home now, but you can to talk to her later." He glanced at Kelly. "She's read all your books. Twice."

"Three times," his mother added, beaming.

Kelly brightened at that and was about to say something. He gave her hand a deliberate tug. "If I let her get started, she'll ask you about every single book."

"I don't mind."

He smiled, but nonetheless dragged her toward the elevators. "I'm sure you don't. But you have a deadline looming, and I know damn well you haven't had time to write lately."

She glanced back toward his family and as the doors opened, he stepped on and pulled her with him.

As the doors closed, she turned to face him. "Exactly where am I going to find peace and solitude so I can write?

"You brought your lap top, right?"

"Yes."

"Then you'll go to my place."

"*Your* place?"

"My place," he repeated, slipping a finger beneath her chin. He leaned closer, his lips hovering over hers. "The thought of you there waiting for me will probably—"

The car lurched to a stop and the doors slid open again.

"Sorry to interrupt, but you forgot me," Gabrielle announced. Barely containing a grin, she stepped inside, coffee cup in hand.

"Your boyfriend isn't at my place, is he?" Derek asked.

Gabby checked her watch. "No. He'd better be home getting ready for a photo shoot. Frankie set it up for him."

"Your boyfriend is a model?" Kelly asked.

"No, her boyfriend is Mr. Enchantment." Derek leaned his head against the elevator wall, remembering the way Jared had gone through women at the conference.

"Jared? But he's so..." Kelly glanced from him to

Gabby and back again. "So... *friendly.*"

"She knows." Derek said as the elevator lurched to a stop. "But he's changed his ways. Or, so he says."

Gabby nailed him with an elbow to the ribs as they stepped off the elevator. "Yeah, there's a lot of that going around."

As they descended to the parking garage, Derek was conscious of his sister's amused gaze moving from him to Kelly. He wondered what sort of questions she had pummeled her with while he was with his grandmother. Probably nothing half as bad as what she'd ask once she had Kelly alone.

The elevator slid to a halt and they stepped into the garage.

Gabrielle held out her hand. "Gimme your keys."

"You're not taking my car, Piglet."

"It was a long shot, but I thought I'd try."

They reached his sister's red Toyota and she deactivated the alarm, the sound echoing in the nearly empty garage.

She made no attempt to get in.

"Well?" he asked.

"Oh, did you want privacy?" She flashed a smile at Kelly. "This must be serious."

He opened the car door and gave his sister a nudge. Giggling, she climbed in. Derek closed the door and leaned against it to block her view.

Kelly stepped closer and he slid his arms about her waist. "Are you all right?"

"What about you?"

"I'll be better when I have more information. Look, I know this is awkward and I'm sorry. But at least you'll have some peace and quiet."

"It's okay. Really."

He took her face between his hands and kissed her. The faint scent of her lavender shampoo reminded him of the bath they'd shared the other night. Pulling back from the kiss, he pressed his forehead to hers. "I'll come home as soon as he's out of surgery."

The car window slowly moved down. "You about finished, or what?"

He walked Kelly around to the passenger side.

Opening the door, he stuck his head inside. "Say anything stupid, and I'll tell Mama everything I know." he warned in a low voice.

She grinned at him, green eyes dancing. "Threaten me again, and I'll tell Mama everything *I* know."

A moment later, the Toyota pulled away. Truth was, she was better off with Gabrielle than anyone else, their personalities were more suited. But he winced, wondering just what embarrassing tidbits his little sister would choose to share with Kelly.

Alone in the car with the stunning Gabrielle, Kelly straightened. As they pulled into the daylight, she felt herself become more alert.

"So how are things going between you guys?"

Kelly slid a glance toward the younger girl. So far Gabrielle had asked her about everything except the actual state of their relationship.

"We're just friends." The words were beginning to ring false even to her own ears.

The brunette snorted. "My brother doesn't know how to be friends with women." She paused for a red light and glanced at Kelly. "The way he looks at you doesn't say 'friend' to me."

"Well, it's new yet." Kelly hedged.

Gabrielle nodded, as if deciding something for herself. "He kept touching you, as if he was afraid you'd disappear. And you should have seen the look on his face when he came out and saw you asleep in the waiting room."

Heat crept over Kelly's cheeks. Gabrielle seemed to sense her sudden discomfort and changed the subject. There was a slight lurch as the car moved forward again. "You guys hooked up at the convention, right?"

"Yes."

"And he made a beeline for you, didn't he? Probably said something crude that some convention slut would have fallen for—only it didn't work on you. How am I doing so far?"

"He told you?"

"Nah. I just know him. And I can tell with one look that you're not a *puttana*. Besides, I know what he acts like when he's in conference mode. I used to go with him.

I'm his personal assistant, you know."

"I'll bet Frankie loves that."

"Hmph. That red-headed witch. She hates me."

"I think she hates everybody." Kelly laughed, remembering her own encounters with the woman. "Were you there this year?"

Gabrielle tipped back her coffee cup and shook her head. "No. You know how they have those Mr. Enchantment contests every year where they pick the next cover model?"

Kelly nodded.

"Well, last year he caught me coming out of one of the contestant's rooms at five in the morning. He couldn't really say anything because it wasn't like he'd been sleeping in his own bed—" She stopped speaking and winced. "I'm sorry. Anyway, he says he'll never take me to another conference." She whipped the car around a corner so fast Kelly had to grab hold of the armrest. "Never mind that the guy he caught me with is now my boyfriend— Jared—and we're sort of engaged."

"You are? Derek didn't tell me that. Congratulations."

"Yeah, he's got that selective memory thing." The girl laughed. "Anyway, the point I was trying to make is I always thought Derek sort of had a crush on you."

"On *me*?"

"Uh huh. I only went to a couple of conferences, but he always used to check to see if you were there."

"He's been posing for my books for a long time. I'm sure that's all it was."

Gabrielle laughed. "Or maybe because you're gorgeous."

Alan's taunt echoed in her ears. *What's a guy like that doing with you*? "I know some people who would beg to differ."

****

A short time later, after a very long elevator ride— Kelly tried very hard not to count just how many floors— they arrived at Derek's apartment.

She wasn't sure what she'd been expecting, or why the thought of seeing where he lived made her so nervous. Tasteful yet contemporary, understated but elegant. The walls and color scheme were a perfect blend of pewter, navy and black, the furniture dark, masculine but tasteful. It looked like something straight out of architectural digest.

What drew her gaze, however, were the knee-to-ceiling windows that took up two walls.

"Wow," was all she could say.

Gabrielle giggled. "Easily impressed, huh?"

Kelly made her way over to the windows and gazed out. "It's incredible. I've never seen anything quite like this." She turned to glance over her shoulder. "Where were the..."

"Twin towers?" Gabrielle stepped up beside her and pointed. "There. You can't see Ground Zero too well during the day time. At night, there are stadium lights that light up the whole thing. It's kind of creepy."

"My God, was he here when the towers were hit?"

The other girl nodded somberly. "He had just moved in a few weeks before. He practically had a front row seat. He won't talk about it, though." At that, Gabrielle turned. "He saw the stuff they didn't show on TV, if you know what I mean. I don't think he slept for weeks afterward." She shrugged. "Just like everyone else, I guess."

Kelly followed her back into the living room. Guilt stabbed at her, an emotion she didn't quite understand. It had happened off and on since the terrorist attacks. Every time she heard about it she felt almost ashamed. She lived in New York State herself, but she hadn't lost anyone. Her day to day life hadn't been terribly affected. Not like these people.

Gabrielle picked up a blanket and absently folded it over her arm. "My sister Gina was supposed to have an interview that morning with one of the brokerage houses in the North tower on the ninety-something floor. They had just postponed it till the afternoon. Can you imagine?"

Kelly could only shake her head.

"Come on, let me show you around. This, obviously, is the living room. It's all nice and neat like this because he's never home. And he has a cleaning lady who comes in twice a week." She paused and gazed at Kelly meaningfully. "Just to clean. Nothing else."

She stepped into the kitchen and pointed to the stainless refrigerator. "That? Empty. Always. Bottled water, the occasional bottle of wine or beer, but that's it. I stay here a lot when he's gone, Jared and I like to have what time alone together we can. Anyway, Ma knew he was coming home soon so there's actually food in the fridge, she sent a bunch of stuff over from the shop yesterday."

She nodded toward a huge contraption that vaguely resembled a coffee maker. "I don't know how that thing works. There's a real coffee maker in the cupboard beneath it."

Back out in the living area, Kelly's gaze was again drawn to the window. Gabrielle's earlier words about Derek seeing the terrorist acts unfold returned to haunt her.

She sensed the younger girl watching her. "I'm sorry. I just can't imagine Derek being here and having such a bird's eye view of what happened that day." She felt herself flush. "You must think I'm so insensitive."

Gabrielle waved a dismissive hand. "Everyone asks about the towers."

"I'm sorry. I know you lost your brother-in-law."

"Yeah," she said, her voice husky. "Mike was a great guy. Derek's best friend. But when it happened—when that tower fell—we knew he'd be inside. He was that kind of guy, he'd have been in there trying to get people out."

"Your poor sister."

"Yeah, they'd been together since high school, married right after. My niece, Brittany, hurried that along a little, if you know what I mean." She laughed. "But Bianca had four kids who had just lost their dad, and she was determined to stay strong for them. She was really brave through the whole thing."

"I can't imagine finding the strength to do that."

"Well, like I said, we knew he wasn't coming home. Bianca says the second that tower fell she felt Mike's spirit leave her. She knew he was gone. They found bone fragments a few weeks later and identified him."

"I'm so sorry."

Gabby sniffled. "Hey, everyone who lives or works in Manhattan lost someone that day, we're no different. My mom's church lost a hundred people from their parish alone. And Mike would have been the first one to say it was his job and he wouldn't have done it any different."

Kelly glanced behind her at the scene outside the window once again. "It can't be healthy for Derek to still live here after witnessing that."

"Try telling *him* that. I know he had trouble sleeping for weeks afterward—we all did—and as far as I know he still has nightmares about it from time to time. But you can't get the stubborn jerk to admit it."

"Sounds about like Derek."

Gabrielle placed her hands on her hips. "Well, I just depressed myself, how about you?"

Kelly laughed. "I think so."

"Come on, let's get you settled."

Kelly could see the girl was exhausted. "Why don't you go on ahead? I'm fine here."

"I will," Gabrielle promised, "but first I want to make sure you have everything you need."

"I'm fine," Kelly insisted. "A place to set up my lap top is all I really need."

"Well, you can sit over there," she gestured to the glass table in front of the windows. "Or you can use his office."

Knowing she'd be distracted by the skyline, Kelly opted for the office. Gabrielle showed her the way, and while Kelly searched for a place to plug in the battery so it could recharge, Gabrielle left the room.

After finding an available outlet, Kelly followed the direction the girl had gone. And stopped short. Derek's bedroom. She was in Derek's bedroom. She closed her eyes, pulling in the familiar scent of his cologne.

She opened her eyes again as Gabrielle re-emerged from a walk in closet holding an armful of sheets.

She set down the pile of bedding. "You okay?"

"It just...smells like him." Kelly explained sheepishly.

"Yeah, I suppose so."

Kelly quickly glanced around the room. The same color scheme, the same masculine furniture. And the bed. "For some reason, I thought it would be bigger."

Gabrielle laughed. "Yeah, I guess with his reputation

you'd expect that. But it's just a king." She whipped the blankets and pillows from the bed and began tugging off the sheets. "Personally, I prefer something smaller. More reason to cuddle up close, you know?"

Kelly bent to help her. "What are you doing, anyway?"

"Well," she grunted as she reached across the bed to untuck a corner. "I guess the maid changed these the other day, but you never know. Like I said, Jared and I sleep here a lot, and we don't always use the guest bedroom." She favored Kelly with a wicked smile reminiscent of her brother. "I'm sure you two will want clean sheets tonight."

Eighteen

In the waiting area off the ICU at the hospital, Derek listened to his family's incessant chatter. Their small talk had gone on like this for hours. He had managed a five-minute conversation with his father about the weather a short time ago. That was the most they had said to one another since arguing this morning

He glanced across from him to where Paul, his older brother, sat beside their father, reading the sports section of the newspaper.

For a moment, he studied his brother. Some ten years older than Derek, it often seemed as if he and Paul were strangers. He had left for college before Derek was even out of grammar school and had married young. He could barely recall the time they had lived under the same roof.

Paul was the only one who really looked like their father, short, stout, his dark hair receding a bit more each time Derek saw him. His older brother was also his father's favorite. It had never been spoken out loud, of course, but Paul had done everything "right." Marriage, family, career. All of it respectable.

Despite Derek's financial success, his profession was an embarrassment to the family.

He glanced toward his mother and grandmother. Nonna's face was pale and tired. She faithfully went to his grandfather's bedside every other hour as was allowed, but each time, the visit seemed to take more out of her.

She looked up at the clock, then tried to rise from her chair. Derek moved to assist her. "You come with me this time," she said, patting his hand. "Maybe Papa will be awake."

He nodded and helped her make her way to his grandfather's room.

Though he'd been in to visit before, he continued to be struck by how small and pale his grandfather looked in that bed. And how old. A slight panic seized him. What if Papa didn't pull through this? He'd always thought him invincible, capable of anything. Right now he looked feeble, vulnerable. Frail.

The minute Nonna sat in the bedside chair, she began to sob. Derek supposed that was the last thing Papa needed just now. He forced his own worries aside and leaned over to take his grandfather's hand.

"Papa," he said. "*È me, il vostro nipote favorito.*" Reminding his grandfather he was his favorite grandson always got a laugh out of him. Never a denial.

His grandfather's eyelids fluttered for only a moment.

"Papa, are you awake?"

The nurse in the room smiled in understanding. "The medication is keeping him drowsy, but he can still hear you."

A moment later, the doctor entered the room. Nonna burst into tears anew. "They're going to take my Angelo to surgery now."

Derek knelt at her side. "Dr. Burke is just here to check Papa. They can't do the surgery until they have a room available."

The doctor smiled politely. "We hope to have something ready soon."

Nonna glared at the woman, then back to Derek. "Don't they have any men doctors here?" she asked in Italian.

He patted her hand and hoped the doctor didn't understand Italian.

"Is there anyone who can help take care of your husband when he comes home, Mrs. Calavicci?" Dr. Burke asked.

Nonna shook her head firmly. "I take care of him."

Derek squeezed her hand. "Nonna, you're in no condition. You can hardly walk as it is."

"Is there another family member?" Dr. Burke asked. "Someone who can come by now and then?"

"What about a private duty nurse?" Derek asked. "Someone who could be there twenty four hours a day?"

"I can get you the name of some agencies." Dr. Burke offered.

"How much will that cost?" Nonna asked, her voice breaking. She turned to Derek, fright and exhaustion evident on her face.

He slipped his arm about her shoulders. "I'll take care of it."

She sobbed and leaned into his chest. "You do too much already."

Derek patted her while she cried. He couldn't think of much to say other than to assure her everything would be all right. He only hoped it was true.

A slurred sound came from his grandfather. Nonna stopped crying long enough to look over at her husband. "Angelo?"

He motioned for Derek to come closer. With great care, he spoke again, carefully enunciating every syllable. "Get her the hell out of here."

****

"Raven, my love, promise we'll never be apart again."

"Nothing and no one will ever separate us, Thorne. I love you. Only you. "

"The end." Kelly said aloud, feeling a surge of pride and satisfaction. Derek had been right about the peace and quiet. And there was more than enough of that here.

Feeling proud of her accomplishment, and perhaps a little lonely, she picked up her cell phone and pressed number three on the speed dial.

"Hey!" Sharon's excited voice came on after only one ring. "I've been wondering what's going on with you."

Kelly laughed and leaned back in the black leather chair in Derek's office. "You were?"

"Mmm. I stopped over last night on my way home from spinning class."

"Oh," Kelly thumped the heel of her hand to her forehead. "I forgot about class."

"Well, your ex was fit to be tied."

"Was he?"

"He said you and Boy Toy took off and left him alone to tend the kids."

"Tend the kids," Kelly snorted. "It's called being a parent."

Sharon joined in her laughter. Kelly filled her friend in on what had been going on with Derek—blushing as

Sharon pulled every last lurid detail out of her.

"I'm proud of you, Kel."

"Why because I've completely shirked my responsibilities as a mother and messed up my kids?"

"You have not. For the first time in twenty years you're doing something for yourself. Your kids are old enough to understand. Don't let Maya guilt you into feeling bad about having a little fun."

"But the look on her face when I turned around from telling Alan how great the sex with Derek was—" Kelly shook her head, recalling the event.

"I'd have loved to have seen Alan's face after *that*," Sharon cackled. "Look, sooner or later Maya was going to find out her mom had sex at least twice, right? And she knows you write about it, has probably sneaked a peek at some of your books."

"Yes, but to hear me say it like that...I'm just worried what she'll do to retaliate."

"Well thank goodness Trevor is in Virginia then."

Kelly sighed. "Yes, that was my thought, too."

"And by the time she finds another guy she likes that well, you and Derek will have gone your separate ways and she'll have forgotten what she was so worked up about."

Kelly brought a fingernail to her mouth and nibbled thoughtfully. "I guess so."

"Uh oh. Do I hear a red alert? Tell me you didn't go and fall for him."

"I didn't intend to. I guess I couldn't help myself."

"Does Derek know how you feel? I mean, you didn't shout out 'I love you' in the middle of an orgasm did you?"

"No. In fact I think we're both reluctant to even discuss why we're still carrying on this pretense when we both know it stopped being a pretense a while ago."

"So you don't know if he feels the same?"

"Oh, Shar, how could he? He even told me he's going to L.A. for a month. Does that sound like a guy who's interested in seeing me again?"

"Well he has to travel for work, and he probably knows you can't just pack up and go with him."

"Right. Which means there's no point in carrying this thing on any longer."

"I'm sorry, girlfriend. I feel like I talked you into doing this and now you're hurting."

"I've been through worse, I'll get over it."

"I know you will. But maybe if he feels the same—"

"That's not likely."

"You don't know that."

Yes I do. "Do me a favor though and check on Maya and Cody, please? As often as you can?"

Sharon's wicked laugh came over the line. "Oh I intend to check all right, if only to see how bad Alan's falling apart."

****

Unaccustomed to so much quiet and solitude, Kelly began to pace the apartment restlessly. The afternoon wore on and though Derek had called once to let her know his grandfather was headed into surgery, she hadn't heard anything since. She paused to study the modern art that graced the walls of the too-perfect penthouse apartment. The art had probably been expensive, but no matter how long she studied it, she failed to find any meaning to it. And there was certainly nothing around to give an observer any insight into the man who lived here.

Of course, Gabrielle had said he was seldom here, so perhaps that's why it felt so impersonal.

Moving on, she once again found herself in Derek's bedroom. The smell of him lingered there, but was most intense in his closet. Now here, at last, was a peek at the real Derek, she decided, stepping into the walk-in closet that was easily the size of her kitchen. Clothes separated by type and color, hung neatly. Designer shirts and slacks were on one side, jeans, T-shirts and more casual wear on the other. Row after row of expensive looking shoes were sorted by color and type as well. The essence of him was nearly overpowering in this room, not just the scent, but the feel of him.

Stepping closer to a row of designer shirts, she pressed her face against them and breathed in. Her nipples tingled in appreciation at the familiar smell and she groaned

Her cellphone vibrated in her pocket a half second before it rang and startled her. The caller ID read "Derek." The thought of talking to him from his closet where she'd been dreaming of him, fantasizing about him, left her a little breathless. "Hello?"

"Hello, Kelly?"

The voice was female, slightly deep but friendly. "It's Ellen Calavicci. Derek's mom."

Kelly's heart lurched. Was she calling with bad news? But she sounded so happy. "Mrs. Calavicci," she said, wondering exactly how one addressed the mother of the guy you were sleeping with. "How—how are you?"

"Please, call me Ellen.

"O—okay. Ellen."

"Did I wake you, hon?"

"No, not at all." *I was just in the closet, sniffing your son's clothing.*

"Good."

"Everything all right?"

"Fine. Pop is out of surgery, he's in recovery now. Derek and Nonna just went down to see him. Hon' I wanted to make sure you knew you were invited to dinner tonight."

"Dinner?"

"The whole family will be there. I mean the *whole* family." Her throaty laugh reminded Kelly briefly of Derek. "Aunts, uncles, cousins—everyone."

"Uh… thank you. That's very kind."

"Well I know Derek won't mention it, he said the two of you had plans."

We do? "Um, no, not that I know of."

"We'll be eating around seven thirty. The girls are at my place getting things ready right now." Another laugh. "So you come on over and get something to eat. Okay?"

"O—okay." The conversation ended then and Kelly frowned at the phone. Weren't Italian mothers supposed to hate their son's girlfriends? And why hadn't Derek told her she was invited to dinner? Did he not want to introduce her to his family? Of course he didn't, their affair would be over in another day, so why bother?

****

Taking a shower didn't invigorate so much as it made her sleepy. Even after two cups of coffee, she was still exhausted. Little wonder after all the lost sleep of the past few days. But she had freshened up and changed into more appropriate attire for dinner with Derek's family. If they went.

In the living room, she sank down onto the leather sofa, the jet black material cool and butter soft to the touch. She glanced at the remote. She recalled Gabrielle showing her how the TV popped up out of what looked like a hutch on the opposite side of the room, but she couldn't remember how it worked. She was too tired to watch television anyway.

The sofa was angled in a way that took advantage of the spectacular view of New York, so she settled for staring out the windows. She yawned and put her head down on the armrest—just for a second—and pulled her feet up, tucking her skirt over her legs.

What seemed like only seconds later, she felt a gentle touch on her forearm. She opened her eyes to find Derek, kneeling down beside the sofa, smiling at her. "We have to stop meeting like this."

The bright sunlight that had lit the room earlier was considerably dimmer now.

"What time is it?" she asked, sitting up. A blanket had been draped over her and she frowned. "Are you just coming in?"

"No, I've been here a while. I had time to shower and change—I understand we have a family dinner to attend tonight."

She put a hand to her cheek, wondering how long she'd been out. "How is your grandfather?"

"He'll be in the ICU another day or two, but he's stable."

"And you? How are you?"

"I'm okay."

She didn't like the hesitation she heard in his voice. "Did you get to see him?"

"Yeah." He rose and moved across the room. A pack of cigarettes sat on the counter and he tapped one from the pack and lit it.

"And?" she prompted, wrinkling her nose as the smell of burning tobacco reached her. She hadn't seen him smoke in days, had almost forgotten that he did.

"It didn't look like him, all those tubes and wires. I know he hates lying there helpless like that." He took a deep drag, and she wondered if it was intended to hide the husky tone his voice had taken. "All I could think about was when I was a little kid, how he used to swing me up onto those big shoulders of his, and how small—"

Kelly rose from the sofa. She wanted to cross the room, take him in her arms, comfort him. But she had no idea how he would react. Most men wanted to be alone to brood when they were upset. Alan always had. "But the doctors think he'll be all right?"

He nodded. "He came through surgery like a champ. The nurse said his vital signs were excellent."

"You must be exhausted."

"Maybe a little, but my family does that to you. Did you write?"

"Derek, don't change the subject."

"I'm not changing anything." There was a sharp edge to his voice. He stamped the cigarette out in nearby ashtray.

For a split second she worried she was intruding on him, but when she didn't respond, he looked up at her. The raw need on his face was all the encouragement she needed. She was across the room in two strides. Reaching up, she placed a hand to his cheek. "Derek," she whispered.

In an instant, he crushed her to him. His lips met hers with a ferocity that rivaled her own. Hot. Hard. Urgent.

A full day of wanting him, longing for him, was pent up in her. She let it out in that kiss, clung to him with the same intensity, pouring out her need for him.

He tugged her sweater and bra up in one motion. She moaned when he cupped and caressed her, then slid the material up to her neck. He bent his head, taking one aching, throbbing nipple in his mouth, his other hand sliding over her buttocks to hoist her against him. Over and over his hot tongue circled her nipple, lips tugging until she moaned and her knees nearly buckled—would have if she hadn't been clinging to him.

His hair, damp and air-conditioning chilled, brushed her skin. The soapy clean scent of him surrounded her, filled her senses until there was nothing left but him.

Her hands began to explore, fingers kneading the

muscles of his back, sliding down the smooth material of his designer shirt until her fingertips grazed his belt, then lower, caressing his firm buttocks, marveling at the tight muscle. He groaned low in his throat and pulled away from her breast long enough to look at her. His eyes were heavy-lidded with passion and she could do nothing more than stare back at him, knowing her own need was reflected in her gaze.

Heat whispered through her. She wanted this feeling to last forever, yet she wanted him inside her. *Now.*

"Jesus, Kel."

Derek scooped her off the floor and headed toward the bedroom, shouldering the door open. He eased her halfway onto the bed, pausing to yank the sweater over her head and toss it aside. He unfastened only two buttons before pulling his shirt up and off. She leaned up, skimming her nails over his taut abdomen, but then lay back as he unbuckled his belt and slacks. In an instant the full erect length of him was freed and he was pressing her into the mattress, hands pulling her skirt to her hips, tugging at her panties.

Bracing himself over her, he paused, gazing down at her. She realized it was to give her a chance to protest if she wasn't ready, but in that instant, wanting to offer him comfort the only way she could, wanting to hold him, she knew. Knew without a doubt that she loved him.

Unable to voice the words, she wrapped her legs high around his waist. "Derek," she breathed, her nails grazing his bare, muscled buttocks.

He entered her with a long, deep thrust. With a mind of their own, her hips moved with him, seeking fulfillment. At his next thrust, she locked her ankles about his back and held him there, unwilling to lose him even for a moment. He slid his hands beneath her buttocks and lifted her. Her cry echoed between them. He rocked his hips against hers, moving with painstaking slowness. Again and again he teased her, rocking, thrusting, stroking until she spiraled over the edge, clinging to him as climax shattered her, followed almost immediately by another. His primal moans mingled with her cries until at long last, the spasms wracking her slowed and stopped.

For a moment his full weight sagged against her, as if she had drained him of every last bit of strength. But then he raised himself up and gazed down at her.

"God, I love making love with you."

Her heart leaped for one joyous second, then plummeted. "I ... me too," she whispered. It wouldn't have mattered if he'd said it anyway, she reasoned, there was no future in their relationship. A tear slid from the corner of one eye.

"Hey," he said, finger stroking her cheek. "Are those tears?"

She forced a laugh. "You know I cry a lot after... well, *after*."

He rolled to one side of her, propping his head up on his hand. "Don't scare me like that. I thought I'd been too rough with you."

"No, it was..." *probably the most beautiful moment of my life.* "Amazing." To her horror, her stomach chose that moment to loudly proclaim how empty it was.

He laughed and pressed a kiss to her belly. "I had planned to just stay in tonight and eat Chinese take out with you." He trailed a finger from her stomach up over one breast, circling her areola and nipple. "Naked. In my bed." He rose to a sitting position and dropped a kiss to her lips. "But apparently I'm not the only one who can't say 'no' to my mother."

"I'm sorry. I didn't know what to say—she sounded so sincere."

"Oh, she's plenty sincere," he laughed. "She'll have you so stuffed full of food you won't be able to move for a week."

"Then I guess we can't disappoint her."

****

A root canal without novocaine. Major surgery sans anesthesia. Sex with a close relative. Any of those would have been preferable to allowing Kelly a glimpse of his old world family.

So far so good, though, Derek mused.

She'd actually claimed to enjoy—enjoy!—the subway ride into Queens. And had declared the tired-looking building he'd grown up in—the same one his family still lived and worked in, "charming." Stepping inside, the smells of oregano and garlic filling the air, she'd inhaled deeply and said "Mmmm."

His father, along with several nephews and nieces were working the pizza shop tonight; he'd introduced her to all of them. He'd seen the puzzled look on his father's face when he'd introduced him to Kelly, but his smile was genuine.

After introducing her to Ben, Bianca's oldest son, Kelly had asked if the boy had a girlfriend and pointed out that if Maya were to meet Ben, she'd quickly forget about Trevor. Derek promised to arrange an introduction, then took her up the stairs that led to his parents apartment.

They'd entered a room nearly wall to wall with relatives

Gabrielle had greeted her like a long lost friend, hugging her warmly and then taking hold of her hand and going around introducing her as "Derek's girlfriend." He was growing used to the title, but wished to hell he knew what Kelly thought of it.

His feelings had almost slipped out tonight, making love to her. It wasn't enough that the thought of her, waiting for him at home, had tormented him the entire day. But seeing her when he returned made him realize how exhausted he was, how much he wanted to be in her arms.

Now, as dinner was served in a haphazard manner—hell, there were people out in the hall eating—he wondered what she thought of them. She probably couldn't wait to get away.

They hadn't had a chance to sit together to eat, and he observed her from where he stood in the kitchen doorway, holding his plate. But it wasn't hard to spot her, pale blonde in a room full of mostly dark-haired people. She sat on a folding chair, chatting with his sister, Gina. He suspected it was pregnancy stuff from the way Kelly nodded sympathetically when Gina held up an elephant-sized ankle.

As he watched, his two-year-old niece slid off what was left of Gina's lap and reached pudgy arms up to Kelly. She looked surprised, but then set her plate aside and scooped the little girl up, kissing her cheek as if it were the most natural thing in the world, then cradled her on her lap.

The sight of that dark-haired Italian baby on Kelly's lap hit him like a bolt of lightning. He'd never wanted kids—had never even thought about having them, too damn many years taking care of younger siblings and after that, the offspring of older siblings had been enough for him.

"Your mouth's hanging open," Bianca said, coming up beside him. "You look like a codfish." She turned her head to follow his line of vision.

"I just realized I'm totally screwed."

"If Nonna hears you talking like that, she'll come after you with her wooden spoon."

Derek forced a smile at her gentle teasing, but a heaviness had settled around his heart. "Nothing like realizing you're in love and knowing she doesn't feel the same."

"What? You know better than to talk like that, every woman in her right mind wants you."

Derek set his plate aside. Bianca linked her arm through his. "Come on, let's go outside and you can show me what fancy set of wheels you drove here tonight, Mr. Big Shot."

"I didn't drive, we took the subway."

"What for?"

"Kel wanted the New York experience."

Bianca rolled her eyes. "What, she wants to get mugged, too?"

Downstairs, Bianca stopped in the pizza shop to check on her kids while Derek waited outside. When she came out, she carried two cups of Italian ice with her, and he could hear their father calling after her. "You gonna pay for that?"

"Dante's payin' for it, Pop," she called back, favoring her brother with a smile.

Then she adopted a stern face and mouthed, almost word for word with Rocco as he roared, "I don't want no money my son earned taking his clothes off."

"So I guess that means these are on the house," she laughed handing one to Derek.

They sat at one of the patio tables outside the pizza

shop, eating in silence for a few minutes as patrons and other people strolled by. Derek caught a few curious stares directed his way, but no one bothered him.

"So what's this nonsense about that woman not being in love with you?" Bianca asked around a mouthful of the frozen treat.

"It doesn't matter."

"Come on, other than that bleached-out toothpick with the double D's you brought around a few years ago, you haven't brought a girl home since Mary Kate Moriarity in tenth grade."

"Jesus, how do you remember that?"

"I remember everything." She shrugged. "So you want me to believe she's not in love with you? She's here isn't she? Putting up with your family, accepting us—you think she's doing it for any other reason but to be with you?"

"Hunger, perhaps?" Derek offered, poking at the lemon concoction in his cup with a wooden spoon, grinning when she rolled her eyes. "Don't tell me Gabrielle didn't fill you in already."

"Gabby's been busy, I don't know where she's been lately, but it hasn't been with me."

"Yeah, that's another story," he grumbled. He sighed, then told Bianca the whole thing—well, the PG version anyway.

When he finished, she stared at him thoughtfully while sucking the end of the wooden spoon. "So you've just been hanging around, pretending to be her boyfriend so she won't look bad in front of her kids and her ex?"

"Basically, yeah."

"And she hasn't complained or asked you to leave?"

"No, but... well, considering how good we are together—Jesus, I can't say this to my sister."

"Are you blushing?" She laughed so loud passersby turned their heads. "Okay, so she's keeping you around because the sex is good."

He tossed his empty cup into a nearby wastebasket and leaned back.

"Wrong." Bianca said. "No woman is gonna keep a guy around just for sex when her family life is in turmoil, unless her feelings go way deeper. Sounds like she wants you around."

"Her daughter doesn't, and that's the deal breaker."

"How so?"

"Remember when you first started dating Steve, the way Brittany acted?"

"Remember? Please, she's still doing it and we're married now."

"Well, this girl makes Brit look like a rank amateur in comparison. She knows what buttons to push, when to push them and how hard. And she can turn on the tears like a light switch."

"*Ouch.*"

"Yeah, ouch. If things keep on like this, Kel's either going to have to break it off with me or face a nervous breakdown."

"I can so relate to that," she said. "But I can't just walk up to her and say, hey, I hear your teenager is an even bigger pain in the ass than my teenager."

"No."

"But I wish I could talk to her. I mean Steve and I went through hell, but after a while Brittany realized her attitude wasn't going to change things. She backed off a little."

"Kelly and I don't have that kind of time. I'm leaving for L.A. in two days. I'll be gone until mid-August."

"Jeez." Bianca looked thoughtful while she scraped the last of the ice from her cup. "Well, I wouldn't let it stop me, Dante. You can still tell her how you feel, maybe you guys can work something out."

"She'll shoot me down."

"Maybe. But you know, shortly after Steve and I started dating, he told me he'd been wanting to ask me out for two years. He hesitated because he and Mike had been friends and he was afraid I'd be creeped out by it or something. But you know, now, I look at how happy we are and think—what a waste those two years were."

"You weren't ready then, it was too soon."

She shrugged. "Maybe it wouldn't have been. But the point is, he didn't take the chance and now we'll never know. Do you want to be looking back two years from now wondering what might have happened if you'd told her how you felt instead of just assuming you already knew?"

"I—" He stopped speaking when a familiar figure came into view, moving down the street at a slow pace. Tall and broad-shouldered with long blond hair, he was studying the buildings as if looking for an address.

Bianca turned to look over her shoulder. "Do you know that guy?"

"Yep."

"Why does he look like someone beat him up recently?"

"Because I did."

She turned to frown at him, just as Jared reached them.

"Derek, I must be in the right place then. Elle told me to meet her here tonight and meet the family."

"Elle?" Bianca mouthed.

"Sure, I'll take you up. Come on," Derek said, taking hold of his sister's elbow. "You don't want to miss *this*."

As the three of them headed up the stairs toward the second floor, Derek turned to Bianca. "Whatever happened to little Mary Kate Moriarity, anyway?"

"She got married," Bianca said. "She's got something like eleven kids. Last time I saw her she was huge, but I'm not sure if she was pregnant again or just fat. Probably kicking herself three ways from Sunday for ever dumping you."

****

Lying in bed with Derek, Kelly realized she'd never felt so content. Certainly not lately. After the way they'd made love when he'd returned from the hospital, she hadn't guessed they'd have the energy to do so again.

She smiled, thinking of the slow, languid way they'd made love just now, almost as though he wanted to make up for how fast he'd taken her this afternoon. Not that she'd minded one bit. She rolled onto her back to look up at him.

He grinned down at her. "So dinner with my family was okay?"

"It was nice. I always wanted a big family."

"As I've told you, you're welcome to mine, any time."

She laughed. "I just might take you up on that. Although your grandmother didn't seem to like me."

"She'll get over it," he said, pulling her against him

and bending to kiss her shoulder. "She saw the pictures of us in the Florida papers. Plus you write dirty books."

"She thinks I'm leading you down the wrong path?"

"Probably. I'm her favorite grandson so she always takes an interest in the women I'm dating. Every now and then I tell her I have a nice Italian girlfriend—as long as she believes I'm going to get married soon and start making little Calavicci's, she's happy."

Children. The word hung in the air between them. "And are you?" She regretted the question the instant it was out, but she had to know the answer.

"I don't know. I've never thought about it."

"You've never thought about marriage and a family?" She couldn't keep the doubt from her voice.

"I assume I'll get married some day, but I don't spend a lot of time thinking about it."

"Will she be a nice Italian girl?"

He chuckled. "Hell, no. She'll be blonde. Successful in her own career, not threatened by mine."

"Beautiful," she supplied for him.

"Beautiful," he agreed, leaning over to kiss her.

"That's a pretty tall order." Yet she couldn't help but notice how closely she mirrored the image he painted. If only she were younger, prettier...

"Kel, can I ask you something?"

"Sure."

"I saw you holding a lot of babies tonight."

"There were a lot of them there."

"You seemed so natural with them." His hand slid lower, splaying over her abdomen. "It made me wonder why you never had more, if you ever wanted more."

A dull pain, like the ache of an old wound, throbbed through her as his words dredged up long-forgotten memories. "Y—yes. I did, at one time."

"What happened?"

"I ... I lost the baby."

"And you never tried again?"

"No," she whispered, shaking her head slowly. "The miscarriage made me realize my marriage was over. It happened the first week of April—the peak of tax season. Alan was too busy to take time away from work. My stepfather stayed with the kids and my mom took me to the hospital. I was alone through the whole thing."

She pulled in a deep breath, trying to force aside dark thoughts of sitting in the hospital room, waiting for a D&C. Alone. "That was the final straw. I knew I could never forgive him. And I knew I couldn't keep pretending to feel something I didn't." She sat up in the bed, rubbing her arms against a sudden chill. "I had a tubal ligation just a few weeks later."

He sat up behind her, pulling her against his chest, wrapping his arms around her and holding tight. "I'm sorry, Kel. I didn't mean to upset you."

"You didn't. I hadn't thought about it in a long time. Sometimes in April, when the anniversary of the miscarriage comes around, I think of it. But usually in October, when we celebrate Cody's birthday, I catch myself thinking, we would have been celebrating two birthdays this month." She closed her eyes as an unwanted tear squeezed out.

He pushed her hair aside and planted soothing kisses to the curve of her neck. "If it's all right with you, next time I see Al, I'm going to deck him again."

****

Kelly opened her eyes, startled to realize it was morning. The place beside her was empty, cold, as though Derek hadn't come back to bed since waking in the middle of the night.

A vague memory returned of waking to Derek mumbling something in his sleep about "helping those people." He'd told her not to worry it, that it was just a dream he sometimes had and she wondered if it was the nightmare Gabrielle had mentioned. But he'd gotten up then and hadn't come back to bed.

She rose and found his robe on a hook near the closet and pulled it on. She opened the bedroom door and descended the stairs only to find Gabrielle in the kitchen, brewing coffee.

"Oh, hey, Kel." She said as if it were the most natural thing in the world to greet a half naked woman coming out her brother's bedroom. "Want some coffee?"

"What's going on?" Kelly asked, nodding when Gabrielle held up a container of milk over the coffee mug.

"Well, technically Derek is back from his two-week

vacation today, so I figured I'd better come by, see what he needs. He's got reporters coming later for some interview, and he'll probably want to stop by the hospital and see Papa. I thought I'd better check his tux and see if it needs pressing, too."

"You do all that for him?"

"That's why he pays me the big bucks," she sing-songed and turned to put the milk back in the fridge.

"Sounds like he needs a wife."

"Yeah, I think so too." She stared at Kelly meaningfully before taking a sip of her coffee.

"Gabrielle—"

"I can't think of anyone better suited—"

"Don't even go there," Kelly warned. "I'm flattered, but it's just not going to happen. I've done the marriage thing once—and failed. I'm not about to make the same mistake twice."

"It was just a suggestion," the younger girl murmured, sulking in a way Kelly was sure usually got her what she wanted. "Anyway, Derek said he'd be back in a while. Something about stopping by the hospital to visit papa, then running a few errands."

"He's already gone?" Kelly asked. She had no idea why that news disappointed her, other than it was her last day in New York and he wasn't even here to spend it with her.

"He'll be back soon." Gabrielle picked up her mug and a stack of mail. "I need to take care of some bills and throw together an itinerary for Los Angeles," she said, heading toward the staircase. "You need anything?"

"I'm fine," Kelly insisted. "I'll just read the paper and—" The call box buzzed and the two exchanged puzzled looks.

"I wasn't expecting anyone today," Gabrielle said, frowning.

"Doesn't the doorman have to announce visitors?" Kelly whispered.

"Most of them, but not people he's used to seeing all the time." Gabrielle headed for the door. "Unless Derek tells him otherwise." She pulled the door open and Kelly had to hold in a groan at the sight of the woman on the other side.

"Frankie," Gabby greeted, gesturing toward the windows. "I didn't see your broomstick fly past."

The woman's eyes narrowed. "Well, if it isn't the Italian princess. Shouldn't you be out making a calzone or stuffing a canoli?"

"What do you want?"

"Just what's rightfully mine." The red head poked her head inside, looking from left to right. "Where is he?"

"Out. I don't expect him back until late."

"He'd better come back with an answer for me about his future plans." She stepped inside without being invited, stopping short when her gaze landed on Kelly. "Well, if it isn't Goldilocks."

Kelly resisted the urge to pull the edges of Derek's bathrobe tighter. Instead she just gave a little wave. "Nice to see you too, Frankie."

"You have better staying power than I guessed. I have to hand it to you; I didn't take you for the Cougar type."

"Cougar?" Kelly repeated. "I don't—"

"A cougar," Gabrielle spoke up, slamming the door behind Frankie. "Is an older woman who only dates younger men. And that's my future sister-in-law you're insulting."

"What?" Kelly wasn't sure if she or Frankie said it first, but didn't miss the playful wink Gabby gave her from behind the redhead's back.

"Derek's in love."

"Derek's a damn fool." Frankie crossed the room to take a seat in the living room. "I'll just wait here for him."

"Can't you feast on someone else's blood today, Vampira?"

"Nope," the older woman replied, picking up a copy of Field and Stream from the coffee table and thumbing through it. "I gave him his two weeks to himself. He's mine again as of—" She flipped her wrist over to check her watch. "Ten minutes ago."

"Why don't I go and get dressed?" Kelly suggested.

"Don't bother," Gabrielle spoke up. "She's not staying."

"I've waited two weeks, I'm not moving. You'll have to bodily throw me out, Princess."

In a move eerily reminiscent of her brother, Gabby placed her hands on her hips. "Which window would you prefer?"

"Maybe I'll just stay right here," Kelly decided aloud, coming to take a seat opposite Frankie.

The older woman studied her, shrewd gaze taking in her attire, or lack thereof, right down to her bare feet. "And to think two weeks ago he was worried he'd never get you into bed. I see he hasn't lost his touch. I thought you had more class than to fall for those well-rehearsed lines of his." She looked up at Gabrielle and snapped her fingers. "Why don't you bring me some coffee."

The younger girl folded her arms over her chest and scowled. "Only if you want to wear it." A buzzing sound from her purse had Gabby scurrying to pull out her cell phone.

Frankie sat back and gave Kelly a smug look. "Which one did the trick? 'It's different with you.' He's never felt like this before? You're the only woman he's ever cared about?" She cackled, as if amused. "I've known him since he was collecting dollar bills in a sequined G-string; he doesn't have a line I haven't heard. And the more desperate he is to get what he wants, the more sincere he sounds."

Kelly tried to ignore a sharp stab of pain as Frankie's words sliced into her. Derek had said *all* those things—in so many words. And like an idiot, she'd believed him. Maybe she was only attracted to men who lied. After all, she had been blind-sided by Alan's lies. Had she really fooled herself into thinking Derek was any different? Thank God she'd never voiced her feelings for him to anyone but Sharon. "Our...relationship isn't like that. You have nothing to be threatened by."

She tossed the magazine back on the coffee table and leaned back. "I'm hardly threatened by you, Blondie."

"You're threatened by any woman who gets too close. You know if Derek ever really fell in love, there'd be a woman in his life with more power over him than you."

"Bravo, Dr. Freud." She put her hands together in silent applause. "But I own him, body and soul, for the next two years, so that's not likely to happen. And if he wants to keep his career, he'll make me happy. And as long as he stays single, I'm happy."

Gabrielle came back into the room. "That was my brother. He's at the hospital with my grandfather. Derek said he'll see you tomorrow, Frankie, bright and early, before his flight to Los Angeles."

The manager rose from her seat. "Poor Grandpa. I imagine he's at St. John's Queens?"

Gabby nodded.

"Good, maybe I'll just go sit in the lobby and wait for him there." Frankie rose from her chair and headed toward the door. Before reaching it, she stopped and glanced over her shoulder. "It'll never work between you two, Goldilocks. I'll see to that."

Kelly folded her arms. "I thought you weren't threatened by me."

Gabrielle pulled the front door open and gestured from Frankie to the doorway. "Derek said to tell you that tomorrow morning, he's going to give you everything you want. And then some. You can wait until then."

"He'd better be prepared to deliver on that."

"Out," Gabby said. "And don't come back."

The instant the woman exited, Gabrielle slammed the door and locked it. "Remind me to tell the doorman not to let her up again."

"What did you mean he's going to give her 'everything she wants and then some?'"

The girl shrugged. "I dunno. That's the message he gave me."

Kelly turned and paced toward the windows, feeling strangely out of place. He had told her once his relationship with Frankie was purely business, so why was she suddenly wondering what *kind* of business?

"Hey, you don't think he means sex?" Gabby snorted.

"Well he has used a similar phrase with me a time or two."

"Look, Derek has done a lot—would *do* a lot—for his career. Changing his name, learning how to talk without a New York accent. But he'd never stoop that low, Kel."

"So what is he going to give her?"

"I wish I knew. But I'm supposed to meet him at her agency at eight thirty tomorrow, he didn't say why, just that it was important I'm on time."

"Is he always so mysterious?"

Gabby laughed. "Yeah, sometimes when he's planning a surprise."

"I guess I should take a shower and get dressed."

"Sure, take your time. I have some errands to run for him in a little while anyway."

Kelly headed toward the stairs, then stopped. "Gabby, what did Frankie mean about knowing Derek since he wore a sequined G-string?"

"She said that?" Green eyes, so like Derek's, rolled dramatically. "She's such a witch. The story everyone has heard goes that Derek was 'discovered,'" she made quotation marks with her fingers in the air, "while jogging on the beach. Not quite the truth. For a while, he worked as an exotic dancer—you know, like those Chippendale guys. That's where Frankie *really* discovered him."

Kelly sank down to sit on a stair, willing away the unpleasant image of Derek giving Frankie a lap dance. "You're kidding."

"It's how he paid for college. My parents thought he worked as a waiter. They still don't know what he was really doing, my dad would have disowned him. Anyway, it's one of those secrets Frankie likes to hold over his head, that she'll spill the beans one of these days. She forgets he's thirty years old now, it's not like he cares if anyone finds out."

There was so much about Derek she still didn't know. And Frankie's taunting her about the lines he used still stung. Added to that, he'd called and hadn't asked to talk to her, after not having seen him since the middle of the night. "With the mood she's in, do you think it was wise to send her to wait for him at the hospital?"

Gabby looked up from plumping the throw pillows on the sofa. "Yeah, I kinda thought it was a stroke of genius on my part."

"How so?"

"Because that wasn't Derek on the phone. Everything I said to Frankie was stuff he told me before he left this morning." She flashed a Cheshire cat grin. "I have three brothers, you know. I never said which one of them called."

Nineteen

For the hundredth time, Derek checked his watch. They weren't late, but he was in a hurry nonetheless. The meeting with his lawyer had taken longer than expected; he'd arrived home just in time to greet the reporters for the interview he'd promised in order to get them to stay away from Kelly's kids. She'd posed for a few pictures with him, said the right things, then excused herself to dress for the ball.

All in all, it went smoothly. But something wasn't right. She'd been distant, almost moody all day. Was she upset that he'd left her alone her last day in New York? Maybe she wouldn't be when she found out what he'd been up to. Or maybe, like him, she was having a hard time coming to terms with tonight being their last night together, which was why he intended to make it special. And why he had to make sure she knew how he really felt.

He wasn't used to feeling so unsure of himself. His profession of love would most likely be unwelcome, he'd heard her many excuses. But like Bianca said, it was better to try than spend the rest of his life wondering.

He reached into his pants pocket, pulled out a velvet box and flipped it open. Gabby had met him at the jewelry store this afternoon. Kelly had shown her the dress she planned to wear tonight, which had made it easier to narrow down his choices. But these were what he'd had in mind anyway.

A knot clenched and unclenched in his stomach as he turned the box so the gemstones caught the light. Flawless, colorless, nearly perfect, emerald-cut diamonds. A bit large at two carats apiece, but he was of the opinion that if a woman was going to wear diamonds, they should make a statement. And these would say: Successful. Sophisticated. Taken. He'd never been much for giving women jewelry, they tended to read too much into it. But with Kel he was willing to let her read whatever she wanted.

He glanced up as she came down the stairs. Gabby hadn't lost her touch; the earrings would look great with that dress. He took a moment to simply drink in the site of her as she came toward him. It wasn't something he'd have chosen, but it was Kelly. Straps with just the slightest hint of sequins went around her neck halter-style. He'd nearly forgotten how sexy a woman could be when she wasn't really revealing anything. The dress flowed gracefully about her feet as she moved, giving him the faintest hint of silver sandals and polished toenails. Red, he realized with a grin. She hadn't forgotten that he liked red.

Her hair was swept up in an elegant twist, leaving her shoulders and neck bare. "Is everything all right?" she asked as she came toward him.

Her one and only flaw. *Insecurity.* "Perfect," he said.

"It's probably not what you would have picked if I'd let you."

"I already chose that dress, you can wear it another time." He offered her his arm and steered her toward the living room. "It's a little more daring, but I think you'll like it anyway."

"Is it red?" Despite the twinkle of amusement in her eyes, he could still feel the imaginary line she'd drawn between them sometime between last night and this afternoon.

"As a matter of fact, it is." He glanced at her earlobes. She wore teardrop pearls with diamond accents. Knowing her as he did, he'd bet they were rhinestones, she'd never spend money on jewelry for herself.

He sat beside her on the sofa. "I have something for you." He reached into his pocket once again. He watched her gaze fasten on the small velvet box and hesitated, trying to read her expression. Curiosity? Fear? Horror? "It's not what you think," he added with a chuckle and flipped it open.

"We got sidetracked the other night when I asked if you'd found time to write, but Gabby tells me you finished the book." She glanced up at him, then back to the box. "So I wanted to give you a little memento for the occasion.

And I thought these would go with your dress."

Her eyes widened as the diamonds sparkled and winked in the light. "Derek, I can't—"

He placed the box in her hand and closed her finger around it. "Yes, you can."

"But they had to cost a fortune."

"You're worth ten fortunes, Kel." His voice deepened with the confession, but it was the truth—and high time he started being truthful with her.

Blue eyes flew to his face, then darkened and looked back at the earrings. "I've never worn anything so ...."

"Big?" he asked, reaching around to unfasten the pearl from the ear nearest him.

"I was going to say beautiful." She sat still while he removed one earring from the box and slipped it into her earlobe.

"I can't accept these."

"You already have." The call bell buzzed, and he rose from the sofa and crossed the room. He pressed the button on the call box. "Yes?"

"Your limo, Mr. Calavicci."

"Thanks, we'll be right down."

Kelly fastened the second earring in and rose from the sofa. She smoothed a hand down the front of her dress and glanced up at him once again with uncertainty. "Are you sure this is all right? Those New York society women are going to take one look at me and know I don't fit in."

"They'll be too busy thinking I'm the luckiest man alive."

****

Try as she might, Kelly couldn't force aside the dark cloud that hung over her head since the encounter with Frankie this morning. For Derek's sake, she gave it her best effort. And she was truly enjoying herself. Dinner had been delicious, and afterward Derek and several others had talked at length about the need to raise money for those who had given their all to clean up Ground Zero.

Knowing the personal loss he'd suffered, it made his speech even more poignant. But unlike the other speakers, Derek had spoken with not just sincerity but wit, and his natural charisma held the attention of everyone in the room. When he finished, she was not only moved by his humor and intelligence, but ridiculously proud.

The crowd was a mixture of who's who; celebrities, politicians and socialites mingled with the very people the ball was held to benefit. More than one person came up to Derek and thanked him for his work on their behalf. Many of them stayed after his speech to tell Kelly how much his efforts meant to them.

If anyone recognized her from the tabloids, no one mentioned it, and she was more than happy to just be Derek's girlfriend for one night.

When the tables were cleared and the lights dimmed, a well-known entertainer took the stage.

Derek took Kelly by the hand and led her to the dance floor. Unlike the first and last time they had danced, she didn't hold herself away from him, wasn't trying to keep their bodies from touching. She didn't fight the sensations sizzling between them. And he couldn't.

His hand moved from her waist to the expanse of bare skin beneath her shoulder blades. She sighed. The sound, reminiscent of the way she sighed when they made love, shot straight to his groin, threatening to cloud his senses. He was half-tempted to suggest they leave. *Now.* Instead he eased his hand into safer territory, away from her warm, soft skin and forced his thoughts onto the topic he had been pondering all night. "You haven't been yourself today."

"Just nervous, I guess."

He only half believed that. "Gabby tells me Frankie stopped by this morning."

Blue eyes met his, then looked away, over his shoulder. "She was her usual pleasant self."

His hand strayed upward again. "I'll talk to her."

"No, no. She didn't say anything I couldn't handle." Something crossed her face for a moment, dimming her expression like a cloud covering the sun. And then she smiled up at him again.

"What did she say, Kel?"

"Nothing, really. Well, there was that thing about you and a sequined G-string."

Christ. "It was a long time ago."

"I know."

"Does it upset you to know I used to take my clothes off in front of hundreds of screaming women?"

"I... no, but it left me with an....*image* in my head."

"It's not so different from what I do now."

"Oh, I'd say it's plenty different." There was a definite edge of disapproval in her voice.

Ahh, now they were getting somewhere. Not good for the kids to know mom's boyfriend used to be an exotic male dancer. He bent closer, until his lips brushed the sparkling diamonds at her earlobe. "You can have a private lap dance anytime you want."

"*That's* the image I'm trying to forget." She pulled away, apparently not amused by his teasing. "I need some air." The song ended, and she left him on the dance floor. He watched her make her way through the room toward the exit. Dammit, the last thing he wanted to do tonight was argue. And the last thing he'd allow her do was push him away again. *Not tonight.*

He followed, though it took him longer to make his way through the crowd than it had her. Well wishers, friends, acquaintances. People who just wanted to shake his hand and say thanks. He couldn't be rude and walk away. But as he engaged in small talk, his heart wasn't in it, and his gaze kept straying to the exit.

By the time he reached it, she was out of the ladies room, if she'd ever even gone in. The hallway was busy with partygoers. The ball was held in the Museum of Natural History this year and ball attendees had the museum to themselves for a private viewing. Not surprisingly the aisles were filled with elegantly clad guests.

He found Kelly browsing an exhibit. Her gaze met his in the glass case as he approached. "I'm sorry," she whispered. "I'm not usually the jealous type, but..."

"It was ten years ago."

"I know. Just..." She turned to glance over her shoulder to make sure no one was within earshot. "Just tell me Frankie was never given one of those... *private* dances."

"Is that what you thought?" He couldn't hold back a chuckle of amusement. "I've told you before, it's all business. She may take a little too much interest in my personal life, but believe me, it all comes down to money with her." He placed a hand on her shoulder. "Anything I do that might affect how much money she can make off of me really sets her off." And falling in love with Kelly would definitely fit into that category.

"But Derek, we're not even—"

He stroked a finger from her shoulder down her arm, enjoying—as always—her reaction to the touch. And the way it ricocheted through him. "I need to talk to you, Kel. Alone. I've wanted to say it all day, but the time hasn't felt right." It still didn't. He glanced up as a couple exited a pair of glass doors and smiled at them as they walked past. "In here," he said, heading toward the exhibit they had just exited.

"Is something wrong?"

He glanced around at the tropical plants, the bluish-white fluorescent lighting. The soothing sound of trickling fountains and piped in atmosphere that sounded strangely like the rain forest. Overhead, several monarch butterflies fed at a nectar station. The Butterfly Conservatory. He couldn't have chosen a better setting had he planned it.

He took hold of her hand and pulled her farther into the room, walking until he found a spot well away from view of the doors with a visitor's bench.

Behind him, he felt Kelly pulling against him. "Derek—are we in—are those—"

"Butterflies."

She let out a strange wail and he stopped. A blue-and-black winged insect had landed on her shoulder.

"Get it off," she whispered, an edge of panic in her voice. "Please get it off."

With a chuckle he took the insect on the end of his finger, then blew gently to send it on its way. "A gardener who's afraid of butterflies?"

The bug flitted away and she shuddered. "I can't explain it, I just don't like them."

"Do you want to go someplace else?"

She met his gaze, then swept a glance around at the serene setting. "No," she said, her tone gentle. "Just keep those—*things*—off of me, and I'll be fine.

He shrugged out of his jacket and draped it around

her shoulders. "This should help."

She gazed warily at the plants behind the bench, checking for butterflies, before sitting. He settled down beside her, draping an arm protectively behind her, poised to discourage anymore "things" from landing on her.

"Still a girlie-girl, I see," he teased, wondering how she'd ever spend a weekend at his cabin. Maybe she wouldn't want to. But he'd been entertaining fantasies for a while now about getting her alone out in the wilderness. No cell phones, no intrusions. Just the two of them.

"I touched that slimy worm when we went fishing," she said defensively. "And I don't know what it is about butterflies. They give me the willies."

He grinned and blew gently at another butterfly taking an interest in her hair. "I think they like your perfume."

"We probably won't be alone in here for long," she said. "What did you want to talk about?"

The gemstones in the earrings winked at him. He fingered one, then lingered to stroke her cheek. "Us."

A half-smile played over her lips, and she dropped her gaze. "Let me make this easy on you."

He frowned. How did she intend to do that?

"I know what we agreed to going into this, Derek, and I don't expect anything more from you. Even if I did, it's impossible. We've got our lives to get back to."

"Wait a minute—what's impossible?"

"Please, let's not make good-bye speeches or promises that we don't intend to keep."

Something hit him hard in the gut, twisted. It was fear talking. She didn't realize his feelings had changed. "What sort of promises?"

"To stay friends, to keep in touch," she said, much too quickly. "Nonsense like that."

"Kel—"

"I mean it's been wonderful—more really than I ever imagined it might be. But at the end of the day it was just sex. *Incredible* sex, but—"

"Just sex," he said flatly. "You think what's between us is just sex."

"Isn't it? I'm not naïve enough to think it would be

that way with any other guy because he wouldn't be you. And it's not that I'm about to do this again anytime soon, but—"

"Whoa, wait a minute—I'm still stuck on the 'other guy' part." He took one of her hands in his, stroking her knuckles with his thumb. "Don't you think this is worth holding onto?"

She frowned as if she hadn't fully heard him. "Do I think *what's* worth holding onto?"

"Us," he emphasized.

"But we agreed going into this that—"

"We agreed to two weeks of pretending," he reminded her. "And we stopped pretending a long time ago."

She tugged her hand from his. "So what are you asking?"

"I'm asking for more time," he said, frowning as she slid a few inches away.

"More time for what? Sex?"

"This is about more than sex."

"No," she said, rising to her feet. "It isn't. That's all that's been between us, and we've both been surprised by how wonderful—" She walked away a few steps, stopping when a butterfly fluttered across the path. "It won't work."

He came up behind her, settled his hands on her shoulders, felt the warmth of her skin through the jacket, and breathed in the sweet smell of her hair. "That's fear talking. You've been pulling away from me all day. You do it every time I get too close."

"I'm simply being realistic."

"About what?"

"Long distance relationships. Ours would be doomed before it ever started."

"Why?" He tried hard to keep the edge from his voice, but a warning prickled along his skin. She was determined to push him away and he could guess what excuse she'd use.

"You told me yourself." She turned to face him, shaking off his touch. "You've never had a monogamous relationship."

Yep, that was the one. "No, I told you I avoided commitments because I didn't think it was fair to ask someone to wait around when I'm gone so much."

"So why me?" Her voice wavered with emotion. "Why is it fair to ask *me*?"

"Because I'm in love with you, dammit."

Her mouth dropped open. "You tell me this *now*—when you're going away for a month?"

"If I could change that, I would. But I've already postponed it once."

"I'm not asking you to change anything, Derek. But you'll forget me long before those four weeks are up."

He slid his hands into his pockets. "You think so?" It wasn't a question. He had to swallow past a lump of emotion in his throat. Forget her? Not likely. He couldn't imagine his life without her.

"I know so."

"You're wrong."

"And if I'm not?"

The anguish in her eyes half killed him. Not because it hurt to know she didn't trust him, but dammit, how could she even think it? "You're shooting me down on a 'what if?'"

"You've never had a long-distance relationship—you've never had *any* relationship that lasted longer than a night or two. I don't want to be your guinea pig."

"My *guinea pig*? What the hell does that mean?"

"The one you try it out on. The one sitting by the phone every night waiting for you to call. What about *my* feelings, Derek? What about the first time you get too busy—or too distracted by some hot, young body and forget to call me?"

"That's not going to happen."

"I'm not willing to take that chance."

"So you want to throw away what's between us because I *might* screw it up?"

"No! *Yes*—I—" She put a hand to her forehead, then pulled in a deep breath. "I have enough to handle right now without adding a broken heart to my problems."

"Really? You married Al because he seemed like a safe bet and look how that turned out."

The color drained from her face. "How dare you throw that up at me?"

"It's true, isn't it? You thought with him you'd have a

safe, boring marriage. But the only thing you got right was the boring part."

Her hand twitched as if she longed to slap him.

"I'm not safe, am I, Kel? You can't control me, and you can't control the way I make you feel." He stepped closer, practically daring her to strike him, knowing she'd never let go of her emotions with him, but wishing she would. "I know you're afraid to take a chance. But I'm not Alan. I'm not going to let you down. *Trust me.* That's all I'm asking."

The anger drained from her expression, he could almost see her warring with the desire to believe him. "Derek, you're an international sex symbol—"

"I'm a *man.* Just a man."

"A man with women throwing themselves at him on a regular basis. Women, I might remind you, who are far younger than me."

"The age thing again." He threw one hand up in frustration. "I thought we were past that."

"*I'm* not past it! You may not believe it now, but someday you're going to want a family like the one you grew up in. What's going to become of me when you realize you I can't give you even one baby let alone six?"

He raked a hand through his hair, scarcely able to keep up with the reasons she kept throwing his way. "Babies? Now it's about *babies?*"

"Partly."

"Well, here's a news flash for you. I don't want kids. I've spent my entire life taking care of them, whether they were my younger siblings, my cousins or my nieces and nephews. Babies, toddlers, right on up to teenagers. I like them—*love* them—but I don't happen to want any of my own."

"And you want to begin a relationship with a woman who has kids?" she asked. "What am I supposed to do with Maya and Cody, send them off to boarding school?"

He released a sigh of frustration. "You're twisting things, Kel. Giving yourself an excuse to push me away."

She folded her arms and gave him an icy stare. "And you aren't taking no for an answer. As usual."

"Because I know you. You couldn't make love with me if you didn't feel something besides physical need."

"You have to realize this isn't about *you*," she said much too calmly. "It's about me, about my need to protect myself from getting hurt again. And I'm not going to begin a relationship based on hot sex."

When she started to turn away again, he grabbed hold of her shoulders. "It goes deeper than that and you know it."

Kelly couldn't stare at the hurt in his eyes another second. Couldn't stand the confusion and pain she saw there—hated knowing she caused it. "It's just sex," she whispered. Didn't he realize she couldn't put her heart on the chopping block this way? She'd known she was in love with him for days now and couldn't allow herself to dwell on it—because it didn't matter, she couldn't allow it to change anything. "I have a daughter I don't even recognize, an ex-husband who thinks he's moving back into my life so I can take care of him, and a career I've neglected... I can't do this now, Derek. I just can't." She turned away, unable to look at him another second without losing control of her emotions. "I have a life to get back to. And so do you."

"Tell me you don't feel what I do and I'll back off."

The familiar buzz of her cell phone—Gilligan's Island—sounded from her purse. She glanced at the bench where she'd left it but made no attempt to move toward it.

"Aren't you going to get that?" There was a challenge in his tone.

"It can wait." She pulled in a shaky breath. "Derek what I feel—or don't feel—doesn't matter right now." The phone stopped ringing and for a moment it was silent but for the tropical atmosphere coming from the overhead speakers.

"Dammit, why are you so stubborn? You can't give even one inch." He turned away, his jaw set tight. "Does this have anything to do with Al coming back?"

She frowned. "*Alan*?"

"Are you going back to him? To keep Maya happy?"

How could he even think it? After having been with him, what man could possibly compare? "I'm not willing to give up my independence for anyone, Derek. Certainly not Alan."

"And certainly not me."

The phone rang again and she forced herself not to move toward it. She saw the brow Derek arched at her. He was undoubtedly surprised that she chose this moment to suddenly stop answering when her kids called. Right now he—the two of them—had to come first. "It's just Cody," she explained. "He probably can't find the microwave popcorn."

It stopped abruptly and a second later Derek's phone buzzed. He hesitated for only a second.

"It might be about your grandfather."

He pulled it from his pocket, glanced at the caller ID. "Alan Michaels?" He glanced up at her out of eyes still dark with hurt and anger. "This should be interesting."

He put the phone to his ear, and she heard Alan's voice almost immediately. "Where is she?"

"Who?" Kelly had the feeling Derek was purposely toying with her ex.

"My wi—Kelly. Look, Boy Toy, this is an emergency."

He handed the phone to her.

"Alan?" she said, her heart immediately in her throat at the word emergency.

"I can't find Maya."

"What do you mean you can't *find* her?"

"She was supposed to be at Heather's. But this afternoon Heather's mom called here looking for her daughter."

"Did you try her cell phone?"

"Of course I did." His voice dripped sarcasm. "It must be shut off or else the battery is dead, it goes straight to voice mail. So does Heather's."

Kelly put a hand to her forehead and squeezed her eyes shut in an effort to think. "The mall. They may have gone to the mall."

"Which one? There are six malls around here. Besides... it gets worse."

"*Worse?*" She squeaked, her gaze seeking out Derek, who stood a short distance away watching some butterflies feed. Despite herself, despite her resolve not to rely on him, for some reason she wanted him near right now. As if feeling the weight of her stare, he turned.

"Cody says she's been texting Trevor."

"But he's in—"

"When we couldn't find her, Cody checked her lap top. She Googled driving directions to Virginia Beach yesterday. Trevor's house. And Heather's mom's car is missing."

"*What?*" Her knees began to tremble. Her baby? On the interstate? But she only had a learner's permit!

She felt Derek before he touched her, before she felt the heat from his body at her back, surrounding her. She reached out and grabbed hold of his forearm and held tight.

"Cody and I are on the way there now, I'm still a couple of hours from Virginia but I wanted you to know."

"Did you call the police? Did you call Trevor's parents?"

"There's no answer at the Bradford's house and Heather's mom called the state police, they're looking for the car."

"Oh my God. If Maya sees a police car in the rearview mirror, I don't think she'll know what to do."

Alan's reply was broken up, then the signal totally disappeared.

Derek took the phone from her. "Breathe."

"I... I can't." She put a hand to her stomach as every bite of food she'd had tonight—hell, in her life— threatened to come up again. "This isn't... this isn't like Maya. This isn't my daughter. It's that *boy!*" Damn that Trevor, if she ever got her hands on him, she'd kill him. "How far is it to Virginia Beach from here? Where can I rent a car?"

He took hold of her hand and led her toward the doors. "I'll get you there, but driving will take hours. You don't have that kind of time."

"But it will take too long to find a commercial flight, plus the wait for the security check—"

"There's a room full of millionaires next door. Someone is bound to have flown here tonight on a private jet."

"I couldn't ask—"

"Do you want to get to Virginia tonight—or sometime tomorrow?"

Nicole McCaffrey

Twenty

Less than an hour later they were seated on the private jet owned by a Hollywood producer. The man and his wife had been more than generous about loaning them the plane. They had teenagers themselves and understood the situation. They had even arranged to have a car waiting for them when they reached Virginia.

Kelly stared out the window at the night sky, willing her mind to stay calm. She didn't know which worried her more, what Maya intended to do once she reached Trevor's house—or Maya not reaching it at all.

Derek's hand slid over hers. She didn't deserve his compassion after the things she'd said to him. Didn't deserve any of this. *My* needs, *my* feelings. When had she gotten so selfish? She glanced at the strong, lean-fingered hand covering hers. She had never needed to guard her heart more fiercely than she did around him.

"We'll find her, Kel," he said. She closed her eyes, grateful he didn't say something foolish like "everything will be all right"—they didn't know that and she couldn't believe that anyway. It was so tempting to lean against him, to rest her head on his broad shoulder and draw strength from him. But she couldn't.

The bottom line was, if she'd stayed home and been a good mother like she should have, this wouldn't have happened. If she hadn't left her kids in Alan's care—selfish, childish Alan—this wouldn't have happened.

She didn't blame Derek. She really didn't even blame Alan. There was no one to blame for this but her. And whatever happened to Maya tonight, it was no one's fault but Kelly's.

Like a zombie, she allowed Derek to lead her to the waiting limo once the plane landed. They gave the driver the address, and Derek slipped him a handful of bills to drive as fast as he could.

She was too numb to be scared even as the limo

seemed to be moving way too fast. The same prayer was on her lips the entire way "please, God, let her be all right."

She had no idea how much time elapsed between the time they got in the limo and the driver pulled up in front of the Bradford's address.

Derek got out and pulled her along with him. Cars spilled out of the driveway and down the street. Loud music blared from inside the house. Walking up and down among the parked cars, Kelly spied one with a New York plate and recognized Maya's school sweatshirt in the back seat. She exhaled for the first time in close to two hours.

Derek looked up at the house. "So this is why she wanted to come."

"I can only imagine what's going on in there," Kelly said. She was about to head for the front door when headlights cut through the darkness. She recognized her own mini van moving slowly down the street. Alan pulled up beside them, then turned into the driveway next door. Jenn's house, Kelly realized. The house where her ex had lived for the past two years. She waited while he, Cody and Barney piled out of the van.

"Is that noise coming from in there?" Alan asked.

"Yes."

"I told you it was probably a party, Dad." Cody spoke up. "Hey, mom. Hey, D. Nice tux."

Derek affectionately ruffled Cody's hair.

Kelly turned and headed back toward the house.

"What are you doing?" Alan called after her in a stage whisper. "If you go pounding on the door and demanding to see her, you'll embarrass her."

"Oooh," Kelly said, feigning horror. "Wouldn't want to do that now would we?"

Derek took hold of her arm and pulled her aside. "Thing is, if you knock on that door they're not going to let you in. And they'll have time hide whatever it is they're doing."

"Like what?"

"Drugs, alcohol, sex." He shrugged. "I'm sure it's all there."

"You don't think Maya—"

"I don't know. But I'd like to find a way in other than

the front door." He glanced toward the back of the house. "Come on."

They followed the sound of the surf until they came to the beach. Kelly's heels sank into the sand, making walking difficult, but she continued until they were standing near Trevor's house.

Glass patio doors were closed, but the curtains were open and they had a clear view of the inside. "I'll bet those aren't locked," Derek whispered. "All we need to do is spot Maya and we can go right in."

"*We?*" Kelly asked. "Derek, I can't ask you—"

"And I'm not about to let you go in there alone. Besides you're too emotional right now."

Alan and Cody came up behind them.

"What the hell are you doing?" Alan asked. "Spying?"

"Looking for Maya," Kelly shot back over her shoulder.

"It's just a party," Alan said, "Leave her alone, give her some time to enjoy herself."

"*Just* a party?" Kelly echoed.

"Come on," her ex scoffed. "We all went to parties when we were her age."

"There's no one in there even close to Maya's age," Derek spoke up. "She's got no business being here."

"There she is," Cody said, pointing toward the house.

As Kelly turned to look she saw Maya rise from a sofa and speak to two boys who looked to be in their early twenties. Another boy, blond and clean cut, reached up from the sofa and grabbed her arm.

"That's Trevor," Cody supplied.

When Maya yanked away from him, he laughed and pulled her back onto the sofa, then handed her a glass, and motioned for her to drink.

"I don't like this," Derek said.

"So it's alcohol, "Alan reasoned. "She already knows it makes her sick, she won't drink it."

"I'd be more concerned about what might be in the glass besides alcohol," Derek reasoned.

"I'm sure in the circles you run in that's true," Alan sneered. "But Trevor's a good kid—"

Derek hauled him up by the collar of his polo shirt. "After the night I've had, Al, I'm in the mood to hit

304

something. It can be that door, someone inside—or it can be you."

Alan cast Kelly a quick, pleading glance, but she turned away and headed toward the back door.

"You go right ahead," she heard Alan rasp from behind her. "Just make sure it's you they sue, Boy Toy, and not me."

Kelly had just reached the bottom of the steps when the patio door slid open. A boy staggered out and barely made it to the rail of the deck before he vomited.

"Here's our chance," Derek whispered. "He left the door open." He grabbed her hand to tug her behind him as he moved up the steps and inside.

It took Kelly only a split second to locate her daughter. "I want to check on Heather!" Maya called over a break in the music.

The blond boy said something to her, then leaned around to kiss her. His hand came up to squeeze Maya's breast.

Motherly rage shot up Kelly's spine, not just that the boy could grope her daughter like that but that he could be disrespectful enough to do it in front of a crowd. She shoved her way through the partygoers and without even thinking smacked the boy in the back of his blond head. "Get off of my daughter!" She whacked him a few more times for good measure.

Trevor turned, looking furious. Maya looked mortified—but relieved. "Mom!"

"That's your *mother*?" Trevor sneered.

Maya leaped up. "Something's wrong with Heather."

"Where is she?" Derek asked.

"I don't know, she had a drink and then she, like, passed out or something. They took her to lie down, but they won't let me check on her."

"They who?"

"I don't know where she is," Trevor insisted.

Kelly closed her eyes as Derek hauled him to his feet. Recalling his earlier threat to Alan, she winced as she heard Trevor's body slam against a wall. "I guess you didn't hear me the first time. *Where is she?*"

Maya chose that moment to rush into Kelly's arms.

Two of Trevor's friends tried to come to his aide, but

before she could even shout a warning to Derek he'd knocked one of them flat with a punch. The second boy quickly changed his mind about helping his friend.

"They took her down here," Maya tugged Kelly's hand. She led her down a hallway that was obviously the bedroom area. Knots began to from in Kelly's stomach. She opened the first door and found a couple too engrossed in sex to notice her.

She moved on to the second room and pushed the door open. Heather lay sprawled on the bed, not moving. Her blouse was undone and a boy on the bed beside her was reaching for her pants. Another boy held a camera.

"Oh, my God," Kelly cried, rushing into the room. "Get away from her."

The boy leapt up. "I wasn't doing anything."

"Maya—get Derek." Kelly rushed to the bed and scooped Heather up in her arms, pulling her blouse closed. "Heather," she called, frantically patting her cheeks. "Honey, it's Mrs. Michaels. Can you hear me?"

The girl mumbled something incoherent. Kelly clutched her to her chest, as heartsick as if it were her own child, and faced the two boys who stared at her dumbfounded. "What did you give her?"

They turned and ran, running smack into Derek and Maya.

"Is she okay?" Maya wailed. "She only had one drink and then she just kind of passed out."

"Did *you* drink anything?" Derek asked.

"Just a sip, but it made my lips feel funny and then Heather started acting strange—I got scared."

"How long ago?" He crossed the room in two strides and took Heather from Kelly. "Let's get her outside for some fresh air."

"She's only been in here a few minutes—right after she passed out."

Kelly breathed a silent prayer that the boys hadn't had time to do anything else to the girl. A crowd of onlookers had gathered but no one attempted to stop them as they stepped outside the room.

Trevor sat in a chair while a college-aged girl held an ice pack to the back of his head. One side of his face was bruised. Kelly was tempted to say something to him but was more concerned with getting help for Heather.

As they stepped out onto the deck, Derek nodded toward Cody. "Call nine-one-one. Tell them there's a young girl who overdosed, probably on a date rape drug."

"Oh *shit*," a near-panicked Alan said. "Now Heather's parents will probably sue, too."

****

Heather's parents arrived right before the ambulance and the police. Kelly hated having to explain what had happened, but to her credit, Maya took full responsibility, insisting it was her idea, and not Heather's, to come in the first place. Not that Kelly really thought Mr. and Mrs. Baldwin were listening, they were too worried about their daughter.

Kelly stayed until the paramedics had loaded the still-unconscious Heather into the ambulance, then prepared to follow them to the hospital. What surprised her the most, however, was that Derek also stayed.

Now as they made their way from the beach toward the front of the house, where the cars were parked, Kelly noted Derek standing nearby, talking to one of the police officers. The party-goers had scattered immediately after she and Derek had left with the girls, and now Trevor was left alone to answer to the police.

Alan volunteered to stay behind and talk to Trevor's parents, who were on their way home, but Kelly suspected his real intent was to talk with Jenn, who had come out of her house once the police and paramedics arrived.

"I suppose I'm grounded," Maya spoke up from behind her.

Kelly stopped in her tracks. "To put it in words you can relate to—you are *way* grounded." She held out a hand. "Give me your cell phone."

Her daughter heaved a sigh but nonetheless handed over the trouble-making device. "I expected that."

"Turned off, I see."

Maya offered no excuse, just looked away.

"Funny, this thing was supposed to bring me peace of mind. But it doesn't work that way unless it's turned on. And I'm beginning to think it wasn't such a good idea after all."

"How long are you taking it away for?"

"A long time." She turned and headed toward the surf, trudging awkwardly in the sandals that were now killing her feet. She pulled her arm back and hurled the phone as far as she could toward the water. It landed several feet out with a satisfying splash. Behind her, Maya groaned.

"*Go* Mom," Cody said, running past with Barney.

"Don't be so amused, young man. Yours could be next."

He grinned, then flipped a Frisbee a short distance down the beach. The golden retriever romped after it, paws splashing through sand and water.

"Car," Kelly called to him. "And make sure you wipe his paws off before he gets in."

She turned to find Maya heading toward the street, and after making sure Cody and the dog were behind her, Kelly followed.

On the street, she spied Derek leaning against the limo that had driven them from the airport. He had loosened his tie and unbuttoned his shirt. With his hair tousled by the breeze from the ocean and the tie, undone, hanging loose about his neck, he looked amazingly as he had the first night she'd seen him in Florida, when he'd carried her shoes.

A pang of utter loss pierced her.

As she neared Derek, Maya suddenly ran toward him. He opened his arms just as she threw herself at him in a hug of pure gratitude. Kelly heard a sob tear from her throat, saw her body tremble with the force of her tears. Derek stroked her hair for several moments, then leaned down and said something to her in a soft, low voice. Maya nodded, clung to him for a few more minutes, then at last pulled away.

She popped the back hatch open on the van so Cody could pull out some towels to wipe down the dog, then headed toward Derek and Maya, uncertain of what she needed to say, but unwilling to leave without speaking to him. She stopped, smoothing a hand over Maya's long blonde hair out of habit. "Do you mind if I talk to Derek alone for a minute?"

"Sure." Maya started to go, then turned to Derek. "I'm really sorry for causing so much trouble," she said, her voice thick with emotion. "And I'm sorry I was so mean to you before." She placed a hand on his shoulder and went up on tiptoe to quickly kiss his cheek before heading for the van.

Kelly waited until Maya had climbed into the van, then turned to look at Derek. For long, silent seconds they only stared at one another.

"I don't know what would have happened tonight if you hadn't been here," she finally said.

He slid his hands into his pockets as if he didn't know what else to do with them. "You'd have been fine. Those kids didn't run off because of me—you scared the hell out of them when you started screaming and hitting Trevor."

She smiled at his teasing. "I don't think so."

"I like what you did with that cell phone, by the way."

Heat crept over her cheeks. "She'll be grounded for a long time." She dared a look into his eyes once more. God it hurt to think she'd never be this close to him again. "Derek, I don't like the way we left things, but I don't ... I don't have a better answer."

"I know." He shifted and folded his arms over his chest. "I won't say I like it, Kel, but I know once you've made up your mind, that's it. I'm not about to pressure you to come around to my way of thinking."

"Thank you." She stepped closer, intent on kissing his cheek, but whether it was habit or whether one of them moved at the last second, she met his lips. Her heart lurched painfully at the contact even while her body reacted as it always did. By the time she pulled away, hot tears ran down her cheeks.

"Do you want me to come to the hospital with you?" he asked.

She swiped at the moisture on her cheeks. "No. I'll only stay until we know how Heather is. I'm sure her family will want some privacy afterward."

"Will you be all right to drive home?"

"I think so. As angry as I am, I'm not the least bit tired."

He smiled. "Don't be too hard on her, she learned a lesson the hard way tonight."

"She's not through learning it yet," Kelly resolved.

"But by the time I'm through taking away privileges, she might come close."

"Meanie," he teased, his tone gentle.

"Where are you off to now?"

"I have to get that plane back to New York. Then I have an early meeting with Frankie and a flight to Los Angeles to catch." He shifted again. "Can I ... call you sometime?"

"Sometime." She whispered. "But let's not say for sure when, okay?" *Because you'll forget, and I'll be crushed all over again.*

"Okay." He reached out to brush her cheek. "You can call me anytime, you know."

"I know."

"But you won't."

"Probably not," she admitted. What if she called and he was with another woman? She forced a bright smile. "You won't be late getting back to New York, will you?"

"No." His voice had gone husky.

She reached up to unfasten the earrings from her ears.

"Kel—don't."

She held them out, but he refused to take them. She tucked them into his breast pocket. "I could never wear them again, Derek, and I could never even look at them without thinking about—"

"I know."

He walked with her to the van and held the door open while she climbed in. After she'd buckled up and closed the door, he turned and headed back toward the limo. But he made no attempt to get in. Instead he lit a cigarette and stood watching while she adjusted her mirrors.

"You okay, Mom?" Cody asked from the back seat.

"I'm fine," she lied, turning the key in the ignition. "Where is your father, anyway?"

"Talking to Jenn," her son replied. "I think he wants to get back with her."

Undoubtedly. She pulled away from Trevor's house—away from Derek—and onto the street. She glanced over at Maya in the passenger seat beside her. But her daughter was looking behind her, where Derek still stood.

"Mom?" she said, drawing Kelly's gaze from the rearview mirror where she had been watching Derek, too. "He really is the model man."

Twenty-One

Derek stepped through the doors into the familiar offices, pausing for the first time in years to read the name on the glass doors "Francesca Levine Agency." He tried to remember how this had all looked to him a few years ago when he had simply been a kid from Queens, but the memory was so distant it might as well have belonged to someone else. He adjusted his tie, then pulled open the doors and stepped into the lobby.

"D, my man, she's waiting for you." Blaine said, smashing a fist to Derek's arm in greeting. "You look like you're up for a fight."

"I never fight in Versace."

"Frankie doesn't have any qualms about it. Give her hell, man."

"I'll give her more than that," he promised, forcing a grin he didn't feel. In fact, he wasn't sure what he felt. Lost. Like he'd lost his best friend, like his world had just been ripped apart.

He made his way toward Frankie's office, taking his time, pausing to greet those he recognized. Lots of new faces, too. He could tell because they all stopped short at the sight of him. One poor girl dropped an armful of papers she'd just taken from a copy machine, and got even more rattled when he bent to help her.

He supposed his effect on the female gender was something he would never understand. Still, her flustered reaction reminded him of his first meeting with Kelly and the thought left a smile on his face. He reached in his jacket pocket, feeling for the earrings she'd given back last night. He had no idea why, but he wanted a piece of Kel with him for this. This was something he was doing for her as much as for him.

He opened Frankie's office door without knocking, as was his usual habit.

She did a double take when she saw him. "You look

terrific. I haven't seen you do the suit and tie thing in a long time." She motioned for him to have a seat. "I'm glad you're here. The new owner is coming in this morning."

He arched a brow in her direction. "So you finally found a buyer for the agency."

"I'm sure half the reason he wanted to buy has to do with you."

He wouldn't deny that. "What made you decide to sell?"

"I want to spend more time with Mort. Ever since he had that prostate cancer scare he's been after me to slow down, take time to smell the roses." She paused to light a cigarette and rolled her eyes. "So I'll work sixty-five-hour weeks instead of eighty."

"I wouldn't think you were ready to give up that control."

She blew a stream of smoke, her gaze thoughtful. "It will be a relief to let someone else worry about the big money decisions for a change. But I'll still have a hand in the day-to-day operations."

Derek leaned back to study her. "I can't see you taking orders from anyone else."

She muttered an expletive. "Take orders my ass. It was hard enough having to always work through this guy's lawyer. Some ego. He insisted on doing everything anonymously. I don't even know his name." She paused to check her watch, then stamped out the cigarette and produced a can of air freshener. "Can you still smell it?" she asked, waving her hand to fan the smoke.

He shrugged.

"So, have you come to your senses yet?" She sat back down.

He nodded. "A long time ago."

"That's my boy."

She checked her wristwatch again.

"This new owner really has you nervous."

"I'm never nervous," she sniffed. "But you've made the right choice." She shoved a paper across the desk. "Read that and sign it. It's only another two years, you can handle it. Of course, by then you'll be thirty-two, almost thirty-three, and I've got new boys in here every day ready to fill your shoes."

"They can't afford my shoes."

She laughed. "That's the attitude." She leaned back in her chair and studied him with an almost maternal look. "You've come a long way. If I do say so myself, I did a hell of a job when I decided to manage your career. I knew what I had on my hands and I wasn't about to let anyone else get a piece of it."

"I'm a person, Frankie, not an 'it.'"

"To me you're a commodity." She shrugged. "I taught you how to dress, how to walk, got rid of that God-awful Queens accent. And that year in Europe didn't hurt either. You came back knowledgeable about art and wines and architecture." She laughed. "I not only dubbed you the model man, I turned you into him."

"You're a real Dr. Frankenstein."

"Come on, it's not like you aren't making a fortune doing this."

"It helped, but I've made more money doing other things."

"Investing?" she waved a hand. "Nobody's got any money left from that now."

"Except those of us who invested wisely and got out before they lost their shirt."

"Lost their shirt," she repeated, chuckling. "Coming from you that's very funny. You wouldn't have had a shirt to take off if it weren't for me. Not to mention what your career has done for your sex life"

He rose and moved toward the window. For some reason the comment nagged at him, reminding him of a past he'd outgrown. His gaze moved along the skyline, seeking out the towers that were no longer there. Their absence was always a reminder. Just as the country had been more innocent before that day, he'd been more arrogant.

"So are you and Goldilocks over and done with, or what?"

"Over," he said, the word sticking in his throat.

"Smart boy, I knew you'd dump her. I taught you better than that."

"You taught me everything I know, Frankie," he said, turning to look at her. "You know that, don't you?"

"Of course I do."

"No personal attachments, take no prisoners. Never let anyone stand in the way of getting ahead."

Her face lit in a rare smile. "So you *were* paying attention."

"Oh, I paid attention all right."

Blaine suddenly appeared in the doorway. "Your eight-thirty is here."

A moment later, Gabrielle strolled into the room, dressed in a sedate black suit, hair pulled back, looking more grown up than Derek had ever seen her.

"You're late, as usual," he growled.

She pulled a face.

"What the hell is *she* doing here?" Frankie asked. "I've got an important—"

"You're in her seat, Frankie," Derek said.

"Have you lost your goddamned mind?" Frankie howled.

"You didn't tell her?" Gabrielle asked.

Derek shrugged. "We were busy reminiscing, I never got around to it." He placed a hand on Frankie's shoulder. "Sorry, love, but I'm CEO now. Gabby's going to manage day-to-day operations. You'll stay on part time, as per our agreement. There's a nice little office for you down the hall."

Still in her chair, Frankie whirled to face him, her face red with rage. "That's a broom closet."

He smiled and helped her from the chair. "You'll figure out something." He gave her a little push toward the door. "Oh, and remember, this is a non-smoking facility."

Gabrielle closed the door behind Frankie with a squeal and leaped at her brother. "Am I really out of that pizza shop forever?" she asked, hugging him tight enough to cut off his circulation.

"Yes, it's time a new generation of Calavicci's learned to make pizza. But I'm warning you, screw this up and you're out of here."

"I won't screw it up," she pouted. "I happen to have a degree in business management."

"Yes, I know. I paid for it."

"You'll get your money's worth." She swept a glance around the room. "So what's my redecorating budget look like?"

He laughed. "We'll discuss it. Anyway, didn't I tell you I was working on your graduation present?"

She sat in the chair Frankie had exited and swung her feet up onto the desk. "Yeah, but I was hoping for a Mercedes."

"You'll be able to buy your own soon enough." Derek picked up the contract Frankie had left for him to sign and tore it in two. "Guess I won't be needing this."

Gabby flashed him a satisfied smile. "I'm Jared's boss now, right?"

He grinned at her. "Nothing new about that, Piglet. Nothing new about that."

****

Kelly jabbed her trowel in the ground, dug down a bit, then plopped a plant in the hole. As she scooped the earth back around it, something flitted past her. She started and held perfectly still as the orange and black butterfly moved past her. But the sight of the insect wasn't what caused a sudden, unexpected ache in her chest. It was the memory it evoked.

Seven weeks and the pain hadn't lessened. Oh, she had some days where she thought about Derek less than others, and some nights where she didn't dream about him at all. But they were rare.

The butterfly moved on, and she patted the dirt around the flowers she'd just planted. Her yard was nearly restored from the beating it had taken when Derek had been here and fans and paparazzi had descended. The paparazzi had been back only once since they had gone their separate ways. Turning the garden hose on them may not have been the social thing to do, but it had worked. They left and didn't come back.

Surprisingly, there had been very little in the tabloids, but then a well-known actor was involved in a sex scandal, so perhaps she and Derek were old news this week. The only place she'd even seen Derek was in print ads for his new cologne.

A familiar yellow convertible pulled in the driveway, drawing her from her gloomy thoughts.

Sharon stepped out. The mid-day sun on her newly-dyed white blonde hair was blinding. Kelly watched as her friend pulled a lap top case and her purse from the back seat and tottered toward her on her ever-present spike-heeled shoes.

"Am I late?" she asked.

"Nope, haven't seen a truck yet."

"Good, I don't like to make it too obvious."

"Shar, the landscape guys come every Thursday afternoon—and every Thursday afternoon you're sitting out here with your lap top pretending to work. You don't think that's obvious?"

"I'm not *pretending* to work. I'm doing research. On the very young, very hot male physique." Sharon set up her folding chair and settled in. "What'cha planting anyway?"

"Marigolds."

"I thought you hated marigolds."

"I do, but I needed to plant something and these are easy to come by right now."

"Where's the kids today?"

"Cody is at Brian's house and Maya is at work until seven."

"You mean ol' mom you," Sharon said, nudging her shoulder. "First you take away her cell phone and lap top, then you make her get a job."

"There are worse ways to spend your summer than scooping ice cream down at the lake all day."

"I'd imagine there are lots of lifeguards around." Sharon sighed. "But then I do like to imagine lifeguards..."

Kelly rolled her eyes, accustomed to her friend's lustful musings. "To listen to you, one would never guess you've been happily married for thirty-five years. Or that you write *inspirational* romance."

Sharon laughed. "My soul is pure, Kel, but my mind...well that's another story. Hey, speaking of hot and young. Have you heard from..."

"No." Kelly stabbed her trowel into the earth again. She hadn't expected him to call, had asked him not to. But somehow she had thought he would. "Cody has e-mailed him a few times."

"How come?"

Kelly shrugged. "They hit it off like long-lost friends.

In fact, Derek invited him to his cabin in the Catskills. I guess he takes his nieces and nephews there for a week around labor day every year."

"Is he going?" Sharon asked.

A landscaping truck pulled up in front of a neighboring house and a twenty-something guy with shoulders as wide as a barn door stepped from the truck. He waved to them before opening the trailer on the back and climbing onto the riding mower.

"I hate to disappoint him," Kelly continued. "I know he'd have a great time, Derek has a lot of nephews and nieces Cody's age. It's just if I take him and pick him up, I'll have to see Derek."

"Would that be so bad?"

Kelly focused on her flowers. "It might be. It's not like he's called or tried to talk to me. Which pretty much tells me he's moved on."

"You didn't give him much *choice* but to move on, Kel. At least not from what you told me."

"I know, but I guess I thought we'd stay in touch."

"What for?"

"To..." Kelly sat back on her heels, observing the row of orange and yellow flowers she'd just planted. "Well, just to..."she heaved a sigh. "You're right. I guess there really isn't a reason."

"I can think of *one* reason."

"I'm not interested in being friends with benefits. Besides, he could never make a commitment to just one woman."

"Seems to me he offered to do just that."

"That was the sex talking." Kelly wiped a hand across her forehead. "Long distance relationships are doomed to failure—why are we even having this discussion?"

"So are you going to take the kid up there next weekend or not?"

"I don't know. I hate to disappoint Cody, he never asks for anything."

"Why don't you go, and if Derek acts like you don't exist, then you know he's over you. You might be surprised."

"Seems to me last time I took your advice I ended up

regretting it."

Sharon laughed. "Hey, I just offer opinions. I never said you had to act on them."

"Nothing but trouble," Kelly said, rising and gathering up her gardening tools. "That's what you are."

"Yeah, but you need me to trim your run on sentences and pull the emotional angst out of your characters."

"Which is exactly why I let you come sit in my yard every week and ogle men young enough to be your sons."

"Grandsons, but who's keeping tr—uh oh."

"What?"

Sharon nodded toward the street where a dark blue SUV had just pulled up. "Your ex."

Kelly groaned. "What's he want now?"

"You want me to leave?"

"No, stay. I might need help disposing of the body."

Alan stepped from the vehicle and removed his sunglasses, reaching inside to set them on the dash.

"Is that a new suit?"

Kelly eyed the conservative grey suit her ex wore. "I don't know, but it's not a Hawaiian shirt and shorts, and *that's* unusual."

"When did he get rid of the—" Sharon fluttered her fingers behind her head.

"Ponytail?"

"Is that what it was?" She waved as Alan came up the walkway. "Hi there."

"And I don't know when he lost it," Kelly finished in a conspiratorial whisper. "This is all new to me."

"Can I talk to you, Kelly?" He cast Sharon a sour glance. "*Alone?*"

"Oh don't mind me, I'm just working," Sharon said.

"I was just going inside to get us some lemonade. You can talk while I make it." Without giving him time to protest the offer, she headed for the house.

"Don't forget the sugar, Kel," Sharon called after her. "You always forget the sugar."

In the kitchen Kelly pulled a bottle of lemon juice from the fridge and set it on the counter. "Well?"

Alan raked a hand through his thinning hair before taking a seat at the kitchen table. "I'm buying the house up the street."

Reaching in an overhead cupboard for a pitcher and measuring cup, she paused. "You are?"

He nodded. "I've taken a position with one of the big firms downtown. I'll be coming in as a senior partner, I made a pretty sweet deal."

She rolled her eyes and poured juice into the measuring cup.

"I was going to look for something closer to work, but then..."

"Then what?"

"I started thinking about how much the kids hate being away from their friends all summer long and on holidays. And how stupid our custody arrangement is."

She could think of nothing to say to that, it seemed silly to point out that was the only option once he'd moved out of state. "And?"

"And I thought how much better it would be if they didn't have to leave their friends to come stay with me. If they could just stay right in their own neighborhood."

Liquid sloshed over the sides of the measuring cup as Kelly overflowed it. He couldn't have surprised her more if he'd said he'd suddenly grown a conscience.

"It's four houses down from you," he continued. "Not so close that you and I will have to see each other all the time, but close enough that the kids can live between the two houses. It has a nice finished basement; I thought I might put in a game room down there or a home theater." He rubbed a hand over the back of his neck, as if searching for the missing ponytail. "I know we'll have to keep in touch about where they are and who they're with. But I wondered what you thought of the idea."

She couldn't think of a thing to say. For a moment the only thought that came to mind was she wouldn't be spending summers and every other holiday alone. "Um...I think..." Tears blurred her vision as she filled the pitcher with water. "I think you should tell the kids."

"I will. I just wanted to make sure you were okay with it."

"Sure ..." she cleared her throat and concentrated on adding the juice to the pitcher, hoping the emotion in her voice wouldn't give away just how okay she was with it.

"Was that all you wanted to say?"

She finished mixing the lemonade and set a glass before him.

"No." He placed his hand on hers. For a second she could only stare at the short fingers and ragged cuticles. She closed her eyes against the memory of long, tanned fingers with perfectly manicured nails.

"I wanted to say that I know up until now I haven't been the best father," Alan said. "Spending time with the kids this summer made me realize how fast they're growing up and how much I've missed out on."

Kelly pulled her hand away, resisting the urge to wipe it on her shorts.

"And I wanted to say I'm sorry I wasn't a better husband to you."

"What brought on *that* revelation?"

"Jenn said some things when we broke up," He glanced up at her before taking up the glass. "Do you know she actually said I was selfish in bed?"

"Imagine that," she deadpanned.

Alan took a sip, then rose from his chair and rushed to the sink to spew lemonade. "I see your kitchen skills haven't improved any," he rasped.

Kelly frowned and turned to the counter where the cup of sugar still sat. "Guess I forgot to add the sugar again."

Twenty-Two

He wasn't watching for her. That's what Derek kept telling himself. He'd been outside for the past hour, on the pretense of making fishing lures. His seat at the picnic table gave him a view of the dirt road leading up to the cabin. He still couldn't believe she was coming.

Bianca took a seat across from him. "You sure you're okay with this? You've never had as many kids here as you do this time."

"That's because the girls decided it was sexist for me to just bring the guys every year."

His sister grinned. "Well, it really is."

"I'm not driving anyone home because they forgot their hair spray."

"The only one likely to do that is Gabrielle, and she's Jared's problem now." She laughed. "Tell me again why you hide out all the way up here?"

He looked beyond his sister to the thick copse of trees that surrounded the cabin, the blue-purple haze of the mountains in the distance. He liked waking to the sounds of chirping birds outside his window, the fresh air tinged with the smell of pine and earth. All things he was separated from high above the city in his Manhattan penthouse. "Privacy."

"Well, you've got that. I have trouble finding it every year." She waved a hand in front of his face; he realized she'd caught him staring off down the road.

He grinned sheepishly. "I still can't believe Kelly is bringing her son here."

"That makes two of us."

"Why did you invite him?"

"Because he's a good kid and his father's a selfish idiot. This is the kind of stuff he likes to do and I don't think he's ever had the chance."

"So, what are you, adopting him?'

He set the lure aside. "When I mentioned it to him,

Kelly and I were still together. I wasn't about to tell him he couldn't come after we broke up. Like I said, he's a great kid."

"And maybe you were hoping she'd be the one to bring him?"

He glanced back down the road again. "She'd better be." The last thing he needed was another encounter with Al.

"I'd say that's a long shot since you've never even called her." She picked up one of the brightly colored lures to examine it.

"You and Gabby both told me not to."

"I told you to give her some space, Dante, give her time to miss you. Not pretend she doesn't exist."

"By now she thinks I've forgotten her."

"So prove her wrong."

"Listen, I appreciate the advice—"

"But mind your own freakin' business." Laughing, she rose from her seat. "Sorry, my not-so-little brother, telling you what to do is an old habit." A volleyball landed in the middle of the table, scattering the lures. She shook her head. "I'm glad it's you and not me that's got to put up with a dozen teenagers the entire weekend."

"I'll give 'em a few beers, they'll be passed out cold before dinner," he teased, ducking, as she reached to smack him. "Gabby and Jared are coming, and Anthony and Melinda will be here tonight so I won't be alone."

"Where you gonna sleep all those people?"

He gestured to the tents set up beside the cabin. "The girls sleep inside, the guys sleep outside."

She rolled her eyes and tossed the volleyball back toward the group of kids. "You'd better hope it doesn't rain."

A moment later a familiar dark green mini-van came into view. Bianca put a hand to his shoulder. "Play it cool, just not *too* cool. By the way, you look great."

"You think I dressed for her?"

"Dante, you've been in cargo shorts and an old T-shirt all week. Now you're all spiffed up in one of those fancy designer shirts."

"It's old."

"Uh huh," she laughed. "Go get her, Model Man."

Kelly had barely turned off the ignition before Cody was clambering out the passenger door, eager to show Derek his new fishing pole.

Maya, still in the passenger seat, scanned the crowd of teenagers. "Did you say he has a cute nephew?"

"I said he has a *lot* of nephews."

Her daughter shrugged. "So at least one of them is bound to be cute."

Just what you need, another long-distance boyfriend. "I suppose so."

"Can we stay a while?"

Kelly resisted the urge to roll her eyes. Half an hour ago Maya had been complaining about having to come at all. Now she wanted to stay. She climbed out of the van just as Derek approached.

"Yo dawg," Cody greeted, half hugging, half hand-shaking. "Where's the beemer?"

The sound of Derek's laugh washed over Kelly's already-frazzled nerves. "It's not exactly practical up here, kid." He pointed to a mud-spattered black SUV. "That's my ride."

"Dude—is that a *Cayenne*?"

Kelly cast Derek a puzzled glance. "Isn't that some kind of pepper?"

"It's a *Porsche*, Mom," Cody breathed. He held out a hand and waggled his fingers. "*Keys*, my man."

Derek dropped them into his outstretched palm; Cody was off to examine the vehicle.

Kelly ducked as a volleyball came flying their way. It landed at her feet and Maya bent to pick it up. As she straightened, a tall, jet-haired boy came running toward her. Kelly recognized Bianca's oldest son, Ben. She also recognized the spark of interest that lit her daughter's eyes.

"Sorry, Mrs. Michaels," he called out, grinning. "Hey," he greeted Maya, reaching for the ball she held out. "You play?"

Maya shrugged. "Not really."

"I'll teach you," Ben said. "Come on."

And without so much as a glance over her shoulder, Maya followed.

"You realize that was on purpose, don't you?" Derek

asked.

"I figured," Kelly admitted, walking around the van to grab Cody's duffel bag from inside. "Besides, she's on the school volleyball team."

He laughed, coming around to take the bag from her. Kelly caught her breath. Didn't he realize she'd done this to avoid having to stand beside him?

"How has she been?"

"Busy," she admitted. "No internet, no cell phone. She had a summer job, so she stayed busy."

"And Heather?"

This from the man who claimed to never remember names. "She's fine. She was touched that you called to check on her."

He gestured for her to move ahead and started up the path toward the cabin.

"Of course, the girls don't see much of one another right now. The Baldwins were pretty upset and blamed Maya, which is understandable. But they'll see each other every day once school starts next week." She glanced up at him, then wished she hadn't. Damn him. Had she expected him to look anything but gorgeous? The khaki shirt he wore pulled taut over his wide shoulders, and though she couldn't remember ever seeing him in jeans, the well-worn pair he wore fit him perfectly, faded denim straining over muscular thighs. Thighs she remembered digging her fingernails into on more than one occasion... "Um, how is your grandfather?" she asked, forcing her thoughts onto more neutral topics.

"Cranky," he said. "He hates the changes he's had to make to his diet, hates exercising, but it gives him more to complain about, so he's doing all right."

And with that they seemed to have run out of conversation. She stared awkwardly up at him. "Thanks for inviting Cody—"

She was saved from fishing for more conversation when Bianca ran up to her, enfolding her in a warm hug. "It's so good to see you," she said, sounding sincere. "Will you stay for dinner?"

"Oh, I don't know," she hedged. "If I wait too long, I'll have to drive back in the dark and I had a hard enough time finding my way up that mountain."

"You'll be fine, Dante can lead you down if need be, he's driven it a million times."

"We'll see." Kelly recognized when she was good and truly cornered and didn't want to hurt Bianca's feelings.

She spent most of the afternoon avoiding Derek as much as possible and cursed herself for being such a coward, for not having the guts to confront him about not calling. But it was easy to keep busy, and as more people arrived, cousins, friends, relatives, she relaxed a bit more and found herself reluctant to really leave.

As they sat down at the picnic table to eat dinner, Gabrielle stuck close to her side. She had already filled Kelly's head with tales of how "miserable" Derek was without her, and taken complete responsibility for him not calling.

"He misses you," she insisted. "Just stay the weekend, give it a chance."

"I didn't bring any extra clothes."

"Oh, you'll be fine," she insisted. "We'll find you some."

"I'm not exactly dressed for getting him back," she said, gesturing to her T-shirt, hooded sweatshirt and khaki capris, something Cody referred to as her "mom uniform." She had intentionally not dressed up for Derek, but now wished she'd taken time to do more with herself.

"That's easily fixed." With that, Gabrielle picked up a bottle of ketchup and shook it. Without even trying to be subtle she squirted a blob on Kelly's white T-shirt. "Well that was clumsy of me," she announced loudly, drawing the attention of everyone at the picnic table. "Come on, Kel, let's get you out of that shirt before the stain sets."

She stood, tugging Kelly along behind her.

"What are you—"

"Trust me."

"Where have I heard those words before?"

Inside the cabin, Gabrielle shoved Kelly into the bedroom. "Take off the T-shirt."

"Wait a minute, why did you squirt me?"

Gabby laughed. "You'll see, just take off the shirt."

Kelly unzipped her sweatshirt and turned away to slide out of the tee.

"Now put the sweatshirt back on."

Frowning, Kelly did, zipping it up to a comfortable height. Gabrielle reached out and tugged the zipper down. "Cleavage, Kel. It's all about the cleavage." She stood back to survey her creation. "Lose the ponytail."

"My ponytail?"

Gabby nodded. "Take your hair down, then bend at the waist and shake it, kind of like you're shampooing." She gave a quick demonstration.

Kelly did as instructed. "Gabby, this is crazy. Derek and I have made our choices, he—"

"He can't take his eyes off of you," Gabrielle insisted. "You come out missing your shirt with your hoodie unzipped, and he'll spend the evening wondering what else you might have taken off." She grabbed a can of hair spray and spritzed Kelly's hair. She fluffed and scrunched until she was satisfied.

"I don't usually wear my hair so messy."

"But I'll bet it looks this way after you've had sex."

Kelly arched a brow. "You're not related to a Sharon Lewis, are you?"

"Not that I know of. Is she Italian?"

"Half. And right now you remind me of her. A lot."

"Good."

"Not really. Sex causes more problems for Derek and I than it—"

"What's going on?" Bianca asked from the doorway.

"I'm trying to give Kelly and Derek a push," Gabby explained. "They may be too stubborn to admit they're more miserable without each other than with, but I'm not going to stand back and let them throw it away."

Bianca stepped into the room and closed the door behind her. "So what exactly are you doing to Kelly?"

"Well when she comes outside, he'll see her and—"

The older sister rolled her eyes. "He already can't keep his eyes off her. I think the only push they need is some time alone—and someone to keep the kids away so they can talk."

"Or *not* talk," Gabby laughed.

"Hold it," Kelly said, raising a hand. "As much as I appreciate what you're doing, Derek and I are over. We didn't break up because we're incompatible, we broke up because we have separate lives."

Gabrielle folded her arms over her chest. "Did he tell you he's practically given up his career?"

"What?"

She nodded. "He bought Frankie out. He owns the agency now."

"Why would he do that?"

"To get out from under her thumb," Bianca explained. "And because he wants to settle down, not travel so much."

"His life is still in New York and mine is still in Rochester."

"I manage the agency," Gabby said. "He doesn't have to be in the office every day. He still has some obligations that will keep him in the public eye, but he can work from pretty much anywhere."

Kelly frowned.

"Your house, his place. Any where." Gabby emphasized. "He's been *here* more than not since he got back from L.A."

Kelly glanced around her at the cabin. She'd pictured it as something rustic when he'd mentioned it, but it was hardly that. Livable, homey, cozy. A bit masculine, but it gave her more of a sense of Derek than the New York penthouse had.

"He even quit smoking," Gabrielle continued. "He said it was for health reasons but I know how you hated it."

The sound of footsteps coming toward the bedroom reached them.

"It's him," Bianca whispered. "Kel, stay put, I have an idea."

"Wait—"

A knock sounded at the door. "Everything all right in there? "came Derek's voice.

"See," Gabby nudged her. "He's worried about you."

Bianca opened the door a crack. "Do you think you could come in here a sec?"

"Something wrong?"

She nodded and opened the door a bit wider. When he stepped inside, she gave him a shove toward Kelly. "You two need to talk." She grabbed Gabrielle's hand and yanked her out of the room.

"Come on you guys—" Derek said, but the door slammed shut.

Outside the bedroom came the sound of furniture sliding across the floor. "You two aren't coming out until morning."

"The door opens *into* the room, you know," he called out.

"So stay in there anyway."

Kelly couldn't tell which sister the voice belonged to.

Derek gave her a look that could only be called reluctant. Kelly's stomach plummeted. He didn't want to be alone with her. Not a good sign. She swallowed. "This is... the cabin, I mean. It's lovely. Did you really build it?"

"Yeah." He paced across the room, finally coming to rest against the door, arms folded across his chest.

As always, his presence seemed to fill the room, taking up all the oxygen. The sight of his muscular, tanned forearms against the light-colored shirt had memories teasing at the edges of her brain, making her insides warm and jittery. She pulled in a deep breath. "Derek, I—"

"I didn't forget," he said, his voice so soft she wasn't certain she'd heard him right. "Not after two weeks, not after four." He shifted his stance and met her gaze, green eyes tormented. "And not after seven."

She wanted to speak, but something—emotion, guilt, fear—lodged in her throat.

He pushed away from the door, one hand tucked into the pocket of his jeans. "I still remember what you smell like, your laugh. The sounds you made when I was inside you," he continued. "I haven't forgotten a damn thing."

Tears blinded her vision. She forced them back and tried to swallow the lump in her throat. "I ...miss... you."

He leaned one hip against a chest of drawers. "The sex, you mean." He didn't sound angry, just resigned.

"No, I miss *you*." She could no longer control the emotions that fought for release, the same feelings she'd kept a tight lid on for weeks. Hot tears scalded her cheeks. "Half the reason I came here was because..." she tried to collect her thoughts and pulled in a shaky breath. "I just wanted to be near you again. Even if it was only for a day."

"I thought I was the last person on the planet you'd feel that way about. I barged my way into your life, your bed. I caused trouble between you and your daughter."

"No," she said. "*Alan* caused trouble for Maya and me. You just happened to be caught in the middle." She shifted on the bed, hugging her arms about herself. "You were right, you know."

"About?"

She released a shaky breath. "Pretty much everything. I'd never thought about it before—never examined my feelings that close. But I think I did marry Alan because he seemed safe. And he did to me exactly what my father did to my mother."

"What do you mean?"

"My father ran around on my mother through most of their marriage, only I never saw it. I thought he walked on water. I didn't want to believe my daddy could do that. They had just separated when I started college, and that's when I met Alan." She swiped at the tears spilling freely down her cheeks. "So maybe he did seem safe at a time when my world had just been ripped apart. But you—you don't feel safe. You scare the hell out of me."

"Why?"

"Because I love you."

She sought out his gaze, wishing she could read something in his expression, but he was too guarded. "You might have mentioned it a little sooner."

"I was... scared. I wanted to believe in you, Derek. But—"

"But I never even called. After I told you I would."

She shrugged. "I figured you'd forgotten me and moved on. But... Gabrielle told me why you didn't."

"I shouldn't have listened to her."

"She meant well. For both of us, I think." She felt rather than saw his gaze skim the length of her. Felt it because her entire body tingled with awareness.

He stepped away from the dresser, coming closer. "Did she mean well when she did that to you?" He gestured to the sweatshirt that was still half unzipped.

"It got your attention."

"You've always had that, writer lady." The mattress beside her sank from his weight. "You don't need red dresses or half-zippered sweatshirts for that."

The familiar soapy-clean smell of him, the heat from his body surrounded her, clouding her senses. Her eyes filled with tears again, blurring her vision. "Derek, I don't know how to do this," she whispered. "I can't for the life of me see a way we can ever make this work. But I love you too much to try living without you again."

He pulled her into his arms. She breathed it all in, the warmth, the security. Everything she thought she'd never feel again.

"You love me," he repeated, sounding pleasantly surprised. "I still can't get used to you saying it."

"You said yourself I couldn't have made love to you if I didn't."

"But you never said it, Kel. You never gave me a hint."

"We never talked about what we felt." She pulled away just enough to look at him, reluctant to leave the sanctuary of his arms for even a second.

"There wasn't time."

"Well, it was pretty clear you didn't want me to go with you to your parents' for dinner that night."

He pressed his forehead to hers and groaned. "I didn't."

"Were you ashamed of me?"

"Hell no. But I thought you'd look at me differently if you saw my blue collar, old-world family."

"I loved getting to see the real you—*Dante*." She rested her head onto his chest once more, enjoying the feel of his hands smoothing up and down her spine. Something intruded on the edges of her brain, dimming her happiness for a moment. "You know the last time I saw Frankie—"

"Dammit, I knew she had something to do with it."

"I shouldn't have let her get to me." She slid a palm over the khaki material warmed by his body, fingers lingering to trace a button. "But when she asked what line of yours had finally gotten me to sleep with you—it just reminded me all over again how everything between us had started. And that all you'd wanted was to get me into bed."

"It was," he admitted. "And I used every line I had.

But by the time we finally made love, they weren't lines anymore. They were the truth." He stroked her cheek. "And you don't have to worry about Frankie."

"Did you really give up your career?"

"Not completely. I still have some commitments to fulfill over the next year, and the skin care and cologne, a new clothing line for men that will be out next spring. And I think there's one certain writer that will still insist I pose for all her covers."

She laughed. "I've been researching my next pirate book. You're the only one who can fill out those leather pants."

When he laughed, she was reminded how much she missed the crinkles at the corners of his eyes.

"I'll still have to travel now and then." He gazed down at her. "But from what I hear, you'll be able to come with me."

"What?"

"Cody tells me his dad lives just down the street now, and that you've thrown out the old custody agreement. The kids just stay with whichever one of you they want."

She hadn't considered how their new arrangement could benefit her in that way. She'd simply been glad to have Alan taking an active interest in the childrens' daily lives. "What kind of example am I setting if I just go off with you on a whim?"

"Mmm," he agreed, reaching for the zipper on her sweatshirt. "Not a very good one if you're running around with your much younger boyfriend." He eased her onto the mattress, tugging the zipper to the end.

It was getting hard to think with him pulling at her zipper. "No, so that leaves us in the same quandary—"

"Face it, Kel," he whispered, slipping his hand between them to unfasten her bra. His breath hitched when he parted the lace to reveal her breasts. "You'll just have to marry me."

"*Marry* you?"

He bent his head, nuzzling her skin. "Mmmm hmm." His tongue swept over her nipple.

"Are you serious?"

Laughter rumbled through his chest. "Would I joke about a thing like that?"

She laughed—for the first time in weeks, she actually laughed. "I suppose not."

"I only have one condition."

"Anything," she whispered, wrapping her arms around his neck.

"Make it soon. I don't want to wait another minute to make love to you." His hands slid beneath her buttocks, cupping them, pulling her against his hard, thick length.

"Then don't wait," she whispered.

"What about your kids?"

"They don't know where I am right now and believe me, they don't care." She trailed her fingers over his shirt, slipping one button out of its hole, then another.

He moaned low in his throat. "You haven't answered my question yet."

"You didn't ask."

"Will you marry me, Kelly Michaels—put me out of my misery and make me whole again?"

"Yes, but... why me?"

"Why *not* you?"

"You can have any woman you want."

He shook his head. "The only one I want hasn't made it easy on me."

She sighed. "I still don't get it."

"You're real, Kel. There's nothing artifical or phony about you—not even these." He slipped his hands between them to cup her breasts, eliciting a groan from both of them. "You make me want to be a better person—hell, you demand it. Besides, I'm lost without you."

"Yes," she sighed, recognizing her own feelings in the words he'd just spoken. Derek completed her, too. In more ways than one. Flutters of nervousness and excitement flitted about in her stomach. "Are you sure about this?"

He sat up, shrugging out of his shirt. "About what?"

"Getting married."

He lay beside her, propped up on one elbow. "Yes," he whispered, the sound rich with emotion. "I've never been more certain about anything. I swear my life flashed before my eyes when you drove away from me that night, Kel."

For the second time that night, tears squeezed past her eyes. "I was so afraid of getting hurt—I never dreamed not having you would hurt even worse."

He trailed a finger over her cheek, her chin. "Are you having second thoughts?"

"No, that's the strange thing. I'm really not. It feels... right."

"Will the kids be all right with it?"

"Yes," she said, reaching up for him. "Cody will be delighted to have a stepfather who likes the things he does—and has such cool cars."

"He hasn't even seen my Bentley yet," he teased.

"Isn't that an old man's car?"

"No, not this one. But it's definitely a family man's car." He bent to kiss her, then pulled back. "And Maya? How will she feel?"

"I don't think she'll mind having an excuse to see Ben on a regular basis." She wrapped her arms around his neck. "Derek, what would you say if I told you I wanted you that first night in Florida? Outside my hotel room door?"

His deep chuckle surrounded her. "I'd say I'm surprised. Especially after I came on so strong."

"Yes, you really were an arrogant ass."

"And you were in denial about what was between us." He bent to kiss her, the touch sweet, tender. "But I'm glad you made me wait."

"Me too," she sighed, giving herself up to his kiss.

His mouth found hers, and any more thought of talk was lost as he took what he wanted, tugging at her lower lip with his teeth, gently stroking with his tongue until she moaned and moved beneath him, her hands sliding into his hair.

He bent his head, closing his lips over an aching nipple. The hot velvet warmth of his tongue surrounded her and she arched against him. His hand moved between them, sliding up her inner thigh to press against the place that needed him most.

"I think these need to come off," he murmured.

She sat leaned up on her elbows while he unfastened her capris and slid them down her hips, tugging her panties down with them.

Derek caught his breath at the feel of her satiny skin beneath his hands. He'd thought he'd never touch her like this again, never hear her moan and cry out at his touch as she did now. He bent to place a kiss to her bare hip, fully intent on sampling every inch of her sweet skin.

The sight of her, leaned back on her elbows, legs slightly parted, a look of pure desire on her face was all the encouragement he needed.

But before he could sweep her beneath him and continue his assault on their senses, he felt her hands on his chest. "I want to touch you," she whispered, fingers unfastening the buttons down the front of his shirt. She parted the material and slid her hands over his bare skin, fingernails skimming over his nipples, then down the center of his chest, and over his abdomen. Every muscle in his taut stomach flinched at her touch, and he couldn't get his breath as she moved lower.

She pushed him back onto the blankets, continuing to trail her fingers over his skin, lower, sliding over the rigid bulge in his jeans before unfastening them. "I want to reacquaint myself with every inch of you." She slid the zipper down and he sprang free, groaning as hot skin met cool mountain air. She trailed her fingers lower, grazing over his abdomen. *"Every inch,"* she whispered.

Oh Jesus. The words, thick with desire, rocked him to the core. No woman had ever turned him on so thoroughly, but Kel knew—had always known—how to play him like a fiddle.

To further prolong his agony, she bent and placed her lips to his stomach, tongue circling his belly button while her hand moved lower. The feel of her palm closing around him sent a hot thrill straight to his brain, even though it was far from the first time she had touched him.

Still cradling him in her palm, she followed the thin strip of hair that led from his navel to the gates of heaven with her tongue. He couldn't breathe. Couldn't do anything but wait. It was hardly the first time a woman had ventured there, but this was different somehow. It was...torture. She was hell bent on torturing him, and from her wicked laugh he guessed she was determined to enjoy it.

She rained kisses over his lower belly, his thighs. Her hair fell forward to tickle his overly-sensitive skin, adding another level of torment to her machinations. She glanced up at him from beneath a veil of blonde hair. Along with the pure desire that darkened her blue eyes, there was something else. A hint of victory. She had him at her mercy and she damn well knew it.

Half a breath later, she stroked him with her tongue. Up the length of him, then around the head of his shaft. When she took him completely into her mouth, inch by agonizingly slow inch, he couldn't move. He grabbed a fistful of blankets and held on for dear life. His mind became a haze of rigid control, fighting not to let go, yet not wanting to miss a moment of the bittersweet agony she was putting him through. He wanted to look, wanted to see everything she was doing to him. But adding visual to the sensory would probably finish him off completely.

She released him at last from her mouth. He had a split second to suck oxygen into his lungs before he felt it. A cool breath of air along his erection, then the warm stroke of her wet, velvety tongue. He shuddered. This time she slid her mouth down him even slower. And just as slowly back up.

He released his death grip on the blanket with one hand, just long enough to cradle it over her head, savor the up and down motion. Raising his head from the pillows, he glanced down and was treated to the sight of her delicate pink tongue slipping out to stroke him once more. "Aw, Christ."

She raised her head up to look at him, her hair still veiling half her face. "Did I hurt you?"

"*Hurt* me?" He scooted slightly away to catch his breath and to reign in the ol' trusty steed—which didn't feel so damned trusty at the moment. "Do you have any idea how close to the edge you were pushing me?"

"Is that a bad thing?" Her tone was gentle, teasing

Laughing, he pulled her atop him. "Where did you learn to do that?"

"Actually, I've never done it before."

For some reason he liked hearing that. Another first. "Then how did you ... no, let me guess. *Sharon.*"

"She told me to just pretend I was eating a popsicle."

Damn did he owe Sharon a world of gratitude. And he hoped to hell he never had to endure watching Kelly eat a popsicle. Nevertheless, an image of her doing just that filled his mind as she straddled him, easing herself onto his throbbing shaft. Her moan mingled with his.

The first stroke nearly tore him in two. He was sure he couldn't hold out, couldn't last until she had been fulfilled. He held still, willing to surrender control to her, afraid to move and force his own climax too soon. He leaned up to caress one breast and take the peak of the other into his mouth.

She moaned and trembled, her movements suddenly rhythmic. The spasms that followed wrung forth his own soul-shattering release. He twined his hand with hers, riding the wave with her until at last a cry of primal satisfaction was torn from his throat.

As his heartbeat slowed to normal, he became aware of the sound of rain pattering the windows and roof, of shrieking, laughing teenagers running into the cabin.

Kelly collapsed onto his chest, and he pressed a kiss to her temple, her ear, the curve of her neck.

"Will it always be like this?" she asked with a purr of contentment

Bianca and Gabby could handle the kids, he and Kelly had all night. He rolled over, pulling her with him so they lay side by side. "No," he whispered, smoothing her hair back from her face. "It'll be even better."

Epilogue

For a haphazardly arranged wedding, put together in
less than two weeks, it was beautiful, if Gabrielle did say
so herself. The late September weather had cooperated
with sunny blue skies and warm breezes for a perfect
outdoor wedding. Kelly's picture-perfect suburban
backyard was the ideal setting.

Derek stood looking proud and impatient at the
makeshift altar, while a yard filled to overflowing with
Calavicci's looked on. Only two rows were taken up by the
bride's family, Gabrielle realized, the rest were
Calavicci's. The couple had wanted to keep it a private
affair, but private included immediate family. And that
was enough to have the yard overflowing.

Still as she looked around, she had to congratulate
herself. Even a few stray golden leaves had fallen from
the trees in the last couple of hours, creating an idyllic fall
scene. Years of looking after Derek as his personal
assistant had prepared her for this job. Arranging this
wedding—and keeping the paparazzi unaware it was even
taking place—was her part of her gift to him. As far as
the press knew, Derek and Kelly would be getting
married in high style in late October. But that was
actually going to be Anthony and Melinda's wedding.

She flashed a smile to Cody who stood on the deck
with his sister, awaiting the bride, whom they would
escort down the aisle.

Pretty blonde Maya seemed more interested in
flirting with Ben, who stood beside Papa, Derek's best
man, than she did in anything else going on around her.
Gabby smiled, she'd caught Maya and Ben kissing a short
time ago. Her nephew was a good six months younger
than Kelly's daughter, so apparently the apple didn't fall
far from the tree.

The newlyweds would be busy for a while, adding
office space to Kelly's house for Derek, and Gabby knew

her brother was planning a surprise for his bride—he was giving up his New York penthouse. Too many bad memories, he said. They'd start their married life shopping for a new home when they were in New York. And since Kelly was willing to spend their honeymoon at that Godforsaken cabin in the Catskills, there was no doubt it was true love.

As the organist began to play, all eyes turned toward the door. Gabby started down the aisle, followed by her older sisters, Bianca, Gina and Angela and Kelly's best friend Sharon.

Nonna's wails nearly drowned out the organist and it was hard to tell if she was crying for joy—or because Dante wasn't marrying an Italian girl. As her mother's happy, tear-filled gaze met hers, she swallowed back the tears threatening to ruin her make up. Her brother, a married man. Who'd have ever guessed it?

Once on the altar, she strained to catch a glimpse of the bride, wondering what Kelly had finally decided to wear today.

This wouldn't be a traditional wedding by any means, the bride insisted on that. Kelly had done the white dress and veil thing once before she said, no way would she jinx this marriage by doing it again.

Oh, Nonna and some of the aunts would probably be scandalized, but they'd get over it. It was Derek's reaction Gabby was most interested in, and when she turned to look at him, his eyes had gone wide and a huge smile had broken over his handsome face.

Kelly started down the aisle, escorted by her children, and a gasp went through the crowd.

Gabrielle stuck a hand out behind her to Sharon, who slapped it in a silent high five. Kelly had taken their advice.

The bride wore red.

About the author...

If it's possible to be born a writer, then I certainly was. I'd probably have started sooner if there had been pen and paper available in the womb! But for as long as I can remember, I have heard voices in my head. Fortunately for me, they're all characters—begging me to tell their stories.

It's ironic that my first two sales were contemporary-set, since my real passion is American history, particularly the Civil War and the old west. But I do enjoy a break back to "modern" times now and then and am so thrilled to be able to share those stories with you.

Married to Peter, my best friend, for ten years, I'm a work-at-home mom with two busy boys ages five and seven. When I'm not working, writing, or buried nose-deep in a research book, chances are I'm baking, fussing over my many houseplants or just kicking back and hanging with my guys.

For news about upcoming releases and to read excerpts from some of my other stories, please visit my website at
www.nicolemccaffrey.com
or check out my blog
http://nicolemccaffrey.blogspot.com.
I love to hear from readers!
E-mail me at nmccaffreyauthor@yahoo.com.

Also available

Small Town Christmas

By

Nicole McCaffrey

All Holland McCall ever wanted—for Christmas or any other occasion—was Tucker Callahan. Unfortunately, he was the high school jock and she an overweight, unattractive nobody. But things have changed. Holly has left the small town they grew up in and made a career for herself, with plans to move on to even greater things. Tucker, on the other hand, has just returned to town, divorced and the single father of two young girls. A visit home for the holidays and a chance encounter leaves both of them questioning everything they thought they ever wanted.

One

Fat, wet snowflakes splattered the windshield as Holland McCall waited for the red light to change. Three turns of the darned thing and she still hadn't made it into the grocery store parking lot. She hated to drive in the snow. And only a fool would be caught dead anywhere near this place on the Wednesday before Thanksgiving.

Guess that makes me a fool.

The radio DJ announced a news break, and with a frustrated sigh, she jabbed the seek button on the car stereo. Officially on vacation from her job as the early morning newscaster in Syracuse, the last thing she wanted to listen to right now was world events. The scanner landed on "sounds of the season." She glared hard at the radio as "Let it Snow" poured merrily from the speakers.

"Bah friggin' humbug," she muttered, switching the thing off altogether.

It was twenty minutes before she found a spot at the far outer edge of the lot. As she stepped from the car, heavy snow began to pelt her head. She had showered at the gym before leaving Syracuse, and while her hair had air dried on the five hour drive to Castleford, the last thing she needed was to catch cold. With a foul-natured grumble, she reached into the back seat and found the hat her grandmother had knitted for her last year. It was brown and lopsided, but better than a bare head. She tugged it on and made her way inside.

Here, too, the holiday season had arrived with bells and whistles. While Bing Crosby crooned "White Christmas," she passed two women battling to the death over the last remaining shopping cart and felt a smug sense of gratification that she wasn't the only one in a rotten mood. But she wouldn't be staying long. A quick stop in the frozen food aisle, a few minutes in the express checkout, and she'd be on her way.

1

Thanksgiving was never her favorite holiday; she had dreaded it since she was a kid. Being forced to sit at a table surrounded by relatives she could barely pretend to tolerate, and listen while everyone bragged about their accomplishments—it was less a time for giving thanks and more an opportunity for boasting. She still didn't like it. Even though she had plenty to crow about. On the outside, at least.

As she rounded the corner to the freezer aisle, she saw, even from a distance, that the cases were empty. "Oh, no." She quickened her pace, as if getting there half a step sooner would change anything. It didn't. All that remained was one smashed up box way in the back. In desperation she went up on tip toe and reached for it; maybe it was salvageable.

She grasped the box at last and gave a little yelp of triumph—which quickly turned to a moan. *Blueberry*? No one brought blueberry pie to Thanksgiving dinner. She heaved a sigh. She'd promised Mother she would bring the pie. Days—weeks, actually, of procrastinating and a busy work schedule had kept her from making good on the promise.

But there was only one kind of pie you brought to Thanksgiving dinner. Unless you wanted to look like a total idiot in front of people you really didn't want to see. Cousin Tiffany was making apple pie—undoubtedly with apples grown on a tree she'd planted herself. From a seed. But Holly was in charge of the pumpkin pie, and since her domestic skills were lacking she'd hoped to play it safe with Mrs. Smith's. No such luck.

Following the signs hanging from the ceiling, she headed for the baking supplies aisle. She would simply whip up a pie from canned pumpkin. How hard could it be? She might not be able to compare to the super moms of this world, like Cousin Tiffany, but she had spent many a winter afternoon in the kitchen with Gran baking cookies and cakes and all sorts of comfort food.

And she'd had the figure to show for it, she thought ruefully as she jostled her way through the crowd. But that had all changed. *She* had changed. Moved away from the small town to a big city. Lost weight in college instead of gained. Had blossomed in the anonymity a large city offered.

For some reason, coming back to the town she had grown up in always made her feel like a kid again. A fat, unattractive kid in coke bottle glasses with mouse-poop-brown hair. She forced her chin a bit higher and squared her shoulders. She wasn't that girl anymore. She was a success story all on her own.

As she was about to turn down the main aisle, the sound of laughter reached her ears. Not just any laughter; the happy, belly giggles of a delighted child. Or two. She turned to see two cherub-faced cuties, dark hair pulled back in pony tails, giggling with delight as their father zoomed a shopping cart up and down the aisle. And then her gaze came to rest on their daddy.

"Oh, dear God, not now." Ducking down the nearest aisle, she hid there, heart racing as though she had just run a mile. The face was older, less boyish, but the smile was the same. And what her eyes might not have recognized at first, her heart certainly had.

As she stood there, too panicked to move, the three raced past her aisle. She gave a silent sigh of relief. Gran had told her Tucker Callahan moved back to town a few months ago. Divorced, she had made it a point of mentioning. Said he wanted his two little girls raised with small town values.

That's where you and I differ, Tucker. I want nothing to do with this place.

She shook off the momentary shock and glanced around to see if she was anywhere near her destination. Tugging the hat farther down her head in a pathetic attempt to remain invisible, she whipped out of her hiding place—the baby food aisle, of all places—and followed the signs to aisle Eleven-A.

If the frozen pie section had looked like a Middle Eastern war zone, then the baking aisle was Ground Zero. For a brief moment, she wished she'd played football in high school. At the very least, attended a game. Because it was fourth down with no time outs left. Gearing up like a receiver intended for a Hail Mary pass, she focused her sites on the goal line—the lone, dented container of canned pumpkin. And went for it. Her fingertips were just about to brush the can when a gloved hand snatched it away.

Without so much as a backward glance, the other shopper plopped the can into her cart and shoved off. Frustrated but not finished, Holly stood there for a moment, mentally calculating the distance to the grocery store the next town over. But Castleford wasn't like Syracuse; there was only one grocery store in this town. Heck, it had been big news when they'd changed the flashing red light at the corner of Main Street to a full fledged three-cycle traffic light. She sighed. Next year, she'd buy the pie the first part of November. No, better still, the day after Halloween.

Halloween! Pumpkins. With a cry of triumph, she put her feet in motion. Sure, it might take half the night, but she could make a pie from scratch. She'd Google up a recipe once she got to Mom and Gran's house, tie on an apron and go for it.

Fighting her way back to the produce department was like swimming upstream. It took twice as long as it should have to wade through shoppers fighting over bundles of celery and a near-empty bin of chestnuts. But luck was on her side. As she rounded the last aisle, she spied two orange blobs in a bin marked "pie pumpkins." The familiar sounds of a fast-moving cart and little-girl giggles bore down. She quickly turned her back as he raced past. Not that Tucker Callahan would recognize her. Or even remember her.

While he paused to look at the pumpkins, she felt a familiar pang of longing for the well-remembered sandy-brown hair, wide shoulders and long legs. One little girl stood in the back of the cart, a half naked Barbie doll dangling from her hand. "Pick that one, Daddy!"

He turned over a broad, denim-clad shoulder. "This one?"

She nodded, face animated with excitement.

The other girl, who appeared to be her twin, plucked a thumb from her mouth. "Are we gonna make a zack-o-lantern?"

A deep laugh preceded a gentle explanation about baking a pie. Her gaze wandered to the contents of the cart, a small turkey, a box of stuffing mix, eggs, milk, and several spice jars. The girl with the thumb in her mouth caught her watching and waved.

Holly offered a quick smile and turned away once again. Tucker plopped a pumpkin in the cart and moved on without noticing her. *Some things never change.*

The minute he left, she seized the remaining pumpkin from the bin. Like a linebacker with a Thanksgiving game football, she clutched the pumpkin under one arm and dove back into the crowd. What were those ingredients again?

Eggs. Milk. Spices.

This was getting easier. All she had to do was follow the crowd. And sure enough, back in the baking aisle, they were all clustered around one area. The spices. She stood back, watching as shopper after shopper grabbed things like allspice, cloves, ginger, and cinnamon. Until her gaze happened across an ingenious little item on display in the center of the aisle. Pumpkin pie spice.

She snatched one of the tiny containers and half ran toward the dairy cases. *Eggs. Milk.* The handle of the cold half-gallon container dug into her fingers as she awkwardly juggled it along with the pumpkin, spice and her purse while trying to check the eggs as she had seen her mother do so many times. It was a ritual really, where she lifted the lid and wiggled each egg once or twice to be sure it wasn't stuck.

She shifted, hefted the milk a bit. The egg carton toppled from her hand. She let out a cry and tried to catch it, but it flopped upside down onto the floor. Other shoppers passing by flashed her the "you're such an amateur" look. Feeling like an idiot, she sheepishly reached for another carton of eggs while keeping an eye out for a store employee she could alert to the mess she'd made.

This time she set both the milk and the pumpkin on the floor and knelt beside them as she checked the eggs.

She had just lifted the lid when she heard it again. The giggles and shrieks of "Faster, Daddy!"

"Coming up on dairy," he called out, sounding like a tour guide, the cart barreling toward her. "To our left we have a lovely display of elbow macaroni at three boxes for a dollar. And to our right, the dairy case, where a dozen large grade A eggs are on special this week for—"

5

"Daddy, watch out!"

With a wild grope for the pumpkin, Holly tried to scramble to her feet. But she slipped on the broken eggs and went sprawling. The pumpkin rolled from her arms. She lunged for it once more, one eye on the cart coming at her like a runaway train. The carton of eggs tumbled from her lap. She darted out of the path just as Tucker spotted her. He tried to stop but skidded through the broken eggs with a "whoa" of surprise. She covered her eyes as the cart continued down the aisle

When she dared peer between her fingers, Tucker was sprawled on the floor, covered in raw egg up to his thigh. The cart had come to rest at the far end of the dairy cases. Two little girls laughed hysterically and chanted "Again, again!"

"Miss, are you all right?" Tucker scooted to his knees. "Did I hurt you?"

She put a hand to the floor to push to her feet; it came away wet, soaked from a puddle of milk. Raw egg and bits of shell covered her coat and jean-clad legs. It dawned on her the cold sensation beneath her wasn't the floor. It was spilled milk.

He rolled to sit up, made a grimace and pulled out something from beneath him. Her pumpkin. "I believe this is yours."

Holly let out a little wail of dismay at the sight of the ruined vegetable.

"Can I at least help you up?" He rose to his feet and held out a hand.

She lifted a wet hand, grimaced, and spied the stringy orange goo and seeds clinging to his leg. So much for wanting to slip in and out of the store, for not wanting to see or be seen while in town. The absurdity of it all sent her into a fit of giggles.

"I suppose if you can laugh, that's a good thing." His face, alight with humor, suddenly sobered, and he crouched down in front of her. He plucked the hat from her head. "Holly McCall?"

Self-consciously, she raised a hand to her hair. A sticky egg-and-milk-coated hand, she realized belatedly. But her gaze was riveted on the fingers that still held her hat. Long, lean and calloused. A working man's hands.

Her heart flipped over backward. She looked up at his face and took in the lines at the corners of his blue-green eyes, the denim jacket, the collar of a flannel shirt tucked over it. Not flannel in the icky beer-belly-and-pretzels way, but in the warm, inviting way. Oh, plenty about Tucker Callahan had changed. And yet he was exactly as she remembered him.

He smiled. "I haven't seen you—"

"Since graduation," she said, brushing bits of egg shell from her coat.

"Has it been that long?"

"Yes." She hated the bitter edge in her voice, hated the memories that rushed over her. Soft, warm lips against hers. The heart-fluttering thrill of a requited crush.

The stinging pain of rejection.

She shook off a sudden stab of agony. No longer Fat Holly; she was Holland McCall, News Channel Eleven reporter on the fast track to bigger and better things. He was just some small town guy.

He rose and walked over to his grocery cart, and returned with a roll of paper towel. He tore it open and knelt down. "Let me help you clean up."

He began to dab at her coat, and she stiffened, resisting the urge to run off somewhere and cry. "I can do it." She took the toweling from him. A million times she had played out this moment in her mind, the surprise in his eyes when he saw her, the way she would ignore him as if he were nothing.

She had never imagined their next meeting would come with her sprawled on the floor of a grocery store, covered in broken eggs, milk and overripe pumpkin.

To purchase Small Town Christmas, visit www.thewildrosepress.com.